The
SACRED
RIVER

A NOVEL

WENDY WALLACE

SCRIBNER

New York London Toronto Sydney New Delhi

SCRIBNER
A Division of Simon & Schuster, Inc.
1230 Avenue of the Americas
New York, NY 10020

First Scribner hardcover edition July 2014

SCRIBNER and design are registered trademarks of The Gale Group, Inc.,
used under license by Simon & Schuster, Inc., the publisher of this work.

For information about special discounts for bulk purchases,
please contact Simon & Schuster Special Sales at 1-866-506-1949
or business@simonandschuster.com.

The Simon & Schuster Speakers Bureau can bring authors to your live event.
For more information or to book an event contact the Simon & Schuster Speakers Bureau
at 1-866-248-3049 or visit our website at www.simonspeakers.com.

Interior design by Erich Hobbing
Jacket design by Matthew Johnson
Jacket photographs: background © Jill Battaglia/Arcangel Images,
woman © Lee Avison/Arcangel Images

Manufactured in the United States of America

1   3   5   7   9   10   8   6   4   2

Library of Congress Control Number: 2014001520

ISBN 978-1-4516-5812-5
ISBN 978-1-4767-6472-6 (ebook)

To MG, SG, and DG

What you seek is seeking you.
　　　　　　　—Rumi

The
SACRED
RIVER

ONE

❦

"Oh, Lord, what is that?"

Louisa, out in the fog with a pair of scissors, explored the soft obstruction with the toe of her shoe. A rag, she decided. A cloth dropped by Rosina from a window, back in the summer. Stooping to pick it up, feeling for it on the brick path, she gasped. The thing was warm under her fingertips. She crouched down and peered through the vapor at a yellow beak, jet plumage around a glassy eye. It was a blackbird. Newly, beautifully dead.

The fog was sour on her tongue. It tasted of iron and smoke mixed with a primeval dampness, made her eyes water and her cheeks sting. Enveloped in the yellow cloud, Louisa could make out nothing. Her own garden might have been a limitless place stretching to eternity in all directions or it might have shrunk to the very spot where she stood.

All over London, birds had been dropping from the sky— thudding onto the leather roofs of carriages, falling down chimneys, and splashing into lakes in the great parks under the gaze of statues. Everyone said that they were an omen, although there was no agreement on its meaning. Louisa wouldn't allow this one to be an omen. She would rid them of it.

Pulling on a glove from her pocket, she made herself pick up the bird. It was light for its size, all feather and quill and claw. Balancing it on her palm, she made her way along the path to the wall at the end of the garden and stretched out her arm to toss the corpse into the stables. As she did so, she felt a scrabble of claws, sudden and intimate against her wrist. The creature lurched, unfurled its wings like a black umbrella, and vanished into the morning.

Louisa stared after the soft sound of wing beats. "Fly away home," she said.

It wasn't until she was indoors, her cloak off, standing at the stone sink in the scullery and running the tap over her fingers, that she remembered her purpose. She'd gone into the garden to cut a sprig of buds for Harriet's breakfast tray.

Drying her hands on a dishcloth, she felt in her pocket for the scissors and returned them to the dresser drawer. She wouldn't go out again. It was she who cherished the tiny shoots of quince and viburnum. She, not Harriet, who loved to inhale the intense, vanishing scent of wintersweet.

"I suggest that you take her for a change of air, Mrs. Heron."

"We intend to, Doctor, when summer comes." Standing in front of Dr. Grammaticas on the top-floor landing, outside Harriet's door, Louisa smiled at him through closed lips and touched the round complications of hair on the back of her head. "We shall go to Boscombe in July, as we always do."

Dr. Grammaticas shook his head.

He'd put on his gauntlets, was stretching the fingers wide and interlocking them with the other hand. "Harriet needs to go somewhere warm. Dry. The climate in Egypt is said to be beneficial."

Feeling herself gaping, Louisa closed her mouth. "I couldn't."

"Travel? Why not?"

She crossed her arms over her chest, raised her eyes to the gas lamp suspended from the ceiling above the doctor's head. It seemed to give him a yellow halo, a small dirty sun set against the months of darkness.

"I . . . I shouldn't like to go so far from home," she said.

Dr. Grammaticas frowned.

"Her breathing is accelerated, the post-respiratory rest almost lost. And there's something else." He glanced at the closed door and lowered his voice. "Something I cannot measure."

Straightening his muffler, he stepped past Louisa and began his descent of the stairs. They were uncarpeted at the top of the house and too narrow for a man of his build, scaled for the hips of maids and children, the struts of the banister wobbling like loose teeth under his hand, the treads creaking underfoot.

Louisa hurried behind him as he took the lower flights of stairs, reached the dim hall, the fanlight obscured by a red blind that cast a warm glow over the pattern of tile. He brushed past the fern case and accepted his coat from the maid who'd hastened forward with it. The girl was new, one of a succession to have passed through the house in recent months; Louisa couldn't for a minute remember her name.

The doctor was still shrugging on the coat as he swung open the front door, admitting a gust of foul air.

"Talk to your husband," he said, descending the stone steps to the street. "See what he considers best."

"Should I get in more tincture?" Louisa called after him. "A new bottle of friar's balsam?"

Silence. A boy loomed out of the fog, walking along the pavement in front of the house, and for the second time that morning, Louisa almost screamed. She shut the door and rebolted it, top and bottom, pulled across the heavy tapestry curtain, then stood, leaning her back against it. Harriet thought the world of the doctor, although Louisa couldn't help asking herself why that should be, when in all the years he'd been attending her, he had been unable to cure her.

Louisa would not break the habit of a lifetime and go away. She dared not.

"Impossible," she said aloud. "Unthinkable."

Hearing the maid's step on the stair, she tried to compose herself, pulling her cuffs down over her wrists, smoothing her skirts over her hips, before she looked up. It wasn't the maid. It was Harriet. She stood on the landing, her feet bare under the hem of a plain white nightdress, her auburn hair loose on her shoulders, crinkled from nighttime plaits, the old pink pashmina shawl she insisted upon thrown around her narrow shoulders. She looked as if she'd stepped out of a painting on the walls of the National Gallery.

"Why is it impossible?" she said.

"Where are your slippers?"

"I wish it, Mother. More than anything."

"We're not going to Africa, Harriet. It's too far away."

"Too far away from what?"

"Home, of course. *Home*."

Louisa kept her voice low. Dr. Grammaticas always warned against excitement, unnecessary dramatics, tears, or laughter. Besides, she and Harriet had—after the passions of her teen years—arrived at a form of speaking with each other that was cautious and careful, exhibited in each syllable their mutual wariness. On Louisa's part, it held too the certain knowledge that many years of enforced companionship lay ahead, yet to be navigated.

"Did the girl bring up your breakfast?" Louisa asked, her voice softened.

Harriet had descended to the hall and was standing in front of her. Her pale face displayed the oddly adult look it had assumed when she first became ill at not more than seven or eight years old, and that she had never quite grown into.

"I'll die here, then. If that's what you wish."

Louisa flinched. "How can you say such a terrible thing, Harriet? All I want is your health. Your happiness. That's all I've ever wanted, since the moment you were born."

"What's best for me is to go away from here, Mother. To a place where I can breathe."

Sitting on the unmade bed, Louisa poured a glass of water from the jug. She couldn't be sure whether she heard or imagined the muffled strains of carols rising from the street below. *May nothing you dismay.* The fog made everything so quiet, as if all of life was being lived secretly.

It was the most injurious kind—sulfurous, yellow as mustard powder. The death rates were exceptional, according to the reports in the newspaper, and there were fears of an epidemic of Russian influenza. Harriet couldn't leave the house without suffering fits of coughing that racked her narrow body, turned her lips and the tips of her fingers mauve, risked bringing on a full attack.

Louisa had done all she could. She and Rosina had sealed the gaps along the edges of the sash window frames with folded strips of newsprint. They stuffed rags into the keyholes of the outside doors each night, fitted the plugs in the drains of the basins, and drew the winter curtains at mid-afternoon. It made no difference. The fog crept down the chimneys, stole in between the floorboards, penetrated the very bricks and mortar. Insinuated itself into Harriet's chest.

The previous night, she'd had an attack as bad as any she'd ever suffered. Louisa pictured Harriet's shoulders lifted high, her mouth open and gasping, the room filled with the smoke from a burning niter paper. In the small hours of the morning, Louisa had begged Harriet to let her send for Dr. Grammaticas. Harriet had shaken her head. "It's o—ver, Mother," she'd said, in the halting cadence produced by her shortness of breath. "The wor—st is over."

Minutes later, the dog had jumped up on the bed. After an hour, Harriet said she was hungry, would like a cup of tea, a slice of toast. Louisa had fetched the loaf from the kitchen with a toasting fork and a kettle. Harriet insisted on making the toast herself, over the bedroom fire. She ate it spread with butter, at four o'clock in the morning, saying what was the point in being alive if you couldn't ever do as you pleased.

Let peace and health and happiness . . . As the ghostly strains continued to rise from the street, Louisa began to pace the old silk rug that lay on the floor at the end of the bed. It was a week before Christmas and she had other worries. Her elder sister Lavinia, next in age to herself, was due to arrive in two days' time with her husband. Letters came by every post, detailing Lavinia's requirements. She needed a daily dose of liver salts, must sleep with the window open despite what she read of the foul fog in their filthy city. Lavinia lived in Northumberland beside a gray, slapping sea, breathing air that had never been breathed before.

Stopping in front of one of the two long bedroom windows, Louisa drew up the slats of the venetian blind. The houses on the other side of the street had disappeared, and below, the gas lamp still burned at ten in the morning, illuminating nothing more than itself. She pressed her forehead against the cold glass. Harriet knew nothing of the circumstances that had caused Louisa all her life to shun travel, to avoid society beyond their own small community of family and friends.

Staring sightlessly into the street, Louisa could think of only one course of action. She would seek advice from her own mother.

TWO

The omnibus came to a halt at the terminus, that dispiriting point where every remaining passenger must climb down and proceed on foot. Louisa, who'd dropped a glove, been groping on the floor for it among chestnut peelings and sharp stalks of straw, was the last to alight. Usually, she took a cab from Canonbury to Antigua Street, but since the fog descended three weeks earlier, drivers could only be persuaded to travel south of the river only for three times the regular fare.

The horses' steaming breath mingled with the vapor as she set off through the square and past a noisy tavern into the ladder of streets beyond, her handbag hidden under the wing sleeve of her wrap. Robbers were flourishing in the obscurity. Murderers too, according to Rosina's cousin, who was a police officer. The wooden pavement was slippery underfoot and Louisa walked close to the walls and hedges that separated the houses from the street, reaching out her hand, feeling through the kid of her glove the prickly brush of privet, the graze of brick.

A half-moon emerged, low in the sky over the top of the roofs of the Greenwich terraces, lighting a dingy-looking circle of cloud. It pulled Louisa along Antigua Street and through the iron gate of number 27, where a congregation of faded silk roses hung from the gatepost.

Mrs. Hamilton opened the door, a raw-chinned baby imprisoned in one arm.

"If you could see yourself in, missus," she said. "I've got my hands full."

The woman pressed herself against the coat stand and Louisa edged past her along a narrow hallway, walked down the decrepit wooden steps to the back parlor. The little window was draped in its customary swag of purple velvet and the air was heavy with the scent of a burning incense tablet, the room dimly lit by a single oil lamp hanging from a beam. Despite the thickness in the air, the powerful scent of musk overlaying a reek of tomcats and burnt potatoes, it was cold, the fireplace empty. Mr. Hamilton's clients were staying away, Louisa supposed, due to the atrocious weather. She wouldn't have come herself if she'd had any choice.

From his place behind a table, Mr. Hamilton nodded at her. "I saw your note. Be seated, Mrs. Heron."

Louisa settled herself on the chair opposite him and rested her hands on the softly furrowed cloth, palms upward. Malachi Sethe Hamilton was Romany by origin; it was the source of his special gift and, she thought sometimes, of his peculiar manners. All year round, he wore a broad-collared coat that reached to his ankles, the hem embroidered with fishes and bulls, scorpions and prancing goats, a pair of twins holding hands. His hair, neither gray nor white, issued from the sides of his head in two matted pelts, leaving the dome naked and exposed. Louisa imagined the inside of it, stuffed like an overcrowded drawer with visions and voices and dreams.

People said that he'd adopted the name of Hamilton on arrival in London, the day he stepped off the boat. Many things were said about Mr. Hamilton, but in her years of consultation with him, Louisa had found no reason to doubt him. He had never been wrong.

"I have a question for my mother."

Mr. Hamilton nodded.

"You want Mama's advice, about a journey."

Mr. Hamilton's powers of discernment gave Louisa a sense of safety. In the cramped back parlor, she felt as she had when their father, a sea captain, used to tell her and her four sisters stories around the fire, in his periods of shore leave. All too soon, Father would be gone, but the stories remained. Thinner and less satisfactory than by the firelight, but present nonetheless, worlds in themselves, resistant to time or breakage, pilfering by older sisters.

"Yes, Mr. Hamilton. I want you to ask her whether I should take my daughter abroad. Her doctor insists on it. But I . . ."

"Somewhere warmer than our own island? A place far away from here?"

Louisa nodded, overcome with gratitude. Mr. Hamilton knew the questions before she uttered them. It was remarkable.

He closed his eyes, his face creased in effort.

"Speak, dear lady," he intoned, taking hold of Louisa's hands on the table. "Speak to us, by your kindness."

Louisa's hands were cold and his warm around them, rough-palmed, one finger constricted by the bright wedding band he'd affected lately. The new Mrs. Hamilton had appeared one day in spring, visibly with child, answering the door with an unspoken challenge in her eyes. The baby was crying upstairs and there was a faint disturbance of the air that could be something or nothing.

Louisa's voice was a whisper.

"Do you hear anything, Mr. Hamilton?"

He didn't respond. Mr. Hamilton sat not more than three feet away from her but Louisa had the distinct sense that he'd left the room, no longer inhabited the large and flesh-rounded body that she saw before her. The silence around them altered. It became full and complex, layered with possibility, and the hairs rose on Louisa's arms and spine as Mr. Hamilton's lips parted, seemed to struggle.

"I expected you sooner." A high, true voice, quavering a little, issued from the mouth of Mr. Hamilton. It was the voice of Louisa's mother. "My poor Izzy."

The childhood nickname that her mother invariably used now, although when she was alive she'd called all of the older girls by their full names. Hearing her voice again, Louisa saw in her mind her mother as she'd been when Louisa was a child, when Amelia Newlove had seemed to represent through her slight frame the entire mystery of womanhood. For a moment, Louisa forgot what she'd come about. She bowed her head and blinked back tears.

"Oh, Mother. I miss you so."

For what she estimated afterward had been a whole minute, there was silence. When Amelia Newlove's voice came again, the tone was altered, a bleak authority entered into it.

"Death is near," she said.

Louisa felt a chill that began at the base of her spine and spread through her body. Her teeth began to chatter.

"What shall I do? Tell me, Mother, please."

"The way is far," said the voice. "Make haste, Izzy."

Mr. Hamilton closed his mouth and shuddered. He dropped Louisa's hands and began mopping at his brow with a spotted handkerchief, sweat pouring from him, drops scattering like rain from his chin and cheeks as if he had undergone a great exertion. Taking a swig from the pint pot on the table, he cleared his throat. "Clear as day," he said, his own voice returned to him in all its gruff depth. "I take it you heard her?"

"I heard her." Louisa's throat was so dry she could barely utter the words. "I almost wish I had not."

"No cause to take fright, Mrs. Heron. Death's always near, when you come to think of it. You walk on bones in London."

"But what shall I do? What does it mean?"

"That's for you to decide."

Mr. Hamilton shifted his chair back from the table and stood up. Something about him had altered. His lined forehead appeared not a map of other realms but the face of a tired man, and the coat looked shabby, faintly ridiculous, as if he'd stumbled out from a fancy-dress party. His voice, when he spoke, was hoarse.

"Awful foggy, ain't it? They've suspended the shipping again."

Louisa handed over the half-sovereign, climbed the wooden steps, and let herself out. Pulling her wrap over her shoulders as she closed the door behind her, drawing it up around her cheeks, she groped her way back along Antigua Street toward the terminus.

She had a peculiar feeling of recognizing nothing, of the way back being different from the way out, as if already she had traveled far from everything that was known to her.

THREE

Harriet lay back on a pile of feather pillows, staring at the window. The fog hung like a dirty curtain on the outside of the glass, and in his basket by the fire, the dog snored softly, sounding as if he were far away. Shifting her gaze, Harriet looked about the room at the familiar faded white of the walls, the dark wooden footboard of her bed. The attic bedroom had been the night nursery; Harriet had slept in it for as long as she could remember, had spent long stretches of her life confined to the same bed looking at the sky.

Whether she was well or ill, she thought of it as a sickroom. The air weighed more than air in other rooms; it bore the memory of the repeated burning of niter papers, fumigant powders of belladonna or carbolic, stramonium cigarettes made from the dried roots and stems of thorn apple that she was required to inhale, alternated with vaporous basins of menthol, camphor, and eucalyptus, emergency whiffs of chloroform from a sprinkled handkerchief. The smoke and steam cleared but the odors lingered on, clinging to each other in the walls and blankets, the old red rug that waited in front of the tiny fireplace.

A quill was poking into her back through her nightgown and she shifted her position on the pillows. Her breath was shallow and her heart still beat fast. She could feel it thudding away, scurrying along like a friend running ahead on a pavement, in more of a hurry than she was herself. Harriet had read once that every person was born with an allotted number of heartbeats. That when the count was reached, the person died. Her heart was hastening toward the total, careless of the cost to her in days.

All winter, she'd urged Dr. Grammaticas to recommend going away. Every time she raised the subject, he refused. It would be dangerous. Reckless. The death of her, perhaps. Then, the previous morning, he had arrived early. After he'd examined her, he sat down on the chair drawn up to her bed and looked at her with his soft brown eyes.

"What is it, Grams?"

"It's you, Hattie."

"What of me?"

"There is a thickening of the membranes of the bronchial tubes. Percussion of your chest reveals emphysematous hyper-resonance. Forced respiration produces rhonchus and sibilus."

"Speak to me in English."

"Your condition's worse, Harriet. It saddens your old doctor to see it."

Harriet pressed her hand against her chest. The bones under her skin felt sharp and light as wishbones, lifting slightly as she breathed in, falling almost imperceptibly as she breathed out, the effort unmatched by the movement. No one knew better than she the state of her health. This winter, more than ever before, she'd wearied of the struggle for breath; no one wanted to hear that the thought that she could cease to struggle, could one day stop breathing, was a comfort to her. Only Dr. Grammaticas nodded his old head when she told him that she was tired.

"Help me, then," she said. "Help me to get away."

"Where did you want to go? Bournemouth? Bath?"

"D'you mean it?" She pulled herself up on the pillows.

"Boscombe? Broadstairs?"

Harriet took hold of his liver-spotted hand with both of hers and kissed it. Shook her head.

"Where, then? Menton? The Riviera?"

"Far—" She broke off in a fit of coughing. "Farther."

Dr. Grammaticas removed the rubber tubes of his stethoscope from around his neck and stowed the instrument in a case, fitting its curves to the empty, waiting spaces.

"I've a nephew in Sydney."

"Egypt. I want to go to Egypt."

The doctor barked with laughter. "Sightseeing amid the tombs." Closing the brass clasp of the case, he sat down again, resting his elbows on his knees. "A tonic climate might benefit you, Harriet, but it's risky. My opinion is that you're not well enough to travel."

"I'm not well enough to stay here."

"You may rally, when spring comes. You have before."

Harriet met his eyes with her own and the doctor looked away first. "All right. I'll do my best for you."

He stood up and when he spoke again his voice was loud, filled with artificial cheer.

"Meanwhile, rest! Do you hear me, young lady? Rest."

Groping under the bed, Harriet picked up a book. The corners and spine were bound in leather the color of fallen leaves, the nap worn to the texture of peach skin. Lying back on the pillows, she balanced the volume on her knees and opened it. Her books were her medicine. It was her books that kept her alive.

Great-Uncle Redvers had instructed in his will that his collection on ancient Egypt be passed to Harriet's three older brothers. Not one of them was interested. The books remained on a high shelf in the study, dusted and unread, until the day Harriet happened to retrieve one and began turning the pages.

In it, she found a dictionary of the hieroglyphics used in the writing of the ancient Egyptians. Looking at the tiny images of birds and beetles, stars and moons, legs walking, Harriet was entranced. The pictures were thousands of years old yet many were as recognizable as if she'd drawn them in her own hand. There were horned vipers and serpents, sickle moons and sun disks, stems of lotus flowers.

Some of the meanings were transparent. A man with upraised arms meant *to praise*, an eye *to see*. Others could not have been guessed at: a bird with a human face represented the *ba*, the aspect of a person that made them different from all others. Immediately, the *ba* bird became one of Harriet's favorites.

Losing herself in the dictionary, Harriet had a sense of having come home. The ancient Egyptians had named things that still needed naming; there were dogs and cats, sparrows and swallows, loaves of bread. They depicted the male phallus, a woman in childbirth, prisoners of war. And in their language, breath was life, the gift of the gods, symbolized by the ankh, a cross with a rounded top.

She began to make up her own symbols. A cup-shaped crinoline for her mother, who in those days had still worn them, and for her father a sovereign bearing the profile of Queen Victoria. A four-fingered hand for Rosina, who'd lost a digit in childhood to an iron gate. Boots for her three brothers, in three sizes. A stethoscope for Dr. Grammaticas.

Aunt Yael had a symbol straight from the hieroglyphs. The drooping ostrich feather stood for Maat, goddess of truth, and symbolized balance and justice. To Harriet, the feather represented the bonnet festooned with bedraggled gray plumes that her aunt wore winter and summer alike.

As Harriet grew older, she understood more clearly that the pictures did not always stand for themselves. Some indicated sounds or had a general meaning. Over the years, the signs she devised for herself became more opaque. An open book signified a kind of escape for which in English there was no satisfactory term. She drew narrowed eyes for envy and weeping ones for grief, official, justifiable grief such as that felt after a death. A head resting at a slant on a hand for the other kind, the kind she mainly felt, sadness that had no cause, that crept into her like the fog crept into the house. She used the symbols, mixed with words, in her journals to ensure no other eyes could read what she wrote.

Harriet closed the book and inhaled its odor of dust and gravitas, felt its familiar weight and heft in her fingers. Along with the elation prompted by Dr. Grammaticas's words, she felt another, more mixed, emotion. All the while traveling to Egypt had been an impossibility, she'd been certain that she wanted more than anything to go there. Now that it had become a possibility, she felt a sense of apprehension that was new to her.

FOUR

❦

"Yael! What a pleasant surprise."

Louisa hadn't expected her sister-in-law. She'd been upstairs in the old day nursery, looking at the globe, when the girl had announced Yael's presence in the drawing room. It was late for calling and the smell of roasting beef was escaping from the kitchen downstairs.

"What does Blundell wish to see me about?" Yael said, glancing at the nearest of the several clocks that ticked at discordant intervals. She removed her gloves. "I've a meeting to attend but he said in his note that it was urgent."

Louisa felt further taken aback. She had no idea that Blundell had summoned his sister, or why.

"Father, probably," she said, tugging the thick silk tassel on the end of the bell pull. "I hear he hasn't been well."

"He has a sore throat from the atmosphere. He refuses anything for it but whisky and hot water. I don't think whisky right, in the mornings. But I don't suppose that's what Blundell wishes to discuss."

Yael discarded her bonnet on the chesterfield and lowered herself onto a chair, its upholstered velvet arms a snug fit around her hips. Her hair, silver since she was thirty years old, was wound into the customary coils over her ears and she was dressed in the muted grays and lavenders and mauves that she'd adopted since her mother passed away ten years earlier. Louisa found such prolonged mourning an affectation. Yael had refused outright her suggestion that she

15

could consult Mr. Hamilton, discover whether the late Mrs. Heron might come through with words of comfort.

Louisa reached for her workbag. She'd made her decision, sitting on the omnibus the previous evening as it swayed back over the river, while a man walked in front of the horses ringing a hand bell. Despite the motion of the bus, she'd had a sense inside herself of stillness. The advice from her mother was clear. For Harriet's sake, Louisa must take the risk and make the journey. She would travel to the ends of the earth, if need be. She would not allow her daughter to die.

The maid appeared in the open doorway. *Mary*. That was it. "A tray of tea, Mary. We'll have Earl Grey. The silver pot."

Her mind made up, Louisa had wasted no time. After dinner, when Harriet went up to bed, she'd reported to Blundell the doctor's advice, then immediately given her own opinion—that they should waste no time in arranging the journey. She hadn't mentioned her visit to Mr. Hamilton. That her mother had confirmed the need for the voyage could be enough for Blundell to deem it unnecessary.

Blundell had remained silent for some time, sighing occasionally. They were still in the dining room, sitting next to each other along two sections of the octagonal oak table, under the light of the gasolier, the curtains tightly drawn, the fire low. Waiting for her husband's decision, Louisa felt the deep comfort of her home. She looked around her at the darkly gleaming sideboard, the Japanese wallpaper behind it, the set of Crown Derby dishes arranged face forward in a glass-fronted cabinet lined with soft green velvet that made her think of moss.

They'd moved to Canonbury from the house in Wren Street when Harriet was barely two years old, following Blundell's promotion at the bank. He'd paid a thousand pounds for a ninety-nine-year lease and Louisa had felt an abiding satisfaction at the prospect that she would see out her days in the Georgian crescent.

Blundell gave another sigh.

"If the doctor recommends it, she must go." He reached for her hand and patted it. "And you with her, of course. I'll find a means of releasing the funds immediately. My chief concern is that I cannot come with you, Louisa. The country's in a wretched condition, by all accounts."

"Thank you, Blundell," she said, relief and alarm coursing through her in equal measure. "I knew I could rely on you. We will set off after Christmas."

"I shall miss you most terribly," he said, lifting her hand to his lips and kissing it. "But that hardly needs saying."

Louisa met his eyes, unable to speak. She couldn't allow herself to think about leaving Blundell behind. If she did, she might change her mind.

Harriet's dog began to bark downstairs. Louisa glanced up to find that, from behind her spectacles, Yael was regarding her. Her sister-in-law snapped shut a tin of peppermints.

"Is something wrong, Louisa? You look drawn."

"I'm quite well, thank you, Yael. You?"

Yael nodded.

"Nothing to complain of, dear."

Louisa took a needle from the little silk pouch that Harriet had made for her, more years ago than she cared to remember. She and Yael shared neither the ease nor the heartfelt quarrels that Louisa had with her own sisters and she didn't feel inclined to discuss the events of the last two days.

The dog's bark intensified, the front door opened, and from the street the sound of turning hooves floated up the stairs. Blundell's voice preceded him into the room.

"Has my sister arrived? Ah, there you are." He poured himself a measure of gin and pulled up a chair in front of Yael's. "I expect Louisa's told you what's afoot?"

Louisa shook her head.

"Not yet, Blundell. There hasn't been the opportunity."

"I won't beat about the bush, Yael," he said. "Harriet's no better. Grammaticas prescribes a trip up the Nile."

"I see." Yael looked startled. She sat straighter on her chair, her bulk lightly balanced. "It sounds an extreme measure."

"Extreme measures are called for," Louisa said. "Harriet is failing."

"Poor girl," Yael said. "I shall pray for her."

Blundell got to his feet again.

"I have something to ask of you, Sis."

"What might that be?"

Yael's tone was wary. It was unfair, Louisa thought privately, that the care of their father fell entirely to her sister-in-law. Blundell paid the bills but it was Yael who sat with the old man morning and evening, listened to his complaints, read the newspaper aloud from cover to cover. Blundell barely sat down when he visited; he stood at the writing desk issuing checks and totting up accounts. He was speaking again.

"Louisa is ill equipped on her own to go halfway across the world," he said, neutrally, as if he was relaying a known fact.

"What on earth do you mean, Blundell?" Louisa's hand ceased stitching.

Yael was staring at him through the thick glass spectacles that seemed to serve the purpose of enabling others to see her more clearly, by the way they magnified her gray, serious eyes. Louisa had been unable to escape the realization, years earlier, that Harriet had her aunt's eyes.

"It will only be for a month or two," Blundell said. "Three at most, the doctor says."

"Who will care for Father?"

Blundell put down his glass, lowered his hands toward the flames rising from an ash log.

"Mrs. Darke knows his routine better than anyone."

Yael levered herself up from the seat, gripping the arms with her hands. "You wish to entrust our father to a housekeeper?"

Blundell spoke gently. "He barely knows who you are, Yael. He won't suffer from your absence. Harriet needs you more."

The girl had arrived with the tray and was fiddling with the teaspoons. Louisa dismissed her with a look and went to the table, carefully filled the first cup; the best pot had always had a dribble down the spout. She couldn't imagine embarking on a journey with Blundell's sister. She and Yael had no common ground. Louisa had time for neither charity work nor Bible study, and Yael took no pride in her appearance, nor was she interested in the spiritual realm.

Yael had retrieved her bonnet. It hung limply in her hand, the tips of the old gray feathers brushing the rug. Like a dead thing, Louisa thought, with a silent, internal shudder.

"Louisa?" Yael said. "What is your view of this fandango?"

"For Harriet's health, I will do what I must." She couldn't think properly, felt as if the season had invaded her head. "I'm sure we shall manage perfectly well alone. Do take a cup of tea, Yael."

Yael stared at her, then turned back to her brother.

"I have never believed Harriet ought to be encouraged in her strange ideas, Blundell. I would have thought the Holy Lands a more suitable destination. But I hope I can always be relied upon to do my duty."

A moment later, the front door slammed again. Louisa went to the window and drew back the lace curtain. The house appeared to float in an ocean of fog and Yael had vanished. Resuming her seat, trying to gather her thoughts, Louisa held up the eye of her needle to the lamplight.

"She's a brick," Blundell said.

"But she didn't agree to it," Louisa interrupted.

"She didn't disagree. I'll see the shipping agent in the morning. The bank has a villa in Alexandria you should be able to use."

"I cannot picture your sister in the tropics," Louisa said, her tone measured.

"It isn't the tropics. It is the Near East."

He sounded distracted.

"Even so," Louisa persisted, "it will be hot."

Blundell sat down and leaned back in his chair, rested the glass on his chest.

"Yael has always been fond of Harriet."

Louisa pulled the end of cotton through the narrow eye. It was true. Yael took more interest in Harriet than Louisa's own sisters did, giving her prayer books with pages edged in gold leaf, a copy of Bunyan's *Pilgrim's Progress*, tracts on the condition of women. Only Louisa's younger sister, Anna, kept in regular touch with Harriet, writing long letters from whichever far-flung part of the world she found herself in, sending gifts. Louisa suspected Anna of fomenting some of Harriet's eccentricities.

19

Blundell was on his feet again.

"The truth is that Egypt is bankrupt," he said. "It isn't the best of times but I don't suppose that will affect you." He looked around at her. "Don't fret, Louisa. Yael will manage things. She always does."

Lavinia sat at Louisa's dressing table with her back to the mirror. "'Opera glasses,'" she said. "'Twine. Smoked spectacles.' However will you transport it all?"

Louisa shrugged. Lavinia had thrown herself into the idea of the trip to Egypt. Earlier in the day, she'd helped Rosina drag the two trunks up from the cellar, set them to air in Louisa's bedroom, their lids thrown back on their necks. She'd commandeered the guidebook Blundell had brought home and was poring over the list of necessities.

Lavinia lifted the book again, held it close to the candle, and raised her voice.

"'Gentlemen ought to take their firearms for hunting with them. Both weapons and shot are difficult to procure.'"

"We are not gentlemen," Louisa said.

It was Boxing Day, three o'clock in the afternoon, and the sky beyond the window was as thick as porridge. It was a pity to be aggravated by her sister, when they met so rarely. Louisa had thought she might confide her worries to Lavinia, but all through the first two days of the visit, busy with preparations, with a pair of geese and innumerable puddings and pies, with welcoming her sons and Tom's new wife, who was still—as far as the eye could tell—not pregnant, Louisa hadn't been able to get Lavinia alone. Now that the opportunity had arrived, she found herself unable to speak her fears aloud.

Lavinia closed the book.

"Must you go, Louisa? If you don't wish to?"

"The doctor believes the dry climate will be beneficial. And Harriet desires it, more than anything."

Louisa studied the pattern of pink roses on the rug. She wouldn't mention the instruction she had received. Like Blundell, Lavinia was opposed to Mr. Hamilton. Louisa wondered sometimes if her sister envied her, because their mother could speak to her from the afterlife. She shivered, at the memory of her voice, the words she'd uttered.

The sound of coughing floated down the stairs and Lavinia put down the book on the dressing table. She looked at Louisa, her head tilted to one side.

"We all pray that it may help Harriet. But is it wise? For you, I mean. You've always been so . . ." Lavinia looked up at a watercolor on the bedroom wall of a baby crawling among the daisies on a cliff-top. "So careful."

Louisa pulled out a plain linen shirt from the heap of garments on the bed. The shirt was old; she'd worn it summer after summer for picnics on the beach at Boscombe. Holding the collar under her chin, Louisa began to fold the sleeves across the back, turn the shoulders in on themselves.

"I ought to be able to travel with my daughter without fear, oughtn't I? After all these years."

"Yes, you ought. I wasn't saying otherwise." Lavinia hesitated. "I often wonder, Izzy. Do you ever hear anything . . . from those days? Anything of her?"

Louisa shook her head.

"Nothing at all? Not a word?" Lavinia persisted.

Louisa glanced at the closed door of the bedroom. Shook her head again.

"No, I don't. I never have."

"Perhaps it's for the best."

"Of course it's for the best, Lavinia," Louisa said, her voice sharp.

Lavinia pulled the cuff of her woolen dress down over her knuckles and dabbed underneath her eyes, one side and then the other.

"I think I shall go and dress for dinner."

When she'd gone, Louisa threw the shirt down on the bed and hugged her arms over her chest. Pacing over the roses, feeling their soft yield under her feet, she felt disturbed. The company of any of her sisters could give her the feeling that the life she'd worked so hard to construct and maintain, the life of a wife and mother, an angel in the house, might be dismantled as easily as a set at the end of a theater performance. The stage laid bare again, leaving only splintered boards and dust. Emptiness.

All through her life, Louisa had tried to leave behind her childhood. Her father, Amos Newlove, was not often home. Her mother, Amelia, felt poor and lonely all her days and longed above all for a son. Louisa was her fourth daughter, after Beatrice, Hepzibah, and Lavinia, but before Anna. Before poor Antony.

Even prior to the tragedies that later befell their family, a family that Louisa grew to see as precarious as a gull's nest on the cliff side, she grew up resolved that her life would not be what her mother's had been. She would not marry a sailor, would not be poor, would not give birth to a row of daughters like Russian dolls, the female endlessly spawning the female.

The dinner gong sounded downstairs. Dragging a chair to the open wardrobe, Louisa climbed up on it and reached inside, felt for the box hidden at the back of the shelf at the top. She found it and lifted the lid, tentatively, her hands exploring until they met a compact, cold weight. Lifting it out, she stepped down from the chair, holding the gun at arm's length. She laid it gingerly on the dressing table, pointing at the wall, lying between the ivory-backed brushes, the pots of cold cream. The gun was loaded with a cartridge, Blundell had told her when he warned her not to touch it.

Picking it up by the carved wooden handle that emerged from the holster, Louisa wrapped the pistol round and round in the old shirt. She slid it under a folded nightgown at the bottom of the trunk and closed the lid. They would be three women, traveling alone, without male protection. She would protect them. Death would not get anywhere near them.

As the brassy sound of the gong floated up the stairs for a second time, she repinned a falling coil of hair and prepared to join the others in the dining room. They were eight for dinner. Blundell and Harriet. Harriet's elder brother Tom, and his wife, Flossie. Lavinia and her husband, John Day. Mrs. Heatherwick, their widowed neighbor, who often joined them for supper. And herself.

It pleased Louisa to see every section of the octagonal table occupied.

FIVE

❧❧

Harriet fitted her face to the porthole by the pillow. On the other side of the thick glass, the land glided by, steady and fluid, as if the warehouses and sheds and cranes of the docks passed by in a stately procession, as if England was on the move, floating away, and they on the ship were anchored amidst a traveling world.

She lay down again. Beyond the sawing sound of her own breath, she could hear boots treading along the passageway outside, shouted commands between men, the pulse of an engine. The bunk vibrated underneath her, and over her head her journal, in its cotton bag, swung from a peg.

They'd left the house in London at first light, Harriet keeping the dog under her cloak as the carriage jolted toward Waterloo. The fog thinned as the train steamed through the outskirts of London and had cleared entirely by the New Forest, puffs of black smoke from the engine trailing over a landscape of skeletal trees and frozen ponds, drifts of steam striping a pale sky. All of them stared out of the train windows, mesmerized by being able to see distance again. Harriet's father and eldest brother were coming to the port to see them off.

Louisa was against bringing Dash.

"It'll be nothing but a nuisance having him with us," she said.

"He'll be no trouble, Mother. I'll look aft—"

"I refuse to quarrel with you, Harriet."

"A dog deters rats," Yael remarked to no one in particular as the train pulled into Southampton and in the rush of alighting nothing more was said on the subject.

Standing on the deck of the steamer, Harriet's father had intervened. "Let the little chap come with you, Louisa. It's a companion for Harriet."

The words were barely out of his mouth when a voice announced through the speaking trumpet that non-passengers should disembark. Her father had opened his arms and hugged Harriet to his chest. Feeling his solid presence, the rough brush of tweed on her cheek, she experienced a sharp and dismaying sense of regret.

"We're going so far away, Father."

"You'll be fit and well by the time you come home," he said. "Don't come back until you are, eh? Look after your mother. And your aunt, of course."

He'd shaken hands with Yael, then gripped Louisa's arms through the sleeves of her new traveling coat.

"Write, Louisa," he said, looking down at her. "Write as soon as you are able. We shall miss you at home."

Louisa's face caught a gleam of wintry sun and Harriet thought she saw tears on her cheek.

"I will, Blundell," Louisa whispered. "I will."

Louisa embraced Tom and so did Harriet and Yael and then the farewell was over. Her father and brother turned to join the crowd passing back over the gangway as Harriet picked up the dog and she, Yael, and Louisa made their way down to their cabin.

Harriet had just enough strength left to climb up onto the raised bunk on one side of the tiny room.

"This surely can't be meant to accommodate all three of us?" Yael said, edging through the doorway.

She opened up a large leather bag and retrieved a tin of flea powder that she began to shake over the dark blankets.

"You must rest now, Harriet," Louisa said, dabbing at her eyes with a corner of her handkerchief. Sitting on the edge of the bunk below Harriet's, Louisa removed her hat, leaning her head and shoulders forward, checking the chignon at the back of her head with little pats of her hand.

"I've lost a hairpin. I can't think where it's gone."

"Don't fret, dear," Yael said, hanging her ulster on the back of the door, stowing the bag in the overhead locker and maneuvering herself onto the single bunk on the other side of the cabin. "I daresay you'll be able to buy a card of pins when we arrive. The women in Egypt have hair, after all. They must do something with it."

Yael rolled over, with difficulty. From above, her aunt reminded Harriet of the whale they'd seen beached on the mud one year at Boscombe. Harriet had stood in the crowd on the promenade, looking down on the mighty creature in its helplessness. Her brothers joined the people on the shore who were splashing buckets of water over it, trying to keep it alive until the tide came in. Next morning, the same individuals were back with knives and whetstones, cutting steaks and rectangles of white blubber from the open-jawed corpse, sharpening their blades with as much enthusiasm as they'd previously filled buckets.

"I can't imagine why I didn't bring spares," Louisa said. "When I think of all the useless things I've got in the trunk. A few pins wouldn't have occupied any space at all. Will you take a drop of tincture, Harriet?"

"No, Mother."

Pulling a pair of blue velvet curtains along the side of the bunk, closing herself away, Harriet breathed through her nose, toward the pit of her stomach. *One, two . . .* She breathed out again, slowly, counting, as Dr. Grammaticas had taught her to do to measure her breath and steady it. *Two, three, four.*

Her chest ached and her breath was short, made worse by the cold air and the fumes from the engines, but she didn't want to start the voyage feeling queasy with the nausea that the tincture provoked. The medicines—foul-tasting, headache-inducing—could be almost as bad as the asthma. She had tried scores but not one fulfilled the promises made for it, of bringing about a lasting change in her health.

Harriet got the red journal out of the pocket and held it to her chest. Despite the roar of the engines, the cry of seagulls outside, the stink of fish and coal, she felt as if she might be dreaming. Putting her face to the porthole again, she watched as the coast grew indistinct and was lost to view. She pinched the back of her hand and told herself she was leaving England. She was on her way to Thebes.

Yael's bunk was empty. *Gone to Divine Service*, read a note on the pillow. Louisa moaned in her sleep and rolled over to face the side of the ship, tugging her blanket over her head. Lifting her cloak from the hook on the back of the door, Harriet picked up the dog and let herself out of the cabin.

She walked past a line of numbered doors to a circular iron staircase, pulling herself up by the handrail. Pausing at the top to steady her breath, she glanced through the windows of the saloon cabin. At the far end, a circle of a dozen people were on their knees, their heads bowed. Harriet recognized Yael's gray skirts spread on the floor like a puddle.

The stairs up to the weather deck were grand and polished, made of wood. Stepping out to the rush and freshness of sea air, she gasped as the wind whipped back her hair and blew her cloak out behind her like a sail. The sky was immense, a soft silver bowl over her head with long fingers of pearly cloud on the horizon. All around, the sea glittered and rolled, looking grand and clean and alive.

The deck was deserted apart from a couple sitting on a bench, and at the bow, just visible between the masts, a man setting up an easel. As Harriet put down the dog, the couple rose and walked toward her, arm in arm, the woman clutching a hat to her head with one hand. The height of the woman's hat, the aigrette of iridescent turquoise feathers attached on one side, gave her the appearance of a gorgeous bird herself. She nodded at Harriet as she passed by.

The sun emerged between the scudding clouds and Harriet became aware of her shadow in front of her on the scrubbed planks. Her own head, in a close-fitting winter bonnet, looked small, her body like a narrow giantess's. Her brown tweed traveling skirt, chosen by Louisa at Marshall & Snelgrove for its warmth and durability, announced her as an invalid, unfashionable and unmarried, set apart from other women of her age. Everything about her carried the same message: her five feet and nine inches, which her brothers used to say made her look like an etiolated plant, shooting up in search of the light; her pale complexion and forced avoidance, often unsuccessfully, of the emotions that she seemed to feel more strongly than others.

Raising her head, she took a gulp of salty air and began a tour of the deck. Passing by a row of upturned lifeboats, she noticed the man again. He stood at his easel, a little distance in front of her, black hair flying out behind him in the wind. She watched as he wiped a brush clean and began to load it with paint from the palette balanced on his forearm. An oily cloth fell to the deck at his feet and as the wind lifted it, Harriet's dog sprang forward. Seizing the rag between his jaws, he began to worry it, shaking it as if it were alive, growling with all his might.

Harriet laughed as she walked toward him. "Here, Dash. Give that back."

"Drop it, brute."

The painter aimed the tip of a laced, two-toned shoe at the dog.

"Don't kick him," Harriet said, her voice half carried away by the wind. "Dash. Let go!"

She knelt down and pulled the rag from the dog's jaws, handed it to the painter.

"You ought to keep it on a leash," he said, taking the cloth and securing it underneath the palette.

"Not it. Him," Harriet said.

The painter looked at her without interest. He was broad-faced and clean-shaven, his hair swept back over a low forehead. He wore a white shirt in an unevenly woven and unbleached fabric, the kind of cloth that Rosina might use to apply beeswax to furniture. No collar. A red scarf decorated with peacock feathers fluttered at his neck. Harriet had never seen a man dressed in clothes like his.

She was staring, she realized, feeling the start of a blush. Turning away, she caught sight of the canvas clamped on the easel. The picture was barely begun; a few arcs of sea spray in shades of pewter and olive and charcoal flew upward into a naked canvas sky.

Dash was shivering at her feet. Harriet gathered him under her arm and walked slowly back along the starboard side, past a stall with two cows lowing from within, a stack of rabbit hutches, a sailor in a chef's hat disappearing down through a hatch with a basket of eggs. The deck was filling with other passengers, English people, shouting and laughing in a way that interrupted the lonely meeting between sky and sea. Harriet felt breathless, the exhilaration she'd felt when she emerged on the weather deck spent.

On her way back down, she stopped again outside the grand saloon. Behind the glazed doors, groups of people sat in the red plush seats, talking and reading newspapers. A fug of pipe smoke rose in front of the mirrors, wreathing the swags of red velvet curtain, the framed illustrations of ships. On the carpeted floor, children played with dolls and toy lambs, the boys hopping and jumping, pretending to fall over from the movement of the ship. Harriet had a familiar sense of looking in on life from outside.

"Are you unwell?" said a voice.

It was the woman she'd seen earlier, alone now, picking her way down the wide steps from the deck. Harriet shook her head.

"I'm only catching my breath."

"Pardon me, I thought you looked a little pale." The woman reached the bottom of the steps and stooped to pat the dog. "What an adorable fellow."

She rose, two pearls swinging on fine gold chains from her earlobes as her blue eyes scanned Harriet's face, her high-necked bodice, then ran down over the robust skirt and reached Harriet's feet, shod in flat boots; heels were out of the question for a female of Harriet's height, Louisa said.

Putting her head on one side, the woman held out a gloved hand.

"I'm Mrs. Cox. Sarah Cox."

"Pleased to meet you." Harriet extended her own bare hand. She felt the softness of Mrs. Cox's kid glove and the firmness and quickness of the hand inside it as it squeezed rather than shook her own, as if conveying some message of sympathy. "My name's Harriet Heron," she said, stiffly. Harriet was quick to detect pity and disliked it.

"Are you alone, Miss Heron?"

"I'm traveling with my mother. And my aunt."

28

"How pleasant for you." Mrs. Cox smiled. "I'm on my honeymoon." Mrs. Cox looked about the same age as Harriet yet she was an adult woman, traveling with her husband. Next to her, Harriet felt as if she were an outsized and overgrown girl. She was twenty-three, but might as well have been twelve years old. Her chest tightened and the familiar struggle for air began to make itself felt more strongly.

"Please excuse me," she said, picking up the dog. "I must go back to my cabin."

SIX

"In the midst of the street of it, and on either side of the river, was there the tree of life . . ."

Aunt Yael perched at the tiny table, her knees twisted round to one side, reading aloud from Revelation. She'd announced on the train her intention to use the time on board ship to persevere with her reading of the Bible. Since the death of her mother, she'd read it through five times and was close to completing the sixth cycle.

"And what will you do then?" Louisa had asked. "When you reach the end?"

"Start again, dear," Yael had answered. "What else."

It was the third day of the voyage and all three women were feeling queasy from the movement of the steamer. Louisa reclined on the bottom bunk, leafing through the pages of a magazine, and Harriet lay on the top one, holding her journal. The journal had arrived in the post a month before Christmas, sent from Penang. Aunt Anna, her mother's youngest sister, traveled the world with her husband, Dr. Lucas St. Clair, establishing missions to sailors in foreign ports. She sent Harriet notebooks from whichever country she found herself in and this one was the most beautiful yet, bound in soft leather in a brilliant red, its pages bearing within their weave flattened shapes of petals and leaves. It had a red-ribbon place marker and could be closed up by a pair of fine leather ties of the same color.

At first, Harriet hadn't written in the book. Feeling that no words could match its thick, expectant pages, she left it blank and new, occasionally turning it over in her hands, opening it to breathe in the sour, woody scent of the paper, returning again and again to an idea she had that excited her and frightened her at the same time.

The fifth volume of Bunsen's great work on Egypt's place in universal history contained Samuel Birch's translation of a funeral ritual that he called the Book of the Dead. The ritual consisted of a set of spells and instructions that the ancient Egyptians had used for defeating death. If successfully followed, they believed, the magic ensured that the *ka*, or spirit, of the departed would be able to emerge from the tomb each day to hunt once more in the fields of reeds, dance again to the music of harps, train monkeys to pluck figs.

Harriet had been forced to contemplate her own death since she first became ill, when she was seven years old. If she had to die, that was the kind of eternal life she wanted. The English heaven had never appealed to her. Sometimes, comparing it to the one the ancient Egyptians had lived, she wondered if even the English life appealed to her.

The Egyptian spells were written on papyrus, by scribes with reed pens and palettes of red and black ink. The dead kept their instructions close; the scrolls were buried with the bodies, on the breast or at the side, between the legs or feet. Some people were buried with the texts unfurled, pressed against their chests under the bandages used to preserve their bodies.

Harriet had persuaded Rosina to buy her a bottle of red ink. She wanted to write her own spells, not for when she was dead, but to help her in her life. In the new book, she had her papyrus. The idea kept pressing at the edges of her mind, occurring to her at odd moments, demanding to be heard, but she put off carrying it out, fearing that it might be blasphemous, that the spells might succeed or that they might not succeed, she hardly knew which. Late one December night, with the London fog lying low and heavy outside, she got out her pens and inks.

The Egyptians had written their magic for the dead, to help them past tests of knowledge and judgments, into the state in which they were considered worthy of eternal life, their hearts weighed against the feather of Maat and found true. Harriet wanted to live before she died. It was life she longed for and it was life that her illness was denying her. Listening to the deep slumber of the household, the soft, interrupting rasp of her own breath, she opened the journal. Across the middle of the first pristine page, using red ink like the scribes of ancient Egypt, to give the words extra power, she wrote the title.

Harriet didn't want what most young women wished for from life. Her dream was to see for herself the tombs of the ancient Egyptians and study the hieroglyphs carved and painted by their hands. And if, one day or night, she was no longer able to continue the fight for breath, she wanted to die there, in Luxor. Above all, she did not wish to end her days in the room in which she'd spent almost all her life.

Wiping the nib, dipping the pen into the black ink, she turned to the next page and began a column of pictures. The first was of the house at Cloudesley Crescent; its five stories stood for home. The next was of an open book, her symbol of escape, followed by a pair of legs walking, the hieroglyph for movement. Below that, she shaped the rounded lines of a steamship, its chimney smoking, and next, she drew herself, a head taller than others, her hair in crinkled locks down her shoulders, her feet flat and pointing forward, like ancient Egyptian feet, certain of their direction. Then her name, enclosed in a cartouche or circle, like the ancient Egyptian royals'. *Harriet* was written in sounds, followed by the heron hieroglyph.

In the second column, she drew the coastline of Egypt, flat, dotted with windmills as she had read that it was. For health and life, she drew Hathor, daughter of the sun god, Ra, and goddess of pleasure and enjoyment, associated with life and laughter. Hathor stood too for that love between men and women of which Harriet knew nothing, feared that she might never experience. Hathor was straight-spined and almond-eyed, the sun disk balanced on her head between two long cow's horns.

For death, if she were to die, Harriet drew herself again, lying on the ground in an Egyptian rock tomb, with her hair fanned out around her, holding her book to her chest with her left hand, lines of lotus flowers painted on the wall behind her and above them the protective eye of the god Horus.

Finally, she drew a hand holding out an ankh, the symbol of breath. She laid down the pen and looked at the spell. Her magic was to ensure that she would reach Luxor. That she would live there and if she could not live, then she would die there. It was complete. Blotting the ink, she closed the book and secured its red leather ties.

She'd kept the journal close ever since. Slept with it under her pillow and carried it by day in a cotton pocket tied around her waist. Louisa said that it made her look like a bluestocking. Lying on her bunk in the cabin, Harriet undid the ties around its covers and for the first time looked again at her magic. She'd hardly dared to believe, when she wrote it, that it might be effective. And yet she was here, on her way. Closing the book again, shutting her eyes, she let the ever-present slosh and roar of the sea, the cries of a child in the next cabin, the murmur of her aunt's voice, wash over her.

And the sea gave up the dead which were in it; and death and hell delivered up the dead which were in them: and they were judged every man according to their works.

SEVEN

"What're you going to Egypt for?" Mrs. Cox asked. "If you didn't have to?"

"My doctor believes the climate will benefit me. And I have always wanted to go there."

"Why?"

Harriet felt for her journal, gripped the top of it between her fingertips. She paused before she answered, steadying herself by breathing into her stomach.

"I was a sickly child, Mrs. Cox. From a young age, I read books. The ancient Egyptians, their writings and pictures, have been my consolation. They were for me what fairy tales were for other girls."

Mrs. Cox raised her elegant eyebrows. Since their first meeting, Harriet had seen Mrs. Cox every day. In the afternoons, while Louisa rested in the cabin, Yael joined the Bible-study group in a corner of the dining saloon, and Mrs. Cox's husband occupied himself with reports of the stock exchange in old newspapers, Harriet and Mrs. Cox strolled on the top deck, weaving between the thick cobwebs of rigging, stopping sometimes to rest on the curved back-to-back wooden benches or to watch other passengers play a game of quoits.

If Harriet was short of breath, or too fatigued for walking, as today, she and Mrs. Cox remained in the grand saloon, at a table they'd made their own.

Mrs. Cox wore a different outfit every day. She was dressed in a raspberry-colored gown; a panel of ruched pink satin stretched from the high neck of the dress under her chin, down to the floor, and gave her the look of a curvaceous and elegant mermaid, her stomach rounded under the glove-like fit of the gown.

"I suppose you will look for a husband at the same time?" she said.

"I'm not looking for a husband."

"Why ever not?"

Harriet couldn't immediately answer. It was Louisa's oft-repeated belief that Harriet was unlikely to marry. That with her delicate health, her ill fortune in the matter of her looks, the best place for her was by her mother's side. Often, as she said it, Louisa reached out and touched Harriet, a gesture upward to her shoulder which Harriet experienced as some form of arrest. She felt sorry more on Louisa's behalf than her own that she'd inherited her father's red-gold hair, his blush-prone complexion, and his pale gray eyes, in place of her mother's dark, dramatic beauty, still evident even now. It was a disappointment to Louisa that her daughter didn't resemble her.

Harriet shrugged.

"I suppose it's because I'm not well. Why are you going to Egypt, Mrs. Cox?"

"My husband has business interests in Cairo. He decided we should take our honeymoon there. He said we could kill two birds with one stone."

"How delightful."

"I wanted to go to Italy," Mrs. Cox said, turning her head in a sudden movement that caused her earrings to swing. "But they are already well supplied with parts for flour mills."

Harriet felt uncomfortable. Mrs. Cox surely couldn't be being disloyal to her new husband. Looking around for Zebedee Cox, Harriet spotted Yael, sitting on the far side of the saloon, her feet in their polished brown boots braced on the floor, her hands gripping the seat on either side of her. Yael nodded in their direction and Harriet waved at her.

"She looks like a fish out of water," Mrs. Cox said.

"My aunt wouldn't be here if it wasn't for me. She'd be at home in St. John's Wood, pouring a whisky for Grandfather on the dot of six, or going off to her refuge for fallen women. My father made her come with us. She's a spinster, so she couldn't refuse."

The floor below them rolled and they both leaned sideways in order to stay upright. Mrs. Cox looked queasy. Harriet enjoyed the sudden shifts to the perpendicular, the capriciousness of the horizon. It seemed to say that change was possible, that it could occur at any time, unexpectedly.

Mrs. Cox took a sip of her chamomile tea and picked a round yellow flower from between her teeth.

"You don't want to live like your aunt, do you? I'll tell your fortune, Harriet," she said.

Producing a leather pouch from a bag that matched her dress, she began laying out a spread of cards in rows, face upward, with some placed sideways, others with their pictures upside down. Harriet sat in silence, watching. She hoped Yael couldn't see. Aunt disapproved of what she called soothsayers and was more than capable of arriving at the table to say so, delivering her views on the inadvisability of trying to peer into the future, which she considered God's business.

"You will marry," Mrs. Cox said, as if in answer to a question Harriet had asked. "And have children. I see three, but only two births." She looked up at Harriet with shining eyes. "Perhaps you are going to have twins. Do they run in your family?"

"Really, Mrs. . . ."

"Oh, call me Sarah."

"Sarah, I . . ."

"You'll recognize the man when you meet him. You will know him immediately. His occupation is something quite out of the ordinary. He won't be a banker or a businessman or work in any kind of office. He'll work with his brain and his hands together."

Mrs. Cox peered at the spread.

"You won't believe this." Her voice was incredulous. She reached out and touched Harriet's wrist with small fingers that were unusually even in length and with a row of three diamonds glittering on one of them. "You'll encounter him on a voyage. A nautical one."

36

Harriet felt herself blushing, but whether with embarrassment or annoyance, she wasn't sure.

"I doubt that."

Mrs. Cox looked around the crowded saloon and Harriet's eyes followed, roaming over elderly Mrs. Treadwell, a suet-pudding-like couple with four round, pale children, two spinster sisters who conversed solely with each other. The only unmarried man present was Reverend Griffinshawe, a widower, who explained to everyone from under bushy white eyebrows that he was taking copies of the Bible in Arabic to his parish in Egypt and would appreciate most kindly any support they could offer for this worthwhile venture.

"He's here somewhere," Mrs. Cox said. "He must be."

"I hardly think so."

Harriet picked up one of the cards and examined a man hanging upside down, his ankles suspended from the branch of a tree. It was humiliating to have one's fortune told and even worse to experience the rush of unaccustomed hope she'd felt on hearing the prediction.

"Do you really believe I could marry?"

"Of course. Why ever not?"

"There's my poor health. And some people think red hair is unlucky."

"It's clear as day, Hattie. You will join with a man whom you meet on the water." Mrs. Cox gathered up the cards and slipped them back into a worn wallet of morocco. "I have seen one eligible gentleman," she said, raising her finely shaped brows. "You must have seen him too, that day we first—"

Harriet rose from the table, accidentally stepping on Dash's tail as she emerged from the bench seat, making him whimper.

"Excuse me, Mrs. Cox. I must return to my mother."

Bidding her friend goodbye, she picked up the dog and left the saloon, made her way down the spiral of iron steps to the second-class cabins. At the bottom, she stopped by a porthole, resting her elbows on its inside rim.

On the other side of the glass, the sea was agitated and unsettled, rearing up around the ship as if it were trying to communicate something from the deep. The sea was becoming a companion, true and constant; Harriet felt a new pleasure every time she looked at it. Perhaps that was the union that Mrs. Cox foresaw.

With Dash at her heels, she continued along the narrow passage-way, bracing herself to meet Louisa's anxious solicitude.

EIGHT

⚜

Three times a day, all passengers sat down to meals in the dining saloon. They took up the same places, on the same turning chairs, at breakfast, luncheon, and dinner. Harriet's was at the end farthest from the captain's table, an isolated spot but with the advantage that she could see the whole saloon.

The painter sat a few tables away. More than once, Harriet had seen him staring in their direction with a brooding look, his sketch pad open on the white cloth, chin resting on his knuckles. At first, Harriet believed that the man looked at her. He regretted having tried to kick her dog on the weather deck, she told herself, and was wondering how to make amends. Quickly, though, and reluctantly, she formed the impression that it was not herself who attracted his attention. It was Louisa.

On the evening of Mrs. Cox's soothsaying, the painter entered the dining saloon late. He stood in the doorway as his eyes roamed the room and came to rest on their table. Louisa was in a good mood. As they'd sat down, Captain Ablewhite had complimented her on keeping her sea legs, then sent two glasses of sherry to the table. Aunt Yael took only a small glass of wine once a year, on Christmas Day. Louisa had finished her own and begun on the other.

In her dark satin evening dress, with the necklace of marcasite around her throat sparkling by the light of scores of candles in the crystal chandeliers, reflecting off the mirrors, she looked elegant and assured, like the subject of one of the paintings she admired. Louisa loved to walk to the National Gallery on a Sunday afternoon and stand in front of the great portraits in oil, identifying the fabric of the women's costumes, speculating as to the meaning of the look in their eyes, the significance of the items in the background. Sometimes she ventured to recognize the tints and pigments used in the paintings, murmuring their names to herself in a private incantation that, when she was a child, Harriet had mistaken for prayer.

Louisa chinked her schooner against Yael's water glass and Harriet's tumbler of Indian tonic.

"I do believe you're looking brighter already, Harriet," she said.

Aunt Yael put down her soup spoon.

"Louisa, dear," she said. "Do you know that man?"

Louisa glanced up and Harriet followed her eyes. The painter was heading toward them with an air of purpose. Harriet felt the start of a blush.

"I can't say that I do," Louisa said.

Before Yael could continue, the man arrived at the table. He bowed.

"Good evening, ladies. May I join you?"

"Why not?" Louisa said, smiling at him as he eased himself into the chair next to Harriet's. "We are all travelers together."

"Indeed."

He picked up the menu and began reading the courses aloud. "'Barley broth. Steak pie. Mutton chops. Spaghetti in cream. Cabbage. Apple tart with *sauce anglaise*.'" The usual muck," he said, putting down the card, looking around for the steward.

"There are plenty who would be glad of such fare," said Yael, pleasantly.

The captain rose to his feet, ringing on his glass with a knife, and the dining saloon quieted to a churchlike hush as the passengers turned their faces toward him.

"Good evening, ladies and gentlemen. A few announcements. The Reverend . . ." The captain consulted a piece of paper. "Ernest Griffinshawe conducts divine service at eight each morning in the grand saloon. He would appreciate the attendance of a greater number of fellow worshippers.

"We have in our midst a pair of honeymooners. I extend my congratulations to Mr. and Mrs. Zebedee Cox."

A murmur of approval went up and there was a general lifting of glasses. Zebedee Cox got to his feet, looking flustered.

"On behalf of my wife and myself, thank you, Captain Ablewhite," he said.

The male passengers banged their tankards on the tables and the women looked at each other, resettling themselves on their chairs like a twittering flock of jeweled, powdered birds. Harriet caught a drift of recent cigar smoke, mixed with a sweet, woody scent, and took a sideways glance at the painter. Even dressed in a black tie and tailcoat, his dark hair greased, he looked different from the other men. The clothes failed to tame him and in place of a starched handkerchief a small sketchbook protruded from his breast pocket. He'd turned his eyes back to Louisa and was watching her, his expression intent.

Captain Ablewhite cleared his throat.

"Enjoy your dinner, ladies and gentlemen. The *Star of the East* makes good speed. We traversed the Bay of Biscay without encountering any storms but we anticipate strong winds in the Mediterranean."

He sat down and the voices rose quickly to their previous pitch. The painter summoned the steward and ordered a bottle of red wine.

"I suppose you are traveling to Egypt?" he said, addressing Louisa.

"Yes. Alexandria." Louisa's face was flushed and her eyes bright. "We are so looking forward to seeing the River Nile."

"Alex isn't the place to see the river."

"Where should one see it?" Yael said, raising her head from her soup bowl.

"It is at its best at Aswan in Upper Egypt, where it flows over the cataracts. But that is a thousand miles away."

"Upper Egypt?" said Yael. "I would have thought it was Lower Egypt, farther down."

"Yes. But it isn't."

"Imagine seeing where Moses was put in his basket among the bulrushes," Louisa said.

She took the last of the second glass of sherry, tipping back her head, her white throat exposed and swanlike under the delicate neck-lace. Yael's napkin was tucked under her double chin like a baby's bib; she began sawing into a bread roll with a great, blunt knife.

The man leaned forward and seized his soup spoon. He ate silently, tipping the dish away from him. Harriet pushed away her own empty bowl. Printed around the rim, in a loopy flourish, was the name of a ship, but it was the wrong ship. SS *Tanjore*.

Putting down his spoon, the painter wiped his mouth and turned to Harriet.

"You're the girl with the dog, aren't you?"

Under the table, Harriet felt Dash's back with her toe.

"I have a dog, yes. The one you feared would kill your rag."

She dropped the remains of her roll off her lap and pushed it in the dog's direction as the steward returned with a large, high-sided tray, the floor rolling under his feet. He pulled the cork from a bottle and splashed red wine into a glass.

"Good health," the painter said, raising it.

"We haven't been introduced," Louisa said. "I am Mrs. Heron, this is my sister-in-law, Miss Heron, and my daughter, Miss Harriet Heron."

"Heron." He rolled his wine around the inside of his glass. "I don't know the name."

"Why should you?" Louisa said gaily.

He turned to Harriet again. "Would you like a glass of wine?"

Harriet pulled strands of meat from a chop with the large knife and fork. She'd never tasted wine. Throughout her childhood, Lou-isa had said she was too young. Later, when other girls her age were marrying, giving birth, running households, Louisa had insisted that wine might bring on an attack.

"I believe I would," Harriet said. "Yes."

"She doesn't take it," Louisa said. "My daughter is an invalid."

"Mother, I—"

"I see. And Miss Heron, being the mainstay of the Reverend's congregation, will most likely be a teetotaler. But Mrs. Heron"— he carried on looking at Louisa—"will join me."

He reached out and poured another glass. Putting down the bot-tle with a bump, he held out the wine to Louisa. There were streaks of oil paint on the back of his hand, bronze and sage and dark mustard, raised spots of it on his nails thrown into relief by the light from the chandelier. Louisa's eyes were fixed on the man's hand. She hesitated as she took the glass.

"You must be a painter," she said.

"I am. Why, Mrs. Heron? Are you interested in painting?"

Louisa shook her head. "Not especially."

Her voice was flat. Harriet shifted on her chair and glanced at her aunt.

"Do you intend staying long in Egypt?" Yael asked, peering at the man through the spectacles that magnified her eyes and made her appear as if she were capable of clairvoyance.

"Until it becomes tedious," he said. "Which I expect will be soon. I've been a half-dozen times before."

Louisa interrupted the silence that followed.

"I don't believe you told us your name, Mr. . . . ?"

The air of giddiness and elation had leached away from her and her voice was clipped.

The man leaned back in the revolving chair. "I don't believe I did. It's Soane. Eyre Soane."

It seemed to Harriet that Louisa flinched. "You have an unusual name," she said.

"You are not familiar with it, Mrs. Heron?"

"There are so many names, these days," said Yael.

Louisa had barely touched the slice of steak pie, the mound of tinned peas, before she laid down her knife and fork, declared herself unable to eat another morsel, and asked Mr. Soane to excuse her. Picking up her fan, she began ushering her skirts out from under the table.

"Will you take some water, Mother?" Harriet said. "Oh . . ."

Louisa, half out of her seat, had knocked over her wineglass. A ruby sea was seeping over the white damask.

"Come, Harriet. It's time we retired," she said. "If you would excuse us, Mr. . . ."

"Soane." He raised his glass to her again. "Not an easy name to forget."

"Come, Harriet," Louisa repeated.

Calling the dog out from under the table, concealing her chop bone in her napkin, Harriet had no choice but to follow Louisa out of the saloon.

As she reached the sliding doors, Harriet glanced back at their table. The steward who had poured the wine now dabbed at the spilled wine with a napkin. Yael was eating pudding as if she were alone, her head bent over her dish. Eyre Soane sat upright in his chair, an unlit cigar between his lips, one ankle crossed over his knee. Mrs. Cox's prediction made its way unbidden into Harriet's mind and, as if he could read her thoughts, the painter turned and looked straight at her, his dark eyes fixing on her own gray ones. There was no doubt this time that it was she who attracted his attention.

Feeling her face begin to burn, Harriet hurried after her mother.

NINE

The wind blew a shower of spray against the porthole and the ship pitched. Under the pressure of Eyre Soane's hand, the point of the pencil broke, a fragment of lead skidding across the page to the floor. He felt in his trouser pocket and found his penknife. Testing the sharpness of the blade across the pad of his thumb, he began to shave wood from lead with swift downward strokes.

The page where he'd been working lay open on the table. It was filled with the same portrait, repeated a dozen or more times. Each picture was different but the woman was recognizably the same, multiplied as if in a hall of mirrors. Her face was oval, pleasing in its regularity, and framed by curling hair. She was young in several sketches, in the middle years in some, and ageless in others. Here, her eyes were lowered, and here, raised as if in challenge or looking into the distance.

In every drawing, exaggerated to the point of caricature, one thing distinguished the woman. Her hairline was strikingly irregular. On the left side of the parting, the hair at the top of her forehead grew in a straight line. On the right side, it grew back in a pronounced widow's peak.

In the final drawing, the woman's head appeared shaven. Her face was reduced to its features—a straight nose, a well-shaped mouth— and above the large eyes the curiously asymmetrical line ran starkly across the top of her forehead.

Eyre had seen her at dinner on the first day of the voyage. He'd begun to feel a sense of sick unease familiar from his childhood, had wondered what prompted it as he pushed mutton around the plate. The curious hairline had caught his eye and as he returned to studying the woman, examined it further, he knew whose it was. She had aged, of course, was altered in every particular except that one and a way of carrying her head that was birdlike, inquisitive, and as if poised for flight.

With the sharpened pencil held in his fist like a dagger, Eyre began to score out the faces. By the time he'd finished, the paper was pitted and torn, the lead broken again, and all but one of the sketches obliterated. Only the picture that looked like a living skull remained.

Throwing aside his sketchbook, Eyre dropped the pencil and rose from his chair, rubbing condensation from the inside of a porthole. No moon or stars were visible outside and he couldn't distinguish sea from sky. Lighting a cigar, walking up and down the cabin, he remembered the way the younger Miss Heron had looked at him across the dining saloon and he smiled.

Louisa, once she'd understood who he was, had been guarded; even her spinster sister-in-law had appeared to regard him with suspicion. But the girl was open, her eagerness for life transparent.

What he would do with her willingness, he didn't yet know. Only that he would make full use of it.

The ship rolled in a great lurching movement that made him feel as if his stomach rose in his body. Opening the cabin door, he poked out his head and shouted for the steward. The passageway was empty; his call went unanswered. Eyre absorbed these facts with equanimity. Other than escaping the English winter, making some desultory additions to his Oriental portfolio, he'd had no particular purpose in setting out for Egypt. Now he had found one. By sheer good fortune, he had the opportunity to wreak a revenge he'd awaited all his life.

TEN

❧❧

Seawater ran over the wooden boards of the weather deck like a tide flooding a beach. The pair of rattan chairs in which Harriet and Mrs. Cox sometimes sat had been overturned, their curved rockers upended. Sailors were lowering the remaining sails, hurrying and grim-faced, some with ropes around their waists that secured them to the masts.

Harriet stared as a crate of live chickens floated toward her. She'd woken from a dream of falling, found Louisa sitting down below on her bunk, gripping its sides, her head hung over a bowl on her lap. Yael's bed was empty, the pillow straightened and blankets folded. Dash slid to and fro across the floor of the cabin with the movement of the ship, whimpering as he went.

"Can you find Yael, Harriet? I'd go myself but—" Louisa began to retch.

With Dash under one arm, Harriet had made her way up the iron steps, clinging to the rail with her free hand. There was no sign of the prayer group through the window of the saloon. She'd come up to the weather deck on impulse, to see if Yael was here and to see the storm for herself.

"Get below, miss," a sailor called to her over the roar of the wind. "You'll fetch up in the briny."

Gripping the banister, she made her way back down the stairs. At the bottom was Zebedee Cox, his collar askew and his hair uncombed.

"Rough, ain't it?" he shouted. "Damned queasy-making."

"Yes," she shouted back. "How is Mrs. Cox?"

"Indisposed. As a matter of fact, I was looking for you. She asked if you'd be kind enough to—" Water streamed down the polished stairs, soaking Harriet's boots, filling Mr. Cox's trouser cuffs. "To call in on her, Miss Heron."

Harriet's chest felt tight and she was shivering. She had to get back to Louisa and she still hadn't found Yael.

"I cannot, Mr. Cox, I'm looking for my aunt."

"I saw her just a minute ago, on her way back to the cabin," he said. "My wife begged you to come to her."

Harriet pictured Mrs. Cox. She knew what it was to be ill and to need someone by you.

"All right," she said. "Take me to her."

The Coxes were traveling first class; their cabin was on the port side of the middle deck, off a small, private sitting area shared with two other cabins. Mr. Cox opened the door and ushered Harriet inside. The cabin was bigger than their own, longer and wider, with a padded seat along the inner wall. Brushes and combs and clothes lay on the floor in disarray and a pair of satin shoes tumbled in a corner with the movement of the ship. In the gloom, Harriet didn't immediately see Sarah Cox.

When she did, she cried out in surprise. Mrs. Cox was sitting on a chair wedged up against the curved wall at the end of one of the beds, bent double, her arms clutched over her stomach. Her hair was undressed, tied in a ribbon on the nape of her neck, and her face looked gray.

"You're ill." Harriet crossed the cabin, kneeled beside her. "Whatever is the matter?"

Mrs. Cox wiped her forehead on her sleeve and sat up in the chair. "I'm sorry, Harriet. I didn't know who else to ask for."

She raised the salts clutched in her hand to her nose. "I'm in trouble," she said. "Awful trouble."

Without warning, she began to shriek, making a series of staccato cries as if she were being murdered. Harriet felt terrified.

"Mrs. Cox? What is it?"

The cries subsided and she sat up again, her eyes wide; perspiration was running down her face and neck, soaking her delicate nightdress. The ship pitched violently and Harriet grabbed the back of the chair.

"You must fetch help, Mr. Cox," she said, raising her voice over the thumps and cries that were going up from nearby cabins. "Your wife needs a doctor."

Zebedee Cox was still by the door, braced against the frame. "I'm not calling any doctor," he said. "Keep your voice down." There was a knock on the door and Mr. Cox opened it partway.

Harriet caught a glimpse of one of the crew, outside, saluting. "Pardon me, sir," he said. "Got to fit the deadlight. Over the porthole. Won't take a jiffy and it'll keep Mrs. Cox safe."

"There's no need," Mr. Cox said. "We shall be quite all right."

"But, sir—"

"I'll leave you two ladies for the time being," Mr. Cox called. And he left, shutting the door behind him.

Harriet stared at the closed door, then turned back to Mrs. Cox. "Don't worry, Mrs. Cox. I'll go for the ship's surgeon. I'll bring him straight to you."

Mrs. Cox covered her face with both hands and moaned. "You mustn't."

"Why not? I don't understand."

Mrs. Cox began to keen again, the cry piercing, her head thrown back and her mouth open. The moment passed and she pulled herself up to standing.

"Look," she said, gesturing behind her with one hand. The pretty nightgown was soaked at the back and stained with blood, the seat of the chair slicked with a sticky wetness. "I don't know what to do," she wailed. "It's too early."

"I'll fetch the surgeon," Harriet repeated.

Mrs. Cox shook her head.

"Everyone knows that we're on our honeymoon. Zebedee won't have me shamed in front of the captain."

The ship tipped again and threw Mrs. Cox forward so she almost fell. Helping her back onto the chair, Harriet cast her eyes around the disordered cabin, struggling to take in this new view of Mrs. Cox. The motion and the noise made it hard to think, but she knew how babies came to the world; she'd persuaded Rosina to tell her how it could be that she always said she saw Harriet's red hair first, before she saw any other part of her. Rosina had helped her own mother attend her older sisters in childbirth, from when she was a girl. She'd answered every one of Harriet's horrified questions, then lain down on her back on the kitchen floor and demonstrated, shrieking and wailing in a way that had made Harriet hysterical with laughter and fear. Babies came when they wanted, Rosina said. They pleased themselves and there wasn't a lot anyone could do about it.

With her hair hanging in rats' tails around her face and her eyes swollen, Mrs. Cox looked like a different woman.

"I'm frightened," she said, her voice soft and broken.

Harriet put her arm around her and squeezed her shoulders. "Lie down on the bed. If it will come, you cannot prevent it." The certainty in her own voice surprised her. There was a newspaper on the floor under a table. Harriet opened out its pages and spread them on the bunk, helped Mrs. Cox to lie down. She held her hand as the woman's body arched in the air with the next pain. Harriet was afraid that Mrs. Cox might die. It could happen, Rosina said. Did happen.

The pains started coming more frequently. Sarah Cox gasped and cried, gripping Harriet's arm, her face contorted, her body racked with effort. She pulled herself up into a kneeling position. Seeing her sitting on her calves, her knees wide, Harriet remembered the hieroglyph for giving birth. She wondered if she would ever get to Egypt or whether they would all be lost before they made land.

After an hour—perhaps more, Harriet had lost her sense of ordinary time—something emerged from between Mrs. Cox's white thighs. It came easily in the end, a clotted mass, not large, slithering out as if in a hurry, in a sea of purplish blood. As it lay on the newspaper, a feeble movement came from it. Mrs. Cox cried out again.

"Look. Oh, look."

She reached forward and lifted up a tiny, curved form. The head appeared translucent and the back was curved, the fingers spread like a starfish. It was a boy.

"He's alive," Mrs. Cox said. "It's a miracle. Zebedee, come and see him."

Mr. Cox had returned and was standing by the door, sucking on his pipe, the smell of smoke mingling with the strong scent of blood. Throwing down the pipe, he reached the bed in three strides. Harriet scrambled to her feet.

"What are you—"

He dashed the little thing out of Mrs. Cox's hands, onto the newspaper, bundled it up, forced open the porthole, and stuffed it through. Closed up the brass catch.

Harriet opened her mouth to speak and a tide of nausea overwhelmed her. She lurched to the basin and was sick, then sick again, spitting up a thin white liquid that burned her throat, until her entire body seemed emptied.

"That was wrong," she said, as soon as she was able, turning around to face him, clinging to the washstand to keep herself upright. "What you did was wrong, Mr. Cox."

Mrs. Cox had rolled over to face the curved side of the ship, the sheet drawn up over her face. Harriet felt suddenly weak. Her chest was tightening and she had an urgent need to lie down and rest, could think of nothing but reaching her own bunk, trying to breathe to her stomach. As she groped her way toward the door, a wall of water hit the side of the ship. The floor shot up at an angle and the porthole burst open again, water rushing in over the bed.

The sheet clung in wet folds to Mrs. Cox's body; she looked like a marble statue.

"It's God's punishment," she wept. "We're going to drown."

"Hush, Sarah." Mr. Cox got the porthole closed and knelt down beside his wife. He took hold of her hand and kissed it, glanced over his shoulder at Harriet.

"Leave us now. Please go."

Harriet made her way out of the first-class cabins and back the quickest way she knew to the lower deck, past the galley. A line of copper pans swung from their hooks over the stoves, crashing against each other like cymbals. Amid the pieces of smashed china that littered the floor, the cooks were down on their knees, holding hands and praying.

At the foot of the iron steps, water was running backward and forward in the corridor. The passage was deserted, but behind closed cabin doors, women screamed and children cried; trunks banged and crashed against the flimsy partitions.

Bumping from one side to the other along the corridor, her feet squelching inside her boots, her strength exhausted, Harriet neared their cabin. Through the portholes, she caught glimpses of the sea. It didn't look like water any longer but like molten lead, gray and menacing, forming in mountainous waves. It could swallow anything, it seemed to say. Lives. Secrets. It could even swallow time.

She felt dazed, fielding Louisa's urgent inquiries about where she'd been, Yael's entreaties, alternated with appeals to the Lord to save their souls, that she get out of her wet clothes before she caught her death. During the long hours that followed, as she lay in her bunk, her legs braced against its sides, her mind pitched and turned as if it too were buffeted by the storm. Harriet had wanted to embrace life. Death, if that was to be her fate. She hadn't imagined that life could include those small, stretched fingers or understood that they might all perish at sea. She remembered Dash and groaned aloud. She'd last seen him in the Coxes' cabin.

ELEVEN

The morning dawned still and bright, the sky cloudless. Dash made his own way back to the cabin, his coat still plastered to his body. At ten o'clock, leaving Louisa to rest in her bunk as she insisted, Harriet and Yael went to the dining saloon. The passengers were ashen-faced and few in number, their voices subdued as they ordered dry toast and black tea, refused offers from the stewards of kedgeree, deviled kidneys, tinned asparagus.

Mrs. Cox was unwell, her female neighbor from the next-door cabin informed Harriet as she passed their table. She'd been removed to the surgeon's suite in the early hours and no one knew what ailed her. Harriet felt sick again. Mrs. Cox's condition must have worsened overnight. Either that or her husband had come to his senses and gotten the doctor to her.

Yael tucked into her usual poached egg, emptied a pot of strong tea. Harriet ordered rashers of bacon and a cup of cocoa. She cut one rasher into pieces and fed it to Dash, looking around the deserted saloon, letting the dog lick her fingers. The painter's chair was empty. She drank the cocoa then raised her fork and put it down again.

"No appetite?" said Yael. "I hope Mrs. Cox will recover from whatever troubles her."

Harriet picked up her cup and scraped at the sugar at the bottom with a teaspoon, avoiding her aunt's eyes.

"She was seasick," she said.

"Indeed." Yael's expression was unfathomable.

. . .

At mid-afternoon, the *Star of the East* docked at the Italian port of Brindisi. The town looked solid and comfortable, its red-roofed buildings clustered like skirts around a great forbidding castle. Once the steamer was cleared by the Italian medical officer, Harriet, Louisa, and Yael took their turn to cross the gangplank to the shore behind an elderly man who, when he reached land, got down on his knees and kissed the worn flags along the edge of the quay.

"Poor Father," Yael said under her breath. "I wonder how he fares."

"Yes," Louisa said, looking around her with a distracted air. "I wonder."

It was the first time any of them had set foot on the soil of Europe, but Harriet, shaken by the night's events, disoriented by the sudden warmth and brightness, couldn't find words to share the experience with her mother and aunt. Louisa's face was blanched and even Yael appeared tired, her clothes crumpled and her face creased.

The sun was warm on Harriet's skin and the air drifting toward them from inland felt soft, scented with damp earth and leaves and blossom. She breathed in, feeling her body respond to its warmth and sweetness, as they climbed a flight of steps to a row of hotels and grocery shops that surveyed the harbor.

Walking past the stores, with their displays of unfamiliar cheeses and liqueurs and dried fruits, Harriet felt as if the stone flags were rolling under her feet, the ancient-looking buildings rocking on their foundations. They sat down at a table under a tree, outside a small hotel. Oranges hung from the branches over their heads. Harriet had never imagined that oranges might grow like apples, with as little ceremony and as much profusion. She stood up and picked one, tore off the greenish, spongy peel, parted a segment from the whole, and sucked out the juice, savored its tartness.

Yael refused the piece Harriet offered her.

"I only take orange in the form of marmalade, dear."

Louisa didn't want any either, on the grounds that unripe fruit might unsettle her stomach.

Harriet finished the orange herself, slowly, picking pips from her tongue and flicking them into the gutter, looking down at the steamer. The blackened funnel was as quiet as an unlit pipe, dwarfed by the three high masts, the riggings hung with coats and breeches. The stern was carpeted with sodden blankets and boots, steaming in the bright sunlight. The crew baled out water, passing bucketfuls up from the lower decks and flinging it back into the sea, while Italian dockers carried carcasses of meat on board on their backs.

After breakfast, on the pretext of needing fresh air, Harriet had sought out the medical rooms. She hesitated before she knocked on the door, wondering whether the surgeon knew what had happened to Mrs. Cox, and her part in it. She felt first embarrassment, then a surge of indignation at the shame of her friend's situation. Mrs. Cox was a good woman. She was sure of it.

She knocked on the door and the surgeon opened it, looking her up and down. His solid body, encased in a navy tunic, blocked the entrance.

"Yes?"

Harriet made herself raise her eyes.

"I've come to visit Mrs. Cox. I heard that . . . she was unwell."

"She can't receive you."

"Could you tell her it's Miss Heron. I only want a few minutes with her."

The surgeon frowned.

"No one but her husband is to have admittance. Captain's orders. Good day, miss."

Sitting in the sunshine, breathing in the balmy air, Harriet thought again about the baby. Even if he couldn't live, it was wrong that he'd been cast into the waters without a burial. Still alive. If he had been an ancient Egyptian baby, he might have been preserved for all time. She'd seen in one of the books a drawing of a mummified fetus, thousands of years old. A being that had never lived and yet had outlived all humanity. It perplexed her to think about the length of life and its brevity.

Shouts from the quayside interrupted her thoughts and Harriet stood up, shading her eyes with her hand, looking down at the harbor. The dockers were crowding around something on the quay.

The gang parted to reveal a large object wrapped in sacking. It looked like a great flat-topped, spindly-legged animal, trapped and bound up with ropes. Harriet watched as the men secured it to a crane, then winched it up and swung it slowly out over the edge of the quay. Midway between the ship and the dock, the cargo lurched and slipped in its ropes, to shouts of alarm. It rocked, then stabilized and landed like a clumsy bird.

As the crew released the piano from the sling, Harriet saw a man standing on the deck, watching. He was a head taller than any of the sailors, wearing a suit the color of sand and a straw hat. As she watched, he stepped forward and slit open part of the sacking with a knife, then lifted the lid and struck a key. A bass note resounded into the silence that had fallen. He played a couple of chords and the crew applauded.

"What's all the commotion?" Yael said.

"It's a piano, Aunt," she said, sitting down. "A grand piano."

"How absurd," said Louisa. "Don't get sunstroke, Harriet, it's very warm."

"I won't, Mother." Draining the sweet dregs of her coffee, Harriet looked again at the deck. The man's hair was down to his shoulders, bleached at the ends as if by long exposure to the sun, and he stood very still. Harriet willed him to turn around; she felt curious to see his face. "Who can he be?" she wondered aloud.

Yael had finished her seltzer water. She picked up her bag and pulled her bonnet more tightly onto her head.

"Your grandfather never traveled, Harriet," she said, as they walked back down the steps and joined the stream of people making their way back on board. "He has spent his whole life in England, as I believed I would do. We none of us know what plans the Almighty has for us."

TWELVE

The weather grew milder each day, and when the winds were sufficient, the ship traveled under sail, the noise of the engines stilled. Louisa felt as if she were neither in the world nor out of it, as if she were nowhere at all. At night, lying in the darkness with her eyes wide open, her mind turned to the girl she had been. Louisa had stifled her memory for so many years, it was as if that girl had died.

Louisa was fifteen when she first encountered Augustus. In those days, she was a hoyden. She never wore a bonnet or gloves except to church, her skin was brown as a gypsy's, and she clothed herself in red as often as she could, from a secret conviction that it was the color of life.

Her mother, ever since she could remember, had insisted that Louisa was beautiful. Beatrice was clever, Amelia Newlove declared. Hepzibah had an artistic gift and Lavinia was born gentle. But Louisa was a beauty. Peering into the old oval looking glass in the hallway at home, Louisa could see no evidence of it.

Her brows were thick as a boy's and demanded constant close attention with tweezers. Her mouth was too large, too definitely shaped, as if it had been drawn on her face with a pencil. Her hair was impossible. Was it true, she asked silently, walking the beach alone, listening to the midair squabbling of gulls. Was beautiful what she was?

Louisa did not know what she was. She didn't share the trust in God that her older sisters professed. She saw no evidence of any God yet was ashamed to admit her unbelief to anyone but herself. Frightened as well, since if there was no God, for girls like the Newloves, what was there?

Still, she knelt by her bed each night, thanking the Lord for his blessings and asking him to help those in greater need than she. Who could be in greater need than she, Louisa wondered, sliding between darned sheets in a darned nightdress, brushing sand off her knees, curling up to try to generate some warmth.

On Sundays, after lunch, she put on her favorite dress—a hand-me-down from Hepzibah, the color of rubies—and walked on the beach, dreaming of the life she would have. Its details were uncertain but it would be far from Dover and she would be at its center, not at the edge of everything, as she felt herself to be. After their father died, they had no society at home to speak of and Louisa longed for company. For a suitor. Even a glance from a man old enough to be her father, a lingering look while his wife's fair head was turned and his small son watched mutely—even such an impoliteness was welcome. She nodded as she walked past, feeling his eyes drawn to her like iron to a magnet, sensing his gaze as she carried on over the sands.

It was late May and the summer was beginning cool and wet. The next Sunday was rainy, the sand scarred with shallow depressions, the beach deserted. Louisa walked for an hour, then went home in low spirits, but the following week, she saw the man again. He was alone, standing on the shore as if he were waiting for an omnibus, puffing cigar smoke into the air over his head in short, fierce bursts.

"There you are," he said as she approached, pretending not to have noticed him. "At last."

"Good afternoon," she said stiffly.

He fell into step beside her, walking along the water's edge, the dark stink of tobacco mingling with the smell of salt and rotting seaweed. He wasn't much taller than she and he labored as he walked, his breath heavy, his watch chain rattling on the horn buttons of a check waistcoat under his overcoat. The tide was coming in, surreptitiously, flicking its tongue over the sand. A wave reached his boot and he kicked at it, splashed foam in the air.

"Damned stuff."

Louisa giggled.

"It's just the tide. It's coming home, sir," she said.

"Home?" he said.

They had reached the end of the bay, under the cliff, and could walk no farther without wading out through the water, over the rocks, around the point. He threw the end of his cigar into the sea, turned to Louisa, and put his hand under her chin. His fingers were roughened and bent, the nails flecked with blue and black paint. He turned her face one way then another, tilting it to the sun.

Louisa wasn't given to blushing, to displaying her feelings on her face, as some of her sisters were in the habit of doing. Her burning was all on the inside and the gesture, the sureness of his touch, lit a fire in her.

The man let go of her jaw.

"I'm going to paint you. We stay at the dower house. Come in the morning, early."

She shook her head.

"I cannot. My mother won't—"

"Yes, she will. Tell her Augustus wants you for a model. I'll be waiting."

He looked at her again, up and down, as if he owned her. A faint, urgent ringing traveled through the still air. Lavinia was summoning her from the garden of the house on the top of the cliff, banging on the old saucepan with a flint. Louisa looked up, shading her eyes with her hand, squinting into the distance. High up above was the figure of a boy, dressed in a sailor suit and so still that for an instant she thought it was a statue that looked down at her.

"I must go now," she said to Augustus. "Good day."

Turning back in the direction of the house, she walked away, faster than she knew she could, weightless, skirting around her footprints in the sand, and his, as the water began to fill them. She felt as if she could have walked on the surface of the sea, all the way along the bay.

And so it began.

• • •

As the ship proceeded southeast through the Mediterranean Sea, past shoals of porpoises and huge floating turtles, past fishing vessels and, occasionally, a steamer traveling in the other direction, Louisa kept to the cabin. She rested on her bunk or sat at the small table with her tatting. She'd brought a pattern and a quantity of silk, intending to complete a tablecloth while they were away. One purl, one plain. Two purl, two plain. One purl, one plain. The repetition soothed her.

There was nothing to worry about, she insisted to herself. If Eyre Soane had recognized her—and she couldn't be certain that he had—she would avoid him. They would never meet him once they arrived in Egypt; she had seen from the globe what a large country it was. The idea of not encountering him again prompted a sense of loss. As much as Louisa dreaded it, she found herself longing to see Eyre Soane, to hear tidings that only he could provide.

THIRTEEN

Harriet's first impression of Alexandria was its color. The city looked white, made up of white flat-roofed houses, white domed mosques flanked by delicate minarets, and pale-trunked palm trees topped with explosions of upward-reaching leaves. Standing on the crowded deck, almost shaking with excitement, Harriet felt as if it were impossible that the port should have looked anything other than exactly the way it did. She had an odd sensation, as if she already knew it.

An Egyptian pilot came aboard and steered the ship between a solid stone lighthouse and a reef of black rocks into a wide natural harbor, full of ships of every description, the sky overhead smudged with smoke from their funnels. The ship received clearance, the surgeon blasted a whistle, and a flotilla of small boats that had been waiting at a distance began streaming toward the *Star of the East*, rowed by men in robes of blue and scarlet and green, their heads wrapped in turbans or covered in close-fitting caps. Egypt was coming out to meet them, the Arabs waving and gesturing at the passengers, their cries filling the air.

The deck was packed—with men, women with babies in arms, old people who'd scarcely been seen for the length of the journey. Harriet scanned the hats of the women, looking for one elegant enough to belong on the head of Mrs. Cox. She'd been back to the medical room to leave her another note. Since the storm, Zebedee Cox had avoided her when she'd seen him on deck, turning on his heel and walking in the other direction.

Glancing around again, Harriet saw the man who'd embarked with his piano. The same back in the same pale jacket moved up onto the bridge, following behind Captain Ablewhite's dark blazer. As the man ducked through the door, Harriet glimpsed his profile, serious-looking and straight-nosed.

"Fine morning!"

The Reverend Ernest Griffinshawe was standing by her aunt.

"The Dark Continent lies before us," he said, his eyes fixed on the horizon. "Awaiting the light of our Lord."

"I shall go no farther than Alexandria," Yael said, raising her voice over the shouts of the porters, the clank of the anchor chain still unspooling into the clear turquoise sea. "Alexandria is on the Mediterranean and the Mediterranean is part of Europe. Europe is England's next-door neighbor. I declare before God that I shall go no farther than this city."

She got down on her knees on the deck and began to recite the Lord's Prayer.

Our Father, who art in Heaven . . .

Some women standing near by began to titter behind their hands.

"Really, Yael, I am not sure that this is the time or the place," said Louisa, as Reverend Griffinshawe frowned at the women and knelt beside Yael, adding his louder voice to hers.

Give us this day . . .

Some of the older female passengers joined them, sinking clumsily to their knees behind Yael and the parson.

And forgive us our trespasses . . .

Harriet barely heard them. At the front of the crush of people stood a man dressed in a brown velvet jacket and breeches. The red scarf at his neck fluttered in the breeze as the painter handed a folded easel to an Arab who'd boarded the ship. He oversaw the unloading of a pair of matching portmanteaus, then disappeared over the side and down the accommodation ladder, his paintbox under his arm.

Since the night of the dinner, Harriet had only glimpsed Eyre Soane at his easel, intent on his canvas, his posture inviting no interruption. She felt as if she might have imagined that he had ever watched them, ever come so purposefully to sit with them, as if—it seemed to her now—he had some mission that he had not declared.

The man had imprinted himself on her mind. Each time she remembered the way he'd looked at her after she and Louisa left the table, a current of an unfamiliar feeling ran through her and left her disturbed.

Pushing her way in between the crowd, Harriet looked down over the railing. Brightly painted boats crowded under the prow, with barefoot men standing up in them, holding out their hands to receive trunks and parcels, calling for business in a soup of languages. Half a dozen or more of the little crafts had their sails hoisted and were tacking back toward the quay with their passengers. Mr. Soane had disappeared.

"Miss Heron!"

Looking to starboard, she saw a red boat bobbing on the translucent sea, the painter seated in it. He raised his head from the match cupped in his hand and lifted his arm in a wave.

"Good morning," he called over the water in a pleasant voice, as if they were old acquaintances.

"Good morning, Mr. Soane," she called back.

"Welcome to Egypt. Tell your mother I shall visit you."

Too surprised to speak, Harriet nodded, reaching automatically for her journal in the pocket around her waist. As the boat carried Eyre Soane toward the dock, she watched, feeling the strong beat of the sun on her face, breathing in air that smelled of salt and sun, that carried a trace of cigar smoke.

FOURTEEN

Harriet sat on one side of the worn leather seat, Louisa in the middle, and Yael at the far end. The horse slowed to a walk as they passed along a narrow alley, past dark cavelike shops stocked with bolts of cloth, glassware, tinned goods. Over everything was a geometric pattern of light and shade, cast by lengths of sacking stretched overhead between the roofs of the buildings. The streets teemed with people, with color, with life and the cries of voices and animals.

Harriet felt the strangeness physically, like heat or cold; every part of her body tingled with impressions, as if the surroundings were both more real than any she had ever experienced in her life and at the same time utterly unreal.

"Arab town, Sitti," Mustapha shouted, turning his head to them from where he sat at the front of the cab, next to the driver. Mustapha had met them on the quay and introduced himself as their housekeeper.

"Pleased to meet you," said Yael. "How did you know it was us?"

"Three ladies," he'd announced, helping them up, hitching his robe to display narrow, scarred ankles, naked feet clad in pointed slippers. "I know he is three ladies."

A girl was hurrying beside them, squeezed into the gap between the carriage and the mud walls. Her eyes, half closed, oozing a yellow secretion, were trained in their direction and she held out a palm, calling for baksheesh.

"That poor child," Yael said. "Can you see her, Louisa?" The driver touched the horse with his whip, and as the animal broke into a trot, the girl caught hold of the armrest and was pulled along. "Slow down, driver," Yael cried, reaching forward and tapping the man on the shoulder. "Stop."

Mustapha issued instructions in a strange, harsh tongue and with a yank of the reins the driver pulled up the horse. Yael began fumbling in her bag. Extracting two English pennies, she leaned down from the cab, pressed them into the girl's hand.

"God bless you, dear," she said as the child darted away.

"The guidebook advises against giving alms on the street," Louisa said.

"She was half starved," Yael said, closing up her Gladstone bag. "And did you see her eyes?"

"Poor," Mustapha said, turning his head to them, smiling, showing a row of the whitest teeth Harriet had ever seen. "She is poor."

He laughed and the carriage moved off again.

"We have poor children in London, Mr. Farr," Yael said loudly. "But they do not go naked as the day they were born."

Her hands gripped each other in her lap as the carriage swayed on through the old town and out under a stone gateway and into a grand square, lined with gracious buildings, made of white stone and adorned with balconies and striped awnings. The strolling people wore European dress and red felt hats. Harriet saw an African boy, laden with packages, running behind a fashionable woman. She had a sick, certain feeling that she saw a slave.

Minutes later, the driver drew up the horses outside a pair of high iron gates. A watchman scrambled to his feet and Harriet followed Louisa and Yael into a garden dominated by a huge tree. Its branches curled upward like the legs of spiders and its leaves were sharp and dark, as if they had been folded into triangles.

"*Araucaria araucana*," Yael announced, pausing to look up into it. "The monkey puzzle. We had one at home."

It didn't resemble a living thing at all, Harriet thought, passing underneath it and along the path to a square stone house with shuttered windows. Mustapha ushered them through the double wooden door, across a vestibule, and into a courtyard in the center of the house that, she realized with delight, stood open to the sky.

Louisa looked around her. She tilted back her head, the sun falling on her white face.

"Where is the roof?" she said. "A house must have a roof."

In a large, airy bedroom with long wooden shutters at the window, Harriet undid her pocket from around her waist and slid her journal under the pillow on the bed. Kicking off her boots, she lay flat on her back on a mattress with a dip in the middle and breathed into her stomach.

She felt filled with an unexpected happiness. She'd feared she was coming to Egypt to die, but now that she was here, she had the peculiar sense that her true life, the one that had always awaited her, had at last begun.

FIFTEEN

Louisa entered the room to see Yael and Harriet sitting opposite each other at one end of a long table. She pulled up a chair next to Harriet's.

"Did you hear the racket?" Yael said. "Late last night and again before dawn? I thought it was a funeral but Harriet says it's the priest."

"It's the call to prayer," Harriet said. "Mustapha explained it to me."

"You must have heard it, Louisa. Such a queer-sounding dirge and we're to be subjected to it five times a day."

"I believe I did," Louisa said, shaking out a napkin and spreading it on her lap. She smiled at Yael. "I can't be sure, I slept so deeply."

It wasn't true. She had slept badly, then risen early and taken a shower, standing under the trickle of water and looking up at a small, high bathroom window through which bright light poured. It was peculiar to be naked in a foreign country. She felt more exposed than if she were in her own bathroom, clothed by the familiarity of her house and city and country.

Back in her bedroom, drying herself on a towel stiff as a board, she dusted talcum powder under her arms and put on her lightest dress. It was one of her favorites, a fitted jacket and skirt in emerald green with a darker, bottle-green train over the hips of the skirt, falling in a fishtail at the back, but once she'd fastened the jacket, draped the train over the bustle, it felt wrong. The fabric carried in its folds a whiff of fog, something sour and dirty, mixing with the smell of her soaped and powdered skin, the odors of salt and pine that drifted through the open window.

Louisa surveyed the table. The cloth bore pale stains of days gone by and the food was spread on unmatched china plates. The fare consisted not of the raw sheep's eyeballs she'd feared but slices of white cheese, flat round loaves the size of saucers, piled high, and a tall jug of what smelled like coffee, strong and aromatic.

"Are these eggs?" she asked, reaching out and touching one.

"Hard-boiled," Yael said. "And perfectly edible."

Louisa sipped her coffee and listened to Harriet's breathing. It was shallow but soft, neither badly impeded nor quite clear. It was foolish to hope that Harriet would be completely cured as soon as they reached Egypt, yet in some primitive part of herself Louisa had hoped exactly that. She had wished for a miracle, a means to silence the words Mr. Hamilton had conveyed from her mother and that she had continued to hear, as if they had planted themselves in her ears. *Death is near.*

Harriet rose from her chair, brushing crumbs from her lap.

"I'm going to look around the garden," she said, standing between the long, open doors.

She was wearing a tea gown in a floral print and Louisa, seeing her slender waist, the curve of her long neck, had the sense that still afflicted her sometimes, of loss, because Harriet was taller by a head than she, a woman, not a child.

"Shouldn't you rest for a few minutes?" she said. "Digest your breakfast."

"I am perfectly all right, Mother." Harriet turned to face back into the room and the sun lit up her hair from behind in a scarlet halo. "By the way, Mr. Soane said he would call on us. He asked me to tell you."

Harriet walked into the garden. Louisa stared after her as the dog rose from under the table and trotted out, his claws tapping on the tiled floor.

"Dear Harriet is in better health already," said Yael, spreading jam on a piece of bread.

"Sea air always agreed with her," Louisa said, cracking the shell of the egg on the rim of her plate, peeling the sharp shards from the softly solid albumen. Her mind was racing. How could Eyre Soane call, when he did not have their address? It was impossible. He was taunting her.

"Perhaps some of our fellow passengers have lifted Harriet's spirits. I believe she enjoyed making the acquaintance of Mrs. Cox, and Mr. Soane." Yael chewed and swallowed, took a sip of coffee. "You seem troubled, Louisa."

"Is that so?"

"You know that . . ." Yael regarded her with her earnest gray eyes. "That if I could aid you by any means, I would."

Louisa put down a half-eaten slice of cheese, rolled up the napkin, and pulled it through its ivory ring, looking at the carved elephants condemned to walk forever in a circle.

"Thank you, Yael," she said, more stiffly than she intended. "You mean well, I'm sure, but I am not troubled by anything. Please excuse me. I must finish unpacking."

Back in the bedroom, surveying the peculiar contents of her trunk, wishing again she had thought to slip in a fourpenny card of pins, Louisa found that her hands were shaking. She had a feeling of time having turned inside out, of the present being flimsy and contingent, less real than the past.

Sitting on the bed, closing her eyes, she found herself again back in the flint house of her girlhood, hearing the cry of gulls. Louisa was home from her walk on the sands, her head spinning, unable to sit down as her mother urged and take a turn with shelling the glut of peas. Amelia Newlove looked up at her from her chair by the fireplace.

"Whatever is it, Louisa?"

"I met a man," she said, "and his family. On the beach. An artist." She avoided her mother's eyes. "He wants to paint my picture."

Louisa had never heard of a person famous enough to go by their first name alone. But her older sister, Hepzibah, staying with the family for a summer holiday following her marriage, informed her that all England knew about the painter Augustus, member of the

Royal Academy, whose pictures of goddesses and muses sold for vast sums.

"*Diana the Huntress* fetched a thousand guineas. Imagine! Did he offer you money, Izzy?"

Louisa shook her head.

"How very proper. He is an honorable man. He will reward you afterward. He will make you celebrated."

Next morning, Hepzibah woke her early with hot water and said she must bathe and brush her hair, couldn't arrive looking like a gypsy. After her sister's scrubbing of her, Louisa discovered she didn't want to wear the red dress. She took her church dress, navy, with a ragged white collar that hung lower on one side than the other, out of the chest and stood with her hair lifted in her hands while Hepzibah did up the row of hooks and eyes at the back. Downstairs, perched on a stool in the scullery, she drank a cup of tea, refused Hepzibah's pressing offer to accompany her to Augustus's house, and set off along the cliff-top path, carrying a cloth bag containing a dozen new-laid eggs, sent from Louisa's mother to Augustus's wife.

Once she was out of sight of the upstairs windows of the flint house, Louisa dawdled, spinning flat disks of chalk along the path with short, violent kicks from the toe of her boot, looking in the springy turf for four-leaf clovers. Down at the beach, a group of village girls played hopscotch in the sand, their boots discarded, lined up in a row. Louisa stood watching, wishing she were one of them, not herself, alone on the cliff top and expected at a big house.

She didn't lift the rusty ring of iron that hung from a lion's mouth. She rapped on the wood with her bare knuckles. The door opened immediately and Augustus stepped out of the house, into the morning brightness. He looked older than he had the day before, the skin under his eyes falling in soft pleats, the beard around his lips flecked with white. He appeared rumpled, as if he had just risen from his bed.

"It's fortunate that I was expecting you," he said as he closed the door behind him. "No one would have heard that."

He went ahead of her across the garden and into what looked from the outside like an old barn. On the inside, it was unlike any barn Louisa had ever seen. No straw or mountain of hay. No ani-mals. It was a great, high-roofed place, almost empty. The top half of one wall was made of panes of clear glass through which light flooded down onto the wooden floor. She felt for a moment as if she'd walked into a church.

Two enormous easels on wheels stood next to each other along one wall, as well as a stuffed peacock perched on a stand. In the mid-dle of the room was a large table bearing a collection of shells and feathers and carved stones. Something oily and sharp pervaded the air and Louisa sneezed three times in a row, light, quick sneezes that she couldn't prevent.

"Pardon me," she said, when she could get the words out.

Augustus sat on a stool looking at her, his face frank and curious.

"Your father agreed?" he said.

"My father is away."

Something prevented her from telling this man that her father was dead, had been dead for three years. Augustus couldn't have asked anybody about her, locally, or he would have known. Every-one knew about the drowning of Captain Newlove, within sight of land and home. Married to the mermaids, the village boys said he was. The man's eyes shifted.

"Your mother, then?"

At the memory of the conversation that had taken place around the hearth, Louisa felt the burning begin inside. Hepzibah, altered since her wedding from the crosspatch she'd always been, now per-petually sunny-tempered, had spun the whole family into a tale of their altered fortunes, of what would occur once Louisa's painting too was sold for a thousand guineas and eminent painters beat a path across the cliff to the door of the flint house. On the advice of her twenty-one-year-old newly married daughter, Louisa's mother had agreed that she should go for her portrait.

"My mother saw no objection," she said, looking at the toes of her summer shoes, which had been Lavinia's, the white leather stained grass-green.

She did not know where, apart from the ground, to look. Around the walls of the studio, on the floor or balanced on chairs, there were pictures of women. Women as she had never seen women before. From the back, from the side, from the front. Standing, seated, or reclining. Draped with gauzy silks and chiffons, wisps of cloud or ribbons of mist that accentuated their nakedness rather than hid it.

"Don't look so frightened, girl."

He reached forward, gripped her arm, and squeezed it. Louisa dropped the eggs. They hit the ground with a soft, crumpling sound and she looked down to see the bag gaping, yolks and whites slithering out onto the floor.

"What do you want with them?" he said.

"They are for your wife."

Her voice was shaking and she didn't know whether it was from the loss of twelve good eggs. She felt that she ought not to be here, that between the flint house and the barn something had gone awry.

Augustus frowned.

"My wife doesn't require eggs."

He fetched a cloth and wiped up the mess himself, rubbing broken yolk into the floorboards, muttering about the patina.

Louisa had never seen a man on his knees, with a cloth in his hand. As she stared, her eye was caught by a movement outside the open barn door. A shadow passed over the beam of sunlight that fell in a column on the dark floor. She looked up and it had gone.

Augustus was on his feet again, his back turned to her, busying himself at the far end of the studio. He continued for so long that Louisa decided he'd forgotten she was there. Changed his mind. She felt relief and some disappointment.

"Shall I go now, sir?"

"Go?" He turned and flung out an arm. "There's a screen over there, where you can disrobe. What did you say your name was?"

Disrobe. What could the word mean? She knew, although she had never heard it before in her life. It sounded different from "undress," as if to be disrobed was worse, but she couldn't think why or how that could be so. Her mouth was dry when she spoke and her tongue seemed twice its usual size. "My name is Louisa Ellen Newlove."

"Let your hair down. Don't comb it. Leave it as it is."

"I've combed it already."

"You can keep your shoes on, for now. We don't want you catching your death, do we, Gypsy?"

Louisa didn't know how to answer. It didn't matter. Preparing his canvas, rubbing it with a dry brush, the man appeared to have forgotten her again.

Louisa was too ashamed when she got home to tell the others what had happened. That Augustus had expected her to pose, not with a half-smile on her closed lips, a prayer book in her hand, dressed in her demure lace collar, as they'd rehearsed in front of the old mirror in the hallway, but without any apparel.

Naked and with a certain expression in her eyes that he said was the reason he'd brought her there in the first place. He wanted her looking as she did on the beach when he first saw her, he said. Like a Gypsy. Sullen. Her lips not half-smiling or closed but parted.

That she hadn't dared to refuse or explain the misunderstanding. That when she'd managed to extricate herself from her dress, her hands shaking like an old woman's, her fingers fumbling as if they'd never before encountered hooks and eyes, when she'd come out from behind the screen that was painted with sprays of yellow flowers, he had arranged her body as if she were a dressmaker's form, his fingers brushing her flesh. That she had agreed or at least not disagreed. That she stood on a drafty floor for three whole hours, naked as the day she was born, her nipples standing up like strawberries, with one hand holding a shell, the other resting on a great rock that somehow had been brought inside. Only her shoes to cover the part of her that could not be seen anyway, the soles of her feet. She'd felt she might die of shame.

Hepzibah's eyes shone. She clapped her hands.

"I want to know everything, Izzy. Absolutely everything."

Louisa threw her shawl over the rocking chair.

"I'm thirsty. Get me a glass of water first, can't you?"

Hepzibah ran to the scullery, returned with a brimming glass. Lavinia had come in from outside and their mother was in her chair. Amelia Newlove sat by the fireplace even in summer. Louisa emptied the glass, swallowing down the clean, cold water, concentrating on the vase in the grate that held a great mass of stems, the flat-topped, white-headed bloom that sprawled in the hedgerows, that they called Queen Anne's lace and that was meant to keep away flies.

"It was all very well," she said.

Hepzibah caught hold of her hand.

"Tell us, Izzy," she said. "Tell us what happened."

"I stood there, that's all. It was dull," she insisted, looking past Hepzibah's disappointed eyes and her mother's pensive gaze. Lavinia had her hand clamped over her mouth. "And I'm not going back."

"You are," Hepzibah said into the silence that followed. "You have to. We're counting on you, Louisa."

The singsong wailing from outside began again, a long lament in a man's voice. Louisa opened her eyes and found herself looking at an unfamiliar ceiling, the rough plaster crazed with cracks. She rose from the bed and began to walk about the room, hugging her arms across her chest. Sweat dampened the underarms of her bodice, a cold sweat that came not from the mild warmth of the morning but from fear. She must conquer it.

Sitting at the washstand, she examined herself in the mirror. Her dark hair was drawn back into the style she'd adopted on her marriage, copied from the pages of a magazine that had furnished step-by-step instructions on how to create it. Her tasteful costume, her cloudy opal earrings and plain gold wedding band, reflected her position in the world as the wife of a successful man of business, mother of his four children. An accomplished and careful housekeeper.

If Blundell knew even a part of what had happened before their marriage, he would cast her off. The life she had made for herself would be destroyed. Her sons would be disgraced by the knowledge of what their mother was and Harriet would see her as a stranger. Just to think of it made Louisa feel sick. And yet a part of her persisted in longing to see Eyre Soane again. She hungered to know what had happened to his family in the long years since.

Rising from the stool, she opened the bedroom window and leaned her head out. The call to prayer had given way to the cries of a man selling vegetables from a cart. Down below, Mustapha was standing by the barrow with an open basket, receiving a quantity of potatoes. Louisa turned back into the room and lowered the window.

Drawing herself up straight, she prepared to go downstairs and arrange the week's menus. She was a woman in her middle years, wintering in Egypt to save the life of her daughter. She was no longer a girl in a hand-me-down robe who knew nothing and hoped everything of life. Eyre Soane could not harm her family. She would prevent it, by whatever means proved necessary.

SIXTEEN

※❦❦❦※

The sound was growing louder. Yael stopped and lifted her head, listened to the sonorous tone of a bell, coming from somewhere in front of her, somewhat to the right. East, she supposed it might be called. Or west, if she was facing south. She did not know which way she was facing. No matter. All she had to do was to follow the note of the bell, incongruous in this harsh light, this dry street, where the shadows of the mud buildings lay deep and angular across the way.

Yael had resolved before leaving London that on arrival in Egypt she would find some useful work with which to occupy herself. Cooped up in the bank's villa with dear Louisa and Harriet, she felt even more at risk of cabin fever than she had on the steamer. She intended to approach Reverend Griffinshawe at the church and offer her services in his endeavor, the promulgation of the Bible to the native women.

She'd breakfasted early, put on her bonnet, and left, rejecting Mustapha's urgent wish that she have someone accompany her. She could not wait, as he entreated, for his nephew to guide her.

The Mohammedan boy was unlikely to know the location of the church, and if the bell ceased, she would have no means of orienting herself. Yael quickened her step.

The wind was cold; she felt chilly. She'd been misled by the brightness of the sunshine, hadn't thought her ulster necessary. As she walked underneath a branch hanging over the wall of a hidden garden, her eye was drawn by bright vermilion petals. She stopped and stared up at the papery blossoms, which seemed to vibrate with their own brilliance.

Yael had always believed that England, English flora and fauna, English people and ways, were the summit of His creation. But these flowers were a marvel. She had never witnessed such a hue in nature. Reaching up, she broke off a stem, slipped it into her Gladstone bag. She closed it, snapping the clasp on the flash of vivid scarlet, and lifted her head again, listening. She would press them, later, between the pages of her Bible.

The sun grew stronger as she walked, stinging the backs of her hands and her face. She wasn't certain now if she was too warm or too cold. Surely it was impossible to be both. Following the slow peal of the bell, which did not sound as if its source was getting any nearer, scanning the blue horizon for a spire, seeing only flat roofs, interspersed with domes and minarets, she continued on into a poorer-looking, native neighborhood. Hobbled donkeys nosed the ground outside dim doorways; red and orange rugs hung out of open windows above caged white doves. A man had slit open a mattress and was spreading the cotton stuffing in the sun, along the edges of the alley.

Sunday was not a day of rest for the Mohammedans. They observed Fridays. Yael hurried on, thinking about Fridays, their potential as holy days. There was Good Friday, of course. Fridays were clearly holier than Mondays, except at Easter. Preferable to Wednesdays or Thursdays but not as inevitable and right as Sundays. Not by any means. The Jews observed Saturdays, which she had always considered the most utilitarian of days.

A little girl appeared in front of Yael, hastening toward her. For a moment, Yael believed it was the same girl they'd seen from the carriage, that the child had recognized her and wished to greet her, but as the small figure came closer, she became aware that it was not the same girl. This one was even younger, not more than three years old, naked except for a scrap of fabric tied around her head. Her curls were matted, her cheeks and chin smeared with dirt. Only her eyes were the same as the other girl's, oozing a yellow secretion, the lids beginning to turn inward. They commanded attention the way the raised bloom of a birthmark might, or a harelip. It was odd the way the eye was drawn to what was wrong in a face. "Hello, child," she said, wishing not to frighten her, sounding, to her own ears at least, absurd.

The girl held out her palm. Yael couldn't be sure if the child could see, but it was clear that the little mite had heard. Yael had coins with her, intended for the collecting plate at St. Mark's. She would give them to the girl. As she fumbled for her purse, feeling inside her capacious bag, other children began to gather around. Boys, jeering and elbowing each other in the way of lads anywhere, calling out English phrases, the words oddly conjoined.

"Goodmorrning." "Thankew." "Gowaway."

Sweat trickled down from under the hair coiled over Yael's ears. She was now certain she was too warm, although the air still held a chill, and confined between the windowless mud walls of the houses on each side of the street, she, and all of them—a number of lads had gathered now—were in shadow. Her fingers at last encountered the silver mesh of the purse, the weight of coins. Yael smiled down at the infant as she drew her purse out into the air, held it aloft.

"Here it is, dear. Now, let me see . . ."

She hesitated. She wanted to give more than pennies, but the half-crown she'd earmarked for the collection plate was a considerable sum. Standing in the alley, looking at the tattered smocks of the boys, their feet bare on the mud, she decided to give it all to the child. Half a crown might mean her mother was able to seek treatment for her; it could even save her sight. As Yael shook the heavy coin out of the purse and onto her palm, a silver threepence slid past it into the dust. The clamor around her increased and several of the boys dived for the coin.

There were fifteen or twenty of them gathered around her in a circle, eager and smiling, their teeth in various conditions of evolution, their heads cropped. All boys, aged seven, eight, nine—it was hard to tell; so many had hardened, wizened faces on slight and childish bodies. Every last one of them appeared half-starved. More were arriving, tumbling out from the narrow paths and stairways that led into the alley, racing and shouting.

"This is for you," Yael announced, extracting the silver half crown and stooping down to take hold of the girl's hand, trying to fit her fingers around the unwieldy coin. "Stand back, boys. The baksheesh is for this little one."

At the word *baksheesh*, the older children surged forward. The coin dropped to the ground and a boy lunged for it, knocking the child off her feet. The little girl began to bawl.

"No," Yael called sharply, trying to put her foot on the silver disk. "It's not for you."

Two larger boys jumped on top of the first one, elbowing and shoving at each other. Others hurled themselves into the scrum, one falling heavily against Yael. She staggered and righted herself.

"I am sorry. I must insist—"

Her voice was lost in the noise all around her. Boys pressed against her from all sides, stretching out their hands, shouting for baksheesh, drowning out the sound of the bell. Several fought like men for possession of the half crown.

"You must stop this."

"Goodafternoon. Godblessyew. Damnfilthybeggar."

She was taller than any of them but imprisoned, as if she were Gulliver among the Lilliputians. The little girl was nowhere to be seen, and hands were plucking at her arms, her bag.

"Excuse me," she cried. "Let me through. I am going to church."

Yael looked up at the carved wooden jalousies protruding from first-floor windows all along the alley, then down, at the seated figures positioned inside dim doorways, fingering their tasseled amber beads, watching. Craning her neck for a police officer, she saw a woman, dressed in black from head to toe, her face shrouded, approaching down the dusty street.

Yael freed an arm, waved at her, and called out, her voice high and strained, more fearful than she knew herself to be.

"Please, ma'am, I need assistance."

The woman skirted around the youths and passed by, as if she had not seen Yael, as if not she but Yael were the invisible one. Just then, a voice shouted something from behind her. The noise died suddenly, as if the needle had been lifted from a wax pressing.

Seated on an Arabian horse, his silver-tipped stick raised in the air, a man was bearing down on them.

The boys fell away as quickly as they had gathered. In seconds, they were gone, vanishing into the dark doorways, racing away up twisting flights of steps. Yael stood alone on the churned ground, her bag gaping open.

She felt in it for her handkerchief. Her peppermints. Her hymnal. Her purse. Nothing remained. Only the stem of flowers. She closed the bag, mopped her forehead on her cuff, and attempted to straighten her bonnet. Her legs felt weak and for a moment she believed she'd have no choice but to sit down in the dust, there where she stood. She thought of the dear Queen, beset by every kind of trouble and grief, and made herself remain on her feet.

The man had dismounted. His neatly trimmed beard was stained orange and he wore a green turban wound innumerable times around his head, a long striped kaftan cut from what looked like silk, girdled at the waist, with a light, embroidered woolen robe worn open over the top. He was looking at her with piercing brown eyes set in a clever, mournful face.

She spoke loudly, enunciating clearly.

"Thank you, sir. I am most grateful for your assistance."

"At your service," he said, speaking more softly than she, inclining his head. "Where are you going?"

Men were approaching now, half a dozen or more of them, drawn not by Yael but by her rescuer, crowding around to pay respects to him, raising his hand to their foreheads, kissing his hem.

"St. Mark's Anglican Church," Yael said loudly. "I am a Christian."

"You are lost. Come."

Leading the horse by the reins, he dismissed the men and set off on foot. Yael looked around her. The street was empty again, as if the incident had never occurred nor been witnessed by anyone at all. The bell had fallen silent; she didn't know when. The man and his horse were already fifty yards away. Yael clamped the new flatness of her bag under her arm and hurried to catch him up.

· · ·

The church was a white building, recognizable by its spire, the wooden cross mounted in the alcove of the porch. There was a little graveyard around it, some bleached stones, but no wall or fence. It stood in sandy waste ground, adorned only by rocks and boulders, looking as exposed as she felt herself.

The man led the horse to the shade of a tree and walked back toward Yael, gestured at the open doors, at the threshold, where Reverend Griffinshawe stood, watching.

"Your church," he said.

Yael was prevented by some instinct from extending her hand to be shaken. The walk was longer than she'd imagined and she was tired, her legs trembling with the effort of keeping pace. It would be all she could do to get herself inside the doors, sink to a pew, in the blessed shade.

"Thank you. You have been very kind."

"Our children are not bad children," he said. "They hunger for many things."

"May I ask your name?"

"I am the Sheikh Hamada."

"Miss Heron," the Reverend called, over the stony ground. "Is the fellow bothering you?"

Sheikh Hamada didn't hear.

"It is our duty," he said, "to receive guests. Your servant should not have allowed you to go alone."

Gripping the back of the pew in front, Yael pulled herself to her feet as the congregation, a thinner gathering than the Reverend Griffinshawe had suggested, rose for "Onward, Christian Soldiers." She opened the hymn book and began to sing.

Marching as to war.

She could hear her own voice, a little out of key, slightly out of time with the rest, as she had always felt herself to be with other people and not only in choral matters.

With the cross of Jesus . . . Going on before.

Hearing the familiar words, Yael felt the pull of England. The high, tremulous voices, the faith expressed in them, however imperfectly, dignified their country more than the Union Jack pennants in the harbor, the British consul's residence in its grand and formal square. It was faith in a Christian God and England's capacity for charity that made the nation great, not their talent for trade, their subjugation of other lands, whatever Blundell might believe. Curious how, thousands of miles away from him, it was easier to think thoughts different from her brother's.

The hymn finished and the Reverend announced a period of private prayer. Yael eased herself onto her knees, to a plain hassock on the stone floor. Closing her eyes, resting her forehead on her hands, she asked God for guidance on what help she might offer in the time she was here.

As the vicar embarked on a reading from Corinthians, she pulled herself back onto the seat. Light poured through the panes of crimson and blue and gold glass set into the round high window over the entrance of St. Mark's and threw a rainbow along the aisle, between the rows of carved pews. The altar, spread with a white cloth, was dressed with a trinity of tall, lighted candles, a vase of flowers so bright and vivid they too might be aflame. The church was beautiful, she saw. As beautiful as any she had worshipped in.

On the way back to the villa, sitting in a rusty brougham as it lurched through the narrow streets—its driver miraculously avoiding haughty-faced camels, donkeys laden with swollen, dripping water skins, barrows piled high with carrots and tomatoes, blind beggars, sherbet sellers rattling brass cups—the answer came to her clearly. The little girl was a messenger. Both of them had been. She would establish a first-aid post, to treat eye disease. She could offer simple cleansing and rudimentary treatments. Alum could be procured here, she assumed, and supplies of gentian lotion. Soap. She had had experience in tending the sick at home, who could not be so very different from the sick here. She would make herself useful.

Yael gripped in one hand the pound borrowed from the Reverend for her fare, as the cab moved along a gracious avenue lined with opulent Greek and Turkish emporia displaying in their windows imported groceries and gowns and perfumes. The clinic would need to be in the Arab city, where the poor children were, not the broad and imposing thoroughfares of the Frank quarter, where the Europeans made their home. If she found a simple room at street level, put herself there with soap and water and medicines, the children would come. Their mothers would bring them.

SEVENTEEN

Harriet felt restless. They had been in Alexandria for a fortnight and at Louisa's insistence had developed a routine for their days. They rose at eight, breakfasted at nine, and spent the mornings in the house and garden. In the afternoons, after the daily rest prescribed for Harriet by Dr. Grammaticas—and weather permitting, because it rained often, a drenching, cool rain blown in off the sea that seemed to fall horizontally, or sometimes even from below, as if defying the rules of nature and rising from the ground toward the sky—they went on excursions.

Pompey's Pillar was the first of the sights they visited.

"Smaller than the Monument," Yael announced, walking around the plinth of red-speckled stone. "And why do men always want to build things pointing up into the sky?"

They walked in the public gardens on Friday afternoon, admiring the blooms in pink and scarlet, to the strains of a brass band. Took a carriage to see the Mahmoudieh Canal, from where people set sail to Cairo.

Most of their time, they spent at the villa. Mustapha had a wife, Suraya, who lived with her four small children in a room at the back, beyond the yard that serviced the kitchen. The room was built from mud bricks and roughly plastered with more of the same mud. It was roofed with palm branches, and the interior, reached through the ragged curtain that served as a door, was smoke-blackened and low-ceilinged.

Harriet took to visiting Suraya, picking up Arabic words from her and teaching her a few English ones. Ignoring Louisa's objections, she sat on a rope-strung stool in the tiny apartment, playing with the children, as Suraya went about her housekeeping. From the pictures in her books, Harriet had believed that all Egyptian women would be slim and beautiful, watchful under their heavy black wigs, half-smiles playing on sealed lips. It wasn't true. They were as unalike in looks as Englishwomen were.

Suraya was plump and purposeful. In the privacy of her home, she wore her hair uncovered, in a long plait down her back, the thin strands at the end always coming undone. Her blue-and-black-striped robe bore marks of flour and cooking oil. Are you married? she asked repeatedly, by means of gesture. Not married? No children? She shook her head and frowned. Why?

Harriet couldn't answer, in any language. Everyone except she and Aunt Yael seemed to be paired with a male. Even Aunt Yael had God. Harriet found herself waiting for Mr. Soane's promised visit. As the days passed and the painter did not come, her disappointment grew.

At night, alone in her room, she got out her books and studied the dictionary of hieroglyphs, the spells in the Book of the Dead. The little symbols possessed even more power for her, by the light of Egyptian candles. She wasn't here to look for a husband, she reminded herself. It had been true when she left London and it was still true. She was here to reach the place that the pharaohs had called Waset, the ancient Greeks had named Thebes, and was now known as Luxor, from the Arabic for *palaces*.

Harriet got out her inks and her journal and arranged her things on the small table in her room. As before, she wrote the title of the spell in red ink, to give the words extra power. Underneath, in black ink, she embarked on a series of pictures. First she drew herself: a tall, thin figure, taller than other people, which she was in life, and which was how the royal females were always shown. Next was Louisa's cup-shaped crinoline, Dash's paw print. In the second column she drew a boat, with a sail hoisted to show that it was traveling upriver against the current. She followed it with a sinuous, meandering stretch of the Nile, and below that the leaning columns of the temple at Luxor.

Harriet held the book away from her and looked at the page. The column of symbols appeared incomplete. Picking up the pen again, dipping it in the neck of the black ink bottle, she drew another image below the pillars of Luxor: a figure of a longhaired man, holding a paintbrush aloft in one hand. He looked straight at her, seemed to summon her to him. .

Blotting the ink, she closed her journal and secured the ties around the cover. She was short of breath; the effort had tired her. Lying on her bed, she held the book against her chest, feeling it rise and fall with her breath. Harriet felt almost afraid of the power of her spells, or if not of the spells, then of the strength of the longing that lay behind them. It was that longing, she had an instinct, that had made the first spell come to pass.

EIGHTEEN

❦

The piano, a Bösendorfer, had been unloaded by crane at the harbor at Alexandria. A tugboat transported it to the dock, where it was hoisted onto a flatbed cart pulled by two asses and, at the railway station, transferred to a freight train to Cairo. Reaching the old port of Boulak, the piano was trundled on a dolly along a ramp and onto a barge; it was secured by the side of a cargo of cedar from the Lebanon that was destined for a new hotel at Luxor.

Eberhardt Woolfe was traveling with the piano on the barge, sleeping at night in a hammock on deck, listening to the sailors' plaintive dirge. They sang to their Prophet, their voices becoming part of nature, like the sounds of the wind and the water. *Ya Mohammed, ya Mohammed, ya Mohammed.*

Eberhardt was impatient to get back to his house on the mountainside and resume his work. More than once, he'd cursed his own folly in bringing the piano all the way from Heidelberg. Everyone who'd learned of the plan had given the same verdict. The instrument would be damaged, perhaps catastrophically, by the clumsy porters he was sure to encounter in Egypt. The fine wood was bound to be eaten by foreign beetles; the wires would certainly rust and the ivories yellow. As for tuning! Each rested his case.

He listened patiently to the objections of his friends but did not waste his time in attempting to counter them. Not one of the fellows had been to Thebes. None had experienced the silence there, the immense and engulfing quietude, which, more than the rock tombs, more even than the loss of Kati, had shown Eberhardt Woolfe the meaning of death.

Only his mother thought to ask the question that discomforted him. How would he get the piano back home again, when his work was finished? That question he did answer, promptly and confidently. "*Mutti*, you worry too much. The same way as I took it there, of course, but everything backward." His mother nodded. She knew and he knew that he would not bring back the piano. That he would not return to Heidelberg except as a visitor.

Apart from the small matter of a grand piano, Herr Professor Doktor Eberhardt Woolfe—as his trunks were labeled—was traveling light. He had in one sturdy wooden box the tools needed for excavation and exploration: pickaxes; hammers; trowels; chisels; scalpels; sable brushes. In a small leather suitcase, he'd packed three of the same lightweight and light-colored suits and white shirts that he wore in all seasons and for all occasions. One spare pair of boots. A few books of sheet music. His binoculars. A framed photograph. All other needs could be supplied locally. *Mutti* had insisted on a hamper that he hadn't had the heart to refuse.

As the barge plied on to the south and the dwellings grew smaller and simpler, the factories fewer, the railway line came to an end, Eberhardt felt content. Even Cairo had been too crowded, too noisy, too full of clamorous life. He would soon be back in the Necropolis, in the only place where he belonged.

NINETEEN

❦

Louisa surveyed a drawing room furnished with two long low-backed sofas upholstered in striped cream and green satin. The few English scenes on the walls—a pair of watercolors depicting milkmaids with bucolic brown cows, a small and indistinct oil of the Thames by moonlight—only added to the sense of England being impossibly far away.

The room wasn't tasteful, contained nothing of beauty or value, and yet with the vase of trailing white flowers shedding petals on the sideboard, the French doors draped with a pretty, tattered lace curtain and standing open to the garden, it was relaxing. She had thought she would feel the loss of her home more than she did. It was only Blundell she missed. The hook flew in her fingers around the skein of silk, producing neat and even stitches.

"Yes, Mustapha?" she said at the tap on the door.

"Visitor, Sitti."

Louisa put down her handwork. They'd had few callers. The manager of the local branch of Blundell's bank, the Anglo Ottoman, had been twice to offer his services. Mr. Moore, a Yorkshireman, had seemed relieved when Louisa had insisted that they would not need to call on him except in case of emergency. Their neighbors on the other side of the brick wall at the back of the garden, a Dutch family with a line of noisy, fair-haired children, had welcomed them with a tin of sugar biscuits imported from the Low Countries. Reverend Ernest Griffinshawe arrived at the gate one morning and was persuaded to take luncheon. Louisa had hinted to all of them that they were in Alexandria for the sake of Harriet's health and intended to pass the time in a state of seclusion.

"Who is it?" she asked.

"Soane, ma'am," Mustapha said. "It is Mr. Soane. I shall show him in?"

"Well, Louisa?" Yael said, her voice mild. "Give the man an answer."

"I . . . Tell Mr. Soane we are not at home."

As she said the words, a figure entered the room from the garden. Louisa felt confused. She knew it was Harriet, by her height and the way she moved, but the person in front of her was not her daughter. She was hidden under a black robe, only the toes of her boots visible. A pair of light-colored eyes looked out from between two strips of black cloth.

"Well, Mother?" came the well-known voice. "Does Suraya's veil suit me?"

Louisa sprang to her feet and reached for a corner of the fabric, tugging it from Harriet's face.

"Harriet, please. Take that dreadful thing off."

"It looks charming, Miss Heron."

Eyre Soane stood in the doorway, smiling. "Mrs. Heron. Miss Heron."

He nodded at Louisa and Yael in turn. Harriet had blushed scarlet and was still standing in the center of the room, the folds of black cloth lying on her shoulders.

Yael put down her pen.

"Do come in, Mr. Soane, and take a seat."

"Thank you."

He sat down on the empty sofa, arranging his leather satchel on the seat beside him, stretching out his legs. He wore a suit made of fustian, the color of cocoa powder, a white calico shirt under the unbuttoned jacket. Leather shoes, in brown and cream. His hair was waxed, smoothed back on his head. Despite his clean-shaven cheeks, he reminded Louisa of his father. She looked away.

"Would you care for a sherbet?" Yael said.

"I believe I would, Miss Heron."

"I'll go and tell Mustapha," Harriet said, heading toward the door.

Yael blotted her letter, smoothing the paper with the side of her fist.

"The weather is warm today," she said. "It might be spring."

"The weather is warm most days." He turned to Louisa and assumed a smile of polite inquiry. "Are you enjoying your stay, Mrs. Heron?"

Louisa took a deep breath. She would not be bullied in what currently passed for her own home.

"We spend our days very quietly, Mr. Soane, for my daughter's health. She is an invalid, as you may remember."

The door opened again and Harriet entered with Mustapha following behind, bearing a tray. He set out woven mats on the scarred surfaces of the tables, put down the cold drinks, and withdrew. Harriet sat next to Yael, her hands clasped over her knees. Eyre Soane regarded her.

"I would scarcely have recognized you, Miss Heron. I believe Egypt agrees with you."

The blush reappeared like a sunrise on Harriet's neck, spread upward to her cheeks.

"Aren't you going to inform me of the sights you've seen?" he said.

"I . . ." she said. "We—"

"We have explored the town a little," Yael said. "And visited the monument, of course. How have you been passing the time, Mr. Soane?"

"I'm continuing work on my Oriental portfolio. I intend to paint Cleopatra while I am here. I shall seek out some beauty to serve as a model."

Louisa remained quite still, looking through the open French doors into the garden. In the early afternoon sun, the flowering shrubs and bushes looked bleached, the deep pinks and purples robbed of their strength and richness. The lace curtain, which had possessed a certain beauty earlier, was limp and shabby. No doubt could remain. Eyre Soane intended to torment her.

"It is airless in here," she said, reaching for her fan, flicking it open.

"In fact, Miss Heron"—Eyre Soane fixed his gaze on Harriet—"I should like to sketch you, just as you are now. Native dress becomes you."

Harriet raised her head and Louisa caught sight of her eyes, bright with a look Louisa didn't recognize. Louisa had a feeling inside, of plummeting, as if some structure were collapsing like a card house.

"It is time for your rest," she said, getting to her feet.

"Mother, I—"

"No arguments, Harriet. Mr. Soane," Louisa continued, "you may care to see the monkey puzzle tree in the front garden on your way out. We are told that it is two hundred years old."

Louisa walked to the door and held it open. Eyre Soane rose from the couch, retrieved his satchel, and bowed to Harriet.

"Until we meet again, Miss Heron."

Louisa led the way through the shadowed courtyard. The thin stream rising from the fountain, falling into the shallow pool surrounding it, sounded like a gutter discharging into a rain butt. Opening one half of the front door, she walked into the garden. Through the soft leather of her summer shoes, the points of the fallen cones underneath the tree were sharp against the soles of her feet.

At the great iron gate, she turned to face Eyre Soane.

"My daughter is ill, Mr. Soane. I would not wish her to be disturbed by anything that does not concern her."

"Disturbed? What do you mean, Mrs. Heron?"

On the other side of the gate, the watchman lifted the catch. Louisa lowered her voice.

"I am asking you not to call on us again."

The gate opened and Eyre Soane stepped through it. He hitched the strap of the satchel higher on his shoulder and got out a cigar case from his pocket.

"It's a fine specimen," he said, gesturing back into the garden toward the tree. "They're considered unlucky, as I'm sure you know. Goodbye, Gypsy."

Louisa turned away, breathing in the odor of dry earth and drains and blossom. She had just time to get behind the scaly trunk of the monkey puzzle, to notice that it looked like a blackened pineapple, before she was silently and violently sick.

TWENTY

꧁꧂

Yael put down her spoon and looked at the French door. "It can't be getting dark at this hour," she said. "Can it?"

The three of them were sitting in the places they had made their own around the long table in the dining room. Harriet pushed back her chair and went to the window. On the other side of the glass, the mulberry trees and palms waved in silent salutation. Opening the door, she stepped out into the garden and looked up at the sky. The sun had disappeared and the air was hazed with brown, carrying the scent of brick and cinders. Somewhere nearby, women were shouting to one another in Arabic. The peculiar quality of the light, the sound of the wind, made her shiver.

"It's dusty," she announced, coming back inside, the wind banging the door behind her. "That's why the sky's overcast, Aunt Yael."

Harriet returned to the table and took another mouthful of a jelly that contained pieces of a sweet, soft-fleshed fruit. Nothing could dim the sense of happiness she'd felt since Eyre Soane's visit. He wanted to paint her. Each time Harriet remembered the fact, she experienced a little jolt of pleasure. On deck, the first time they met, the painter had barely noticed her. When he joined them for dinner, he had seen her for the first time. Now he wished her to be the subject of one of his works. Despite Louisa's discouragement, he would call again. Harriet felt certain of it.

Mustapha entered the room with a tray. Setting out small cups with no handles, he began to pour the coffee, holding the pot high, filling the little cups with a dark, steaming stream. The room was growing dimmer by the minute.

"What is happening, Mustapha?" asked Louisa.

"It is the wind, madame. The Khamseen."

"I think we ought to investigate, Louisa," Yael said, getting to her feet.

"If you insist," said Yael.

With Mustapha following, the three of them walked through the front part of the garden and out of the gate, onto the wide, unpaved street. The watchman had enveloped his entire head in his white turban, leaving only a slit for his eyes.

Their dresses blew against their legs as Harriet, Louisa, and Yael stood staring at the horizon, at a dim, dark shape bearing down on the city like a soft, moving mountain. Harriet felt a sense of foreboding. She enjoyed extremes of weather—found thunder and lightning exhilarating, relished the drama of high wind—but the brown cloud looked ominous. She'd never seen anything like it.

"'For, behold, darkness shall cover the earth,'" said Yael.

"There's no need to be dramatic, Yael." Louisa rubbed her eyes and turned her back on the horizon. "Come inside, Harriet."

By the time they had finished the coffee, they could barely see each other across the dining table. *Khamseen* meant *fifty*, Mustapha told them as he took away the cups. It was the fifty-day wind and it had arrived early. There was no saying when it would leave.

Parting the curtains of net around the bed, Harriet swung her legs out from under the blanket. A shutter was banging against the wall outside the window. She leaned out over the vanished garden and pulled the shutter back into the frame as the wind blasted dust at her face.

Back in bed, exhausted by the effort, she listened to the sound of her own breath, harsh on the air. She felt empty, devoid of the hopes and thoughts and ideas that had been filling her mind. In the weeks since they had left London, she'd allowed herself to begin to believe that she had left her illness behind. She'd been deceived. Asthma had stowed away inside her, waiting for the moment to spring out and make itself known.

If she couldn't be well here, a voice in her head insisted, she couldn't be well anywhere. Propped up on the pillows in the position meant to ease the constriction in her chest, Harriet wiped her eyes. The hope and excitement she'd felt on first entering this room seemed to mock her. How could she live, when it was all she could do to keep breathing?

She turned down Louisa's offer to sit with her, Yael's suggestion that she might read aloud. At mid-morning, Suraya arrived.

"Good morning, Suraya," Harriet said in Arabic, rousing herself. The greeting translated literally as *morning of light,* and Harriet enjoyed using it. Arabic seemed able to inject poetry into anything. Suraya didn't answer. Putting down a glass of black tea on the chair by the bed, she fetched a can of water from outside the door and began scattering it on the wooden floor, casting drops as if she were sowing seeds, then picked up a grass brush and began sweeping in quick, efficient strokes, hinging from her waist, the silver bells around her ankle tinkling as she moved.

She dropped the brush and sat down on the edge of the bed. Reaching for Harriet's hand with her small, strong one, she squeezed Harriet's fingers.

"You're well, by God's will?" she said in Arabic.

Harriet nodded.

"I'm well," she said, using the Arabic Suraya had taught her. "Thanks be to God."

She didn't know how to say that she was ill, that she felt hopeless and lonely. That more than anything she was filled with a bitter disappointment.

Suraya's dark eyes, lined with a sooty cosmetic, were unconvinced. Glancing toward the door, she reached into the neck of her robe, pulled out an envelope, and handed it to Harriet. It was addressed to Miss H. Heron. Harriet turned it over. There was no name on the back but she knew who had sent it.

"From where, Suraya? Who?"

The tinkling receded, and when Harriet looked up, Suraya had gone. Harriet tore open the envelope and unfolded a single sheet of paper.

Parthenon Hotel
March 15th 1882

Dear Miss Heron,

*Quite unaccountably, I find I'm missing you awfully. In fact, I
long to see you again.*

*I will call on you as soon as this wind subsides. We shall take
a picnic in the Palace gardens and perhaps you will be persuaded
to pose for sketches. Above all, I should like to paint you.*

Believe me, I shall pay no heed to your mother's opposition.

Yours very sincerely,
Eyre Soane

Harriet turned over the sheet of paper but the other side was
blank. Returning it to the envelope, she caught a faint smell of cigars.
Lying back again on the bank of pillows, Harriet looked about the
room. Nothing had changed. The Turkish rug lay flat on the floor,
forming an imperfect rectangle, one side longer than the other.
Brown light filtered through the slats of the shutters, throwing a soft
ladder of shadows onto the wall. "Eyre Soane longs to see me," she
said aloud. The room made no response.

Her breathing seemed looser. Lighter. She took a sip of tea and
grimaced. The water in Alexandria was brackish, its saltiness impossible to disguise even with the quantities of sugar the Egyptians used.
How could he long to see her again? It wasn't possible. She didn't
believe it. But perhaps it was true. Why would he say it if it was not?

Closing her eyes, Harriet slipped away from the rapid rise and
fall of her chest, the fast thud of her heart, and into a dream. Eyre
Soane admired her. He painted her portrait and, in doing so, fell in
love with her, begged her to marry him. Harriet Heron, spinster and
invalid, became a woman like other women. Mrs. Cox's prediction
was fulfilled.

Opening her eyes, Harriet felt disoriented. She got out of bed and
wrapped her old pink pashmina around her shoulders. Brushed her
hair at the washstand and splashed her face with water. Retrieving
her pen and travel bottles of ink, a sheet of paper from the trunk, she
got back into bed.

Dear Mr. Soane,

Thank you for your note.

I should be glad to sit for a painting when the weather improves. I am perfectly able to make up my own mind, in all matters.

Yours,

Harriet Heron

At three o'clock, the hour that Yael dubbed "Egyptian lunchtime," that Louisa had tried and failed to alter, Suraya brought up a tray covered with what looked like a conical woven hat. She removed it to display a plate of tomatoes stuffed with rice and minced meat, sprinkled with green herbs.

As she balanced the tray on Harriet's lap, Harriet passed her the note. It was addressed to *E. Soane Esq., care of the Parthenon Hotel.* Suraya couldn't read but she would know who it was intended for, Harriet was certain, and would find a way to deliver it. Suraya slipped the envelope down the neck of her robe.

"Eat!" she commanded in Arabic, as she twitched the edge of the sheet, straightened the tray. "Eat."

TWENTY-ONE

The room was lit by two pairs of candles, held in sconces on the walls. The shadows they cast reminded Louisa of antlers, as if she and Harriet were in a dim and misty forest, surrounded by wild beasts. Harriet's breath was shallow and harsh; she could barely speak. Dash was cowering in a corner.

Harriet began to cough, her face contorted and mouth open, gasping for air between spasms. Louisa got off her knees and hurried to the medicine chest, extracted the bottle of friar's balsam. "Will you take this?" she asked, measuring out a teaspoonful of the black liquid, dripping it onto a lump of sugar. "I am sure Dr. Grammaticas would think you ought."

Harriet made the ghost of a nod and Louisa put the spoon to her daughter's parted lips, trying to control the trembling of her own hand. She sat by the bed, straining her ears for any alteration, hearing none. Air was entering Harriet's chest with a hoarse, sucking noise, leaving it almost immediately with a reluctant hiss. Tortured though the sound was, Louisa focused fiercely on its continuance. All the time she could hear it, Harriet was breathing.

Earlier in the evening, Louisa had squeezed a dozen drops of lobelia tincture, twice the normal dose, into a glass of water, held her own breath as Harriet had swallowed it, then tried to make her comfortable on the hard Egyptian pillows. The tincture made little difference. The lit pan of dried stramonium leaves, mixed with belladonna, filled the room with noxious fumes like an autumn bonfire. Afterward, Harriet complained of a headache but breathed no more easily.

At midnight, with the wind whistling down the chimney, Louisa lit the portable vaporizer. The air began to fill with the woody odor of eucalyptus and menthol oils. She placed the device on the chair by Harriet's bed and wafted steam toward her with her fan, felt her forehead. It was clammy, her hair damp. The sound of wheezing, so close, so constrained, contrasted oddly with the great, free wind outside.

"Do you feel any relief?" Louisa asked after a few minutes. Harriet couldn't answer.

By the early hours, she sounded as if she were drowning, her breath coming in desperate, groaning gasps. Louisa took a candle from the sconce and held it near her daughter's face. Harriet's lips were blue and her mouth open, the sinews on her neck standing out. Her glazed eyes had a faraway look and her pulse was rapid.

It was four in the morning, an hour that seemed neither night nor day, an hour at the bottom of the sea. The wind had fallen silent. With her own heart hammering, Louisa pierced the wax seal on the bottle of chloroform, the medicine of last resort, which she'd never administered, although she had seen Dr. Grammaticas do so. She'd delayed using it because once she had, there would be nothing else left to try. She had an urgent fear that she'd delayed too long.

Sprinkling the clear liquid on a flannel, she hurried back to the bedside and passed the cloth under Harriet's nose once, then again, listening and praying at the same time. After a minute, Harriet's breathing altered. The struggle became less frantic. Louisa wafted the cloth past Harriet's face again and Harriet licked her lips.

"I'm . . . thir . . . sty," she said, her voice hoarse.

"Thank the Lord."

The dog shook himself and padded across the room as Louisa dropped the cloth, splashed water into a tumbler, and held it to Harriet's lips. Harriet raised herself on one elbow, took the glass.

"Why is it so dark?" she said.

"Dark?" Louisa's voice shook. She opened the shutter and looked out at the beginnings of a violet dawn over the white rooftops. "It will soon be morning."

Harriet didn't answer. She was asleep, her breathing easier than it had been for days. The dog snored at the end of the bed.

In the privacy of her own room, resealing the chloroform bottle with wax, fitting it back into its compartment in the medicine chest, Louisa wept.

Her mother's voice had refused to be silenced; it came to Louisa at odd hours of the day and night, demanding to be heard. The crisis had passed but Harriet was still unwell, wan-looking and short of breath. She'd been confined to bed for days, raised up on the pillows or sitting in the chair, while beyond the shutters the wind hurled itself at the villa, the trees in the garden creaking and flapping under the onslaught, part of the wall blowing down flat on the ground.

She and Yael had taken Harriet to a European doctor, watched as the Frenchman cupped her back, leaving red weals on each side of her long spine. He had written half a dozen prescriptions but prevaricated when Louisa begged him for advice as to what they should do.

"It is perfectly obvious, Yael. We have to go home." Yael, blinking and looking vague, offered no reply.

"The dust is worse for her than the fog," Louisa said. "I will send Mustapha today to book the tickets."

"I am not ready to go back to England, Louisa," Yael said.

Louisa jumped up from the sofa.

"Why on earth not?" she said as the door opened. "Harriet! Ought you to be out of bed?"

"I thought I heard you talking."

Harriet looked at Yael and Louisa in turn. She had on the slippers that Yael had bought for her on a visit to a bazaar. They made a shuffling sound, imitating the Arabic word for them, *ship-ship*, as she crossed the room and sat down.

"Your mother believes it is time to go home, Harriet," Yael said.

"But your aunt refuses to leave Alexandria." Reaching one hand behind her head, Louisa began to pat at her hair. "Very well, Yael. Harriet and I shall return alone."

Behind her spectacles, Yael blinked again.

"If Harriet wishes to leave. It is on her account, after all, that we're here."

The dog raised himself from the rug at Yael's feet and flopped down on Harriet's. In the wind, his white fur had turned the color of brick. Harriet stroked the top of his head.

"I don't want to leave. We can travel farther south, to Luxor. We'll escape the wind there, Mother."

"Not without Yael."

"Aunt?"

"Forgive me, Harriet. I determined on the steamer that I would go no farther than this. But I see no reason why you and your mother should not go on."

"Mother?"

Louisa didn't know which prospect seemed more dangerous—taking Harriet back to London, or traveling farther into Egypt. The only thing she was sure of was that they could not remain where they were.

"We cannot travel alone, Harriet," she said. "We need assistance."

Mustapha stepped forward from the doorway, his white robe gleaming in the brown haze in the atmosphere.

"Madame must take a dragoman."

He left the room, returning minutes later with a boy that he thrust through the door in front of him and introduced as his nephew, Fouad. Louisa raised her head from her hands. The boy was skinny and small, his black hair cut close to his head. He wore baggy Arab pantaloons and an old, highly polished pair of brown shoes tightly laced around bare feet.

"Does he speak English?" Louisa asked.

"Yes, madame," Mustapha said. "He is your lifesaver."

"I doubt that. He doesn't look more than fourteen." Fouad stared at the floor.

"I think it would be excellent if Fouad came with us, Mother," Harriet said.

Fouad raised his head, looked at his uncle and then at Louisa. His eyes came to rest on Harriet.

"I will travel with you," he said. "*Inshallah*. If God wills it."

TWENTY-TWO

The muezzin began calling the faithful, his words floating over the dusk like another form of ethereal cloud. In a corner room on the first floor of a Cairo hotel, Eyre Soane turned away from the window. The hotel barber had nicked his skin, stuck a piece of cotton on the cut. Eyre pulled it from his jaw and watched in the mirror as a drop of blood gathered slowly on his flesh, spilled like a tear. He sat down in the leather armchair, loosening the cord of his dressing gown and looking around his suite.

He was delaying dressing for dinner. Hadn't pared his nails, applied his cologne, oiled his hair. He was off-duty, in the business of being Eyre Soane, son of the late, great Augustus. Inheritor, said the critics, of his father's wealth but not his talent.

They were wrong on both counts. His father's talent had been for creating voluptuous, creamy-looking flesh that connoisseurs could feel they might reach into a painting and touch. All instinctively wanted to possess it. It was a formula Augustus had repeated scores of times, in different draperies, with different props. Different eyes, necks, breasts. Eyre favored landscapes. Landscapes never lied.

A high-pitched whine near his ear grew louder and Eyre slapped at the newly shaven portions of his neck with the palm of his hand. He hadn't wanted to be in Egypt this winter. He'd undertaken the journey only to escape the London season, the matrons of his mother's acquaintance throwing their female offspring in his path. He'd gotten away, all right, but now that he was here, he couldn't tolerate the crowds of English idlers and investors and adventurers whose laughter and boasts and pointless games of pinochle filled the downstairs bar.

Mother still hoped he would marry. For years, she'd asked constantly whether he had met a suitable girl, or would allow her to find one. Later, when the question fell silent on her lips, she inquired by means of anxious looks or hopeful ones if a female name was mentioned. Recountings of the weddings of the offspring of her friends. Eyre believed himself unlikely to marry. Not cut out for it.

The whine resumed, and with it came a sharp stinging on the rim of his ear, a hot bump rising. He groped in his whisky glass, hooked out what remained of a lump of ice, and applied it to the bite. The ice slipped from his fingers, dropping down inside the neck of the dressing gown, and he threw the dregs of the Scotch toward the shutters. Lighting a cigar, holding it between his lips, he removed the lid from a pot of sandalwood pomade and began to work the grease into his hair.

Augustus had been dead for a decade but the power he wielded in the family was undiminished. Despite all she'd suffered, Mother still worshipped the old man. She kept the London house as a shrine to him, preserving his correspondence, his handkerchiefs, his pipes and boots and belts, his hats and gloves. The gloves and boots bore the traces of the old man's bent, stubby hands and feet, like casts in plaster of Paris, the leather hardened around the spaces where he had been. Eyre disliked catching sight of the boots lined up on the rack in the cloakroom downstairs as if Augustus might step out over the floor, leaving his deep, dirty footprints once again, might don a pair of the gloves on the stand in the hall, ready to reach out with a thick gauntlet, take what he wanted.

Mother spoke of Augustus in a hushed voice as if he were asleep nearby and not to be disturbed. She silenced her son with a wave of her hand if Eyre suggested changing anything, clearing the studio.

"Your father visits me every day and has more to say than he ever had when he was alive. I am under strict and particular instructions, Eyre, to disturb nothing."

The old place on the coast had been sold off decades earlier, when

Eyre was still a child, but the London studio remained as it was on the day Augustus died, an unfinished painting of the latest dark-haired muse balanced on the easel. They were all alike, each one indistinguishable from the one before her, the one after. His mother was a saint.

Much of the work had already been sold. Only a few canvases remained. Among them was the *Thetis*, the sultry, half-clad sea goddess, sitting on the floor in the studio wrapped in an old sheet, along with a few other goddesses and nymphs and some early work that Augustus had disowned. Mother wouldn't have the *Thetis* on display in the house; she insisted that Julia, Eyre's younger sister, shouldn't see it. Eyre refrained from pointing out that the *Thetis* was no worse, morally speaking, than any of the others.

Perhaps he would sell the painting to Louisa's husband. Eyre was not as affluent as his detractors believed. The money was being depleted. The London house, where Mother insisted on remaining, was expensive to keep up, and the price the paintings fetched had dropped in the years since the death of Augustus. His own work rarely sold.

Hair slicked back over his head, Eyre heaved on the bell pull, intending to order another glass of Scotch. There were distractions in prospect. Julia was coming out and Jim Simpson had telegraphed to say that he was arriving with his new wife. *Docking Suez 21st, traveling Cairo same day. Meet Shepheard Hotel, 6 p.m.* They were probably in the bar by now, waiting for him.

Despite his desire to remain in Alexandria, to press on with his plan, Eyre had been obliged to come and meet them. He'd promised over an inebriated dinner before Christmas that he would act as his old friend's guide. Jim had set his heart on a crocodile twenty feet long. Eyre disliked hunting, the paraphernalia of guns and shot, the whole pointless palaver of it.

He intended a hunt of a different kind. He lifted one hand, pointed two straight fingers toward an alabaster statue of an Egyptian princess, and released a single shot in a whistle from his lips. Seeing Miss Heron looking back at him from across the dining saloon on the steamer, he'd remembered something Jim once told him of the way hunters trapped elephants. They rounded up the young, then waited for the mother to approach, tethered by invisible chains to her off-spring, willing to act against every instinct to stay close to the calf.

He must write the girl another note. Assure her of his passionate intentions and explain his obligation to escort his old friends up the Nile. It spoke well of a man, to have old friends.

My dear Henrietta. He screwed up the sheet and threw it in the wastepaper basket. It was on the tip of his tongue. *Helen. Hannah.* He found her name impossible to remember, slipping away like soap in the bath.

There was a knock at the door and he opened it to see a fellow done up in a black-and-white-striped robe, a tarboosh faded to an insipid pink, pointed red slippers. Eyre resented the silent plea in his eyes. There was no dignity in poverty. He took the glass from the tray, signed the chit with an extravagant scrawl and shut the door.

My dear Miss Heron—

Probably best to observe the formalities. The time to play the ardent lover would come later.

Forgive my silence. I have been called away to Cairo. How I wish that you might be here in the same city! Some old friends . . .

Eyre Soane continued to write, his attention only half on the lines forming under his hand. Near his head, the insect whined.

"There you are at last," said Jim Simpson.

"Hello, Eyre," said his wife, putting down her book.

Soane nodded at them. Jim was leaning on the bar; next to him, his wife perched on a high apparatus that was half chair, half stool. They both bore the hallmarks of the newly arrived, their complexions gray from the London winter. Mrs. Simpson was attired in a dress that might have suited a London drawing room but here appeared fussy, and Jim wore a tropical suit made for a taller man.

Jim looked out of place wherever he was, Eyre thought. He'd looked just the same on his first day at school, drowning in a new uniform, his face pink. He could still picture him.

Jim ordered a whisky for Eyre from the barman. "We've been waiting. Expected you at six."

"Did you, old man? Chin-chin."

When discussion of the hire of the dahabeah river cruiser, the likelihood of increasing temperatures on the journey south to Luxor, and the pleasure each felt at the prospect of seeing the antiquities had run its course, Eyre judged the moment right to begin.

"I've met a girl," he said, putting down the glass on the shiny surface of the bar, drawing it along the wood, watching the trail of moisture in its wake.

"Oh, Soanie," Effie Simpson said, leaning forward on her stool, her features expressing a mix of interest and concern. "Tell us everything about her. Where did you meet her?"

His new wife had begun to use Jim's schoolboy nickname for him at the same time that Jim had abandoned it. Eyre glanced up to meet Jim's skeptical eyes, the woman's widened ones.

"On the voyage out, as a matter of fact, Mrs. Simps—"

"Oh, please, do call me Effie."

"She's traveling with her mother and aunt."

"How romantic." Mrs. Simpson's eyes shone. "To meet on the voyage out. Did you hear, Jim?"

"The pity of it is that the mother's set against me."

"What possible reason can she have for that?" Effie Simpson's voice was flooded with a sudden and excessive loyalty. "She's only got to get to know you, Eyre. That'll set her mind at rest."

Jim Simpson shifted from one foot to the other and his wife glanced at him.

"Stop fidgeting, Jim. Eyre's telling you something of significance. Is she beautiful? What's her name?"

Eyre lifted the glass again. The lumps of ice had shrunk to the size of peas. He drank it to the watery, unsatisfying end and ordered another, felt in the inside pocket of his waistcoat for his cigar case.

"She is . . ." He couldn't come up with a word. The truth was that he had no thoughts about Miss Heron. "She has red hair."

Jim Simpson drank pale ale from a glass-bottomed pint pot, his Adam's apple protruding like an elbow. The new Mrs. Simpson sipped from a glass of chilled champagne. She left lip prints on the rim of the flute, creased marks in pale pink.

"Well," she said. "It can't be helped. And anyway, it's not her fault."

"I'd like you to make her acquaintance. Perhaps you'll put in a word for me if we happen to meet them."

Effie clasped her hands against her chest, tilted her head to one side.

"Of course I will. Jim, you might congratulate Eyre."

"Indeed," said Jim, his eyes shifting to a point behind Eyre's shoulder. "Congratulations, old chap. It's about time you settled down. If you really are serious this time."

Idiotic fellow had blushed like a woman.

TWENTY-THREE

Harriet and Louisa had been waved off by Yael from the station at Alexandria at nine in the morning. Now a great clock, marked in both Arabic and Roman numerals, indicated that it was four in the afternoon. Wrapped in her pink shawl, perching on the lid of her trunk while Louisa and Fouad went to find assistance, Harriet felt disoriented. In just hours, she had arrived in another world, a busier, more thoroughly foreign one than that she had left behind.

The Europeans among the urgent travelers that rushed across the tiled concourse of Cairo station looked not as grand or consequential as the Eastern people. The Turkish men were white-skinned, opulently clad in embroidered cloth, looped strings of amber prayer beads dangling from their fingers and silver-tipped sticks held under their arms. Shrouded women took little steps behind them, dressed in more somber hues than their male counterparts, like a species of bird where a drab female attends on a vivid-feathered mate.

Breathing in air heavy with fumes from the train engines, mingled with the sweet scent of jasmine from baskets of flowers that ragged-looking children were pressing on parties of German and French travelers, Harriet found herself scanning the passersby for someone she knew. She was looking, she realized with surprise, not for Eyre Soane but for the long limbs, crumpled suit, and pale straw hat of the man with the piano. The disappointment she'd felt on not seeing his face had stayed with her.

She wondered where, in all the vast continent that lay to the south of here, the instrument had come to rest. Whether the man was playing it now, transporting himself to his homeland through its resonant chords. Picturing his angular body bent over its keys, his hands ranging across them, Harriet heard in her head a wistful piece of music that evoked the wind blowing between the stones in a graveyard.

The haunting notes continued to play in her head as, with a strength disproportionate to his skinny frame, Fouad lifted her bodily into a sedan chair, and from there into another dusty cab. With Louisa looking anxiously out of the window, the three of them set off for the hotel, rattling past domed mosques with needle-like minarets, under the shadow of dark buildings, the upper windows covered in latticed woodwork screens, and along narrow alleys lined with shops that looked as if they and their goods had been there since the dawn of time.

TWENTY-FOUR

The service was over and, with its wide doors standing open and congregation departed, the church had lost its hushed, sacred atmosphere. The bleating of goats floated in from outside over the rows of wooden pews, along with the smell of baking bread.

"There you are, Miss Heron," a voice boomed. "I expected to see you before now."

The Reverend Griffinshawe's white eyebrows waggled as he spoke, distracting Yael from the speech she'd prepared, the appeal she'd intended to make to his Christian charity. Moving toward the dais where he stood, Yael braced herself. She had never liked asking others for help or favors but, she told herself firmly, *needs must*. She intended to inquire of Reverend Griffinshawe whether there was a doctor within the congregation who might lend his services once a fortnight, for the cases that were beyond her scope.

He beamed at her. "I have been considering your offer and I have a particular request to make of you."

"Good morning, Reverend Griffinshawe. What is that?"

"I am in need of a housekeeper. An Englishwoman—"

"Reverend, I don't think I—"

He raised his hands in the air.

"You misunderstand me, my dear Miss Heron. I am not for one moment suggesting that you would undertake the work yourself. I need a woman to train the servants to make English tea and order the groceries, teach my maid how to iron linen. I find myself so much taken up with domestic issues, there is scarcely time to pursue the mission.".

Yael wished that he would step down from the dais. She disliked looking up at him, from a greater distance even than that which nature had decreed.

"Reverend, I have an apology to make."

"Come, dear lady." The eyebrows knitted together as Ernest Griffinshawe looked down on her with a look of benign approval. "I cannot believe you can have anything for which to apologize."

"I had thought that I could devote my spare time to assisting your project here in Egypt," she said. "But I find I am called to other work."

"What other work? Who by?"

"I intend to establish a clinic for children. An eye clinic."

The Reverend took a step back.

"I wasn't aware that you had expertise in ophthalmia." He guffawed. "Should I have been addressing you as Doctor?"

"The clinic will be for first aid and teaching basic cleanliness. I will offer what simple treatments I can. But this is what I wished to talk—"

Reverend Griffinshawe looked up at the rafters.

"If there is teaching to be done, Miss Heron, it should surely begin with the word of God."

Yael did not contradict him, although she was becoming aware since she had arrived in Egypt that the people here, as far as one could see, had their own word of God. From the same God or at any rate through one of His prophets. Not equal to His son, of course, but theirs nonetheless.

She smiled pleasantly.

"I hoped, Reverend, that you might be able to offer me some assistance. I wanted—"

"Don't see how, dear lady," he said, looking past her with a distracted air, his eyes ranging over the parched white ground outside the doors. "I am not much of a one for children. Females. More concerned with souls than runny noses and so forth."

"Please hear what I have to say . . ."

Reverend Griffinshawe was gone, disappeared into the sacristy. A minute later he emerged with three great tomes hugged against his chest, and Yael glimpsed the distinctive brown and gold binding of Shaftesbury's Arabic-language Bible.

"You may have these, Miss Heron," he said, stepping off the platform at last, thumping the volumes down on a pew next to where she stood. "For use in your clinic. I hope you may find some opportunity at least for study with your ladies."

Coated in a layer of dust, their pages still uncut, the volumes looked old already. Yael became aware of her back teeth clenched painfully together. She shifted her jaw experimentally and felt a stabbing pain in the hinge of it, below her ear.

"Reverend, these women are quite unable to read in any language. That much I do know, from my work in London. I wanted to ask—"

"My point exactly," he said, nodding as he spoke, as if to confirm his agreement with himself. "You could serve the flock better by teaching them the English alphabet."

Yael took a sudden objection to the word *flock*.

"I don't believe so," she said. "Children who are blind cannot read, after all."

He looked at her with dislike.

"I must bid you goodbye, Miss Heron. I have a meeting to go to."

His tone had been unpleasant, Yael decided, walking back through the narrow streets of the old town, skirting around a donkey laden with two milk churns. The jovial assumption of common purpose had departed from it entirely. She had omitted to give him back the pound he'd lent her.

She carried on, walking in the shadow of ancient-looking buildings, their foundations made of great boulders of white stone, the upper stories of mud bricks, roughly patched with plaster. Despite what had happened on her first outing, Yael had taken to walking everywhere she went. She enjoyed glimpsing domestic life through half-open doorways, peering into courtyards or the musty interiors of the large cupboards that in the native quarter passed for shops. Her experience with the children, the first time she'd gone out alone, had taught her a lesson. She no longer brought out her purse in public places. She kept half a dozen silver piastres loose in her handbag.

If a child approached her, she slipped one or two of the small coins into his or her hand without fuss or fanfare, as she had seen the local people do. No one molested her.

The smell of food reached her and Yael's stomach rumbled in answer. On the shady side of the alley, a group of men were squatting around a large dish. Dressed in black-and-white-striped sateen gowns, red felt hats, and embroidered shawls, each with the right sleeve pushed up to the elbow, they were dipping their right hands into the bowl, rolling bread and beans into balls and sliding them into their mouths with deft, economical movements. Seeing her looking at them, one gestured for her to join them.

"Welcome," he said in English. "Welcome, Sitti."

Mustapha called her Sitti on occasion. It meant *lady*, as far as she could tell, and was a respectful address to a woman, not only a foreign one. She disliked being called *khawaga. Foreigner*. Harriet had told her that in the ancient Egyptian script the sign for *foreigner* was the same as the one for *enemy*; a person with their hands tied behind their backs.

"Thank you," she said as she passed by, nodding. "I shan't join you but thank you."

The gratitude Yael felt continued as she carried on toward the villa. It was not for the offer of food but for the acknowledgment of a common humanity. The Mohammedans treated her better than her own countrymen did.

Continuing on her way, she had an idea. Ernest Griffinshawe's refusal to help was a blessing in disguise. When she felt ready, she would request a meeting with the sheikh. Tell him of her intention to find a room in the old town, where she could teach the mothers simple hygiene, and inquire whether he would support the venture, whether he knew an Egyptian doctor who might volunteer his services. It wasn't inconceivable that Sheikh Hamada would help her. The idea of bypassing the Reverend Griffinshawe, of appealing to a local leader, and a Mohammedan one, pleased her. It was right.

Thinking again about her plan, Yael felt a surge of excitement. For all of her adult years, she had involved herself in charity work in London, trying to improve the lot of her fellow man or—more often—woman. Although the schemes had been varied, worthwhile, all had been established by other people. The prospect of following her own vision, offering assistance according to her own most dearly held principles, was entirely new.

She reached the Frank quarter and walked slowly across the Place des Consuls, the jacaranda trees making the square look as if it were aflame with violet fire. Stepping over fallen blossoms on the flagstones, walking past the wooden cabin where a man and his son sold long-handled pots of Turkish coffee and hard, twice-baked biscuits, Yael thanked God for bringing her to this far land. She'd agreed to it with the greatest reluctance, had boarded the *Star of the East* with gritted teeth, anticipating nothing more than a test of endurance. Yet she was experiencing a peace in Alexandria that eluded her in London. Searching her mind for its source, Yael found the answer.

By the white wall that ran along the front of the villa, she stopped, looking at the motionless, perpendicular form of a lizard, defying laws of gravity and reason. She could *do* things here. It was this, not language and sunlight, the complexion of the people, their religion and food and mighty river, that made Egypt a foreign country.

TWENTY-FIVE

❧❧

Standing on the landing of a wide staircase, leaning her elbows on the ebonized banister, Harriet looked down at the lobby of the Oasis Palace Hotel. The hotel was for invalids. Mr. Moore, whose wife had been treated here for her nerves, had recommended it to Louisa, and they were spending a few days there before traveling on to Luxor.

It was a place of hushed conversations and little laughter, elderly women with hair like dandelion seed and wizened men with female nurses hovering close by. Harriet found it depressing. She was in the state familiar to her of being neither well nor ill, not in crisis but not able to breathe freely. Even here in Egypt, that condition felt like a half-life. More than anything, it made her feel lonely. However sympathetic, no one else could really understand what it was like. No doctors seemed able to help.

The floor down below was of smooth, polished marble with Oriental rugs laid on top. A green glass chandelier hung in the center over a vase of flowers, and around the edges of the large hall, pairs of chesterfields, dark leather twins, faced each other across tables made from engraved brass trays.

The revolving doors turned, disgorging a man in a safari jacket and pith helmet. Something about his gait was familiar. A moment later, from the next quarter, a second figure emerged, straight-backed, clad in a broad-brimmed hat swathed with a veil that covered her face. Harriet gasped.

"Mrs. Cox!"

The woman threw back the veil. "Harriet!"

Mrs. Cox began to cross the lobby, a lace-trimmed parasol swinging from her wrist, the train of her skirt swishing on the tiles. Ignoring Louisa's protests, Harriet almost ran down the stairs.

"What are you doing here?" Mrs. Cox said, gripping Harriet's elbows.

"We're staying here until we travel to Luxor. And you?"

"I have an appointment with the doctor."

Mrs. Cox glanced at her husband. Zebedee Cox's hands were clasped behind his back, his head tipped back in close examination of the chandelier.

"Afternoon, Miss Heron," he said.

Harriet nodded at him and returned her eyes to her friend. She pictured her in her nightdress, soaked, lying curled up on the bunk in the same shape that the tiny form had been. She hadn't seen her since that awful night.

"I am so happy to meet you again, Mrs. Cox," she said. "How are you?"

"I hardly know," she said softly, looking up at Louisa, who was still standing on the stairs. "The lemonade here is delicious, Mrs. Heron," she called, her voice bright and social. "Have you sampled it?"

The four of them arranged themselves around one of the low tables.

"We've come this minute from a tour of the Pyramids," Mrs. Cox said. "Do tell Mrs. Heron about it, Zeb. It was the most marvelous thing."

Mr. Cox turned to Louisa.

"They used to bury the slaves with the pharaohs, you know," his voice boomed out. "Still alive. Absolute barbarism."

Sarah Cox turned to Harriet. She looked drawn, her eyelashes and the fine hairs on her cheeks and top lip thickened with dust.

"Are you any better?" she asked.

"Yes, I'm much . . ."

Harriet was overcome by coughing. It hurt Harriet to admit that she was still ill; an invalid, like the other residents of the hotel, the old people who belonged there. She was ashamed of her illness, she understood suddenly. She'd never allowed herself to realize it before. She felt responsible for it, as if it were a personal failing.

"This awful wind lays everyone low," said Mrs. Cox. "Zebedee's had bronchitis."

"I was improving until the Khamseen came." Harriet breathed in toward the pit of her stomach, as deeply as she was able. "And you? Are you recovered, Mrs. Cox?"

Mrs. Cox's eyes glistened. She pulled a handkerchief from her sleeve, squeezing the fine lawn into a ball in her hand.

"I see him everywhere, Harriet, dream about him at night. I can't stop thinking about the way he—"

"Here we are," announced Zebedee Cox, as the waiter set down four glasses, their rims frosted with sugar, bright sprigs of mint floating on the drink.

Mrs. Cox blew her nose and smiled at her husband.

"I was just telling Miss Heron that we are traveling to Suez shortly. To meet the shipment."

"What are you shipping, Mr. Cox?" Louisa asked.

"Parts for a flour mill," said Zebedee Cox. "But since the natives cannot afford to buy bread, I don't know what earthly use it'll be."

"What a coincidence it is," Louisa said to Mrs. Cox, "to see you both again."

"Small world," said Mr. Cox. "We ran into another chap from the steamer earlier, out at the Pyramids. What was his name, Sarah? Had his easel set up there under an umbrella thingy."

"I don't recall," said Mrs. Cox. "Have you been yet? Really, Harriet, you simply must see them."

"Soane. That's it. His father was a well-known painter, you know. Julius or Octavius. Name escapes me now."

Louisa had taken her fan from her handbag and was waving it in small, agitated movements. Harriet lowered her face to her glass, swallowed another mouthful of the cool, sweet liquid. Mr. Soane was here, in the same city. He must have followed her. She had misjudged him.

Zebedee Cox got to his feet. He slid his hand into the pocket of his jacket and drew out a watch.

"Ready, Sarah?"

"Yes, Zebedee," said Mrs. Cox. "Do write to me, Harriet, as soon as you're back at home. Come." Linking her arm through Harriet's, leading her to the reception desk, she picked up the old-fashioned quill pen and wrote a few lines. "Here is our address. I insist on your coming to tea."

Blotting the paper, she handed it to Harriet. The handwriting was neat and even, the address in a part of London Harriet did not know. Below, Mrs. Cox had written: *Mr. S. spoke of you most kindly. Wanted to get a letter to you before he travels to Luxor with his friends.*

Harriet folded the note and slid it into her pocket next to her journal.

"I'd like to give you our address," she said to Mrs. Cox, glancing over her shoulder.

Louisa stood a few feet away with Mr. Cox under a grinning crocodile mounted on the wall. Harriet took another sheet of hotel paper. Below the post office box number, the line drawing of the Oasis Palace Hotel, she wrote the Canonbury address. *Tell him I long to see him again*, she added underneath. Folding the paper, she held it out to Mrs. Cox.

TWENTY-SIX

Louisa sat at a breakfast table on the deck of a dahabeah. Amid the clatter of china, the hum of conversation, the screech of birds from the banks, Harriet was quiet.

"Some more coffee, Harriet?"

Harriet shook her head.

Fouad had found a cabin for them, sharing the boat with a party of eight French people on their way to Abu Simbel. Louisa and Harriet had boarded the previous evening, hours after seeing the Coxes. They'd sailed through the night, by moonlight, the captain saying they would take advantage of the wind. Harriet had been wakeful, troubled by fits of coughing, but had announced in the morning that she felt well enough to breakfast on deck.

In the bright sunshine, she looked almost gaunt, her hair thickened with red dust, its color dulled. She'd taken only a few mouthfuls of an omelette.

"Is there anything I can fetch you?" Louisa said. "Do for you?"

Harriet laid down her fork.

"No, thank you. I'm going back to the cabin, Mother, to rest."

Louisa felt sure she was thinking of Eyre Soane. Her heart ached for her daughter. It was natural, that Harriet should want a suitor, should have hopes of a family of her own, a future. It was cruel, that the first man to present himself should be Soane, trying to use Harriet in a game of cat-and-mouse.

Louisa followed her down the wooden steps, wishing she could bestow happiness in the way she'd been able to when Harriet was a child, with a story or a sugar mouse. Louisa didn't know, now, what made Harriet happy. At Christmas, she'd given her a bottle of scent in a pretty cut-glass bottle but she'd never noticed Harriet smelling of lily of the valley. Blundell had given her another great tome on the pharaohs, which she'd insisted on bringing.

"Do you need a lozenge?" she said, feeling helpless. "I could burn a paper?"

The traveling medicine chest was to hand in the cabin, restocked with the prescriptions of the doctor in Alexandria, new supplies of Espic cigarettes, Legras and Escouflaire powders, from France. She'd bought pastilles of ipecacuanha and a salve he'd recommended.

"No, thank you. Leave me now, Mother, if you would."

Harriet was grown up, Louisa thought as she climbed the steps back to the deck. She didn't know why it should have taken so long for this self-evident truth to come home to her. Her daughter was an adult and her life, the preservation of it, was not in Louisa's hands as it had been when she was a baby, an infant, or even a little girl. Harriet's life belonged to Harriet and to God. Her death, when it came, belonged equally to her and the Almighty.

Resuming her seat at the table, Louisa sent up an urgent, silent prayer that they were doing the right thing and that the climate in the south would benefit Harriet, the journey not exhaust her further. She added one for herself, that the voyage to save her daughter's life would not mean the end of her own.

Eyre Soane was bent on creating scandal. Blundell would feel it dreadfully. Blundell cared above all for propriety, for doing the correct things, at the correct time, in the correct way. His sense of what those things, times, ways were, never failed him.

Thinking about her husband, from so far away, Louisa wondered why he adhered so rigidly to what he called good form. Why he found it necessary. She asked herself, not for the first time in her married life, what secrets he might have from her. Where his mind wandered in sleep, in the shared silences of their life together. When she returned to London, to the substantial house, the tree-lined crescent, she had an instinct that they could never go back to how they had been. She felt a yearning sadness that he was not near and might never again be near.

Moving to the little writing desk in the open-air saloon, she wrote to him describing the landscape, the crew, the French fellow travelers. The letter was humorous and even-toned, could not have been more different from how she was feeling.

The *Amon-Ra* plied its way up the great gray-green river, past emerald patches of clover, fields of waving new grain, and flocks of stick-legged egrets. While Harriet rested in the cabin, occupied with her books, her journal, her inks, Louisa reclined in a deck chair, hypnotized by the changing panorama of ruined monuments and tumbledown hovels, farmers astride donkeys in the palm groves. They passed what appeared to be a large and ramshackle factory, from which came the unmistakable smell of boiling sugar, transporting Louisa to her own house, to a dozen pots of strawberry jam cooling on the marble slab.

Accompanying it all was the ghostly creak and groan of water wheels. The archaic-looking contraptions were everywhere, pulled by blinkered asses that trudged in circles, dipping empty vessels on a wheel down into the water, raising them up brimming, for spilling over the fields.

Louisa tried to conjure home again. She strained her ears for the sound of hot water splashing into an enameled bath, Rosina singing in the kitchen, the strike of the several clocks in the drawing room that at midday and midnight made a symphony of the passing of the hours. She could not. Only a high female voice made itself heard, still insisting that death was near. It seemed Amelia Newlove wasn't aware that Louisa had heeded her words, taken her advice.

At sunset, Louisa rose from the chair and wrote another letter, this time to Mr. Hamilton. Did her mother have any more to say to her? Anything at all? Please would he be so kind as to send Louisa a note, care of the British consul at Luxor in Egypt, passing on any message that might come through.

TWENTY-SEVEN

Yael followed Mustapha through a gate and into a mud-walled and mud-floored enclosure, filled with men. A silent crowd was packed into the little yard and most looked impoverished, their robes ragged, bodies and faces lean. They waited in silence, some sitting on roughly turned wooden chairs and stools, some squatting in the shade cast by one wall, elbows resting on their knees. A few turned their heads to glance at her but Yael had the impression that the men were less surprised by her presence there than she was herself.

One, silver-haired, missing a leg, hauled himself up from his chair and, leaning on a wooden crutch under his arm, pulled the chair away from the rest, so it stood alone. He returned to the others, leaning on the wall.

"For you, Sitti Yael," said Mustapha, nodding his head at it.

"Thank you."

Yael sat down, feeling uncomfortable. She didn't like to deny the man his seat but to refuse his chivalry was worse. A minute later, with no audible command having been issued, a boy with his head swathed in a white cloth brought a drink and set it in front of her on a table.

"Thank you," she said again, the words discordant in the gathered intensity of the silence. Yael settled herself on the rickety chair, preparing for a long wait. She would not take the drink. Lord only knew what it might be. Not anything normal, such as elderflower cordial or ginger beer, she was certain. Not iced tea or pear juice. Lemonade.

Licorice tonic. Her favorite seltzer water. She swallowed. Her throat was parched. It was hotter every day and the wind had continued intermittently in the weeks since the girls had gone.

She sat very still, thinking about them and praying for them at the same time. Louisa had written that the Khamseen afflicted Cairo as badly as Alexandria, that they were traveling farther south. They would be on a boat by now, traveling up the River Nile.

Yael had left it to Louisa to communicate this further change of circumstances to Blundell. She had a feeling that he would be displeased, downright angry, that she had not accompanied them even to Cairo. She had preferred not to dwell on that, was instead following another instinct that *sufficient unto the day is the evil thereof,* and she would face the reckoning with Blundell when she was back in London. *The morrow shall take thought for the things of itself.*

Her mouth was so dry she was unable to swallow. She reached for the tumbler, took a sip of something cold and sour. Its taste was unpleasant and appealing at the same time but surprisingly thirst-quenching. It was curious how in Egypt things could be not one thing or the other but both simultaneously. Egypt, she repeated silently, to herself. She'd grown attached to the word. The awkward sound of it, the unknowable thought of it, gave her pleasure. Egypt. She picked up the glass again, took another sip, then drank it to the end.

Mustapha had asked about and found a room for her for the clinic. It was in a Mohammedan quarter, in an alley so narrow that the wooden galleries protruding from the first floors of the houses nearly touched overhead, blocking out the sky, creating a perpetual twilight; the sandy path was dampened by water thrown out of the doorways by Egyptian women, their veils tied over their faces, dusty infants clinging to their necks or backs.

Yael had to duck under the door frame, but once inside the house she could stand freely. The dirt floor was clean and swept, the air scented with some lingering odor that Mustapha informed her was incense, to banish evil spirits. The frames of the small windows were crooked and the wood unpainted; the only furniture was a couple of wooden tables and a bed strung with woven strips of animal skin.

Mustapha had arranged for her to rent the house from a cousin of his, for what seemed to Yael a small amount. Privately, she thought it barely worthy of the name *house,* consisting as it did of just one room on the ground floor and above it another, from which a steep open stairway led up out of one corner and onto a flat roof. Yael had climbed up there behind Mustapha the first time she went to see the house; each step was a different height, all unfeasibly steep.

Emerging into the sunlight, she'd found herself standing inside a low mud parapet, looking out at a world whose existence she had not until now suspected. All around her, in rectangles of flat mud, gaggles of ducks and chickens strutted and pecked, sheets and fruits were spread out to dry, women squatted by bowls picking chaff and stones from beans, or washing clothes. Not a chimney pot to be seen.

She'd gotten the supplies she needed from an apothecary in the Frank quarter, acquired cotton cloths and tin bowls, and set up the little room as best she could. Then she had to contemplate the aspect she'd been postponing. How to reach the children. In London, without barriers of language, it was easy enough to recruit people for any service, on the grounds of entertainment, the likelihood of a little warmth or some food offered for free. Here, she was not certain of how to begin. It occurred to her that she needed a translator. Perhaps Mustapha would agree to assist.

She stood in the open doorway and waited for likely-looking women to pass by. Young mothers seemed suddenly to have absented themselves entirely from the alley, although they thronged every other quarter.

"Good morning, ladies," she said to a pair shuffling past in what looked like black shrouds, every part of them but their eyes hidden. Even so thoroughly camouflaged, they appeared by their gait and outlines beyond the likelihood of having young children but they might, Yael supposed, be grandmothers. *Habobat.* She made a dabbing motion at her eyes.

"Eye clinic," she called after their departing backs. "For children." Neither looked around.

She retreated inside, sat alone in the room, listening to the sounds from outside. A quarrel broke out between two men and Yael got to her feet in alarm, wondering if she would find herself providing first aid to adults. Within minutes, the row had given way to sounds of laughter. Yael had felt confused. She'd heard more laughter since she arrived in Egypt than she believed she'd heard in her entire life.

Returning the glass to the table, Yael became aware of a man standing by her with an expectant air. She rose and followed him through a door and into a dim, almost empty room. As her eyes adjusted to the gloom, she saw the sheikh sitting on a cushion at the far end. In front of him was a row of smaller, plainer cushions for his audience and beside him, on a stool, what appeared to be a copy of the Mohammedan holy book, the Qur'an. Behind him, on the wall, was a set of framed photographs. Yael had the impression they were of the sheikh but, distracted by the prospect of being expected to sit on the floor, on a bolster, surprised by the simplicity of the surroundings, when she had expected a grandeur to match his own, she could not be sure.

He gestured for her to be seated and she became aware that his assistant had brought in the chair for her, placed it behind the row of cushions. Sitting down, she bowed her head. She'd understood that the sheikh did not favor eye contact.

"Good morning, Sheikh Hamada."

"Welcome, Sitti. You require further assistance?"

Yael hadn't meant to pretend it was a social call but the bluntness of his greeting threw her off balance. She found herself answering a query he had not raised.

"I am quite well, thank you, despite the unpleasant weather. Are you in good health? Your family?"

"Thank God."

He blinked but otherwise remained motionless. Sweat trickled down her back, under her dress. She must declare her purpose.

"I wish to start . . . That is, I have started . . . a clinic in the old town. For the children."

The sheikh's beard twitched. If she had expected congratulation, she was not to be gratified. No matter. She was asking the sheikh only for his blessing, which he surely could not withhold, and more practically, his good word among the women of the neighborhood.

If he seemed amenable, she might venture to inquire whether he had any candidates for the post of translator.

Yael cleared her throat, which was dry again. "You told me yourself that the children here lack many things. I want to help them retain their sight."

The sheikh's expression quickened. "You are a doctor?"

"No. I intend to teach the mothers how to keep their children's eyes in better condition. Talk with them about hygiene and the importance of cleanliness. Washing their children's faces."

"Washing their faces," he repeated. "Can you bring food?"

She shook her head. "No, Sheikh Hamada. I cannot bring food."

He looked at her for the first time, his eyes making a brief, incurious contact. His beard was a vivid orange, freshly stained with the powdered leaf that Mustapha's wife stained her nails with, and the rims of his eyes darkened with the antimony that they called kohl. He would have appeared a figure of fun in London, been taken for a theatrical performer or a turn at a fair. Here, he was sage. Powerful.

Yael felt her own peculiarity more strongly than the sheikh's. She pictured the Egyptian Hall in Piccadilly, remembered Belzoni as her mother had told her she'd seen him as a child, nearly seven feet tall and dressed as a mummy, wrapped head to toe in bandages, moving among the crowds, causing women to faint. Yael longed for a peppermint, extra strong, to chase away the creep of mortification that England, the idea of England, kept arousing in her. No one had warned her that when you traveled, you lost your country twice over. Physically were removed from it and mentally suffered a greater distance still.

"What help do you seek, ma'am?"

She leaned forward. "I want you to explain to them, Sheikh, that I can assist them. So that they will come to the clinic. I have a room in the old town, near the Gate of the Sea. I want you to tell them not to be afraid."

"They should not be afraid? Of foreigners? Are you sure?"

"Not of the ones who wish to assist them. Most certainly not."

From the look on his face, Yael might almost have believed he disagreed with this incontrovertible truth.

He ran the palm of his hand over his beard in an affectionate, private gesture.

"Our people need food, Sitti. Without food, we die. And our children perish first. I cannot help you."

The sheikh looked past her shoulder, gave the slightest possible inclination of his head, and a man holding a tattered and thumbed piece of paper shuffled forward from outside, folded himself in one agile movement onto the cushion at his feet.

Mustapha reappeared, his head bowed. He kissed the sheikh's hand and backed away. The audience was at an end. Yael had no choice but to stand up and take her leave. She assumed the vague expression that she found her best camouflage in any situation, blinked and nodded, spoke cheerfully.

"Thank you, Sheikh," she said. "Good day to you."

On the other side of the gate, back in the dusty street, Yael put up the rusty black gamp she'd brought from London in case of rain and had taken to using as a parasol. The spokes were reluctant, sharp on her fingers, and as she raised the struts, a soft shower of dust descended from inside the umbrella. It drifted down, settled on her bonnet, her nose, her shoulders as, walking a couple of paces behind Mustapha, she set off for the villa.

Yael strolled around the garden, as was her habit in the hour before supper. The wind had dropped, but it hadn't rained for days, and the air was humid and salty. She could hear Mustapha's wife, talking to her children in their quarters, making a low, ongoing stream of sound like birdsong.

The Reverend Griffinshawe considered her a potential housekeeper and no more. As a Christian and as a woman, she was beneath the sheikh's dignity. She had thought better of him but inside their formal garb, in their self-regard, the two men were alike. Members of that same family, the brotherhood of man.

"A plague on you," she said aloud. "A plague on both your houses." Yael held her head very straight as she continued around under the trees, enjoying the faint, sweet smell of earth, of blossom and wood smoke, of salt and rotting vegetables, of what she could only call *life*. She would not give in. God had brought her to this place for a purpose.

One of Suraya's children wailed in protest at something and the baby began to cry. "Hush," Yael heard Suraya sing out, in English. "Come to me." She thought of Harriet's patient teaching, the pair of them singing children's rhymes. Of course. Yael didn't know why she hadn't seen it sooner. Suraya. She would help Yael to recruit the patients. She could talk with the mothers. If Mustapha agreed to it, Yael would appoint her as her assistant.

TWENTY-EIGHT

Harriet felt dreamlike. Her feet, in the same flat, laced boots that she wore in London, were treading the ground where queens had walked in beauty, where kings sported in their chariots and citizens listened to the music of drums. She was being warmed by the same sun, breathing the same air, tinged now with rose and gold.

It was late afternoon, and after the fortnight-long voyage up the Nile, she and Louisa had disembarked from the *Amon-Ra*, been carried through the shallows by the crew, and set down on the shore of the village of Luxor by the ruins of a vast temple.

Fouad splashed through the water, holding his shoes above his head, soaking his pantaloons. With a satisfied air, as if he'd conjured it himself, he waved in the direction of a brown-stone building that stood on the other side of a rough road leading along by the river.

"Hotel, Miss Harry. *Kwayis?*"

"*Kwayis*, Fouad. Good."

She smiled at him. Fouad appeared to have made the decision that although employed and paid by Louisa, it was Harriet he was there to serve. He was a faithful shadow, offering help both wanted and unwanted.

"Lord only knows what it'll be like," Louisa said, raising her green glasses and peering in the direction of the hotel.

Harriet and Louisa crossed the road and passed under an arch bearing the name *Luxor Hotel*, picked out in pebbles in the mortar. Inside, behind a reception desk, a man dressed in a threadbare dinner jacket and a lopsided white bow tie, appeared to be waiting for them. He spread his hands in welcome.

"*Salaam alaikum, mesdames.*"

"Rooms," Louisa said, pulling off her glove, holding two fingers in the air. She pointed at herself, then Harriet. "We need two rooms."

The lobby was painted white with earth-colored tiles underfoot. Pushed up against one wall was a shoeshine chair in carved black ebony. With its high step and long back, it looked to Harriet like a dusty, vacated throne. The man was already unhooking keys from a board. He emerged from behind the desk and made a bow to Louisa.

"The ladies will have the best chambers that we're able to offer."

"You speak English," said Louisa, pausing the movement of her fan. "How very fortunate."

"Monsieur Andreas, at your service," he said, bowing again, turning to lead the way up the wooden stairs, past a large thermometer on the wall. "You are most welcome, madame. Follow me."

Minutes later, they'd taken two adjacent rooms with windows looking on to the Nile, at a long-stay rate of thirteen shillings a week, negotiated by Louisa. Fouad would be accommodated in a separate part of the hotel, a room in the garden where Egyptian servants stayed. The trunks had been hauled up the stairs, farewells made to the captain, the crew, and the French passengers of the *Amon-Ra*.

Louisa departed for the neighboring room, saying she intended to rest before dinner. She kissed Harriet on the cheek and looked at her with anxious eyes.

"You will be able to get well here, away from the wind, away from everything."

"I hope so, Mother."

Harriet closed her door behind her and surveyed a wooden bed swathed in a veil of white netting, a simple washstand, two long windows. Pulling her hair loose from its bun, she slid her book under the pillow and went to the window. Opening the wooden shutters, she leaned over and rested her elbows on the warm stone sill.

Across the rough road, the place where the dahabeah had moored to allow Harriet and Louisa to disembark was empty. The water bore no trace of what had recently been their home. On the other side of the river, the mountains looked soft and mysterious, like a pink velvet cloth carelessly thrown down on the floor of the world. There was no sign of what was hidden in them, the painted tombs of kings and queens.

A huge sun sank below the horizon, the color of the mountains changing before Harriet's eyes from rose to crimson to a deep, luminous violet. She was within sight of her destination. Despite the warmth of the air, she shivered.

TWENTY-NINE

Eberhardt Woolfe sat on his verandah facing out over the river to the village on the east bank. In his hands, pressed to his eyes, was a pair of binoculars. He watched as a flock of swifts darkened the sky around a large tree on the far side of the Nile, the birds settling then rising, moving in concert as if magnetized by an invisible force, writing on the sky.

His eye was caught by a flash of color behind the darkening cloud and he found himself looking at a woman leaning out from a first-floor window at the hotel. She had red hair and a pink shawl over her shoulders. A pale face rested on a pale pair of hands. The woman was perfectly still. He adjusted the focus, wanting to see her with greater clarity, but the binoculars could offer no more.

Eberhardt wondered who she was. He tried to focus again on the darting birds; the light was too low, he couldn't make them out. Putting down the glasses, he looked across at the far bank. The birds were reduced to specks, the woman to a fiery punctuation mark against the dark stone façade of the Luxor Hotel.

Rubbing his eyes, Eberhardt reminded himself that he wasn't here to look at women, at tourists, to wonder idly about making their acquaintance. He was here to excavate the tomb of the queen and record his findings. His purpose was to honor the dead, to place himself in their service. The living were not his concern and he sought no place among them.

He rose from his chair and went inside to the large room in which he worked and spent his leisure hours, there being for him now no distinction between the two. Banging the screen door behind him, lighting the lamp on the desk, he lowered himself into the chair, feeling the ache in his shoulders. He was stiff from the day's endeavor, from scraping at the dense wall of rubble and debris that still blocked the entrance to the tomb.

Picking up his scalpel, he began with its sharp, silver point to scrape dried bat droppings from a scarab he had found a few days earlier. The scarab was green, made of malachite, and smaller than his thumbnail. The humble beetle had been for the ancient Egyptians the symbol of resurrection, for the way it rolled its ball of muck, mimicking the sun rising to roll across the sky each day. This one had survived some two and a half thousand years. It was crudely carved, the workmanship unremarkable. There had been shoddy workers among the scribes and craftsmen of ancient Egypt, as well as fine ones. It touched him, to realize it. He had a tenderness toward the imperfect. He reached for a brush and dusted away the specks of dirt and dust he'd dislodged from the carved lines of the beetle's back.

As he did so, Eberhardt saw again the white, oval face, the sideways tilt of it as it rested on the long, linked fingers. The woman had been so very still as she looked out over the river. As if, he could not help thinking, she too inhabited that space between the lands of the living and the dead.

"*Ach*," he said aloud. "Such nonsense. Be quiet now."

He'd gotten into the regrettable habit of talking to himself. He spoke Arabic fluently, had exchanges all day long with the workers at the site and the foreman who managed the hiring and firing, distributed the wages. He could speak with them but he couldn't talk to them. They understood each other to a serviceable degree and no further. If he had anything important to discuss, he conversed with himself. Or sometimes with Kati.

He put down the scarab and went to the far side of the room, to where the Bösendorfer stood, opened the lid. Pulling up his shirtsleeves, inclining his sore back over the ivories, he lowered his fingers to the keys and heard the first notes enter the room like party guests, dancing over the air, reaching the mud ceiling and the rounded corners, drifting out through the netted door to the verandah. He closed his eyes and played on, Beethoven's Immortal Beloved filling his head and heart and mind.

"Kati," he said, his voice drowned out by the music. "Where are you? Where are you now?"

THIRTY

The air in Luxor was dry and clean, composed mainly of sunlight, it seemed to Harriet as she inhaled it. Her chest had gradually ceased to ache and her breathing grew deeper and easier with each day that passed. Sitting in the grass-topped shelter in the hotel garden with Louisa, inhaling the scent of the jasmine that grew up the wooden supports, the muddy, underlying tang of the great river, she felt as if she might take in so much air she could float away like a balloon.

Each morning, Arab men came to the hotel gates to offer their services as guides to the west bank. They pressed around European visitors, offering to procure donkeys on the other side, ladies' saddles, cold water, *antikis* for a good price.

Harriet and Louisa watched from where they sat on the stone terrace at the front of the hotel.

"Why don't we go, Mother?" Harriet said. "I'd like to."

Monsieur Andreas, hovering by a bed of leggy roses in the garden, cleared his throat.

"I will find the best guide for Madame," he said. "The very best."

Louisa lifted her green veil, threw it back over her hat, and smiled at him.

"I fear it may overtax Harriet's strength, Monsieur," she said. "And for myself I consider visiting tombs a macabre occupation."

Monsieur Andreas nodded, looking at Louisa, dipping his dark head up and down.

"As Madame wishes," he said.

Harriet decided not to quarrel with her mother. She would find a way to get to the west bank. When she was fully recovered, she would insist on it. If Louisa refused, she would go alone, with Fouad.

Until she could reach the Necropolis, Harriet occupied herself at the Luxor temple, a short walk from the hotel. She settled to sketching a section of wall that bore a carved depiction of a king offering two round vessels to a god. The king looked boyish, his chest bare and his profile grave and smooth under an elaborate crown. Attached to the front of his crown was his uraeus, the raised head of a cobra, ready to spit in the eyes of enemies.

The deity to whom he offered vessels of wine wore the plumes of Amun, the hidden one, and held a scepter, or *was*, emblem of the power of the gods, in his left hand. In Amun's right hand, hanging from his fingers, was an ankh, the symbol of life and breath. Amun held the ankh loosely, almost casually, as if it was a gift to be lightly given and as lightly withheld.

Above the two figures and running down between them were vertical lines of hieroglyphs, the characters large and beautifully formed. Harriet recognized the seated woman with a single feather on her head that signified the goddess Maat, or truth. The ankh was repeated again and again on the panel of stone. Had some invisible god handed her an ankh, she wondered as she worked. Had she been given the gift of breath, of life, in this place?

While she sketched, Fouad held the parasol over Harriet's head, keeping curious children at bay by means of a narrowed gaze or click of his tongue. Far from Alexandria, out of the shadow of Mustapha, their dragoman appeared taller than he had, and a more effective protector. *Dragoman* came from a Turkish word meaning *to explain* and Fouad, encouraged by her interest in the life of the present as well as the past, had begun to explain all that he could to Harriet.

"Good, Miss Harry?" he said when she raised her head and found him looking at her work.

"*Kwayis?*"

"*Kwayis*, Fouad," she replied.

THIRTY-ONE

Harriet seemed well, which gave Louisa some peace. She was out for long hours, accompanied by Fouad, sketching at the temple. Alone in the hotel room, or continuing with her tatting in the large garden, Louisa found herself once more reliving the days of her girlhood. Through the long years of her marriage to Blundell, she'd never dared to recall that time. Now, considering the events from a distance of half a lifetime, she saw them differently.

All the while she stood naked before him, Augustus had complained of her form. Her legs were bandy; had she had the rickets? She assured him that she had not. Her breasts were overdeveloped. Her hair made her look like a gypsy, and that, as it happened, he liked. It distinguished her from the prissy misses crowding every London salon and now being aped even by the country girls. Gypsy she was and Gypsy she should be called. But her expression was that of a frightened hare, for Christ's sake. How was he expected to render her as a goddess when she looked like a hare? What Thetis ever chewed her own nails? Bit her lip?

Louisa grew accustomed to the judgments. She was clothed by them, armored. Knowing he did not find her pleasing but that he wanted her presence all the same, grew angry if she was late to arrive at the door of the barn, she became bold. Looking at the paintings of other women, she informed him of her opinions, wondered that such an old man could persuade such beauties to pose for him.

Sometimes, at the end of the sitting, when he laid down his brushes, he caught hold of her by her hair and drew her close.

"Here, Gypsy. Come to me."

He put his nose to her neck, tightened his hands around her waist. Then released her, instructing her to put on her clothes and be gone.

Later, when her form was complete, she had to don the red vel- vet robe of Thetis. It smelled of another woman's sweat and perfume and one of the silver buttons on the front of the costume lolled on a length of twisted red thread, ready to roll away. She disliked the way the garment trailed on the floor, emphasizing her modest height. Augustus brushed off her objections. The robe concealed a number of her imperfections, he pronounced, arranging it so that it fell open to the waist. It lent her an air of mystery no woman of her age could hope to possess. Having been already naked before him, Louisa felt no shame in appearing half clothed. In the airy studio that was a world in itself, she became someone different. Her second self, the one in the picture, gave her a power over Augustus.

In the long hours of posing for him, she felt hypnotized by the repetitive swishing of the flat sable brush over the canvas, the earthy, musky smell on the air of linseed oil, the sharp interrup- tion of turpentine. The image forming on the canvas was and wasn't her. This woman's skin was made of lead white, of rose madder and Naples yellow, with cerulean blue in the shadows under her eyes; her hair was umber, the raw and the burnt, the robe orange and Chinese vermilion. In the long afternoons, he taught her the names of the pigments, made her recite them to keep herself awake. Burnt sienna, lake, ultramarine. Cobalt and cadmium. Ivory black. Ivory black was made from the burned tusks of elephants, ground up with oil. Bone char, he called it. Umber was from the Latin. *Umbra.* Shadow.

Her second self was made of color, of Augustus's sighs and squint- ings, his sallies toward the canvas and his steppings back from it, his under-the-breath curses, laughs, expletives, they too were in the thick, daubed texture of the picture that was taking shape on the canvas, coming to life, as if the black-haired, sullen-eyed woman might at any moment speak, or sing, or sigh. Drop her gaze. Louisa felt altered by the existence of the other woman. The painting was something born between them.

Often, the real shadow passed over the doorway. Augustus, standing with his back to it, could not see it but Louisa could. It appeared in its full outline one day and stopped, remained motionless for a minute or more. Louisa saw what she already knew. It was the boy, standing somewhere beyond the half-open door. His shadow, thrown into the room by the afternoon sun, was elongated, taller than his father. Seeing the hang of his arms by his sides, their powerless drop, she flinched.

"What is it?"

Too late, Augustus turned his head. Surveyed the bright empty slant of sunlight.

"Only look, Gypsy. Don't see."

At the end of July, when the cornfields had been cut, when the charred smell of burnt stubble hung in the air and the fields of gold were black, Augustus announced that she was to don the embellishments.

"What are embellishments?"

He produced a pair of what he called sandals, no more than soles and straps. Knelt down and put them on her feet, laced them up her ankles. Lying on a great carved tray, throughout the sittings, were a number of strange and beautiful objects. Louisa sometimes examined them, picking up the sheaf of peacock feathers and brushing them against her cheek, peering with one eye through the stone with a hole through its center or pricking her finger on the pointed ears of a cat carved in black basalt. At the center of the collection was a silver ornament. A ribbed, shallow bowl of a shell, of a type she had never seen on their own beach. She'd never dared to touch it.

Augustus selected the shell, threaded it onto a fine strip of leather. He came and stood behind Louisa, so close that she felt the hairs on the nape of her neck rise. He felt with his finger for the hollow in the center of her throat, then laid the shell over the spot, tied the straps on her neck clumsily, methodically. The piece was cold on her skin, heavy, its edges smooth and rounded.

As he turned her around, pulling her by one hand so that she faced him, she giggled.

"It feels so strange. Not like me at all."

He took hold of her by both arms, his thumbs digging into her flesh.

"It isn't you."

His voice was hoarse, like stones being rubbed together. He was looking at her mouth. She felt a shift in temperature, slight, as if the sun had gone behind a cloud.

"What do you—"

Augustus released her arm and slid his hand inside the open robe as his mouth closed on hers. The sensation of his lips, his tongue in her mouth, was overpoweringly strange. He pulled away from her.

"Go and lie down."

Walking toward the couch, Louisa felt a blossoming between her legs like a flower opening. She lay down, listening to the sound of his belt buckle. She'd known from when she first saw him on the beach that this, whatever it was, was going to happen. That she, because she loved him, was going to allow it to happen.

The shadow flickered past the door.

Laying down her handwork, Louisa strolled around the garden, oblivious to the lush proliferation of leaf and blossom, the cries of the birds. For now, at least, she could bear no more remembering.

THIRTY-TWO

At the sound of the door, Louisa cried out and sat up, her eyes staring.

"Whatever is it, Mother?" Harriet said, opening a shutter, allowing light to flood in over the wooden floor.

"Oh, Harriet. It's you. I . . . I was dreaming."

"Of what?"

"Nothing."

"It must have been something." Harriet sat on the edge of the bed and took Louisa's hand, felt the clammy coolness of her palm.

"I was dreaming about . . . Dover. Where I lived when I was a girl."

Louisa lay down again and closed her eyes. She looked as white as the pillow slip, her dark hair tangled.

"Are you ill, Mother?"

Louisa shook her head. "Take your breakfast without me, Harriet. I've got a headache."

After breakfast, Harriet brought up a tray of tea made from mint leaves with a bowl of coarse sugar lumps, sent by Monsieur Andreas with his compliments.

"Shall I pour you a cup?" She put it down by the bed and Louisa turned her face away.

"No, thank you."

"Can I bring you something else?"

"Rosewater," came her mother's voice. "I wish I had a few drops of rosewater."

"I'll go and look for it in the bazaar."

Louisa opened her eyes and lifted her head. "You cannot go alone."

"Fouad will come with me. There's nothing to fear, Mother."

Louisa raised a hand then let it fall back on the sheet.

"If you insist. Don't forget your parasol."

Harriet breathed in the fresh, swampy scent of the Nile. The trees by the river made a canopy, the leaves shading the dry earth underneath in a shifting, soft-edged dance. Down on the shore, half a dozen women were filling pitchers with clay cups. The women departed, the great round-bottomed jugs balanced at an angle on their heads, two brightly dressed girls following behind them with smaller pots on their heads.

Winding her scarf around her neck, Harriet stopped and looked across to the west bank. Beyond the palms and crops that ran in a strip along the other side of the water, the mountains rose implacably. Already, the heat was visible in layers over their flat tops, shimmering and otherworldly.

Up ahead, Fouad whistled. The dog strained at the leash and Harriet set off again. She was half running, keeping her eyes to the ground as she tried not to trip over tree roots or get her skirts tangled in the lead, when she ran headlong into a warm, angular body. Crying out in surprise, she fell awkwardly to the ground, dropping the lead in the dust. A hand with a silver ring on it, a dark red stone in an oval mount, reached down and took hers. It was a man's hand, the grip dry and strong.

"Permit me to help you."

He pulled her up and Harriet got to her feet, too winded to speak.

"*Ach*, my apologies," he said as he let go of her hand. "I was looking over at the other side."

"It was my fault," she said shaking dirt from her skirt. "I was following my dog, not paying attention to where I was going."

She recognized him immediately. He was dressed in the same pale, creased suit, wearing his fraying Panama hat. The bleached ends of his dark hair still brushed his shoulders. His face, now that at last she was able to see it, was suntanned and his eyes the color of the neem leaves over their heads. The man was younger than she'd thought, not more than thirty years old.

Papers carpeted the ground, their corners being lifted by the breeze off the water. Bending to help him gather them, picking up the last sheet, Harriet saw a drawing of hieroglyphs, a neat, precise rendering of the symbols, surrounded by writing in a language she didn't recognize. She handed it to him.

"*Danke*," he said, flattening the documents back into a folder, putting it under his arm. "Are you certain you're unharmed?"

"Quite certain, thank you."

Her chest was throbbing where his had thumped against it. The man must have the same sure sense of her physical being as she had of his. The dog raced toward them, his lead trailing in the dust, and began leaping up toward the man's knees.

"Have we met before?" said the man, leaning down, rubbing Dash's ears.

"I recognize you too," Harriet said.

"You do?"

"Your piano . . . We watched it being loaded at Brindisi."

"*Ach,* you were on board the ship. You must have cursed the delay."

"No," she said. "I was happy to see a piano traveling to Africa."

"Were you really?" His eyes were alive and searching, at odds with the formality of his manner. They flickered away again, to the far bank, the pink creases of the hills. "I discovered I was unable to live without music. So I brought a piano two thousand miles. Crazy, is it not? The men almost dropped it in the river, over there." He gestured at the west bank.

Some melancholy hung in the air about him, undispelled by the light and heat of the morning. Harriet pushed hair out of her eyes, feeling as curious about him as she had done the first time she saw him. On the steamer, she'd taken him for a European, but here he seemed neither Western nor Eastern but something in between, adapted to this place but not of it.

"Why did you take it over to that side?" she said.

"I live there."

"In the Necropolis?" She couldn't keep the astonishment out of her voice.

"Nearby. I am working at a site, making an excavation of a tomb." They both looked across the water to where a lush band of emerald fringed the far side of the river like a velvet ribbon. A whistle pierced the air and Harriet brought her eyes back to the east bank. Farther along the shore, Fouad was leaning against a tree, his shoulders curved forward.

"I'm on my way to the bazaar," Harriet said.

"Of course." The man raised his hat. "If you're sure you are unharmed."

Harriet felt in her pocket, gripped her book.

"I couldn't help seeing those hieroglyphs, on your papers," she said. "I've been interested in hieroglyphs since I was a girl. I started my own Book of the Dead, in London. I was ill then, and thought I should never get well."

Why had she told a stranger something so private? He would think her absurd.

"Is that so?"

"I wonder, I mean, might we visit the site? My mother and I?"

The man hesitated, and when he answered, his voice was abrupt. "There is little to see. I am still working in an outer passageway. No great finds of gold and jewels. No mummies."

"Oh, of course." Harriet felt herself flushing with disappointment, both at the refusal and at the man's misunderstanding. She had never been much interested in the riches the tombs had contained. It was the hieroglyphs that were the treasure to her. "I suppose visitors must get in the way."

"Some do." He bent to pet Dash again and the dog wagged his tail and grinned. "*Ach*, why not?" the man said, as if he were speaking to himself. He straightened up. "You may visit if you wish, Fräulein. I'll call for you and your mother on Friday. Can you be ready early? It is dusty over on that side and hotter, away from the river."

"We will be ready. But you don't know where we're staying."

"The Luxor Hotel, is it not?"

She nodded as he gave a little bow and went on his way.

Harriet followed Fouad through the area where the tinsmiths and coppersmiths worked, the din jangling in her ears. They continued past the open booths of tailors and shoemakers, where the ground was littered with ends of cotton and scraps of leather, and into the section given over to groceries and medicines.

Walking underneath hanging bunches of strips of gold paper that rustled strangely in the breeze, surveying heaps of dried dates and rough chunks of soap and strings of dried fish, woven baskets piled high with smooth-sided cones of powdered spices in amber and ocher and scarlet, Harriet struggled to remember what her errand was.

She could hardly believe that she had been so bold as to invite herself to a tomb. If she'd had time to consider what she was saying, she might not have dared. She had no regrets, she decided, as Fouad showed her into a little shop, its front shaded with an awning of sacking, its dusty goods displayed on a shelf along the back. Sitting cross-legged on his mud divan, the shopkeeper pressed Harriet to take tea. Emboldened by what had just passed, Harriet broke with convention for a second time.

"Tell him I will," she said to Fouad. "I would like a cup of tea."

As she said the words, she remembered. Rosewater. A stool was brought for her to sit on, then a boy arrived with a steaming glass on a tray. Harriet told Fouad what she wanted, he explained it to the shopkeeper, and the shopkeeper dispatched the tea boy on another errand. By the time she'd drunk the tea, Harriet was in possession of a brown bottle that, according to the label, contained cinnamon cough mixture made in Battersea. She pulled out the cork and caught the soft fragrance of roses, shook a few drops onto her hand, and rubbed them on her wrists.

"*Kwayis*, Miss Harry?"

"*Kwayis*, Fouad."

Stepping back out into the sunlight from the dark interior, skirting around vendors who—Fouad informed her—called out that figs were the food of sultans, licorice water the refresher of kings, Harriet felt as if she was already with the ancient Egyptians, as if their descendants lived on here in Luxor, faithful to some of the old ways, as unchanging as the landscape and the sacred river itself.

THIRTY-THREE

The crew had cleared the luncheon table and the three passengers were lingering over coffee, Eyre smoking a cigar and Effie Simpson retelling the story of their wedding day while Jim nodded in confirmation. It was past the heat of the day and the breeze off the water was cool. Mrs. Simpson interrupted her reminiscing to complain of a chill and her husband went below to the cabin to retrieve her wrap.

Eyre, prompted in equal measure by the sound of a disturbance up ahead and by a desire to avoid being alone with Mrs. Simpson, rose and went to the edge of the deck. The river was in a meander and the bank on the left side loomed high overhead, a cliff of dried black mud. Heading toward them at a clip from around the bend, propelled by the water's fast flow, was a rusty hulk, lying low in the water.

Eyre's first impression was not of the likelihood of imminent collision, although the captain of their dahabeah was heaving on the rudder, shouting at the crew. Eyre was transfixed by the cargo of the craft that was heading straight at them. It was loaded, not with cotton bales or sugarcane but with men. Hundreds of them, packed like sheep, on an unshaded deck. There wasn't sufficient space to allow a single one of them to lie down or even to sit. The babel that rose from the wretches on seeing the dahabeah—the screams and cries and invocations to Allah—was deafening.

Clad in the ragged robes of peasant farmers, most of the men had their wrists bound. The few free men held in their hands long whips, the *korbaj*, or scourge of hippopotamus hide, that was offered for sale on occasion to tourists. As the shouts and beseeching cries increased in volume, the overseers began setting about the captives, lashing them across the heads and faces and backs, cursing them as sons of dogs. Profanities were the one part of the Arabic language that it had amused Eyre to pick up.

"Christ," said Jim Simpson, standing beside Eyre, holding a lace mantilla in his large hands. "Bloody thing's going to run into us."

Moments later, a juddering shock ran through the timbers of the boat, sending the coffee cups skidding off the table and prompting screams from Effie Simpson. Irritated, Eyre tossed the end of his cigar into the water. The collision could mean only two things: delay and further expense.

The captain, Rais Mohammed, sprang into action, pushing the two vessels apart with his bare hands, inspecting the damage to the dahabeah, and issuing orders to the crew. His commands went unheeded. The sailors were in shouted conversation with the unfortunates on the hulk, who were still being belabored by the whips of their captors. One man had fallen overboard and was thrashing about in the water, his hands bound. His head sank and rose and sank again.

Eyre turned away.

"Can't we get going, Rais?"

"In good time," said the captain. "These poor fellows are sending messages to their families, with the men."

"Instruct the crew to get on with their duties," said Eyre. "I'm not paying them to act as go-betweens."

It was risky to get involved with natives in large numbers. He'd made that mistake on one of his previous trips, when a Scotsman attached to their party had shot a small child, mistaking it for a gazelle in the reeds. The boy had lived, but they'd been obliged to pay blood money, and even then things had almost turned ugly.

The hulk floated on around the bend, taking its strange cargo with it. A part of the bow of the dahabeah had been damaged. Rais Mohammed began to explain the details of what had occurred, wanted to show Eyre the problem and, worse, engage him on the subject of forced labor. They were peasants, *fellaheen* from the south, he said, and had been rounded up like goats, taken off their own fields to be transported two hundred miles to the delta to work on someone else's, without reward.

Eyre cut the loquacious fellow short.

"Just tell me, old chap, when will we be on the move again?"

Rais Mohammed looked at him, then shrugged in the way they did when they had no idea of the answer to a question but didn't want to admit it.

"Tomorrow, God willing," he said, his face dark and reserved. "We shall leave tomorrow, Mr. Soane. Or after tomorrow."

In the evening, Eyre opened some red wine from the case he'd brought and began drinking it from the bottle. Jim was cleaning his guns. He sat in his shirtsleeves, humming, surrounded by greasy rags, elongated brushes, abrasive pads, and tins of stinking grease. His feet were bare on the wooden deck and his wedding ring gleamed in the light from the hurricane lamps swinging overhead. Jim's absorption, his unself-conscious contentment, made Eyre, for a minute, loathe his old friend.

They were awaiting the completion of the repair, the boat moored at some village in the middle of nowhere, a mile upriver from where they'd had the collision. Most of the crew had gone off to bake bread, to supply themselves for the rest of the journey. Two remained, squatting on the bank at a short distance from the dahabeah, smoking a hubble-bubble improvised from an old tin can and a length of rubber tubing. Eyre could hear the long, dying gurgle as the smoke passed through the water, the voices of the sailors murmuring in the still twilight. The captain had ordered them to stay, to make sure the *khawagat*, the foreigners, weren't murdered, Eyre supposed.

The low-slung canvas chair enforced an attitude of relaxation that he didn't feel. Pulling himself to his feet, he began pacing the rectangle of deck. It had been a stroke of luck to learn from the Coxes that Louisa and her daughter were going south. Without the aunt, as well, which made matters easier. The aunt could get in his way, he had an instinct.

The danger was that the Herons would leave before he ever arrived. Or, worse, pass him on their own dahabeah, traveling downstream, shouting cordial greetings across a stretch of fast-moving water. He pictured Louisa behind a pair of green glass spectacles—she would adopt them, he was certain—her white-gloved hand raised in a wave.

Leaning on the railing, he looked upriver in the direction of Luxor. The sky on the west bank was crimson and vermilion and madder, brighter and more luminous than even gouache had ever been; if he depicted the sunset as it was, no one would believe it.

He resumed pacing, holding the bottle in one hand. He would tackle Rais Mohammed when the fellow returned from the village. They would leave in the morning, repair done or not done, and whether or not there was any wind. If the crew had to tow the dahabeah all the way to Luxor, then so be it.

Taking another swig, putting down the bottle, Eyre climbed down the companionway to the cabin and brought out his paintbox from the overhead cupboard. He felt easier as he returned to the deck. In the few minutes he'd been in the cabin, it had shifted from dusk to night. Darkness fell quickly in Egypt. The moon was up, bright and almost full; he could see the turbans of the two sailors moving like two great white poppies as they squatted at the top of the bank, the pipe finished and the smell of roasting coffee beans drifting on the air. The fellows lived for the duration of the voyage on tobacco and coffee, with a ration of hard bread and dried dates. When the wind dropped, they were capable of pulling the dahabeah all day and all night. Eyre felt a grudging admiration for them.

Sitting in one of the yellow pools of light shed by the storm lamps, he opened out the tiered lid of his paintbox and began removing metal tubes, china water saucers, brushes and scrapers and bottles of turpentine and poppy oil, arranging them in a circle around him on the wooden deck. He set about cleaning the saucers, arranging the colors, considering which hues he would need for the complexion of Miss Heron, so white it was nearly blue. He would prepare the canvas with zinc white. It would pass the time until they arrived.

Eyre pictured the girl in his mind's eye. She was not in any way his type, insofar as he had one. His tastes, he liked to think, were catholic. He'd felt irritated when Mrs. Sarah Cox had told him the girl longed to see him. Mrs. Cox had showed him the words, apparently written in Miss Heron's own handwriting, under a London address, which he'd memorized.

He intended to seduce her. He would take her body and her heart, then abandon her. Louisa would taste the bitterness of seeing someone she loved destroyed. The symmetry of it pleased him. He felt in his pocket for his cigar case, then thought better of it and let it remain where it was. He was running low. There was a danger that he would be reduced to smoking local tobacco.

THIRTY-FOUR

Twenty or more women sat cross-legged on a swept earthen floor,
their backs bent, sandals piled in a heap at the door. In front of them,
at a rough wooden table, stood Suraya. Her veil was thrown back
off her head, her arms submerged to the elbows in a basin of water.
In her wet hands, glistening with Pears soap, was a white china doll
with blue glass eyes.

Suraya lathered its rounded cheeks and nose, drew her thumbs
over its eyes in a gentle, fluid movement, talking all the time in a
singsong monologue that required no answer, that seemed by its
rhythms to be its own justification, a bath of words as clean and slippery as the bubbles on the water.

Sitting on the only chair, her arms hanging loose by her sides, her
fingers still wrinkled and waterlogged, Yael watched. She'd cleaned
the faces and hands of two dozen or more real infants, swabbed their
eyes with zinc lotion purchased at the Otto Huber apothecary in
the rue Chérif Pacha, spoken at least a few words with each of their
mothers, through Suraya. The connection between dirt and disease was unknown to these women. It was God's will, they declared,
through Suraya, that their children should live or die. They feared
that keeping the children clean would bring the evil eye on them.
Yael thanked God she wasn't a Mohammedan. God's will was all
very well but one could not accept the death of a child. Not without
a fight.

Mustapha had not only agreed to the suggestion that Suraya

could help, he had thrown himself into it. He set about teaching English to his wife and Arabic to Yael. The three of them sat together in the evenings after dark, under the mulberry trees. It was simple teaching, based on drawing pictures, pointing at things around them. The Arabic was harsh in the throat, some sounds impossible to pronounce. Mustapha made Yael repeat words many times over. He considered his own language, it occurred to Yael after the first of these lessons, the primary one. English was to him the supplementary tongue. After quelling her initial indignation at this misplaced idea, she applied herself more diligently to the pronunciations.

Soon, Yael could say more than the few words she'd picked up without trying. She was able to ask after people's health and explain that she did not take sugar in her tea, or want a carriage ride today. She could express that food was good or bad, hot or cold, and that she was thirsty or hungry or content. That yes, the eggs, the day, the city of Alexandria—Iskandariya—were indeed *kwayis. Good. Alhamdulillah. Praise be to God.* She liked the musical sound of that word, the richness of it, ever on the lips of the impoverished Egyptians. Best of all she liked the greeting. *Salaam alaikum. Peace be upon you.* They were fine words, Yael thought, with which to begin any encounter.

Suraya let out another stream of communication, which sounded as if it were a question. The women sat with their veils held in their teeth and their breasts out for their babies. Some appeared to listen, some talked with each other. One volunteered what Yael took to be an answer to the question. She hoped it was the right answer. The right question.

Even when the first of the ladies had ventured inside the clinic, the problem had remained of how to teach them. It was futile to simply clean the children's eyes; the mothers had to learn how to do it themselves, morning and night. She'd spent hours with Suraya, trying to explain how things were done in London, how the same measures could be used here.

The women weren't easy to convince. It was dawning on Yael that they had their own ideas, which they held as firmly as she held hers; they didn't, of course, have any means of understanding that they were wrong and she was right. It was God's will, they informed her, through Suraya, if their children contracted eye disease. Failed to thrive. Died. Yael wished she could explain to the mothers about the Christian God, who wanted all his children to prosper and flourish, who brought the promise of life everlasting to all who believed in him.

"Nonsense," she said theatrically, in response to their fatalism. "Mere superstition. Balderdash. Preposterous."

Yael's initial method of communication—speaking in the most prosaic English, clearly and loudly, patiently repeating phrases about the link between ill health and grime—had proved not to work. Since she could not be understood even by Suraya when she strayed away from the most basic utterances, Yael had taken to performing as if she were onstage, in a pantomime, declaiming with large gestures and polysyllabic words whose vehemence seemed to communicate itself to the women even if their meaning was obscure.

"Poppycock," she shouted, flinging her arms in the air, taking in the faces of the assembled crowd. "Ludicrous tittle-tattle. Old wives' tales. Humbug."

There seemed to be no end to the vocabulary for describing erroneous thought and speech. Perhaps because there had been so much of it, throughout time. Humbug and obfuscation were as common to England as rain, she was beginning to think. It was a sadness, the way distance from one's own country diminished it.

Three little girls had crept away from their mothers and were hovering close to Suraya's knees, eyeing the doll. Suraya reached down and patted each of their heads with a wet hand, then continued with the washing of the doll's face. Its blue eyes remained unflinchingly open as the soap ran over them.

The day after Yael's visit to Sheikh Hamada, she had opened up the clinic again, determined to do what she could to bring people in herself. The little room had filled up shortly after she unlocked the door. The sheikh had given the word, Suraya told Yael later. The women informed her that he had advised their husbands that wives should attend and bring their children.

He had told her he would not help and then had helped anyway.

Yael puzzled over it as she surveyed a table covered with gifts that the women had brought. Speckled hens' eggs; a bunch of limp, lacy green leaves that seemed to be some form of parsley; beads of hardened tree resin, to be burned on charcoal; flowers of different hues and shapes. It touched her that these poor women should make offerings to her. She would pass them on to Suraya, who would know what to do with them.

Yael shifted on the wooden chair, looked again at the assembled women, their faces rapt, their hardworking feet drawn up beneath them. Suraya had concluded the instruction. The doll lay on its back on the table, next to the bowl, its head wrapped for modesty in a cloth. The mothers were getting to their feet and retrieving their sandals, covering their faces and stepping out through the wooden door to the alley beyond. If even one of the infants went through his or her life with sight, rather than blinded, their efforts would have been worthwhile.

One woman stayed behind, positioning herself in front of Yael. She had a child on her hip and two more clinging to the skirts of a ragged black robe; the girls were so close in size that Yael had taken them at first for twins and then, while washing their faces, decided that they were not. The mother looked not more than sixteen or seventeen, thin-faced, with a silver ring running through one side of her nose. She broke into a stream of speech, directed at Yael, waving her free hand.

The speech sounded accusatory. Yael shifted her chair backward. "What is she saying, Suraya?"

Suraya put her head to one side and rubbed her belly. "No money. Hungry."

Nothing Yael could not have seen with her own eyes, without benefit of language.

"What is her name?"

"Um Fatima," said Suraya. "Husband prison."

Yael looked up at the woman. She had a duty to help but she wouldn't give her money. She did not dare.

"Codswallop!" she announced with a smile, banging the side of her hand on the table for emphasis, as she had seen Mr. Dickens do during a reading of his works. "Tripe! God save the Queen. Give her the eggs, Suraya, and the herbs. Tell her I will get some rations for her. Next time. Give her the flowers as well."

The baby sent up a thin cry that sounded like the mewing of a kitten. Getting to her feet, collecting the umbrella, Yael thought of the Europeans on their knees under the scented cedar rafters, praying to a God of love. Saw in her mind the blue velvet collection pouch being passed from hand to hand and resolved to return to St. Mark's on Sunday. She would see Reverend Griffinshawe and plead with him again to support the clinic. The sheikh was right. What use was soap without food.

Yael felt a sudden longing to be out of the small room and back at home. By which she meant, she understood with some surprise, not a wallpapered, picture-adorned, fire-warmed house in St. John's Wood but a sparsely furnished villa in the Frank quarter of a North African port.

THIRTY-FIVE

The man rode ahead on a bay horse, trotting around a thicket of acacia trees. Sitting sidesaddle, her head wrapped in a new orange scarf she'd acquired on the voyage down the Nile, from a woman with twins at her breasts, Harriet followed on a donkey. Sweat was streaming into her eyes; her lips stung from the dry heat. The donkey boy walked behind, cudgeling the creature every few moments, and behind him a small girl with a full, squelching water skin on her back ran after them in her bare feet.

They were going west, away from the river, the sun at their backs as they traveled along the edges of lush fields of heavy-headed maize plants, around forests of sugarcane that came up to the haunches of the donkey. The farmland ended and the horse turned north, leading the way up a stony track into a white mountain valley. Harriet held onto a tuft of its mane as her donkey began to scramble up the path.

Dr. Eberhardt Woolfe had pulled up his horse.

"How do you fare with the donkey, Miss Heron?" he called as she approached.

"Not bad. I used to ride them on the beach, when I was a girl."

"We shall arrive in ten or fifteen minutes."

A smaller track led off from the main one and the horse took it, its hindquarters swaying, tail swishing against the flies. Harriet's donkey followed, its hooves sending showers of small stones back down the slope, Harriet feeling as though she might slide off the back of it.

Louisa had refused the invitation to come to the tomb but at the encouragement of Monsieur Andreas—who assured her that everyone in Luxor knew Dr. Eberhardt Woolfe, and that everyone who knew him respected him—she'd acquiesced to the expedition, on the condition that Fouad accompany Harriet.

Fouad had made clear his opposition to the outing. Despite his claim to be an Alexandrian, and therefore superior in all ways to his fellow Egyptians, Fouad was full of superstitions. He swore that there were men who could with a breath turn silver coins into gold ones and salt into sugar; he believed that the evil eye caused troubles ranging from death or sickness to the failure of crops, and wore a small leather pouch around his neck that contained a prayer from the Qur'an, to counter it.

He'd muttered, as they crossed the river in a small felucca, about evil spirits, ill fortune, the unfailing superiority of the city to the village. Now, as they climbed the path through barren hills, Fouad was silent. Having refused Dr. Woolfe's offer of a donkey for himself, he trudged at the head of Harriet's, his heels rising out of the laced shoes with every step.

A breeze got up and fanned Harriet's face, lifting the hair around her forehead. The donkey quickened its pace, pricked its ears; the sound of its hooves altered on the shale. They rounded a bend in the track and entered a narrow ravine of white rock, the lower part of it in shade, the tops of the slopes on each side blinding to look at. Dr. Woolfe dismounted.

"We have arrived." He gestured toward a dark opening that looked like the entrance to a cave, farther along the valley and up a slope, in the white cliff of rock. "Are you ready, Miss Heron?"

Sliding down from the donkey, assisted by Fouad, Harriet discovered that she felt unready. All through the winter in London, struggling breath by breath through the lonely nights, she had resisted death. With the fortitude that she could summon in her mind if not in her enfeebled body, she'd told herself that she refused to die—until she reached the city of the dead.

Now that she was here, she felt differently. Harriet wanted to live. She wanted it fiercely. She hadn't known that the world could be so expansively beautiful, so full of possibility. From the day when she had landed in Alexandria, she had changed her mind about life. She could hardly explain that to Dr. Woolfe.

She took another sip of water from the tin flask that Louisa had insisted on, replaced the cork, and slid it back into her pocket next to her journal. Blotting her forehead with her scarf, she cleared her throat.

"Yes, Dr. Woolfe. I am ready."

"Come."

He set off along the valley floor and Harriet followed, first walking along the bottom of the narrow gorge, then scrambling behind him up the path to the entrance of the tomb, stepping into a passageway hewn from the rock. It was just tall enough to stand in and inside the entrance was a wooden table, on which stood several small, old-fashioned lamps, matches, and a stack of wooden boxes.

Dr. Woolfe lit two lamps, the smell of the smoking wick reminding her oddly of London. He handed one to Harriet.

"This way, Fräulein. Watch your step."

She followed behind him into the downward-sloping passageway. The walls and ceiling were undecorated and the ground scattered with rocks and chips of stone. A sweet, unpleasant smell hung in the air. She remembered Fouad and turned to see him still standing at the entrance, with Dash cowering by his ankles.

"Come, Fouad," Harriet called over her shoulder. "Hurry."

"I cannot."

"Why not?"

"*Afrit*, Miss Harry. Spirits. This bad place."

His face was ashen. She'd promised Louisa that she would not allow Fouad to leave her side, but he looked as if he might faint.

"All right," she called. "Wait for me there. Don't go anywhere." The dog's mournful yelps echoed into the tunnel behind her as Harriet walked on into the passage to where Dr. Woolfe was waiting. In the lamplight, his suit was the color of the rock. It occurred to her that he looked at home in the tomb, as if he were at ease, more so than he had been on the steamer or even by the river. She smiled at him.

"My dragoman is afraid."

"*Ach*, I thought you had changed your mind."

Dr. Woolfe began talking about his excavation. Sand and rock and rubble, debris from the occasional flash floods that could fill the ravine, had over the centuries been washed into the tunnel and silted up the entrance to the tomb. Artifacts he had already found suggested that the tomb had been robbed in antiquity, the entrance blocked originally by departing thieves. He explained his resolve to cause no further damage to the tomb, either in the excavation or once they gained entry, but only to preserve what was there and record it for posterity, with the help of the Egyptian workers.

"Where are the workers?" she asked.

"It is Friday, Miss Heron. The men are at the mosque. They are faithful fellows."

The air in the tunnel was warmer than outside, almost suffocating. The darkness was so dense it seemed to Harriet as if it were something solid, not merely an absence of light. She made herself keep walking, taking small steps behind Dr. Woolfe, breathing slowly and steadily, fighting the gut instinct to turn and run back toward the entrance, to sunlight and air.

Dr. Woolfe gestured at something on the wall. He held up his lamp to it and Harriet found herself looking at a picture. It was blackened and sooty, as if fires had been lit underneath it, and the plaster on which it was painted was flaking, in some places had been gouged away. Despite the damage, she could make out an elegant seated woman, dressed in a white robe and with an elaborate headdress on her black hair. Her face—calm and contemplative—was in profile, the nose missing. The woman was sitting at a table, playing a board game.

Above, painted on the wall, were hieroglyphs. Harriet saw a cartouche, the circle that enclosed the name of a royal, containing the symbol of a windpipe, with lungs attached. The half-effaced signs seemed to speak directly to her, and despite the heat, Harriet shivered.

"Once, all of this section would have been decorated. This is all that remains. Come. I will show you where I am working, Miss Heron."

Dr. Woolfe continued round a bend in the passage, the light from his lamp vanishing. Harriet's dress was clinging to her skin, her palms damp. The ground here was soft, carpeted with feathers and embers, desiccated animal droppings. She felt as if she were standing inside the nest of a bird. She leaned against the wall of rock, afraid she was going to be sick from the stench.

She stood up as straight and tall as she could and felt for her journal in her pocket. It was for this that she had come to Thebes. Written her spells. Now that she was here, she must explore whatever she could, experience it as it was. Wrapping her scarf over her mouth, wiping sweat from her eyes, she continued along the passage.

Dr. Woolfe was standing by a wall of rocks and debris that made a dead end. He held up the lamp again.

"This is the site of my work, Miss Heron. Not very exciting, as I warned you, but you can see from the lintel above"—he directed the lamp at a white stone beam running across the highest point of the passage, above the rubble—"that there is a tomb behind."

"Whose tomb is it?"

"I think that it belongs to a royal female."

"A queen?"

"Yes. The one you have seen, on the plaster panel. The lady in white."

Harriet thrilled to the thought that the woman depicted in the wall painting might lie on the other side of the rubble, her body preserved, her spells, written on papyri, kept close by her. The sweet smell assailed her again and she put her hand to her mouth.

"The smell, Dr. Woolfe. Is it from . . . mummies?"

He laughed and held up his lamp to the ceiling of the passageway, illuminating a line of black clustered shapes hanging motionless over their heads. One came to life and took off, darted past them. Harriet gasped as its wing brushed her face, soft as cobweb.

"Bats. Don't be afraid. The worst they will do is to blow out your lamp as they pass."

Harriet pulled her scarf from her shoulders up over her head, wrapped it around her face, and tied the ends behind her neck.

"How can you tolerate being down here?" she said.

"*Ach*, one grows accustomed to it. Lepsius, the great German

Egyptologist, even lived in a tomb." Dr. Woolfe put out his hand to the blocked doorway and pulled a pebble from the mass of rubble. A trickling sound, like water, filled the air as a shower of sand and chips of stone ran down to the ground. He held out the round stone to her. "I am called by this work, Miss Heron. I have a sense of connection to those who planned for the eternal life with as much faith as Christians do now. Sometimes, I feel they might be my own ancestors."

Harriet pulled the scarf away from her mouth.

"That's how I felt when I first saw the hieroglyphs and learned about the Book of the Dead. The people were so real, they seemed closer to me than my own relations."

The stone in her palm was soft and cool. She slipped it into her pocket as another bat swooped past their heads in a strange, flitting movement, and the nausea returned. Dr. Woolfe bowed his head toward her.

"Are you finding it too hot? Would you like to get back into the daylight? Come, follow me."

He began to walk back in the direction they'd come. Harriet followed, stepping carefully. She felt something sharp under the leather sole of her boot and couldn't contain a cry of revulsion; she'd read about tombs littered with shards of bones, with skulls smashed like teacups, ribs scattered around like kindling. She might be walking on the remains of the queen.

Reaching the place in the passageway where the painted panel was, she stopped and held up her lamp. The light fell on the last column of the hieroglyphs. At the top was a painted oval, symbol of the protective eye of Horus. Peering at the wall, she made out below it the shape of the seated figure that denoted a woman, facing to the right, which indicated that these hieroglyphs were to be read from right to left. Hieroglyphs were always read toward the faces of the living beings in them.

Looking again, she saw the sign for *neb*, and the feminine indicator underneath it, followed by the two lines that represented Lower and Upper Egypt. *Lady of the Two Lands*, she murmured to herself. It meant *Lady of the Two Lands*.

Harriet felt a sudden and powerful reverence. Human hands had made these marks, perhaps three thousand years ago. They'd made them because they believed that words had power. This was what she had come to Thebes to see and what she had written her own magic to bring about, she reminded herself again. She wanted to understand what their message was.

She called Dr. Woolfe and he returned to where she stood. "Yes?"

"I want to copy down the hieroglyphs and try to read them."

"Read them, Miss Heron?"

"Yes."

Harriet reached into her pocket and drew out her book. Putting her own lamp down at her feet, holding the journal to the light of his, she opened the pages where she had worked on the columns of hieroglyphs from the Luxor temple, accompanied by her tentative interpretations, made in the evenings at the hotel.

"May I?"

He held out his hand. She hesitated and then, for the first time, put her journal into the hand of another. He looked at the drawings, nodding, his face impassive.

"Once again, I must apologize to you," he said, closing the red leather cover and handing it back.

Harriet's heart sank. He was going to refuse. She could hardly return to the tomb without his agreement. She tried to keep the disappointment from her voice.

"Apologize for what, Dr. Woolfe?"

"I did not understand, Miss Heron," he said, shaking his head, the ends of his hair brushing the shoulders of his jacket. "I mistook you for a tourist."

THIRTY-SIX

Yael sat in the courtroom, surrounded by onlookers, dignitaries, and men of all shapes and sizes. Um Fatima, the young mother from the clinic, had pleaded with her, through Suraya, to intercede on behalf of her husband, who was accused of not paying his taxes. Um Fatima was nowhere to be seen; Yael was the only female present and Mustapha, who'd insisted on accompanying her, sat nearby.

Drifts of red dust had collected on the unevenly plastered walls and a portrait of the khedive, the Ottoman ruler of the country, fly-blown, decorated with red tinsel, hung high behind the judge. The judge, addressed by all as Bey, wore the Turkish-style fez, a shirt, and trousers. He held a fly switch in his hand; at intervals he flicked the switch over his face, closing his eyes as he did so. Next to him, at a smaller, lower desk, sat a skinny clerk, writing in a ledger almost as big as he.

The accused was brought into the room by court officials. Yael's first thought was how very young he looked, scarcely more than a boy himself, and yet he was Um Fatima's husband, the father of the three small children she saw at the clinic. He was barefoot, dressed in a peasant's blue robe, had a skull cap askew on his dusty black hair, a wispy beard on his chin. As soon as he was within sight of the judge, he began protesting, his words slightly slurred, as if he had a speech impediment, but no less impassioned for that.

"He calls on the bey to think of the tender heart of his own wife and have pity," Mustapha whispered.

The judge hammered on the table for silence but the man continued imploring for mercy. Yael considered getting to her feet and making the intercession but thought it too soon. She had hoped that her presence might exercise a restraining influence, but the judge had given no indication that he had noticed her at all.

The bey consulted a paper passed to him by the clerk and read out the charge. The accused responded in a torrent of Arabic in which Yael discerned several of the names of the Prophet—the Noble, the Forgiver, the Just. Seeing the vehement and unaffected nature of the man's faith, Yael felt a confusion in her heart. Few of the laboring classes, or indeed, any classes at home, could be trusted to exhibit such unaffected passion for their Savior.

The judge passed his tail of horsehair over his face and, banging a gavel on the desk, issued what sounded like a verdict. Yael caught the word *bastinado*; next to her, Mustapha tensed. The word held a peculiar horror for Egyptians. The time had come.

Summoning all the strength she could muster, Yael rose to her feet. Victoria was not a tall woman but nonetheless she held sway over half of the world. It was said that Her Highness never needed to raise her voice.

"Sir," Yael said quietly. "*Bey*. May I have your permission to say a few words on behalf of the accused?"

The young man turned his head toward her. He was streaming with perspiration, the back of his patched gown soaked. His eyes looked violently and unnaturally dilated. He was a laborer, his wife had told Yael, working on building sites for a few piastres a day, but was required to pay a tax on each and every one of the palm trees at his mother's small farm, an amount that they did not have and would never have.

The judge looked blankly at Yael while his clerk whispered in his ear. After some moments, the bey spoke.

"Permission refused," he said.

Seconds later, before Yael had time to gather her wits, the young man had been thrust facedown on the floor of the courtroom, his knees bent and feet raised to the ceiling, held in position by a wooden contraption fitted around his ankles. His piteous cries increased as he called on Allah for mercy. Two men, each of whom looked almost as poor as the accused, began with leather whips to thrash the soles of the man's feet, taking turns to deliver the lashes.

Fearing she might faint at the awful sound of leather whipping through the air, the man's screams, Yael sat down. He was calling not on his god but on his mother, weeping like a child. Yael made herself watch, observing the contemptuous expressions of the men doing the whipping, the apparent detachment of the bey, now taking a cup of coffee. She had been unable to help the man by preventing the barbarous punishment, she told herself, blinking back tears that were as much of rage as of pity. She would not shirk her Christian duty to bear witness to it.

The man's feet turned first red then purple then raw, like steak meat. Trickles of red ran down his ankles, the ends of the whips grew crimson, and the cracked floor tiles became smeared with blood mixed into the dust. The cries grew less frequent. At the point where she feared he must die, the man let fall from his mouth a small silver coin. One of the policemen snatched it up, wiped it on his gown, and laid it on the table before the bey.

The man's eyes were closed, his body motionless. Yael kept her own eyes on him until he was carried from the room like a corpse.

THIRTY-SEVEN

Harriet sat on a folding canvas chair. She had her scarf wrapped around her head, one end of it covering her mouth and nose. The smell in the tomb was not as overpoweringly strong as it had seemed on her first visit but the air was dusty. Working on a sheet of cartridge paper on a drawing board, by the light of a lamp tied to a stick propped against the wall of the tomb, she was copying the painting of the Lady of the Two Lands.

Dr. Woolfe had called at the hotel and invited her to return to the site. It would be helpful to him, he said, to have an accurate record of the panel in the outer passage. Harriet had immediately expressed her willingness. Louisa, encouraged perhaps by his formal manners, his disinclination to engage in small talk or even to sit down and take a cup of tea, had agreed. Harriet always had a facility for drawing, she told him, embarrassing Harriet. And since her health was so much improved, she believed it would be quite safe. Her only condition was that Fouad should be in attendance.

Each day since then, Harriet had risen early. By the soft gleams of reflected light that spread from the east before the sun appeared on the horizon, she'd put on what she'd come to think of as her tombs dress—an old muslin, in deep cornflower blue. The skirt was frayed along the hem but the cotton was cool and light, the color matched the midday sky. Clothes that might have looked odd in London looked unremarkable here.

Encouraged by the thought, she'd pinned to her bodice a gift Aunt

Anna had sent her from India—a silver brooch in the shape of a tree, its ruby-red fruits made of garnets, dangling from slender branches. However dusty it might be over there, she wanted to dress up to meet the ancient Egyptians, enter their sacred place. She wanted to announce through the vibrant colors that she shared their dream of life, and their reverence for it.

The life conjured up by the spells in the Book of the Dead, the pictures on the walls of the rock tombs, looked more like life than the years Harriet had known on earth. She hadn't realized so clearly until now that people lived not only lives of different lengths but of different intensities, of varying degrees of beauty and joy and pleasure. She didn't just want a long life. She wanted one filled with interest and adventure, a life of her own making. Or, if one day she became ill again, if the struggle became too much, she wanted a death of her own making.

She'd laced on the soft leather boots with the low wooden heels; the ground was rough everywhere in Luxor and the light shoes Aunt Lavinia had insisted on buying for her were no use at all. On this fourth day, on her way out of her room, she'd stopped, glanced at herself in the oval mirror set into the wardrobe door. Looking back at her was a woman: her long, crinkled red hair worn loose, the orange scarf on her shoulders glowing in the dim light. The dress the woman wore was soft and practical, and a brooch glinted at her neck. Harriet was changing. She couldn't identify quite how but she could see it plainly in the mirror. She was altered, in ways that went beyond her improved health. She looked like herself.

With Fouad, she'd crossed over the river in one of the small white sailing boats called sandals that from dawn till after dark flew across the surface of the water like white-winged birds. Looking back toward the east bank, from far out in the river, the village of Luxor appeared small and insignificant. The reflected columns of the Luxor temple lay in long rippling lines on the surface of the water, the stone undulating with its movement.

When the little boat was near the bank, the same donkey that she'd hired each morning had been brought by its boy into the water, splashing its way to the side of the boat. Fouad had lifted her from the sandal on to its back in one easy movement and they made their way to the white valley.

She worked carefully, at pains to copy the shapes exactly, keep the proportions true. Dr. Woolfe was nearby, scraping with a trowel at the blocked doorway. She could hear him but not see him, feel his steady concentration on the task at hand. It matched her own. Two Egyptian workers carried away the spoil in baskets on their heads, hurrying past in bare feet, returning at intervals. Harriet tried to labor as tirelessly as they did. She enjoyed the feeling of being part of a team.

Taking a sip from her water bottle, she applied herself again to the drawing she was making of the queen. Her ceremonial headdress appeared to be made of the wing of a bird, coming down behind her ear. The queen's head was in profile but her chest was turned forward, both shoulders showing. One slim arm curved in front of her body, holding the *sekhem* or "scepter," symbol of authority and power. Her feet were clad in sandals so flimsy they would not have lasted a day in the valley where she was entombed. Harriet found her both beautiful and enigmatic. At the thought that the queen might be only yards away, on the other side of the blocked entrance, Harriet felt a chill run down her spine despite the warmth and closeness of the atmosphere. The prospect of encountering her was becoming real.

"Why did you come here, Miss Heron?" said Dr. Woolfe.

In the near darkness, the question took her by surprise.

"To the dig?" she said.

"To Egypt."

"We came for my health. I persuaded my doctor to insist on it. I always wanted to see Thebes before I . . . if I was going to die."

"Die?" He sounded angry. "Why should you contemplate such a thing?"

"I have been forced to, Dr. Woolfe. I have been an invalid for much of my life."

Harriet concentrated on the uraeus, the cobra poised on the queen's forehead ready to spit in the eye of ill-wishers. Part of this one had been scratched out, was present only as absence. She'd

wanted, on the first day, to fill in the gaps in the images and hieroglyphs, make good what was missing in the queen's profile, restore
what had been defaced or destroyed. Eberhardt Woolfe had stopped
her from doing so. He explained that to make the images and the
signs whole was not the endeavor. The aim was to faithfully record
what was. What was not. The time for making whole would come
later. Draw as if you were a camera, he had repeated.

"And has the mission succeeded?" he said, his voice softer. "Is
your health improved?"

"Since we arrived in Luxor, I'm much better. I can't be certain that
it will last."

Harriet carried on working as she spoke, her answer coming with
the rhythm of her pencil strokes, the light sound of the point moving on the thick paper Dr. Woolfe had brought for her to work on.
There was something pleasant about talking to someone without
being able to see them.

"And now that you are here, Miss Heron, are you happy?"

Harriet licked the end of her pencil, carried on shaping what
remained of the queen's fine, lonely profile. Mr. Soane's continuing absence had marred her happiness. But since working in the
tomb, she'd thought less about him. Her mind was filled not with
Mr. Soane, the picture he had said he wished to make of her, but
with the queen playing her game of *senet*, one brown, gold-cuffed
arm outstretched over the board, about to move a piece in the game
symbolic of trials and obstacles. The passage into everlasting life was
a dangerous one, beset by perils. Perhaps the passage through mortal life was the same.

"I am happy now. This minute. I like this work, Dr. Woolfe. Your
work. I like entering the distant past, seeing their world through
their symbols and pictures. In fact, now that I've gotten used to the
smell, I'm beginning to think I prefer being in the tomb to being
anywhere."

He gave one of his dry, private smiles. She couldn't see it but she
could hear it in his voice.

"*Ach*, you are an Egyptologist."

Putting down her pencil, Harriet took a sip of water from the flask.

She struggled with what she knew she must say. He should know the truth about her. She didn't want to be here under false pretenses.

"I never went to a school, Dr. Woolfe. Because of my poor health, my mother thought it unwise. I picked up a little French from my brothers' governess but not much. Not enough to make sense of Champollion. I know only what I gleaned from books at home."

"You are self-taught," came the voice in the darkness. "In Heidelberg, that is considered an honorable way to begin."

Harriet picked up the pencil and carried on with her drawing. "How did you begin doing this work, Dr. Woolfe?"

"I discovered the ancient Egyptians as a student, reading Lepsius and the other great German explorers. I came here when I left the university"—he pronounced it *uniwersity*—"five years ago, as an assistant on the excavation of Klaus Kranz. I spent half a year working with him and returned on my own account two years later. Since then, I've come every winter, conducting research."

"Do you ever go home?"

"To Germany, you mean?"

"Yes, of course."

"Last year, I returned to Heidelberg only at Christmas to collect the piano and see my family. This year also . . ." He paused for so long she thought he had finished his sentence. "This year also, I will remain here throughout the summer."

"Have you abandoned your poor wife in Heidelberg?" Harriet said. "Are you married?"

Dr. Woolfe was silent; if it hadn't been for the slight scraping noises made by his trowel, she could have believed he was no longer there. As Harriet opened her mouth to repeat the question, it occurred to her that he might think she had a personal interest in the matter. She flushed, as the noises from the trowel—hollow when he applied it to the rubble and mortar, ringing when he tapped on the larger stones in the doorway—ceased.

"In answer to your question, Miss Heron: I am married. But I did not leave my wife at home."

"She is here with you?"

"No. She is not."

The taps recommenced, sharp and repetitive, like a woodpecker on a tree of stone. Eberhardt Woolfe was married but had not left his wife at home. Nor was she here. Harriet could not decipher it. She would leave it as a gap, she decided, returning to her drawing board and trying to regain the concentration she had lost. An absence to be filled in later.

Soon afterward, Dr. Woolfe came along the passage in his long worker's apron, the tools slotted into pockets specially shaped for them. In the largest pockets were the hammer and the trowel, but he used smaller tools too and had showed them to Harriet: a scalpel and a box of toothpicks; a paintbrush, for removing dust.

"Look," she said, pointing at the wall. "This eye symbol is pronounced *wasir*; it stands for Osiris. The flag here is the sign of a god and the *aa*, the long *a* sound, means *great*. I think that this line relates to Osiris the great god."

"It makes sense that it should," he said. "Osiris is the god that gives life. That is, if the heart hasn't testified against the person." The shadow of his profile fell over the page of drawings, the living figure softer and more tentatively outlined than the copied queen.

He cleared his throat. "I believe the light must be fading outside, Miss Heron."

"I've lost track of time," Harriet said, feeling suddenly awkward.

She rose from the chair and rolled up the sheet of cartridge paper.

Carrying the folding chair, Dr. Woolfe accompanied her out of the tomb and walked with Harriet to where Fouad waited in the shade with Dash and the donkey, on the west side of the steep valley. She handed him the rolled scroll of paper and he nodded his head to her, in the stiff gesture that was becoming familiar.

"Will you return in the morning?"

His eyebrows and beard were pale with dust and his eyes green as leaves, searching, as if they held questions he didn't utter.

"I will, Dr. Woolfe."

He nodded again as Harriet, with Fouad's assistance, mounted the donkey from a boulder, seating herself on the roll of faded carpet roped around the animal's back and setting off along the narrow path.

"Hold tight," Dr. Woolfe said.

"I will!"

On the way out of the white valley, Harriet looked back. Dr. Woolfe still stood where she had left him, watching; she lifted her arm in a wave before the donkey lurched down an incline and broke into a trot, Fouad and the boy running to keep up. Donkeys were always in a hurry to get home.

THIRTY-EIGHT

Louisa stood in her room, sniffing the warm, still air. Seeping under the door, mixed with the smell of frying fish from the hotel kitchen, was the stinging intrusion of Cuban tobacco. It wasn't a surprise. She'd known, deep down, that he would pursue them. Eyre Soane had no inkling of what he risked in attempting a revenge on her. He didn't know whose happiness he jeopardized.

She crossed the room and stood by the chair under the window, staring out at a strip of bruised-looking purple sky. The swifts were congregating in the trees in the front garden of the hotel, their shrill chatter hailing the dusk. On the far side of the river, the sun was a gold disk poised over the mountains, the palm trees along the bank no more than spiky silhouettes that looked as if they had been cut from black paper.

At the tap on the door, her heart made a feeble movement. She opened the door to see Monsieur Andreas, dressed for the evening in a white shirt with a small white bow tie at the neck and a golden, soft-petaled flower in the buttonhole of his lapel.

"Monsieur Andreas. Good evening."

"Good evening, madame."

He smiled at her apologetically. "There is a visitor. Downstairs."

"Thank you. You may inform the visitor that I shall come down shortly."

Closing the door again, Louisa sat at the dressing table, propped her elbows on it, and tilted the looking glass forward. The painting must have altered. Her skin, which he used to say was the shade of hawthorn blossom, might by now be darkened, her eyes and lips and breasts crazed with cracks. In its essentials, though, the picture would be the same as on the day Augustus had laid down his brushes.

She, by contrast, had changed utterly. The living figure had not had the immunity to time that, when she'd posed for the painting, she'd assumed was hers. Louisa drew closer to the mirror, searched for the sullen look that Augustus called her gypsy glare. Now her eyes held a wary, guarded expression. Her face had lost its oval definition and her mouth had grown thinner.

One thing had not changed. She smoothed her hair back from her forehead. On one side of the parting in the center, the hair grew in a crescent, forming the top of a heart shape. On the other, it grew in a regular line. Augustus had accentuated the asymmetry in the painting and it was still there. Her distinguishing mark. He had called it her hallmark.

The smell of a smoldering, cured leaf was growing stronger. Louisa picked up her fan, rose from the stool, and let herself out of the room.

For a moment, as she descended the stairs, Louisa saw Augustus again. Full lips and thick brows. Dark, waving hair swept back from a low forehead and a broad, flattish face that had made her think of a bull in the field and had been at odds with her idea of what a painter would be. She'd imagined artists to be ethereal, connected only lightly to the earth, halfway already to the realms above.

Digging the end of her fan into the palm of her hand, she continued around the curve in the stairs. How ignorant they had been of their own youth. Even Augustus, whom she'd considered hopelessly, irredeemably old, had been younger than she was now. How could he have behaved as he did? She'd never understood. She hurried across the floor toward him; she must speak with him, demand to know why.

"What a pleasure to see you, Mrs. Heron. I was afraid you might be gone."

The figure that rose from the wooden bench had clean-shaven cheeks, brown eyes, not hazel ones. He wore a bright scarf at his neck and smelled of a cosmetic preparation. He lacked the substance of the ghost, seemed barely real at all, as if she might reach out and put a hand through him. Louisa gripped her fan, felt the sharp filigree of carved bone, the brush on her skin of the silk tassel that fell from the handle.

"Mr. Soane. What brings you here?"

He made a bow.

"The same as everyone else, ma'am. Exploration of the past."

Louisa made an odd, choking sound in her throat, and Monsieur Andreas, hovering behind the reception desk, flicked over a page of the open ledger.

"Any assistance, madame? Cold refreshments?"

Louisa shook her head. Eyre Soane sat down again on the bench.

"How is your daughter?"

"Harriet?"

"Who else?"

She looked at the floor, at the square honesty of terra-cotta tiles, pitted with use and mopping, and the rich, worn rug laid on top, its fringes flat at either end like combed hair. Monsieur Andreas had retreated to the bar; she could hear the delicate tap of glasses being set down on a brass tray.

"Is this a social call, Mr. Soane?"

"It is not." Soane crossed one ankle over his knee, blew a ring of smoke into the air over his head. "I have come for Harriet."

"What do you mean?"

"I intend to paint her. Didn't she tell you? She has consented."

Louisa opened her fan, sweeping the half-moon backward and forward through the air.

"I forbid it."

"Really? Your daughter will doubtless wish to know on what grounds."

Louisa moved away from him across the dim lobby and took hold of the arm of the raised shoeshine chair.

"Mr. Soane, I believe you said you have a sister. A younger sister."

"I do indeed, Mrs. Heron. What is it to you?"

Louisa swallowed. Without the chair, she felt she might slide to the ground.

"In that case," she said, "you understand how easily a girl's head can be turned, her feelings swayed. Have you no pity?"

"Why should I have pity?"

Soane's face for an instant looked young and frightened; it was the face of the child on the beach, intercepting the look between herself and his father.

The door from the garden swung open and Harriet walked through it, the dog straining in front of her on the lead, her book under her arm, a pencil stuck in her hair.

"Mother, I . . . Mr. Soane!"

"Miss Heron." Soane rose from the seat, took Harriet's hand, and raised it to his lips. His face had lost altogether the look Louisa had just witnessed. It was smooth and expressionless, his lips curved in an eager smile. "What a pleasure. I have longed to see you again."

Harriet's cheeks burned and she seemed at a loss for words. "You have come," she said eventually.

Louisa felt a lump in her throat.

"I arrived this afternoon. I've been having a pleasant conversation with your mama." Eyre Soane took a short, fierce puff on his cigar. "About my late father. The painter, Augustus. I've been telling her about some paintings of his that I have in my private collection. You might care to see them one day, Miss Heron."

He released a slow stream of smoke.

"Yes, I would. Mother would too, I'm certain."

Louisa held her folded fan in front of her mouth. She shook her head.

"You will see them, Mrs. Heron," said Eyre Soane. "Everyone will. I am considering donating the finest one to the nation, to hang in the National Gallery. That is, if I'm not forced to sell it to a rich art lover." He turned to Harriet. "Miss Heron, I am going with my friends in the morning to watch the sun rise at the Karnak temple. Will you accompany us?"

Harriet's expression changed.

"I would like to but I cannot, Mr. Soane. I'm working on the west bank, assisting at a dig."

"Are you really?" Soane raised his dark eyebrows and a smirk traveled across his features. "No doubt you are a great help, Miss Heron, but I daresay your expertise can be spared for one day."

Harriet looked puzzled.

"Yes," she said. "I'm sure that it can. But Dr. Woolfe expects me."

Soane reached to the ashtray on the reception desk, twisting out the stub of his cigar, smiling again.

"The good doctor will excuse you, I am certain, for the sake of friends who have journeyed for a fortnight to see you."

Harriet stooped and unfastened the lead from the dog's collar. She stroked the top of his head.

"I suppose that missing one day won't matter," she said, straightening up, removing the pencil from her hair. She looked at Louisa, her face still flushed. "If Mother agrees, that is."

Louisa had suspected it in Alexandria, had her fears fueled in Cairo when they met the Coxes. It was being confirmed before her very eyes. Harriet thought herself in love. Her heart ached for her daughter and she felt a murderous impulse toward Eyre Soane, for his cruelty.

"Harriet, I—"

"You'll come too, I hope, Mrs. Heron." Eyre Soane's expression was bland and pleasant, his voice persuasive. "I'll call for you both in the morning at five."

"If Harriet wishes it, Mr. Soane." Gripping her skirts in one hand, holding to the banister with the other, Louisa began to ascend the stairs. "Come, Harriet. We shall be late for dinner."

At midnight, Louisa knocked on the door of Harriet's room. She entered without waiting for an answer and sat down on the edge of the bed. Dressed in her white nightgown, Harriet was sitting in the chair, her journal on her lap, her inks out. At Louisa's entrance, she closed the book and screwed down the lid on a red ink bottle. "I thought I heard you moving around," Louisa said. "Can't you sleep?"

Harriet shook her head. Louisa hesitated. "Harriet?"

"Yes, Mother."

"Mr. Soane . . . Do you care for him?"

By the light of the bright, quick-burning Egyptian candles, Harriet began brushing her hair in long strokes, the strands rising to the brush, crackling with electricity.

"Yes, Mother. I do care for him."

"He isn't a suitable acquaintance. Please believe me."

Harriet dropped the brush on the floor.

"You know nothing about him."

"Please believe me, Harriet," Louisa said again. "I know everything that I need to know."

"You don't want me to have a suitor." Harriet walked across the floor and stood in front of her mother. "Why don't you want my happiness? Why do you always try to prevent it?"

"That isn't fair." Louisa jumped to her feet, feeling as if Harriet had struck her. "Your health and happiness are all I want." Her voice softened. "Don't let us quarrel, Harriet. Do you need a glass of water?"

"I need to be allowed to live, Mother. That is all I need."

Louisa stared at her, at the long shining tresses on the white shoulders of her nightgown, the pinkness of her complexion. Harriet had lost the elderly look she'd had since girlhood. She at last looked like what she was, a young woman.

Opening her mouth to speak, closing it again, unable to think of what she might possibly say, Louisa left the room. She would speak to Eyre Soane. She would impart the knowledge that would cause him to desist, to leave Harriet alone. She would do it as soon as she had the opportunity.

THIRTY-NINE

❦

Harriet held the dog more tightly on her lap as her donkey brayed in the fresh chill of the dawn. She was glad of the near darkness. It made it easier to think. Her pleasure at the arrival of Eyre Soane was marred by her unease at breaking her promise to Dr. Woolfe. Riding toward Karnak, along the half-ruined avenue of sphinxes, her mount led along by the donkey boy, she couldn't shake off the feeling she was heading in the wrong direction. Eyre Soane and Jim Simpson were ahead and on either side of her were Louisa and Mrs. Simpson.

"I've been so impatient to meet you," said Effie Simpson. "Eyre has told us so much about you."

"I wasn't aware that Mr. Soane knew much about my daughter," Louisa said.

Mrs. Simpson seemed at a loss. "I hope we'll be able to get to know each other better, now we're here," she said eventually.

Against her wishes, Mrs. Simpson had been persuaded to ride a donkey. It had taken some time to convince her that there were no carriages in Luxor, news she had greeted with openmouthed disbelief until Louisa suggested they either proceed or cancel the proposed visit to the temple. Harriet half hoped that the plan would be called off, but Mrs. Simpson had finally allowed her husband to lift her onto the back of a donkey.

They reached the entrance to the temple, and when Fouad hurried forward to help Harriet dismount, Eyre Soane flicked the glowing tip of a cigar through the air and dismissed him, taking hold of Harriet's hands as she slid down from the saddle.

"We were beginning to think you were lost," he said, squeezing her fingers, keeping hold of them too long in the concealing darkness.

Breathing in the familiar, mixed odors of sandalwood and cigar smoke, startled by Eyre Soane's proximity, his solid physicality, Harriet felt light-headed. She knew Mr. Soane better as an idea in her head than as a man. She pulled away her hands as a dozen or more Egyptians rose from mats on the ground in front of the temple and hurried toward the visitors, winding their turbans while they came, offering their services in a mixture of English and Arabic.

The men crowded around them, thrusting forward scarabs and shards of pottery for inspection. They were skinny fellows, of medium height or less, all dressed alike in gowns that had grown thin and ragged, gray with use.

"Stand back, you blackguards," said Mr. Simpson, getting in front of Mrs. Simpson and thrusting out his chest. "Get away."

"They are guides, Mr. Simpson," Harriet said, collecting herself. "They mean no harm. This man showed Mother and me around a week or two ago. His name is Abdullah."

"They're all Abdullahs," said Mr. Simpson, lowering his fists. "Abdullahs or Mohammeds."

Harriet glanced around for Fouad, who was standing at a little distance. *Abdullah* meant *Servant of God*, he'd told her, and she thought it a beautiful name. More beautiful than *Jim*. The other men retreated and Abdullah held out his handful of souvenirs—scarabs and *shabti*s, the small figures of servants placed in tombs to serve their masters and mistresses in the afterlife.

Dr. Woolfe had warned Harriet against buying what the guides called antikis. It was theft, he said, and anyway, most of the best-looking ones were fakes, made locally, then wrapped in bread and forced down the throats of geese. They came, *ach*, how could he put it, out the other end, looking two thousand years old.

Mrs. Simpson took a shabti from Abdullah's hand. "Is it a doll?" she said.

"They put them in the tombs, Mrs. Simpson. To carry out the work for the dead."

Mrs. Simpson shrieked and dropped the figure on the sandy ground, wiping her hand on her skirt.

"You might have warned me."

"Do you care to have it, Miss Heron?" said Eyre Soane as Abdullah picked it up.

"Oh, no. Thank you."

The party set off behind their guide toward the entrance of the temple. The sun was still below the horizon and the light appeared blue, the colors—of the stone, the trees, Mrs. Simpson's sun hat— oddly bleached, like a tinted photograph. Entering the Hypostyle Hall, Harriet felt the same sense of shock as on the first time she saw it, at the grandeur of the temple and the scale of its ruin. Sand, mud, and rubbish were banked up eight or ten feet high around the bases of the pillars. Some of the columns had keeled over; great chunks of stone from the roof lay like tombstones on the ground.

Mr. and Mrs. Simpson were ahead, talking to Louisa. Reaching for Harriet's hand, Eyre Soane drew her behind one of the massive pillars. He stood in front of her, looking at her intently.

"I set off as soon as I received your summons, Miss Heron."

"Summons?"

"Once I knew you longed to see me, I came as soon as I could."

Harriet felt her face warming at the reminder of the words of her note. It was true that she had summoned him, not through the note but through the spell she had written, the picture she'd drawn of him with his paintbrush. Now that he had come, she felt confused. He seemed to expect something of her and she didn't know what it could be.

"I don't suppose you came just to see me, Mr. Soane," she said. "Did you?"

From the other side of the pillar, Louisa's voice rang through the still air.

"Harriet! Abdullah has something to show us."

The sun grew stronger as the minutes passed, the light altering from blue to pink, to the luminous crimson glow that the ancient

Egyptian priests must have experienced as they made the ritual sacrifices of roasted meat and wine, burned the frankincense that they considered the breath of the gods. They walked on through a series of pylons, across open courtyards and around the maze of columns and obelisks. The scale of the temple gave Harriet a sense of peace. Mr. Soane and his friends had come to see the antiquities, not her. She owed him nothing. She would return to the dig the following day and explain to Dr. Woolfe what had happened.

Mrs. Simpson was walking in front of her, wearing white leather pumps under a fashionably short walking skirt; the narrow footprints she left in the dust reminded Harriet of the story of Monsieur Mariette, the great French Egyptologist, opening up a tomb in the desert and finding in it the footprints of the workers who had sealed it behind themselves more than three thousand years earlier. She considered telling Mrs. Simpson about him and decided against it.

They both stopped to examine a line of hieroglyphs—a lotus flower, a bowl, a pair of walking legs—carved in a granite wall. The symbols were perfect, as clear and distinct as if they had been chiseled out overnight.

"Soanie says you're an expert on all this," Mrs. Simpson said.

"Not an expert but I'm interested. You see? This vulture here symbolizes protection, like a mother." Harriet traced the bird's puffed-up chest and small head with her finger. "I think it's wonderful that they can communicate with us, over three thousand years later."

"How can a vulture be a mother?" said Mrs. Simpson. She yawned, covering her mouth with her hand. "Pardon me, Miss Heron. I'm not usually an early riser."

The party reached the edge of the great rectangular lake, the symbol of the eternal ocean, where Amun's priests had purified themselves. Eyre Soane once again stood beside Harriet.

"Do you admire the temple, Mr. Soane?" she said.

He made a gesture encompassing the whole site.

"Sublime. But I've seen it all before." He lowered his voice. "It is you that I have come for, Miss Heron. Tomorrow we can begin."

"Begin what?" she said, feeling dull and stupid, starting to be dazed by the heat.

"The painting, Miss Heron. Have you forgotten?"

"Oh, of course. I haven't forgotten, Mr. Soane. But I must go to the dig tomorrow. I should have been there today."

"I thought we had an agreement."

"We did. We do. But . . ."

"Harriet," Louisa called.

Eyre kicked a stone into the water as Harriet crossed back over a stretch of open ground and joined the others, who were sitting in the shade of a statue of a king, his false beard carefully shaped.

"That's a corker," Mr. Simpson pronounced, tipping back his head, aiming his wife's opera glasses at the statue. He wiped his face on a handkerchief. "Look at the size of it. Remarkable!"

"Remarkable!" echoed Mrs. Simpson as Mr. Simpson rolled up his sleeves, climbed onto the plinth at the base of the statue, and began to carve his name.

Eyre Soane was walking around the edge of the lake, hands thrust into his pockets, smoke rising over his head in the clear air. Harriet wanted to go after him, explain that she had not forgotten about the painting but, in full view of the others, with Louisa watching her, she couldn't. She sat on the toppled pillar, half listening to Louisa's conversation with Mrs. Simpson about the news from England, while Mr. Simpson carried on with his laborious task, scratching his initials in thin, shallow lines.

By the time he'd finished the inscription, dated it May 1882, the sun was high overhead. Harriet was surprised to be reminded that it was May already, that they had been away for four months. The weeks had passed quickly but the span since they'd left London seemed to Harriet an eternity.

FORTY

The Nile was changing color, turning brown with the mud that it carried from the south. The inundation had begun early, the river rising by five or six centimeters each day. The ancient Egyptians had set their calendar by the rising waters, dividing the year into three parts. Akhet, the time of the flood; Peret, for the growing season; Shemu, harvest time. It was a decent way to divide any length of time, Eberhardt Woolfe thought. A day. A year. A life. He was moving from Shemu to Akhet. But what had he harvested, in this last hard year? What would he sow, this year or next, when the dig was completed and the floodwaters receded, leaving behind the layer of rich silt that sustained and created the country?

Four eggs bumped gently in a pan on the charcoal stove, steam rising from the water. Eberhardt had no servant at the house, only assistants at the tomb. Standing at the table in his kitchen, he sawed into a loaf of black bread by the light of the oil lamp and added another slice to the ones already cut. In the near darkness, he wrapped two plates and two cups in a linen cloth, then selected two knives, their bone handles rounded from use. It was a particular pleasure, to take out items in pairs.

He removed the pan from the fire and retrieved the eggs with a spoon, left them to cool. Rinsed a branched vine of red tomatoes that made him think of a robust, young family, so firmly attached they were to each other. So alike one to the other.

"*Ach*, Kati. What am I doing?"

The eggs were cool enough to touch. Egyptian eggs were white-shelled, all yolk inside. They were either too small, as these were, or too large, like the ostrich eggs that Professor Kranz had considered a delicacy and that Eberhardt found an abomination. Miss Heron, he was certain, would not like to eat an ostrich egg.

What did women eat? He could barely remember anymore. They ate the things one couldn't find here. Sacher torte and strudel. Soup. White meat. That was women in Germany, he reminded himself. In England, everyone had drunk tea. He shook salt into a tin, screwed down the lid. He had packed a cloth bag of dates and dried apricots. An enamel pot. The coffee was ground, ready to brew at the site.

Did Englishwomen drink coffee? His landlady in Holborn, when he had studied at the British Museum, had served beer with every meal including breakfast, a flat, warm tankard of it that left rings on the table. Whether the woman offered it because it was her own custom, or because she believed it must be his, he'd never discovered. On the first morning, he had requested coffee; Mrs. Brown brought something unrecognizable, so much like ditchwater in appearance and taste that he had waited until she left the room, then—unable to open the filthy window—poured it into a plant pot.

Harriet was not like the Englishwomen he'd met when he was passing those dingy, intense months under the great dome of the Reading Room, treading in front of the stacks of books along perforated iron landings, through which you could see the balding heads of the scholars underneath.

The few women he'd met in London had struck him as constrained by living on their island. Short in stature and limited in their horizons. Harriet was more like he was. Not properly allied to her own country. A wanderer by nature. He sensed it. She would drink coffee. Eat black bread. March into a bat-ridden tomb without fleeing.

He wondered whether she was ill again. Her health was delicate; that was why she had come here with her mother. She had not arrived at the dig the previous day, although he had expected her. He'd thought her delayed, had been disappointed to realize, at midday, that she wasn't coming. She would be present today, he was certain. Her interest was serious. She had the feeling, the feeling he had, of tending the legacy of living people and having a responsibility toward them. She would arrive on her black donkey, with the boy walking beside her, the dog on her lap. Wearing the orange scarf that she wrapped around her head like a turban, with her hair loose underneath it. She was tall. When they spoke, he could look her in the eye, not regard the top of her head. He liked that. The thought provoked a stab of guilt. Kati had been small; she barely measured five feet and her hips were narrow. Too narrow for life. Their daughter had survived only hours, long enough for Eberhardt to recognize his own features mirrored in her face, to feel the grip of her hand around his finger. He had named her Rosa, insisted against the doctor's advice that before she was buried with her mother she be christened. He was not a believer except in the importance of ritual, of offering to the dead every paltry assistance available to mortals.

Eberhardt walked into the large salon that was study and drawing room, and picked up the framed photograph balanced on the Bösendorfer. Kati's mouth was open as if to speak. Her eyes watched him, with a wry understanding he hadn't been aware of during their life together. Sometimes he felt that it was he who had abandoned her, he who had disappeared out of their shared life, while she had remained faithful to a moment, her lace shawl draped around her sloping shoulders, her expression steadfast, as unchanging as the cameo at her neck. He had absconded into alteration, who and what he had been dying more with every day that passed.

The basket was full, the oranges nestled on the top, the last of the plum cake Mutti insisted he bring from Heidelberg neatly slid down the side. He lifted the bag by its leather handles, felt its weight. It was an offering to take into the tomb. Not for the dead but for the living. For Harriet Heron, the white woman with the red hair, who had walked into the catacomb with him and stayed there, in the darkness. He wanted to share something with her. He was not sure what.

Picking up the basket, he walked toward the door, then turned back and looked again at the photograph.

"Is it wrong, Kati? *Ich muss nun Abschied nehmen.* The time has come to say farewell."

FORTY-ONE

The British consul's agent inhabited one of the few two-story houses in Luxor; it was narrow, built of mud bricks, with curled iron grilles over the ground-floor windows. A pot of marigolds stood to one side of a faded red door, which opened to a dark hallway scented with a musky incense. The smell transported Louisa, as she stepped inside, to Mr. Hamilton's house in Greenwich.

She glanced around her, half expecting to see Mr. Hamilton's plump, leaking wife, to breathe in the scent of cats and cabbage, be invited to make her own way to the back parlor. She found herself instead looking at a neat, dark-haired woman with an olive complexion, gold hoops dangling from the lobes of her ears. Louisa removed her glasses.

"Good morning. Is Ahmed Bey present?"

The woman shook her head and showed Louisa into a cool, square study. She brought in a pile of letters on a salver. Looking through the envelopes, Louisa found three addressed to her. One was in Blundell's strong, methodical hand, the second in Yael's forward-leaping script that made her think of a horse taking a fence. The third was in handwriting she didn't recognize.

The housekeeper left the room and Louisa sat down on the visitor's chair by the side of the agent's desk. The silence in the room was broken by the light, scurrying tick of a carriage clock on the top of a bookcase. Its urgency seemed redundant in this place of stillness, this place where time had dwarfed itself.

Blundell's letter was addressed to her in Alexandria, care of the Anglo Ottoman Bank, and had been forwarded by Yael. Louisa opened it with the jeweled paper knife that lay on the desk, shearing through the crease on the top of the envelope. She got out the letter and for a minute held it without unfolding it. It was communication enough, that what had been in Blundell's hand was now in hers. How long had she been away from her husband? She hardly knew anymore and no counting of days or miles could quantify how far she'd traveled from their life together.

Opening out the sheet of paper, she read the contents. He'd received the letter she had written on the journey upriver, was glad to hear they had enjoyed the trip, and hoped the climate in Luxor was proving beneficial to Harriet. Their sons were in good health, although he himself had suffered a minor bout of Russian influenza, which was no cause for concern. The weather was wet for May and hardly seemed like spring, although the cherry blossom in the garden was splendid. He was sorry she was missing it, since she appreciated beauty better than he. On a more serious note, the news from Egypt concerned him. He suspected that it might be a good idea for them all to return home soon and would sign off now in the hope of being reunited with his beloved wife.

The housekeeper returned and set down a tray on which was a small glass of spirits, a saucer of Turkish delight. Louisa raised her eyes from the letter, blinking away a tear. She waited until the woman had left the room before opening the next letter. Yael trusted that dear Harriet's health was improving and Louisa was keeping well. She was busy with her charity work. The weather in Alexandria was surprisingly comfortable, not unlike Boscombe in July, and the evenings cool. Louisa scanned the lines, barely absorbing their contents, folding the sheet back into the envelope.

She contemplated the script on the front of the third letter. The initial *L* was embellished at both ends with curling loops. The envelope was coarse, with a dirty-looking thumbprint on one corner. Her surname had been misspelled. *Mrs. L. Herron.* Whenever she received a note in an unfamiliar hand, Louisa knew its provenance. Malachi Sethe Hamilton had so little time and so many calls on it that he always sent missives written by one scribe or another. She tore open the envelope, impatient suddenly to know what message it contained.

Glancing at the letter, taking in its brevity, Louisa first thought that Mr. Hamilton had no news to communicate to her. It wasn't more than a line. Then she read it.

Antigua Street, SE

Mrs. Herron,
  Yr mam came through again. Death is coming for sure.
                              M. S. Hamilton (Mr.)

Picking up the glass from the tray, Louisa downed the brandy in one burning swallow.

As she walked back by the river, Louisa's feet hurt. She stopped to rest, sat down on a great gray boulder, lifting one foot and then the other out of the thin summer shoes that she had purchased for the trip and that had proved quite hopeless for the terrain, watching the coruscant water, its smooth eternal flow. The Nile appeared wider than it had when they arrived in Luxor. Everything changed. Even the oldest river in history, on which Moses had floated in a cradle sealed with pitch, was altering with every moment that passed.

As she sat, the meaning of her mother's message at last became clear to her. Harriet was in better health than she had been for years. She was blooming in the dry heat, breathing freely, had never looked or been stronger. If it wasn't Harriet who was in danger, it must be herself. It was her own death that was near. Amelia Newlove—Louisa never thought of her as *Mam*, that was Mr. Hamilton's term—had tried to warn her. Was trying still. Warn her or welcome her. She didn't know why she hadn't seen it before.

She stopped under one of the trees that grew by the edge of the river. Leaning on it, she felt steadied. A tree was a tree, in whatever soil it grew. The dry rustle of leaves over her head sounded for a moment like the sea, and she felt a sudden longing for the sensation of rain on her face and the sight of a cloudy sky. Walking on, she found herself thinking again of Dover, the place she still called home if taken unawares. The place that Augustus had robbed her of because the flint house where they'd lived, the turf-covered cliff, the night music of the sea as it murmured and roared to itself in the darkness, had come to seem the same as innocence.

"I am homesick," she said aloud.

On the far side of the river, the pink hills stared back, impassive. A noise cut through the air, sounding like a wounded animal. Louisa walked a few more steps and, beyond the line of bushes at the edge of the field, saw a woman. She was on her knees by a short, low mound of earth, scooping handfuls of dust from the ground and raining them down over her head, rubbing them into her grief-ravaged face and her exposed breast, her wails rending the air. She lowered her face to the ground, rubbing her forehead on the earth as if she would crawl into it. At the end of the grave was a bowl of water with a small brown bird perched on the rim. Louisa bowed her head. She felt a pain in her own breast, for all the agony that lived in the world like wind or sun, moving about, falling at random on its human subjects. If she was to die, she must first get Harriet safely back to Blundell. At the thought that she might never see her husband again, she began to weep.

FORTY-TWO

Strips of wicker had uncurled from the bentwood frame: the chair back was scratchy against Harriet's palm. Shards of light fell through a roof made of dried grasses, striping her shoulders, the tops of her bare feet. She was dressed in a loose blue robe, the Egyptian djellaba that Suraya had made for her; newly released from its nighttime plaits, her hair fell in crimped waves to her waist and her feet were bare on the dried mud floor. Every muscle in her body was begging to be allowed to move.

At the other end of the gazebo, his shirtsleeves rolled to the elbow, Eyre Soane mixed pigments on his palette. The paint, or the oil he used to thin it, was irritating her lungs. For the first time in weeks, Harriet could hear her own breathing.

He glanced up.

"You are beautiful, Miss Heron."

Harriet felt embarrassed. She looked at him, her eyes shifting down from the point where he had instructed her to fasten her gaze.

"I'm not beautiful, and I have always known it. You need not flatter me."

"But you are," he said. "The shape of your head. The delicacy of your gestures. I knew from the very first time I set eyes on you that I had to paint you."

"That morning on the weather deck? You barely noticed me, Mr. Soane."

Harriet thought she saw annoyance in his face. She pictured

him as he had been on that day, remembered how handsome and unreachable he had appeared. Harriet felt she knew him barely any better now. It was the fourth day of the sitting and Eyre Soane had once again taken a long time to arrange her in the pose, moving her head right and left, her chin up and down until it was just so, adjusting her arm. Harriet's face had colored at the touch of his hand through the thin fabric of her sleeve.

His treatment of her was making her uneasy. He approached too close, looked too long, rested his hand on her waist in a manner that Harriet sensed was improper. Even worse were the compliments he paid her. She wanted to believe them but something inside, some insistent voice, told her that they were insincere.

"I meant at the villa," he said, "in Alexandria. I didn't have a chance to see you on the steamer, amid all those frightful tourists."

She felt the blush begin again. It would not be deterred. Had he forgotten the way their eyes had met across the ship's dining saloon, after he had joined them at dinner?

The shelter was open on two sides to the breeze, and from where she stood, out of the corner of her eye, she got a glimpse of the aviary. Inside it, the trapped birds swooped and perched, clung to the netting, dipped their heads to the shallow bowl of water.

Outside, the free birds came as if to visit them, landing on the ground, heads cocked to one side, letting out streams of sound.

As she looked, Harriet thought she saw a flash of green, glimpsed the train of Louisa's skirts passing behind a clump of palm trees outside. She waited for Louisa to enter the gazebo and comment on the canvas or announce that she had changed her mind about allowing, or at any rate not disallowing, the portrait. But the minutes ticked on and Louisa did not come. Harriet decided she must have been mistaken.

Louisa had taken it into her head that they must return to London. Harriet had no wish to leave Luxor. She'd agreed to begin the sitting immediately, from a sense of obligation to Mr. Soane and to gain time in which to try to change Louisa's mind.

Standing in the pose, her gaze unfocused, as Eyre Soane had instructed, her mind turned to the west bank. She saw the white valley, the dark entrance to the tomb, and imagined herself walking into it, sitting in front of the panel and puzzling over the signs to the music of Dr. Woolfe's trowel. She'd wanted every day to see him, if only to explain her absence, but Mr. Soane had made it impossible. He arrived at the hotel each morning even before it was properly light and was waiting for her in the lobby by the time she and Louisa came down for breakfast. He worked on the portrait for hours, releasing Harriet at mid-afternoon, too late to cross the river.

Harriet pictured the cartouche, the circle enclosing the hieroglyphs, by the queen in her white dress. She could see each of the symbols individually—the image of the goddess, seated, with her wig long on her back. Aast. Isis. The sign of a windpipe and lungs, which meant *beautiful*, the face, which was in her own name, that made the sound *hr*—but she couldn't read anything coherent from them.

Lifting one foot in the air, she moved her toes, trying to rid herself of pins and needles.

"I must go back to the dig tomorrow. I've been away for days."

"Don't tease me."

"I am not teasing you, Mr. Soane. It matters to me, the work I do there. And Dr. Woolfe expects me. I cannot pose for you tomorrow."

"You will not escape me that easily, Miss Heron," he said, standing back from the canvas, his right arm outstretched, making marks on the rectangle that was clamped on the easel.

Harriet said no more until Eyre Soane walked over to where she stood and took hold of her hand, turned it upward and kissed the palm, pressing his mouth to her hand. She could feel the moistness of his lips. She pulled away her hand. Harriet had a guilty feeling that far from being in love with Mr. Soane, she was beginning to dislike him. Perhaps that was normal. She knew nothing of love, she reminded herself.

The sitting over for the day, Eyre Soane insisted on accompanying Harriet to the dining room of the hotel, where she was meeting Louisa for luncheon. As they walked into the room, Louisa rose to her feet from her place at the table. She looked like a ghost, her eyes huge and haunted, one hand patting her chignon.

"Mrs. Heron," Eyre Soane said. "Please don't disturb yourself."

"What do you want?" Louisa said.

He raised his eyebrows, pulling out a chair for Harriet. "I want to invite you and your charming daughter to dinner. I'm organizing a soirée here on Friday evening, for the Europeans. It is to be a celebration of art."

"When will your portrait be finished, Mr. Soane?" said Louisa.

"Soon, Mrs. Heron. Soon."

He smiled at her and Louisa stared back at him without the smallest pretense of politeness. Harriet felt puzzled. In all her life, she had never known her mother to behave badly.

FORTY-THREE

Harriet applied her pencil to the paper on the drawing board. Things had changed since her last visit. Dr. Woolfe was close to being able to enter the tomb. The whole of the lintel of the doorway had emerged under his patient tapping, and the rubble beneath it was steadily being reduced, carried away for sieving by the Egyptian workers. He had greeted her without commenting on her absence, simply saying that he had thought she would return. Then he made a little bow and apologized for his English. He had not thought she would return. He had *hoped* that she would.

The pool of lamplight where she worked was still and steady; not a breath of the thick air moved.

"Have you made any more finds, Dr. Woolfe?" she called to him.

"*Ach*, just shards mainly, Romans. I came across the feet of a shabti, in faience. And a promising-looking amulet that I haven't had a chance yet to examine. Another scarab."

"I like scarabs," Harriet said.

"I also like scarabs," came Dr. Woolfe's voice. He cleared his throat. "We have missed you here, Miss Heron."

"I wanted to come before but I've been sitting for a portrait. Eyre Soane, the artist, is here with his friends."

"I have heard about the arrival of the dashing Mr. Soane. In fact, I met the man on the ship."

"He would like to visit the dig," Harriet said, "if you had no objection."

"If I had no objection," Dr. Woolfe said, "then he could."

His voice, traveling through the darkness, sounded farther away than it was.

Harriet held up the paper to compare her drawing with the original. She was copying the second column of hieroglyphs, below the oval ring of symbols that spelled out the name of the queen, that she hadn't yet been able to read. At the top of the column was the depiction of a house, which—combined with two walking legs and an empty eye shape—meant *to go forth*. Harriet wondered again whether the queen still lay on the other side of the doorway, whether the magic had worked and the Lady of the Two Lands went forth by day to savor the muddy scent of the rising Nile, feel the sun on her shoulders. The queens wore surprisingly revealing gowns.

Harriet had risen before dawn and walked through the hotel garden in the darkness, the warmth cloaking her despite the early hour. Mornings in Luxor were unlike any Harriet had ever experienced in England. The minutes before dawn seemed to hold some great tension, as if the curtain was about to be raised on an epic drama and the earth hushed itself in readiness, with only the cockerels unable to contain themselves, shrieking their excitement at the coming day.

She'd told Fouad of her intention and he was waiting for her by the gate the servants used. Hurrying behind the mud-brick wall at the back of the hotel, they walked quickly south along the shore to the spot from which the boats departed for the west bank. Soft splashes broke the silence as the boatman pushed the little craft out into the water, waded through the shallows, and scrambled on board in his bare feet, pulling round the sail to catch the breeze.

Fifty yards or more out into the river, Fouad clicked his tongue and nodded his head toward the shore. Harriet followed the direction of his eyes. Eyre Soane was walking in the direction of the Luxor Hotel, his paintbox under his arm. His step reminded Harriet of the way he'd approached their table on the steamer. Then it had been Louisa who was the object of his purpose. Now it was herself. She still didn't know what that purpose was.

Harriet had thought once that she wanted more than anything to be painted by Mr. Soane. It was hard to admit to herself that she wasn't enjoying it. She watched as he dropped his cigar in the dust, ground it out with his heel, then walked through the gate. She'd left a note in the gazebo apologizing for her absence and assuring him that she would be there the following day.

Harriet looked again at what she had copied onto the paper. A sickle shape, an oar, the sign for the sound *kh*, and the name of the god Osiris, giver of breath, followed by a flag, the sign of a male god, and something like a sword that made the sound *ahk*, and meant *great*. Then the feather of Maat, that for Harriet stood for Aunt Yael but for the ancient Egyptians meant order and balance and rightness of all kinds.

Suddenly, the signs fell into place. Harriet let out a shout of pleasure and the tapping from farther down the passage ceased as Dr. Woolfe came hurrying to where she worked.

"Miss Heron? Are you—"

"Look!" She pointed at the hieroglyphs. "This means *Her voice has been justified before Osiris, the great god*. Or at least I think it does."

"That is most helpful," Dr. Woolfe said, examining her drawings. "In fact, it is marvelous."

He smiled at her, then went back to his station by the blocked entrance and for some time they worked in silence.

"How is your mother?" he called through the darkness.

"Well, thank you."

Louisa hadn't been herself for days but she wasn't ill in the way one could describe to another person. She had taken to haunting the garden, veiled against the sun, shaded by her parasol, her hands hidden in white gloves. At lunchtime, when Harriet met her in the hotel dining room after the sittings, she was anxious, her appetite poor. She was still urging that they leave for Alexandria, and then London.

"I wondered . . ." came Dr. Woolfe's voice in the darkness. "That is, I thought . . . Will you join me for dinner on Friday evening, Miss Heron? With your mother, of course."

"I would like to, Dr. Woolfe, but I can't." In the silence that followed, Harriet added an explanation. "Mr. Soane is holding a dinner party."

"*Ach*, I see. Yes, I do see." The tapping resumed.

"I am certain he would be pleased to see you there, Dr. Woolfe, at the dinner."

"How are you certain, Fräulein?" he called over the hammering.

"Well, I would be glad if you attended," she called back. "I know that."

FORTY-FOUR

Yael sat in the front pew at St. Mark's. She attended the weekly service regularly, opening the clinic late that day. The women understood that it was her holy day. On Sundays, the crowd around the little door did not begin to gather until midday. Today she might be later than that in arriving. The women would still be there. They had a talent for patience.

After the service, Yael waited until every member of the congregation had departed. She removed her spectacles and rubbed the lenses on her handkerchief before returning them to her nose. It was as she suspected. Ernest Griffinshawe looked tired. His shoes were dusty and his surplice gray. He had lost weight since the days when he conducted divine service on the *Star of the East*. The man needed a shave and a haircut, she noted with satisfaction.

He hadn't seen her, sitting on in the empty church. People didn't see Yael. She had come to understand it as one of God's blessings. And it was because he hadn't seen her that when she called out his name, he jumped and let out a startled cry.

"I am so very sorry," Yael said, rising from the pew and walking toward him, peering at him through the glasses just as if she had not been observing him closely throughout the service and after it. "I didn't mean to alarm you."

"It is you, Miss Heron," he said.

"Yes. It is me. Reverend . . ." Yael paused, as if what she was about to say was the source of some difficulty.

"Well?"

"Reverend, I am, despite my years and spinsterhood, a member of the female sex."

The Reverend looked alarmed, as if he might be about to contradict her.

"And," Yael continued, "as is well known, women are prone to changing their minds."

Ernest Griffinshawe looked at her with doubt in his eyes. "About what have you changed your mind?"

Yael sighed.

"You had the notion some time ago that an Englishwoman could train your cook, your maid, to do things in the way they're done at home. Of course, having run my dear father's house for many years, I am accustomed to such duties. I well understand the inconvenience of poor housekeeping."

Yael paused and looked up at him, her eyes fastening on the grubby surplice, traveling down to the dusty footwear, in which, she saw, string had taken the place of shoelaces.

"And, Miss Heron?" said the Reverend, sounding hopeful.

"I believe that I could find the time, on two afternoons a week, to make a contribution to the smooth running of your household."

Reverend Griffinshawe beamed.

"Could you, Miss Heron?"

"I could, Reverend. Or rather, I would."

"You would?"

"Yes." Yael paused again, blinked, and looked around the church, assuming her vaguest expression. "If you would be so kind, Reverend, as to do something for me."

Reverend Griffinshawe's voice took on a more guarded tone. "What might that be, Miss Heron?"

Yael cleared her throat and spoke in a businesslike manner, looking the Reverend straight in the eye. "My families need food. I need money to purchase it for them. I will oversee your household affairs, if you will launch a weekly collection among your congregation to feed the hungry children of this city."

Reverend Griffinshawe paused only briefly. "Done, Miss Heron."

FORTY-FIVE

❧❧

A hum of voices was coming from the bar off the lobby. The day had been hot and the heat still lingered; it was 112 degrees Fahrenheit, according to the thermometer on the wall in the hotel lobby. The talk ceased as Harriet and Louisa walked in. All the other guests were already present. The Simpsons; the Misses Fleury, two English sisters who were staying at the hotel while they waited for a paddle steamer to carry them back down the river to Cairo; elderly Mrs. Treadwell, who had a home in Luxor and believed herself in a previous incarnation to have been one of the wives of a great pharaoh; and Dr. Woolfe, who was standing next to Jim Simpson. Harriet smiled at him and he nodded, his eyes lingering on her. She was wearing a tea dress in a deep poppy color and had pinned a marigold in her hair, dabbed on some of the scent Louisa had given her for Christmas.

"Good evening, Miss Heron." Eyre Soane's eyes flicked over Harriet's costume before fastening on Louisa. "And Mrs. Heron," he said, making an exaggerated bow. "Delighted that you could join us."

He and Jim Simpson both wore dark jackets over their white shirts; Effie Simpson wore a gown of pink silk, her breasts raised out of the bodice like two white apples. The Fleury sisters, their faces powdered white, were in evening dresses, limp satins that looked as if they'd expired from the heat.

The sisters began conversing about the warmth of the day, the certainty of hotter weather to come, their relief that they would

201

be departing shortly for cooler climes. Harriet stole a look at Dr. Woolfe. He appeared ill at ease, his hair still damp from washing, his white shirt crisply ironed, and a glass in his hand in place of a trowel.

As she began to detach herself from the sisters, to go to greet him, Monsieur Andreas emerged from behind the bar with a napkin over one arm. Monsieur Andreas had been busy all day, in and out of the kitchens at the back of the hotel, calling instructions in a mixture of French and Arabic, sending the boy who cleaned the shoes on errands to the market. He bowed to Louisa, then clapped his hands in the air in a triumphant gesture.

"*Messieurs-dames*. Dinner is served. Please be seated."

Dr. Woolfe offered his arm to Mrs. Treadwell, helping her rise from her chair, and the guests made their way into the dining room. Several tables had been pushed together to make one long one, covered with a white cloth, laid with silver that shone by the light of many candles. The pink roses from the garden had been cut and were set in a glass vase in the center of the table. The Fleury sisters insisted in turn on bending their noses to the open blooms.

"You simply must smell them, Mrs. Heron," said Annette Fleury, the younger woman. "The scent takes you straight back to England."

She lifted the little vase and held it under Louisa's nose. Louisa sniffed deeply.

"They have no scent," she said, handing back the vase.

She turned away, tugging up her gloves toward her elbows, smoothing the dark satin against her forearms. Harriet felt worried about her. Earlier, she'd sat on the bed watching as Louisa prepared herself for the evening. Louisa lifted sections of hair, tore through them with the teeth of the comb without her usual care, then pinned the thick coils in the chignon at the back of her head. It was a ritual Harriet had watched for as long as she could remember; Louisa had always prided herself on being able to dress her own hair better than any maid could do it.

"Are you sure you wish to attend this charade?" Louisa asked, looking at her in the mirror, a couple of hairpins between her lips.

"What do you have against Mr. Soane?"

"I have told you before, Harriet, that he isn't a suitable acquaintance."

"Why do you say that?"

Louisa shook her head, secured another coil of hair, her eyes fixed on her own face in the mirror. "I am your mother, Harriet."

Louisa was her mother, but not in the way she always had been. Harriet was beginning to feel as if it was Louisa who needed looking after. Walking behind her as they made their way along the landing, she noticed that Louisa's chignon was lopsided, the coils looser on one side than the other. It made Harriet feel oddly lopsided herself.

Miss Fleury proffered the vase of roses to Dr. Woolfe, who sniffed at it politely and agreed that he believed he could perhaps detect some fragrance. He was seated too far away from Harriet for her to be able to speak to him. Eyre Soane had seized the neck of the bottle that Monsieur Andreas had placed in the silver bottle holder and was making his way around the table, splashing red wine into glasses.

"Eat, drink, and be merry," he said as Miss Hannah Fleury covered her wineglass with her hand.

"Oh, I couldn't," she said. "Really, Mr. Soane, I couldn't."

Mr. Simpson stood up and cleared his throat. He made a solemn toast to the Queen and the guests raised their glasses to their lips, then began to eat. The first course was chicken liver pâté, smooth and peppery, served with the flat brown local bread, toasted and cut into triangles.

Harriet took a sip of dark wine. Eyre Soane was sitting at the head of the table, from where he could see all the diners. At the opposite end of the table, Dr. Woolfe was engaged in conversation with Miss Annette Fleury, although perhaps conversation didn't describe it, Harriet thought, since Miss Fleury appeared to be doing all the talking.

"We shot the fellow. Did Eyre tell you?"

Harriet looked across the table at Jim Simpson. For a moment, she couldn't think what he meant.

"No?"

"Been after him all this time. Then yesterday, we found him lazing on the bank, bold as you like. A monster. Fifteen feet long, I'd say. Hit the fellow right between the eyes."

"Oh." Harriet swallowed a mouthful of toast. Jim Simpson and Effie had been making expeditions with the crew on the dahabeah, farther upriver, while Eyre Soane stayed behind to paint her. She wondered whether the pâté might be made from the tail of a crocodile. It was a delicacy, according to Champollion. But he was a Frenchman. They ate all manner of strange things.

"The ancient Egyptians considered crocodiles sacred," she said.

"Blasted thing slid back into the water before the Abdullahs could get a rope around it."

"Not even dead, Mr. Simpson?" Louisa's voice was high. "Only wounded? That really is unforgivable."

"There's no knowing if it was dead or otherwise, dear lady," Mr. Simpson said. "It got itself down the bank and vanished. Only a cloud of blood left behind in the water."

Harriet put down the silver fork. Its tines were bent, almost touching at their tips, like a mouthful of crooked teeth. She'd lost her appetite for pâté.

"Didn't you have time to get dressed?" Effie Simpson, sitting to her right, was scrutinizing her with a look of discontent.

"I did get dressed, Mrs. Simpson."

"I feel sorry for him."

"For whom?"

"He's gone to all this trouble to make a party for you and you arrive late. Don't even make an effort."

Harriet took another mouthful of the wine. It was Louisa who'd made them late. Harriet had found her in a dark room, lying on the bed under a sheet, when she knocked at the door.

"I did make an effort," she said.

"He's told me how your mother's against him, how you begged him to come here, and now that he has, you spend all your time with a foreigner scraping about in the catacombs. It's a disgrace."

Harriet hoped Dr. Woolfe hadn't heard. Her face felt as if it were on fire.

"I didn't beg, Mrs. Simpson," she said under her breath. "And Dr. Woolfe is not a foreigner. He's from Germany."

The waiters moved around silently, clearing the plates, delivering new ones. Harriet felt Eyre Soane watching her and glanced up at him. The look on his face was not amorous or even affectionate. It was calculating. Almost unfriendly. His expression shifted to a bland, cool smile and she dropped her eyes to her plate, to a bony fish steamed with herbs, and occupied herself with trying to detach the delicate flesh that clung to the skeleton. Sometimes she felt that Mr. Soane didn't care for her at all. But if that was the case, why had he pursued her all the way to Luxor? Why was he so determined to paint her?

"When we met on the steamer, you claimed to have no interest in painting."

Eyre Soane spoke loudly, as if it were obvious whom he was addressing, as if no one else was present in the room. Harriet had the sense that Louisa was the true object of his interest, just as she had been on the last occasion when they sat down to dinner together. Under the cotton gown, Harriet's skin prickled with unease. Louisa looked up.

"Did I, Mr. Soane?" she said. "I don't recall."

"Evidently, it is true," said Eyre Soane, "or you would have wished to view the portrait of your daughter."

"She will see the painting when it is complete," Harriet said.

Louisa dabbed her lips with her napkin, laid it down on the table. "I have been spoiled, Mr. Soane, by long years of admiring the work of the masters. Modern painting means little to me."

Eyre Soane looked away, and Mrs. Simpson began talking to Hannah Fleury about the sights at Abu Simbel. Mrs. Treadwell announced suddenly that she had spent some years there, as senior wife of the god-king, and Miss Fleury began to laugh behind her hand. Her sister caught the contagion and the two giggled helplessly as the waiters cleared away the plates, the fish knives and forks, and served roast lamb and dishes of rice and spinach and the little hairy vegetable that they called ladies' fingers.

Harriet felt on edge. Eyre resented Louisa's disapproval of him, she supposed. It occurred to her that it was mutual. Louisa and Mr.

Soane disliked each other. Now that she thought about it, they'd disliked each other from the first night they'd met. She would not allow Mr. Soane to bully her mother. Louisa was so unlike herself these last few days.

"The trouble is, you see—"

Jim Simpson began a lecture on the state of the Egyptian economy, on the twin evils of the greed of the pashas and the laziness of the fellaheen, their inbred unwillingness to pay their taxes unless persuaded to do so by a flogging. New pink skin was growing shinily on his nose and cheeks, where he'd been burned by the sun, and his wedding ring gleamed. Harriet felt a sudden pity for Effie Simpson, yoked to Jim for the rest of her life.

"I cannot agree with you, Mr. Simpson," said Dr. Woolfe. "The cruelty of the Ottomans and the greed of our own financial institutions have much to answer for."

"What greed?" said Jim Simpson.

"Where do you suppose the taxes go?" said Dr. Woolfe. "Straight to London and Paris. Peasant farmers will be in hock to your bankers for generations, for a canal that benefits them not at all. If they are revolting, we should not be surprised."

The Fleury sisters stopped laughing. At the other end of the table, Eyre Soane snorted.

"You surprise me, Dr. Woolfe," he said. "I understood from Miss Heron that your concern was only with the dead."

"I am much concerned with the dead," Dr. Woolfe said before Harriet had a chance to object. "That is correct."

"Death and taxes," said Jim Simpson. "They come to us all."

A cut-glass dish of fruit salad—watermelon and pomegranate and mango—arrived at the table, borne by a waiter. Another man followed behind, carrying a tray of rice puddings. Monsieur Andreas entered the room and surveyed the table, hovering behind Louisa's chair, rubbing his hands together.

"Do you require anything, madame?"

"Dinner was excellent, monsieur," said Louisa. "You can do nothing more."

"Madame is too kind."

Mr. Soane rose to his feet. "This evening is dedicated to the fine art of painting. To paintings and painters, and their subjects. As you all know, I am painting a portrait of Miss Heron. Soon she will don the embellishments." He lifted his glass. "Then the process can be completed."

All but Louisa raised their glasses, and before long the ladies, at Mr. Simpson's prompting, stood up to move into the sitting room for mocha coffee. At the far end of the table, Dr. Woolfe was on his feet. Harriet felt mortified. She hadn't had a chance to speak with him all evening. She approached him, as he stood with Eyre Soane, wanting at least to say goodbye.

"Must you leave already, Dr. Woolfe?"

Eberhardt Woolfe looked at her, his green eyes honest and troubled.

"He must," announced Eyre Soane. "He must return to his catacombs. But I have informed him that tomorrow, at least"—he slid his arm around Harriet's waist—"I shall not allow you to join him."

As Harriet shrugged off Eyre Soane's arm, Dr. Woolfe turned abruptly and left the room.

Harriet returned to the table. Louisa was still sitting in her place, as if she had not heard Jim Simpson's invitation to withdraw.

"Come, Mother," she said, pulling out Louisa's chair for her. "We are retiring to the sitting room."

Louisa turned to her. Her face glistened, despite the breeze that moved through the dining room from the open French doors, carrying the scent of jasmine.

"I have failed you, Harriet. I should never have permitted this." They left the dining room and Harriet took her arm.

"The dinner?"

Louisa shook her head. "No, Harriet. The painting."

"I insisted on it, Mother. It wasn't your doing."

Louisa took hold of Harriet's hand, squeezing her fingers through her evening glove. "We could leave tomorrow. The paddle steamer is due in, Monsieur Andreas told me. It's only the mail boat but they take passengers and the journey downriver is faster. We could be back in Cairo in ten days. With Aunt Yael again, inside a fortnight."

"It's too late, Mother."

"Too late?" Louisa's voice was high and strained.

"You heard what he said. Mr. Soane has almost finished. Soon the sitting will be complete. I can't leave now. Anyway, I don't want to go. I feel well. I can live, here."

Louisa dabbed her forehead with her handkerchief, then wiped underneath her eyes. She refolded the scrap of lawn and closed it up in her bag. "I only ever wanted what was best for you," she said. "Please remember that of me."

"What are you talking about, Mother?"

FORTY-SIX

The gazebo was a rustic affair, a flat roof of woven grass mats, topped with palm branches, supported on six round and sturdy palm trunks. Two sides were walled in with more woven grass panels and two were open, looking out onto a clump of palms in a secluded area of the rambling garden. Eyre Soane had selected the spot for its privacy.

Miss Heron was standing at the far end of the gazebo in the position in which he'd arranged her at the beginning of the sitting. He'd mimicked exactly the attitude in which Louisa had posed for Augustus—her body at an angle, her head half turned, the eyes looking directly at the viewer. The mouth unsmiling, lips parted.

The girl knew the pose well enough now for him not to have to adjust her body, the set of her head, but he began each day with the ritual anyway, calculating the effect his proximity had on her, beginning with her bare feet, kneeling at them, shifting their position in tiny movements that allowed him to rest their bare soles on the palm of his hand, moving up her body, adjusting the angle of her hips, her hand, touching her cheek, pressing her skin with his fingers. Her blush deepened as he arranged her limbs.

His sister, Julia, had telegraphed that she was arriving in Cairo shortly. He would leave the following day to go to meet her there. He was sick of Luxor, bored with the company of the Simpsons. The sight of Louisa's pale, faded beauty was becoming intolerable. He must act, if he was ever going to. Carpe diem.

"Did you enjoy the evening, Miss Heron?" he said.

"I think so," she said, her lips barely moving.

"It was for you."

"I thought it was for art."

He felt irritated, stippling his brush against the palette, mixing cadmium with carmine for the shade of her hair. Adding a squeeze of flake white for the highlights. Umber, for the shadows. Something outside caught his attention, from the corner of his eye. It looked like a glint of light on metal, some rapid movement, among the trees. He raised his eyes but saw nothing. It might have been one of the waiters, hurrying past with a tin tray.

Eyre looked again at the image on the canvas, the tall, slight figure with its half-turned head, half-lifted chin, one hand resting lightly on a chair. The hue of the blue robe was vibrant and the gleam of the ivory-white trim luminous. The face, curious and vulnerable, looked older than its years and yet innocent. Miss Heron's countenance lit up with an unexpected vitality when she spoke of the things that concerned her.

He hadn't been interested in painting this sickly English girl but had made himself undertake the work as if he were and now the portrait held a certain beauty. From where it came, he didn't know.

Miss Heron was not as irredeemably plain as he'd believed on first seeing her. Either that or she was changed.

"What are you thinking of, Mr. Soane?" she said, startling him.

"Me? I am regretting that we are nearing the end of the sittings, Miss Heron."

"Are we? Have you finished your work? You know I must get back to mine, on the west bank. I don't want to miss the opening of the tomb."

"Never mind that, Miss Heron. Today is the day."

"Which day, Mr. Soane?"

"The day of the embellishments."

He felt in his pocket for the heavy piece and lifted it in the air. It was a necklace, a round silver disk the size of a crown, chased all over in the Arabic script, the edges studded with flat-topped, raised beads. He'd acquired it in the bazaar for a few florins from a nomad woman. Beaten her down from her asking price until she'd passed it over, still warm from her own neck. Holding it before him on its silver chain, he walked toward her.

"I chose it to complement your complexion."

"It's beautiful," she said. Her face began flushing but whether with pleasure or because she knew herself to be insulted, he could not be sure.

He held out the necklace. "May I?"

She nodded wordlessly. The skin on her cheeks, her neck, darkened as he moved behind her and lowered his arms over her head, placing the chain around her throat. Standing close to her, he laid the piece on her chest, his fingers grazing her skin.

Eyre found himself unable to use her first name. Often, he could not recall it. Then, when he remembered it, he couldn't speak it. He swallowed and, when he spoke again, employed the same deep tone of scarcely controlled feeling.

"Hold up your hair."

Her hands reached behind her head, lifted up the crinkled mass. The hair was a darker tone underneath, a deeper copper, the skin on the back of her neck milky white. The rounded shapes of the spine bones as she bowed her head reminded him suddenly of his sister's neck.

Eyre felt no appetite for what was to follow, neither desire for her nor hatred. Only the enduring wish to hurt Louisa. Scruples were nothing but a nuisance. He would set them aside. Bending forward, he brushed the back of her neck with his lips. Her skin was cool and smelled of soap. He kissed her again, encircling her waist with his arm, pulling the slender body against his own.

"Stop, Mr. Soane, please."

"Harriet. I cannot wait any longer. If you love me—"

"Love you?"

He pulled her around toward him and locked his eyes on hers. "I've dreamed of this moment."

"What moment?"

Her voice was cool, more collected than he would have expected. She looked puzzled. Eyre drew her to him and again felt the rigidity in her body, the resistance. He lowered his mouth to hers and forced open her lips with his tongue, stifling the noise she made. Thrusting one hand inside the open neck of her gown, he felt her breast, her skin soft as water, and experienced a rush of sorrow at what and whom he had become.

Eyre Soane became aware of two things. The girl was struggling to get free. And there was a noise coming from outside. He raised his mouth from hers and looked past Harriet's troubled gray eyes. Outside, framed by two palm trees, was Louisa. The sun was behind her; her shadow fell long and thin into the gazebo, her head at his feet. She wore the same dark evening dress as on the previous night and her hair was out of its coiled arrangement, fallen down on her shoulders.

For an instant, Eyre Soane saw again the girl Louisa had been, coal and milk, all black curls and white skin, half draped in red velvet. He heard her high, teasing laughter. His father's groans as he rolled off her. Eyre had thought he was dying. He pictured his mother in the house, weeping.

Louisa had lifted one arm and was holding it out in front of her. She waved it at him and again Eyre saw the glint of sun on metal.

"Don't be ridiculous," he said.

The silver piece fell to the ground as Harriet wrenched herself away and turned to face the garden.

"Mother! What are you—"

Louisa waved the gun in the air. "Get away from her," she said.

Eyre pushed Harriet out of the way. He was angry. How dare she threaten him. It was he, he would threaten her. Raising his hands in a mocking surrender, he walked out of the gazebo and into the sting of sun. A few yards from Louisa, he stopped. She looked deranged, her eyes staring and her mouth set. Even now, he could not help but notice the distinctive hairline that Augustus had represented so accurately. It reminded him of something or someone. He couldn't think who. The gun was pointing straight at him.

"I will kill you," she said, waving it in his direction.

"Kill me?" He took another pace toward her and stretched out his hand to relieve her of the pistol. "You wouldn't dare."

Louisa steadied the arm that held the gun. "One more step, Augustus, and I will shoot."

Eyre Soane's palms were sweating. He had a peculiar feeling of satisfaction at facing his foe at last, directly. For what she had done, he hated Louisa. Hated her in a way he'd never hated any other person. Except the unbidden, unwelcome, and unfamiliar thought came to him: one. There had been one other person whom he hated as much or more. The mocking face of his father rose in front of his eyes, as if Augustus were present in the parched garden, as if his feet again filled a pair of the leather boots, the smell of his paints hung heavy in the air.

"Go on," Eyre said. "Go on, Gypsy. Shoot him."

The sound seemed to shatter everything—the morning, the ground under his feet, the clear blue sky that tumbled and spun as he fell. He heard the harsh cry of a peacock and had just time to think that he'd seen no peacocks here, before he felt a warm flood seeping into the sleeve of his shirt. The smell of oils had given way to an acrid stench of burning and a woman knelt by him on the grass, screaming for help.

He need pretend no longer. He turned his face from her, closed his eyes to block out a splintered sky.

"You mean nothing to me, Harriet. You never could."

FORTY-SEVEN

Blundell's letter lay on a tray on the table. Yael looked at it for a moment longer, then went up the steps to the bathroom and removed her dusty clothes. The tap in the shower was dry but a large, filled jug stood next to a tin bowl. After washing herself all over with a soapy flannel, Yael stood in the bowl, trickling what remained of the clean water over her face and shoulders. It was pleasant to stand naked, with her feet in the cool water.

Wrapping herself in a robing gown, she returned to her own room, where she lay down on the bed in a shaft of sunlight and opened the gown. She could not recall a time when her breasts, her stomach, had ever been exposed to the sun's rays. She was a lizard, she told herself as she bathed in the soft, intense warmth and light that flooded through the window, basking in God's sun, and it was neither injurious nor immoral.

In the soporific warmth, Yael fell asleep. She dreamed of a place that, when she woke, she was unable to describe to herself, except through the sense she'd had there of ease, a contentment that in her waking life she had never experienced. Happiness, she thought as she pulled on the dress she'd had made at a little tailor's in the rue des Soeurs, a road with the distinction of having a convent at one end and a brothel at the other. Yael fastened the buttons at her cuffs. The dress was a pale gingham check, the color of the dust at noon. Happiness of the kind she had imagined heaven to offer. That was what it was.

She finished dressing, put on her shoes, and went down the steps. The fountain in the little courtyard in the middle of the house was running again and a drab sparrow perched on the edge of the pool, dipping its beak down to the water and then throwing back its head, allowing the water to run down its throat. It watched her pass, seemingly unconcerned.

Sitting down at the table, she poured herself a glass of water. When she had drunk it, she opened Blundell's letter. Yael had been expecting it. She had continued to postpone writing to her brother. He had put her in charge of his wife and daughter when he forced her to accompany them, she reasoned. He could have no quarrel with the decisions she then made, since he had put her in a position where she alone must make them. Since improving Harriet's health was the purpose of the journey, it had been best for her to travel farther south. Agreed, Blundell might have preferred that Yael accompany them. He might even have expected it. But, having started the clinic, she was resolved to continue it for the length of time she had promised herself and God that she would.

Sister,

I trust all are well and Harriet's health improved. You will be glad to know that Father carries on all right.

News from Egypt is worrying and there may be trouble ahead. I regret that I cannot allow you and Louisa and Harriet to remain any longer. Get back the others from wherever they may be, book your return journey, and inform me by telegraph of your likely arrival date at Southampton.

Yr affectionate brother,
Blundell

Yael sat on at the table, half listening to Suraya and her children, to the beat of the wings of the birds in the garden, giving themselves dust baths. She folded the sheet in half, replaced it in the envelope, and in one gesture tore it through the middle, from top to bottom.

Mustapha appeared with a tray.

"Dinner, ma'am," he said. "No fish in the market today."

"Thank you, Mustapha. Why no fish?"

He made a noncommittal movement of his head. "The boats did not leave."

"I see. Well, never mind. It is not important."

Yael pulled her chair in to the table and began to eat. The omelette was the same temperature as the air, as the fried potatoes and slices of pickled turnips and radishes that surrounded it in a ring. Somehow, she wasn't sure when or how, Yael had adopted the native way of taking food. She found a curious pleasure in eating with her fingers. She ate the omelette slowly, using torn-off pieces of flat bread to soak up the oil and vinegar and juices left behind on the plate, the scraps of slightly burnt potato, the floating shreds of green herbs. Eggs seemed to her the very best type of food, digestible, nourishing, pleasing in shape and appearance, and involving no active methods of slaughter. For pudding there was a fruit salad of irregular geometry, apples and some kind of melon, further sweetened by dates.

When she had finished, she washed her hands and poured a glass of tea, watching as the leaves unfurled, floating and waving from the prison of the thick little glass. The agony of the leaves, tea planters called it.

She dated a sheet of paper *May* and gave as the address *Alexandria*.

Dear Blundell,

I expected to have heard again from you but have received no word. I shall not worry unduly, the post in this part of the world is not altogether reliable.

Alexandria is pleasant, and certainly quieter and safer than London. We are not troubled by drunkenness here or thieving, due to the strong beliefs of the Mussulmans.

Louisa and Harriet have taken a short trip farther south in search of better air. I occupy myself with a little charity work.

Please give my love to Father and remind Mrs. Darke that he likes his whisky at 6 p.m. sharp.

Yr affectionate sister,
Yael

Was there affection between them, she wondered as she put down the pen. There had been. Was there still? Her brother had changed since he was a boy. His eyes had grown grave and distant, his expression harder. That much was obvious and right. But the best parts of him, his sense of fair play, the concern he once showed for the most vulnerable living creatures, when he would rescue every spider and bedraggled fly from the ewer, release them onto a sunny leaf in the garden, those parts had been hidden away when he became a man. Either that or they were lost, left behind as surely as the rocking horse with the balding mane, the skiff on the lake in the grounds of their childhood home.

Theirs had been a happy childhood. They wanted for nothing, had never in their lives gone to bed hungry or walked barefoot except for the joy of it. Nonetheless, to remember it filled Yael with a sadness as deep and sweet and dark as the water in the lake.

FORTY-EIGHT

Louisa stepped carefully, avoiding the goats' pellets flattened into the ends of straw, the rotting skins of mangoes and bananas, picking her way around the ashy circles of fires, stinking fish heads with their attendant bat-eared cats.

The light was pink; the water, the boats, even her own hands, were fire-touched. In the hour before sunset, all living creatures seemed to wait, in anticipation of the sinking of the sun. The birds grew frantic, searching for a place to roost, and the people were arrested, poised between day and night, between life and death.

She had not intended to kill Eyre Soane. She had pulled the trigger intentionally but as she did so, it was not him she aimed at but Augustus. For those few months of her girlhood, she had loved Augustus with all her heart. For thirty years, she had hated him with the same intensity. Louisa had meant to shoot him through the heart. It would have been just, to have wounded Augustus where he had wounded her. She supposed she was glad that she had missed.

The departure of the dahabeah had been delayed while Mr. Soane rested, Mr. Simpson had informed them at breakfast. The bullet had passed through the outer side of his right arm, his painting arm. Mrs. Simpson had dressed it, flooding it with iodine, packing the wound with lint and bandaging it with one of Eyre Soane's own shirts, torn into strips. Her father was a surgeon, Mr. Simpson had informed Harriet, rolling his eyes to the ceiling, avoiding looking at Louisa; he had taught her first aid.

Mr. Soane had not wished to involve the British consul. He'd insisted, when Monsieur Andreas arrived at a run, calling for Madame and brandishing an antique firearm of his own, that it was an accident. His own fault. Louisa hadn't disputed it. It was his own fault.

She looked about for one of the crew to fetch her in the small rowing boat and, seeing no one, walked into the shallows of the river. Wading toward the boat, she felt the pressure of the current running against her legs, her overskirt rising behind her on the water. The cold was a relief. She felt cleansed by it, as if the immersion was overdue.

She had resolved to tell Eyre Soane the truth. She wouldn't waste another minute in informing him of what he had to know. It would prevent him from threatening them, pursuing Harriet any further. Reaching the set of wooden steps on the side, Louisa pulled herself up and boarded the boat.

A pile of drying antelope hides occupied one end of the deck. The stench was sickening. Mrs. Simpson sat in a deck chair under the patched canvas awning, reading a book. She looked as if she had been weeping; her eyes were red-rimmed. She stared out from under her sun hat as Louisa stood in front of her, wringing out the hem of her skirts, twisting the silk like a rope between her hands. "You've got a nerve," she said. "Coming here."

"Good evening, Mrs. Simpson. Where is Mr. Soane?"

"In his cabin. He doesn't want to see you."

"I don't wish to see him either," Louisa said. "But I must."

Mrs. Simpson burst into tears, covering her mouth with her hand.

"I hate it," she said. "All these guns. Shooting everything that moves. I hate guns more than anything in the world. I wish I'd never agreed to come to Egypt."

Louisa felt a wave of dizziness pass over her; the sense kept afflicting her that she couldn't stay upright any longer. That a collapse was coming, whether she liked it or not. She slid down into the chair next to Mrs. Simpson's, her shoes leaking water.

"Why did you?" she said.

"Jim. He'd set his heart on a crocodile."

"I didn't want to come here either," said Louisa.

"Why did you, then?"

"My mother spoke to me from the other side, of a death. At first, I thought it was my daughter's. That we could get away from it here. Then, for a moment, I believed it was Aug . . . Mr. Soane's. Now, I am certain that it must be my own."

Mrs. Simpson reached a small hand over to Louisa's, patted her. Her nails were pink, small as shells on an English beach, shaped, and buffed to a shine.

"There, there," she said. "Don't upset yourself. We're a long way from home, that's the trouble. It was an accident, anyway. Soanie said so himself."

"It wasn't an accident."

Mrs. Simpson got out of the deck chair and returned with a glass in her hand.

"Have a drop of wine," she said, passing it to Louisa. "And calm yourself, Mrs. Heron. Of course it was an accident. What else could it have been?"

The cabin door was ajar and Eyre Soane lay in bed, propped on a heap of cushions with an unlit cigar between his lips. His right arm lay across his bare chest in a sling made from a red silk scarf; the upper part of the arm was bandaged, a dark stain blooming through the thick wad of dressing. The lamp was lit, suspended from a hook on the ceiling over his bed, and the air smelled of iodine and damp wood mixed with sandalwood pomade.

Louisa gripped the door frame. "May I come in?"

"Louisa," he said, shifting his position slightly. "Are you armed?"

She smiled. "How are you?"

"In pain. You missed the bone."

"It was your father I wanted to kill. Augustus. He deserved it."

Eyre Soane turned away his head, lowering his eyelids as if the pain assailed him again.

"Augustus was a great man," he said. "A great, great man, with immoral and unscrupulous women throwing themselves at him all his life. It broke my mother's heart."

He began trying to light the cigar one-handed.

Louisa took the matchbox from him and struck a flame.

"He was a scoundrel," she said without rancor. "A scoundrel and a cad."

"My mother loved him, and my sister. They thought the world of him. Still do."

Louisa crossed the small cabin to the window and gazed out at the sinuous, amnesiac water.

"Your sister?"

Eyre Soane tipped back his head as if to blow a smoke ring, then seemed to think better of it. He breathed out the stream of smoke in a sigh, reached with his uninjured arm for a telegraph on the locker by the bed, and held it up.

"She's arrived. I'm going back to Cairo to show her the sights. We'll return to London together. I believe when I get there I shall make a bequest to the National Gallery. Unless I can find a private buyer for *Thetis*. What do you think, Louisa? Would your husband care to purchase the picture? Hang it in the drawing room?"

A rusted cargo boat chugged past, heading north, and the dahabeah began to rock in its wake, rippling waves hitting the craft in long, sloshing tides of brown water. Louisa returned to the door frame, holding to its upright support, feeling the floor rise and fall under her feet. She could not utter the words she'd come to say.

"I should be glad to meet your sister," she said. "I do hope an opportunity will present itself."

FORTY-NINE

❧✦❧

Harriet sat on the back of the donkey, her feet dangling to one side of its belly; the rein was slack and the animal made its own way through the flooded fields that lay behind the river, continuing around the edge of a thicket of strange human-looking cactus plants, as tall as she was. Fouad walked at the donkey's head, holding Dash under one arm. The donkey boy had a thorn in his foot and had stayed behind.

The night before, Harriet had been unable to sleep. She'd been picturing Dr. Woolfe's house, clothed in darkness on the other side of the river, had looked for it out of her window, wondering if it betrayed its presence by a light, but had seen only darkness on the west bank. Remembering the hurry in which Dr. Woolfe had left the dinner, the boorish behavior of Mr. Simpson and Mr. Soane, she urged the donkey on with her heels. She wanted to see Dr. Woolfe, talk to him. She hoped she wasn't too late. He'd mentioned at the dinner that he intended to visit another dig, to the south, out in the desert.

Harriet could make sense of neither her mother nor her supposed suitor. Louisa seemed to have temporarily lost her mind, firing the pistol at Eyre Soane. She was insisting that they leave Luxor the next day, on whatever boat presented itself. If necessary, her mother said, they would travel on one of the cargo boats that passed through laden with elephant tusks and feet, bundles of ostrich feathers, chattering monkeys tethered to the rails. She offered no explanation for what had happened in the garden.

Eyre Soane had shown himself in the worst possible light. Harriet felt repulsed by the thought of him. Lying under the cotton sheet, in a cocoon of mosquito curtains, listening to wild dogs baying in the distance, she'd made a decision. She wasn't ready to leave. She felt at home in Luxor. She had a sense as strong and unstoppable as the surging river that she could find life in this place of death. It was strange to Harriet how the west bank, the knowledge of the rock tombs concealed in the mountains, made life not morbid, as Dr. Grammaticas had feared, but more vivid.

She would apologize for the embarrassment of the dinner party, then beg Dr. Woolfe to take her on as an assistant, allow her to work on the dig until it was concluded. Harriet had a small amount of money; her father had given her some before they left, for emergencies, and when she'd opened the tin that Yael had pressed on her at the railway station, she found not peppermints but sovereigns, wrapped in a note that, in her aunt's familiar handwriting, wished her *bon voyage*. Away from the hotel, she could live on almost nothing; the little she had would last for months and she could lodge with Mrs. Treadwell. She would think about what had happened with Eyre Soane, none of which she could understand, afterward.

They came through the fields, skirting the two giant statues, and began the climb into the hills. Beyond the floodplain, the ground grew dry and arid; the air was hot and still, the silence broken only by the unshod feet of the donkey striking the ground and the slosh of the water skin behind her on its back. Despite the intense heat, Harriet shivered. She never quite grew accustomed to this landscape, never altogether threw off the feeling it had aroused in her the first time she visited, of fear.

The donkey quickened its pace, pricked its ears, as they entered the steep-sided ravine. It was Friday; the site was deserted and the valley looked as desolate as she'd ever seen it. Fouad halted the donkey, dragging on the rein.

"This bad place. Let us leave, Miss Harry."

"No, Fouad. I must see Dr. Woolfe."

Harriet shook the rein, urged the donkey on, and the animal picked its way toward the entrance to the tomb. She slid off its back, not waiting for Fouad's assistance, her feet meeting the ground with a crunch. At the tomb entrance, the usual lamps and matches were arranged neatly on a wooden box. The guard wasn't at his post.

"Stay here, Fouad. Stay with Dash and wait till I come out again. Don't move from here."

Lighting the first lamp that came to hand, Harriet blew out the match and adjusted the wick. She walked in slowly, her eyes growing accustomed to the gloom, keeping one hand in contact with the wall and feeling the curious softness of the rock under the tips of her fingers as she made her way along the passage.

"Dr. Woolfe?"

No answer. At the panel of plaster, she paused, raising the lamp to the queen, arrested in her game, still undecided about where to place her piece.

At the blocked entrance to the tomb, she held the light aloft. Underneath the white stone lintel, a gap had opened up in the rubble. There was an opening of a foot or more in height, the same across. Harriet's heart leaped. Dr. Woolfe had opened the tomb. He was inside, exploring.

She leaned her head through as far as she could. "Dr. Woolfe? Are you there?"

A faint sound of pebbles shifting and sliding came from somewhere inside. He must be there, working. She brought her head out again, her skin crawling with a mix of excitement and dread at the idea of entering the tomb. Straightening up, she inhaled to the pit of her stomach, counting the breaths in and out until she felt steady. The opening was more like a tunnel than a doorway, the remaining rubble underneath still thick. She longed to see what was on the other side of the wall, to see the resting place of the Lady of the Two Lands. And she had to see Dr. Woolfe. It was vital.

Harriet took another deep breath. She wrapped the orange scarf tightly around her head, tied the ends at the back of her neck. Holding the lamp in one hand, pushing the pocket around to the back of her waist, she maneuvered herself through the opening headfirst, as if she were swimming across the heap of remaining rubble, and half fell through to the other side. Setting the lamp down by her feet, she wiped her face on her sleeve and shook the dust from her skirts. Righted the pocket. Her hands were grazed.

"Dr. Woolfe?"

No answer. In front of her was a flight of fifteen or twenty steps, hewn into the rock, leading downward. She picked up the lamp and walked down the steps, her heart thudding with excitement. At the bottom was another doorway. As she stepped through it, every hair on Harriet's body rose. She was in a rectangular chamber, the walls covered in columns of hieroglyphs, painted on a white background. The symbols were bright, the colors vivid and jewel-like. The writing, she saw immediately, related to the funeral ritual. Harriet cried out in awe. She had stepped inside the books of her girlhood. At last, she had arrived.

Turning up the wick, she held up the lamp. The room was large. Farther doorways led off it and in the center were four tall pillars going from the floor to the ceiling, their sides made smooth by plaster, decorated with more hieroglyphs and pictures, all perfectly preserved.

Holding the lamp close to the wall on her right, moving step by slow step, she gasped again and again. The hieroglyphs were beautiful, each one a work of art. The curving serpent was represented; Maat's feather of justice balanced on one side of a pair of scales; the length of twisted flax; the sickle; the seated woman; the sun disk, colored crimson; and again and again, the ankh that symbolized breath. Her eyes came to rest on the heron hieroglyph. Its long legs were striped with black, its breast tufted with feathers, its pose curious and hesitant.

"Dr. Woolfe?"

She longed to read the story told by the signs. The longing was physical, strong and fierce as hunger. She must find Dr. Woolfe without delay, persuade him to allow her to stay and work with him. Straining her ears for evidence of where he was, she called his name again. No answer came.

Dr. Woolfe was not there. Harriet stood for a moment, absorbing the knowledge. She felt a compulsion to go on, to reach the place where the Lady of the Two Lands lay at rest. The flame in the lamp seemed to flicker, despite the stillness of the air. The tomb was hot, hotter than the passage outside.

Gripping her book in its pocket, feeling the soft leather under her fingers, holding up the lamp with her other hand, she walked down another set of steps and around a pillar painted with priests, recognizable by their garb of leopard skins. In the space between four pillars was a pink granite sarcophagus. The stone lid had been heaved off it and was balanced like a playing card between the coffin and the ground. Harriet inched her way toward it, sweat pouring down her back under her dress. Bending over the side, she held the lamp aloft and peered in. Except for a heap of sticks that looked like kindling, some dirty bandages, the sarcophagus was empty.

The queen was gone from her ornate palace of death. Harriet felt sad. She stood still for a minute, then raised her eyes and held up the lamp toward the ceiling. It was a rich violet blue, the color of midnight, lined with gold five-pointed stars, thick with them. The queen had lain under the starriest of all starry skies, the movement of the hands that had painted them seeming to live on in their shapes. As Harriet gazed up at the ceiling, the lamp flickered again. With a flare that lit up the celestial realm, the flame went out.

FIFTY

A party of Italians had arrived earlier in the day and was taking coffee in the gazebo. The exuberance of their language, its extravagant rise and fall, made it sound as if they were debating matters of life and death. Listening from a table in the dining room, by the open doors, Louisa wondered if they could see daubs of oil paint on the ground in the gazebo where the easel had stood, or found a remaining spot of blood outside on the grass, where the gardener had so painstakingly sluiced and scrubbed, and were piecing together the incident. But perhaps they were discussing the dinner menu, the heat, where they would go next.

Louisa lifted a piece of chicken on a fork and ate it slowly. She was taking a late lunch alone; Harriet had gone to the west bank to say farewell to Dr. Woolfe, with Fouad and the dog. Looking at the white meat on the bone on her plate, Louisa put down her fork. The waiter brought a pot of the English breakfast tea that Monsieur Andreas had procured from somewhere, and which Louisa drank at breakfast, lunch, and dinner. She topped up the pot from a jug of hot water and sat on in the dining room.

She had to get Harriet back to Yael. Her own death might come at any moment. It was right, that if one of them were to die, it should be herself. Louisa had had a generous helping of life, more than many, and Harriet's was at its beginning. Still, it was hard to face death. In all its comedy and pathos, life was dear. Its imperfection, its ridiculousnesses and failures, were its more precious parts. She'd never realized it until now. Before she died, she would absolve herself for the mistakes she had made. She'd borne their weight too long and would not take that same burden into death. If she could only say goodbye to Blundell, look on his face once more, she could die in peace. It was a terrible cruelty to die without farewells.

"Good afternoon, madame."

Monsieur Andreas stood by the table, his hands linked behind his back, wearing the white bow tie in which she had first seen him, the wing collar and rusty-looking black tailcoat. Ruler of his small empire by the Nile, which was, more than anything, an empire of the imagination. One of his front teeth was chipped, she noticed for the first time. Teeth were the only part of the body not capable of healing themselves, she'd read somewhere. If they suffered an injury, it was permanent. Louisa wished she could offer him her own unchipped teeth. Soon she would have no need of them.

She eased the tightness in her throat with another sip of tea and replaced the cup on the saucer.

"Good afternoon, Monsieur Andreas."

"You will depart tomorrow?"

She nodded. His manner toward her, solicitous, almost tender, had not altered since the shooting in the garden.

"Yes, as soon as we can find a cabin."

"They say, madame, that once you have drunk the water of the Nile, you are sure to come back."

Louisa wanted to speak to him frankly. She would have liked to explain to Monsieur Andreas that death awaited her, would unfortunately preclude her from coming back to the Luxor Hotel—but that its proximity made these days, even this moment, among the very sweetest of her life. The hotel had appeared shabby on their arrival. Now she recognized it as an oasis of civilization, an outpost if not of England then of Europe, the polished brass planters and fringed carpets, the fish knives and soft-boiled eggs nothing less than miraculous.

"I shall not return," she said gently.

"I am sorry to hear it. We shall feel your departure."

Louisa nodded. "You have made us very comfortable here, monsieur."

He shook his head, rocked back and forth in his dusty black shoes, the soles creaking lightly as they made contact with the wooden floor. It occurred to her for the first time to wonder where he lived; in the hotel, she supposed, in a room tucked away somewhere. A permanent guest. He'd said once that his family came from Alexandria. She had never seen him go beyond the arch at the front of the hotel.

Louisa wound a loose coil of hair back into its pin as she rose from the chair, leaving her napkin in a heap on the table. Outside, the Italians roared with laughter.

Upstairs, in the simple room, Louisa emptied the chest of drawers and the wardrobe. She heaped her chemises, stockings, and the green veil in a pile on the bed, set about brushing and folding and pairing. One day years from now, a day that she would not see herself, this time would be the past, could be folded away flat in a trunk. Locked and consigned to an attic. Rendered harmless, its colors faded, passions spent. Harriet was an adult and would survive without a mother. Everyone had to, if they lived.

She retrieved the gun from the dressing-table drawer. Its nozzle was blackened but the barrel had grown cold, the discharged shot forgotten. Rewrapping it in the old blouse, she wondered whether Blundell had noticed its absence and felt a twinge of regret. She ought to have told him she was taking it. He might have been disturbed by a burglar; gone to get the gun and found it missing. She hoped Rosina hadn't been careless about locking the doors.

The packing complete, Louisa moved to the stool at the dressing table and looked at herself in the mirror. She was perspiring, too warm in her stays and stockings and the bustle petticoat under her dress. A fallen hank of hair lay heavy on her neck again; she'd lost more pins and had never succeeded in obtaining any in Egypt. Her chignon had become a makeshift affair.

She lifted the fallen lock and secured it with a pin. It fell out immediately, lolled again on her shoulder. On impulse, she took up her nail scissors and snipped it off, close to the root. Holding the tress between two fingers, she felt its silky length and weight. Blundell had loved her hair. She would tie the dark hank in a ribbon for Harriet to give to him.

Her head felt lighter without it, her neck cooler. Another of the coils of the chignon, from the right side of her head, was undone and about to fall. She picked up the scissors again and sheared that off too. Intoxicated by what she had done, by the sense of release it brought, Louisa pulled out another pin, released another coil of hair, and continued. It took only minutes to divest herself of the hair she had worried over and cared for her entire life.

She looked in the mirror again. The Louisa Heron who had set sail from London had died already. Some other creature had been born in her place, an old woman, thin-faced and wary-looking, her skin darkened by the sun despite all the care she had taken to try and avoid it. The woman's eyes looked haunted.

She reached into the back of the dressing-table drawer, groping among rolling buttons, a couple of worn silver piastres, for the note from Mr. Hamilton and read it again. *Death is coming for sure.* The words seemed to dance before her eyes. If only she knew when. Was it to be today? In a month's time? Two months'? It was the not knowing that was difficult.

Sweat was darkening the armpits of her dress; her ankles were swollen and her fingers puffy. Louisa eased off her shoes, undid the hooks and eyes at the back of her dress, stepped out of it, and left it where it lay. Releasing the bow at the waist of her petticoat, she loosened her stays and lay down on the bed, wondering how her life might have been different if she had lived it without corsets.

The bed was soft underneath her; the cotton mattress seemed to hold her in its embrace. She missed Blundell with a sharp, incurable ache, and at the thought that she would never see him again, the pain increased. She considered her sons, one by one, feeling the same awe for each as when they had been newly born. They had seemed miracles, from another realm. They still did seem that.

Closing her eyes, Louisa saw an English orchard, its hardy, bent-limbed trees laden with white blossom. She did not resist; she allowed the memories to come, starting as a feeling in her body of being heavy. A sense of time standing still.

• • •

It was April and Louisa had not left the house on the cliff top since Christmas. Her mother, Amelia Newlove, had put it about in Dover that she was ill, with a wasting disease. Only her older sisters knew the truth. That she was not wasting but expanding, her belly a hard, tight fruit, her breasts doubled in size. Mother even insisted on keeping it from Anna, eleven years old at the time and a strange, half-wild girl who spent her days on the beach, watching, waiting for Jesus.

So that Anna should not see her undressed, Louisa had moved into Hepzibah's bedroom. Hepzibah hadn't visited since the last, fateful, summer. Her boater still hung from its elastic on the nail on the back of the door; her sampler was framed on the wall—*And now abideth Faith, Hope, Charity, these three; but the greatest of these is Charity*—spelled out in uneven scarlet cross-stitch, fading in the beam of sun that fell into the room in the early morning, then moved on, left it in shadow for the rest of the day.

It was a cold spring but no one called it that. They all termed it *bitter*. Everything coming late, said the old midwife who trudged up from the village to look Louisa over every week or two, feel her belly. Amelia Newlove, determined that no one at all should know, was keeping the doctor away. She would die, she said, if they did know; the shame would kill her. Louisa felt as if she had died already. Augustus, who'd told her that he loved her, was gone. She, who had declared that she loved him too, remained.

She stood in the kitchen at the low stone sink, peeling potatoes, gouging out black spots of rot from the white flesh. Burnt umber. Flake white. Ivory black. The words ran around her mind, her mind that had been dull and slow since the autumn, like her movements. As if she, huge and lumbering as she was, was reduced; as if the painting had stolen the life from her.

"Her time's near," Mrs. Ditch said to Amelia Newlove.

"I don't believe so," Amelia said, her lips tight. "Not yet."

Louisa felt restless. She went into the garden after Mrs. Ditch had left and wandered around the inside of the hawthorn hedge, her cloak thrown over her nightgown. The forget-me-nots were out, their little blue heads scattering the earth like beads. The grass was soft and tender, a bright emerald green, and the frogs splashing in the gully. At the sound of hooves approaching in the lane, she hurried back inside and stood behind the kitchen door, listening. Hoping, for the thousandth time, to smell cigar smoke on the air. Hear a deep voice pronouncing her name. A cart rolled on past the flint house, two girls laughing on the back of it.

She'd taken the broom from the scullery and swept the bedroom, banged the rugs out of the window, cleaned the glass with vinegar. She polished the old brass candlestick on the mantelpiece and blackened the grate, then stood on a chair and explored the corners of the ceiling with a feather duster, half hoping she would fall. While her hands were busy, her mind was numbed. It was almost as good as sleep. She was waiting. There was nothing to do but wait for what was going to happen.

Anna had been sent away to an aunt. All the others had gone to a wedding in the town. Her elder sister Lavinia squeezed her shoulders before they set off, then put her hands on her belly, shyly, one on each side.

"I hate to leave you here alone, Izzy. I wish you could come with us."

"You can tell me all about it when you get back."

Louisa's voice was brusque. Sympathy from anyone threatened to prize the lid off some great reservoir inside, of anguish. It was easier to face her mother's fury, Mrs. Ditch's avoidance of her eyes, except when she rolled forward the lower lids to check her blood.

She felt easier once they'd left. She had bread and milk for supper, standing up, looking out at the plum blossom strewn over the grass, sodden confetti, turning brown. Brewed a cup of the raspberry leaf tea that Mrs. Ditch said could bring things on, and went to bed early, before the others returned, lying on her side with her head flat on the mattress, the pillow under her belly.

Louisa woke at three in the morning with a sense of urgency. It was pitch dark, no moonlight and not a hint of dawn either. As dark as dark could be. For a long minute, nothing happened. Then a sharp, rippling pain ran through her belly like a knife slicing at her from inside. With both hands, she felt the contours of her stomach through the sheet, felt the taut intention from within. It was a fortnight before her sixteenth birthday and the waiting was over.

She got out of the bed and knelt by it, praying to God to let her die, resting her elbows on the mattress, the weight of her stomach pulling her forward. Amelia Newlove found her at dawn, still on her knees. She helped her up, sent Lavinia down the lane for Mrs. Ditch, and put on a kettle. In the lull that followed, she stroked Louisa's forehead, bent, and kissed her hair.

"I'm sorry," she said. "This is all my fault."

Lying on the bed at the Luxor Hotel, Louisa woke to darkness, feeling drugged, staring at the roughly plastered wall, unable to reconcile it with anything she knew. Turning over, she slept again, deeply and dreamlessly.

The baby was red-faced, old, and ugly. It looked like its father. A girl, said Mrs. Ditch with what sounded like pleasure. Louisa heard the words with disgust. Another girl. The creature screamed more loudly than she would have thought possible, writhed in her arms, would only be pacified by the production of her nipple.

Amelia Newlove stood in the doorway, looking at them both. "I'm not having it," she said. "I won't stand for it, Louisa. Him getting away scot-free and you ruined. I won't have it."

The baby altered over the weeks. She wasn't ugly, Louisa saw. She was watchful and calm, pale as chalk. Looked like no one but herself. The little stump at her center dried and shriveled to nothing. Her hair came through black and silky, covering a strawberry mark on the back of her head. Louisa couldn't name her. They called her Baby.

The two of them stayed in the house, living in what had been Hepzibah's room, Baby sleeping in a drawer lined with blankets, under the sampler. *And now abideth Faith, Hope, Charity, these three; but the greatest of these is Charity.*

It was Whitsun. Baby was two months old. Amelia Newlove came into the room and Louisa scrambled to her feet, feeling guilty. She had been playing with her. Kissing her tummy, making funny noises with her lips, which the baby watched with eyes that were serious, as if they had already done a lifetime of seeing, several lifetimes.

"Oh, Baby," Louisa had said. "How I love you."

"None of that, Izzy," Amelia Newlove said. "We can't have any of that. And anyway, it's time."

"Time for what?"

"This can't go on, Louisa."

They were outside, cloaks on. Louisa had not been out; the world had altered. It was vast, the grass noisy under their feet and gulls screeching from the cliffs. The scent of life was overpowering, could have choked her. She had Baby under her cloak, wrapped in her arms, asleep.

Louisa followed her mother in the direction of the dower house. Heart thumping, in case Augustus should be in residence, she watched her mother lift the great iron knocker and let it come crashing down, as if the door would split in two, as if it were a tree struck by lightning.

He wasn't there. His wife answered the door. Louisa knew it was she, although she had never seen her before. Dignified, was what she thought. The woman had fair hair, smooth and thick. A kind face, with lips that made you want to look at them and listen to the words that spilled from them.

"Can I help you?" she said.

"I hope so, ma'am," Amelia Newlove said, gesturing to Louisa to step forward, reaching in under Louisa's cloak. "Because no one else can."

Louisa didn't remember what happened next. Only the feeling of emptiness in her arms, the warmth and the small weight gone. Gone, as they walked back along the cliff top, the gulls fallen silent, and the grass, the sky so low over their heads Louisa felt it would smother her.

"This time is finished," Amelia Newlove said. "As if it never happened. Anna's coming home next week."

They passed a line of little girls, dressed in white. They fell silent as they passed Louisa, staring at her with round blue eyes.

FIFTY-ONE

Harriet moved backward, away from the sarcophagus, until her hands encountered a wall, a limit to the darkness. Leaning against it, still holding the lamp in one hand, she tried to think. Dr. Woolfe wasn't here. She should have known it. He'd told her himself that he was going away. She called his name again, her voice high and fearful, and was answered only by an echo.

Her chest had constricted in the moment of the lamp going out; her heart was thudding and her lungs were tightening. The familiar feeling afflicted her of the air having lost its capacity to satisfy. Closing her eyes, she forced herself to breathe down to her stomach. One, two, three. Out through the mouth. One . . . two . . .

The darkness was absolute and Harriet was disoriented. She could not picture where she was in the chamber, or the direction of the steps that led out of it. She took a step forward, pointing her toe in front of her, feeling for obstacles, before putting down her foot. After several steps, she reached a corner. With one hand touching the wall, she inched her way along, moving a little faster, feeling an urgency to get out of the tomb. The ground disappeared from under her. She fell off what seemed to be a ledge, about a foot in height. When she'd recovered her breath, rubbed her knees and her grazed knuckles, she crawled back up to where she'd fallen from, inched her way back to where she believed she must have been standing before.

She set off in the other direction, more cautiously. This time, after moving a short distance, she fell down another flight of steps. She'd seen before the light went out that the tomb didn't end in the chamber that contained the sarcophagus. She pictured herself walking down the steps, farther inside the earth, getting more lost.

Feeling in her pocket for the water bottle, she eased out the cork and took a sip, felt a warm spilled drop run down her chin. The bottle was almost full. She felt tired. She would have to do what she feared to do and sit down. Trying to put out of her mind that she might be sitting on human bones or a nest of scorpions, she eased herself to a sitting position, hugging her knees through her skirt.

She dared not move any farther without knowing which way she was going. It was better to stay still. The tomb was large. A maze of chambers and antechambers. There was air in it and all she needed to do was to keep breathing and remain where she was until help came. Help would come.

"You won't suffocate," she said aloud.

It was a comfort to hear a voice. She spoke again, more resolutely.

"You won't die, Harriet. You're not going to perish—"

At the word *perish*, she began to scream, a series of harsh, staccato cries that flew around the chamber. Then she stopped. Her throat hurt and no one could hear her. The rocks were deaf. Shouting would only exhaust her.

Harriet opened her eyes. She kept them open for a few seconds, hoping they might even now adjust, that some vision would become available. Nothing. She shut her eyes again, tightly, so that the darkness was of her own creation. It was a horrible thing, to have your eyes open in the dark.

Fouad was outside. He would be alarmed when it began to grow dark and he would go to the house on the mountainside. If he was present, Dr. Woolfe would come to assist her. If he was not, Fouad would have to cross the river to summon help. It must be getting toward evening, already. Most likely, Fouad had already gone to raise the alarm.

The silence was roaring in her ears, merging with the darkness and the steady, oppressive heat. Her eyes hurt. She opened them and immediately closed them again. Such darkness was a horror. It was death. The Lady of the Two Lands had endured it, perhaps for centuries. But she was no longer here. Harriet was quite alone.

She brushed away a wetness from her cheek and felt in her pocket for her journal. Pressing it against her chest, she pictured the vivid red hue of the cover. She sniffed the leather and felt the creased softening of corners, the ties, with one side smooth and the other softly rough. She pictured in her mind the creamy paleness of pages, the patterns that covered them, her own signs. The spell she had written in December, in London, that she would escape her bedroom. The one she'd written in Alexandria, that she would reach Thebes, meet the man with the paintbrush. And another she'd written since, of herself playing senet with the Lady of the Two Lands, engaged in her own game of chance, making a path through the trials and obstacles and opportunities of life.

Laying the book on her lap, she pressed her back against the rock. With her eyes closed, she could still see the flame of the lamp as it had been before it went out. The outline of the flame and the pool of light around it. She thought of all the lamps she had known, from when she first became aware of her own life, and used to watch the night-light, trying to stay awake longer than it did, aware that darkness and sleep were almost the same but not the same, that there could be darkness but no sleep. Louisa always expected her to be afraid of the dark but Harriet remembered a time before she was ill, when she was not afraid of the dark. It was only when the dark filled up with the whistling creature that sat on her chest and prevented her breathing, the thing she could hear but not see, that she became afraid.

She pictured herself as a girl in the attic room, listening to the wind outside, trying to hear life itself, fathom her place in it. The bed had seemed huge, a world in itself. She saw herself with Rosina, sitting on her lap, cushioned by her plump thighs and stomach, her smells of boiled onions and cough drops, her even kindness, and remembered how she loved her when she didn't know any better, didn't know that servants weren't for loving. She had wished that Rosina was her mother, had told Louisa so at the age of three or four and been surprised, first by Louisa's laughter then by her tears.

She considered Louisa, who had been so dissatisfied with her daughter, so anxious for her transformation into another girl, for as long as Harriet could remember. From when she was born, it seemed to her now. Harriet had believed as a child that she must have been a foundling. Later, she understood from her reading that it was a common conceit amongst girls who fancied themselves misunderstood. It wasn't the simple truth that she didn't look like Louisa that caused those thoughts to flourish. She did, after all, take after her father. It was the knowledge that on the inside she did not resemble Louisa, that in their hearts and minds they were somehow unrelated. Strange to each other. That as much as Harriet had wished for another mother, Louisa too had wanted another daughter. She never said so but Harriet felt it. The signs were in her voice, her eyes.

In the hours that followed, Harriet grew calm. Opening her eyes, she let the darkness wash over her and welcomed it. She need not fear it. The chamber was the same as it had been by lamplight. A place of beauty and magic. Nothing had changed. What a fool she had been. She had no feelings for Eyre Soane. And he had none for her. She'd always known it, deep down, if she'd only admitted it to herself. She had no wish to see him ever again. In that, at least, Louisa had been right.

If she survived, she would carry out her plan and plead with Eberhardt Woolfe to take her on as his assistant. If she could assist in the exploration of the tomb, help record its treasures of pictures and hieroglyphs, then whatever happened afterward, she would have done something exceptional that could never be taken from her. At whatever age she might die, she would do so in the knowledge that she had lived.

The dust caught again at the back of her throat and she swallowed, tasted its sour, enduring strength. This dust was what every person returned to. The small clay figures of servants and handmaids, the shabtis that the people who made this chamber put in the tombs with the mummies, were longer-lasting than the people they represented. Death was a greater truth than life. The wrapped bodies of kings and queens were no more than macabre dolls, the vain attempts of the ancients to defeat the human foe.

The darkness changed again. It became iron, pressing on her from every direction, constricting her. She hated to breathe it in, feel its intimate reach in her mouth and ears, between her fingers, entering the pores of her skin. It was death, her body telegraphed to her mind. She heard herself whimpering and experienced an animal fear that counting could not tame.

The minutes, even the seconds, seemed to pass very slowly, as if time wasn't a line, as she had always imagined, a line that might have been drawn by a pencil, that went from birth to death, but something in three dimensions, someplace where gravity failed, and she drifted like a leaf caught in the wind. Only now had she appreciated the grandeur of a moment. A heartbeat. Three thousand years in the tomb might be fifty thousand in the land above. Time was an altered thing here; it too had died. Was stilled. She was its frail representative, its ghost from the overworld. It was the Egyptians who had invented time, Herodotus said. It was they who first divided a year into months, a day into hours. Harriet felt as if she was in the time before time, when such divisions had not been devised, when time simply was.

She thought about the queen. She'd been young once, and perfectly alive, must have zigzagged across the Nile in a felucca, eaten the muddy-tasting perch and perhaps had a pet cat that wore gold earrings. She had brushed her black hair, watched the moon out of a window, and dreamed of a man. Harriet felt sorry that the girl who grew up to be the Lady of the Two Lands had not been allowed to rest undisturbed in her coffin of pink stone. As she thought about her, she pictured her cartouche and at last its meaning came to her. The queen was called Nefer-hor, beautiful of face, and she was beloved of the goddess Isis.

Unwrapping the orange scarf from her head, she matched the corners to each other and laid it on the ground. Lying down on her side, she felt for the soft cotton with her hand, rested her cheek on it. Sharp shards of rock, or bone, pressed through it, painfully, into her flesh. She groped in her pocket for her journal, laid it on the scarf, and rested her face on its cover. The leather was smooth and blank, skin against her skin. Resting her head on it, she slept.

FIFTY-TWO

Eberhardt Woolfe was dressed and drinking his first cup of coffee when the pounding on the door began. Setting down the cup, he emerged from the kitchen, swallowing. It was barely light and he felt annoyed. It was the foreman's role to deal with the complaints and problems the workers had, their crises when children fell sick, wives died, or they themselves had accidents and could no longer work. Eberhardt took the view that for every problem there was a solution, was willing in all cases to see what help could be found, but he disliked having emergencies thrust at him. If he could not get away from the dramas of the living here, there could be no escape anywhere. "*Ach*, what is it now?" he muttered to himself, reaching the door, opening it.

On the step, her head wrapped in a green turban, was Harriet's mother, Mrs. Heron. Behind her, in evening dress, stood Monsieur Andreas from the Luxor Hotel.

"Good morning, Mrs. Heron. Monsieur Andreas. What can—"

"Is she here, Dr. Woolfe?" said Mrs. Heron.

He struggled to take in the meaning of the question. "Forgive me?"

"My daughter. Is she here?"

"Your daughter?" He shook his head, befuddled. "*Nein*, she is not."

Mrs. Heron broke into a wail and covered her face with her hands.

"She was over on this side," Monsieur Andreas said. "She has not returned."

"Come in, please."

Eberhardt held open the door, led them into the single large room that he used for study, dining, and sitting, that had no satisfactory name. Swiping dust from the leather seat of a chair, he helped Mrs. Heron into it. Pulled his own forward for Monsieur Andreas. Was Harriet with the Englishman? Had she eloped with the fellow? A tide of anger ran through him and he believed for a moment he would smash something, pick up the scarab that he had been working on the previous night, after his return, and hurl it at the wall. The fury was not with Harriet. It was not even with Soane, cad though he'd appeared from the first to be, in his ludicrous clothing, his sneering superciliousness. It was with himself. He ought to have acted. He had been a coward.

Mrs. Heron was hunched forward on the chair, rocking backward and forward, her hands still clasped over her face. She was dressed in a traveling coat over what appeared to be a nightgown, her head curiously wrapped in a length of green muslin, and she was moaning like an animal. From the other side of the small room, Monsieur Andreas regarded her with a look of helpless pity.

"Take some coffee, Mrs. Heron."

Eberhardt returned to the kitchen, stood by the slab of pink granite on which he kneaded bread, chopped onions. Testing the bottom of the coffeepot on the palm of his hand, he found it still hot, almost burning. He filled two cups, placed them on a tray, with a bowl of sugar, a slender silver spoon. Ritual. Routine. They were always there, present when people died. Vanished. Altered. Eloped. He returned to the room.

"*Bitte*, Mrs. Heron," he said, his voice even, as he put the cup of coffee into her hand. "Let me understand what has happened. Where is Harriet now?"

"We don't know, Doctor," she wailed. "What time did she leave you yesterday?"

Eberhardt stared at her white, upturned face, her swollen eyes. He was confounded again.

"Leave me?"

Mrs. Heron ran her hands over her covered head.

"She was here. She came to say goodbye to you, Dr. Woolfe."

Eberhardt began pacing the room while he readjusted what he thought he knew and tried to reconcile two feelings that rose in him: exultation, at the idea that Harriet had not run away with the Englishman; dread, that some accident had befallen her.

"I returned last night, late," he said. "I've been away for two days."

Monsieur Andreas put down the untouched cup of coffee.

"The boy Fouad isn't back either. Nor the dog."

Eberhardt had a strange sensation in his body, as if everything around him, his papers, his tools, the grand piano, had altered, moved from the foreground to the background, become less solid and real than the urgency that was coursing through him, making it impossible to be seated, causing his palms to sting. He knew where Harriet was.

"I shall go ahead to the dig," he said, bowing to Mrs. Heron. "You can follow. My foreman will conduct you to the site when he arrives."

"It is too late," Mrs. Heron said, her voice flat. "She has perished, Dr. Woolfe. It was all foreseen, before she even left London." She began to cry. "I don't want to live. It should have been me. I believed it was me."

Eberhardt Woolfe felt another spurt of anger. This was a crisis, undeniably, but to give up hope when hope could remain was wrong. It was morally wrong. It hindered fate. His eyes fell on the scarab. It had proved perfect when cleaned, the green malachite divested of its casing of dirt and mortar and bat droppings; by the look of it, it might have left the manufactory last week. He picked it up from his desk and went to where she sat, pressed it into her hand, closed her cold fingers around it.

"Please, Mrs. Heron. This symbolizes rebirth. You must not despair." He left the house on the hillside, leaving the door hanging open. Unable to wait for the foreman to bring up his horse from the pasture, he went on foot, running along the narrow path made by the horse's hooves, toward the valley. By the gathering light of dawn, the landscape of limestone mountains and valleys looked blue, unearthly as the moon.

Harriet's black donkey stood in the entrance to the passage, its head hanging. Next to it, Fouad was sitting on the ground. He scrambled to his feet and saluted. The boy looked frightened out of his wits.

Eberhardt took his hand.

"Don't be afraid," he said in Arabic. "Where is she?"

Fouad gestured toward the passage.

"Miss Harry inside."

"Why didn't you come for me?"

"She said I must stay here," Fouad said.

The dog appeared and began springing at Eberhardt's knees in a frenzy of recognition, the shrill bark echoing up and down the valley.

He reached down and rubbed its head, trying to think clearly. She must have gone through. The opening was too narrow for him but it must have admitted her. She was inside, he was sure of it. The dog continued to yap as Eberhardt Woolfe lit a lamp, grabbed the pickax, and ran along the passage to the blocked doorway. He tried first to force his own broad shoulders through the opening and, failing to do so, began swinging the pick with all his might at the edges of the aperture, smashing through rock and rubble, careless of the amulets and shabtis and scarabs that flew through the air.

Harriet woke to the sound of hammering. For a minute, she remained where she lay, quite still. The sound was faint, so slight and distant, it might have come from inside her own head. Sitting up, she took a drink from the tin bottle and listened again. She could hear another noise. The faint strains of a bark, recognizable by its rhythm, its persistence, still overlaid by the sound of demolition.

Getting to her feet, shaking out her skirt, Harriet wound her scarf around her neck. Holding her journal to her chest with one hand, putting the other straight out in front of her, taking one cautious step after another, she followed the source of the sound. She walked into a stone pillar, bruising her elbow, then moved away from it and continued, inching forward, until she tripped on an obstruction. It was a step. The step led to another, moving upward. As she crawled up them, on her hands and knees, the sound grew louder, almost deafening.

"Dr. Woolfe?" she called, as the faintest glimmer of what was unmistakably light appeared before her.

The hammering ceased. "Miss Heron? Is it you?"

"Yes. It is me."

"Come, Miss Heron. *Ach*, please come to me."

Reaching the top of the steps, shaking all over, Harriet crawled back through the opening. A pair of hands reached for her, helped her to stand, and in the bright light of a lamp she found herself blinking, looking at Eberhardt Woolfe.

"I am sorry," she said. "I thought you were inside. I should not have entered the tomb before you. It is beautiful in there. Miraculous." Eberhardt Woolfe shook his head, then stepped forward and took hold of her, enveloped her for a long, enduring moment in his arms.

FIFTY-THREE

Sitting on the wooden chair, with a table beside her bearing a bowl of water, a bar of soap, a pile of clean white rags torn from a nightdress brought from England, Yael was humming. She encircled the squirming body on her lap with one arm and with the other reached for a scrap of cotton, dipped it into the water, and squeezed it out, dabbing a corner on a thinning oval of translucent soap. "Send her victorious," she said, drawing the cloth over the child's forehead.

She plunged the rag back into the water, squeezed it out again, and applied it to the little girl's right eye, cleaning it from the inside corner to the outside. The lashes were long and lustrous, each one thick and black as a miniature quill.

The infant sent up a scream. "There, there," said Yael.

Wiping the other eye in the same way, she rinsed out the cloth, gave the girl's nose and mouth a rub with the damp, soft cotton. Cleaned her cheeks and ears, dabbed her dry. She looked like a child again. She'd ceased crying, was looking at Yael curiously from between the long lashes. Her eyes were still healthy, the iris clearly defined, delicate as a watercolor. Only the youngest children, and animals, did not know that one was foreign. Or, at any rate, gave one the benefit of the doubt.

Yael experienced a sudden yawning ache inside, that she would never experience her own baby wriggling and warm on her lap. She wanted to tell the mother that her child was beautiful, a miracle, that she *trailed clouds of glory*. She could not, knew better, understood that such remarks risked bringing down the evil eye. "God save the Queen," she said, dropping the cloth back into the bowl, lifting the child up underneath her arm, handing her back to the mother. "Clean water, Suraya, please. Another rag."

Suraya put the other bowl down on the table, took away the used one. Yael added the alum herself, one teaspoonful per half bowl of boiled water, stirring it in until the white powder dissolved. The mothers only wanted her to treat the children who were already affected by eye disease but Yael was trying through Suraya to teach them the value of prevention. She had spent long hours speaking to her, with Mustapha acting as translator, at the villa. Washing the hands and faces of their children. Explaining the meaning of hygiene.

She and Suraya had developed a rhythm for the mornings at the clinic. First, Yael treated the children. Afterward, Suraya demonstrated to the women the washing of the doll, explained the connection between dirt and disease. Only then did they distribute the rations bought with the donations from the congregation of St. Mark's.

Yael heard a knock and looked up. Through the crack in the door she saw a long robe, draped on a tall, upright figure. Sheikh Hamada. He had never been to the clinic. She handed back the child she was about to treat and hurried toward the door, held it open.

"What a surprise. An honor. Welcome, Sheikh Hamada. Come in, please."

He remained outside, his eyes flickering over the inside of the room, then resuming their gaze down the alley. The women were dragging their veils back over their faces and had fallen silent. Suraya was scrambling for her burka. Yael understood that the sheikh could not come in. She removed her apron, dried her hands on it, and dropped it on the wooden bed. Picking up her umbrella, she stepped outside.

"I am honored that you have come to visit us, Sheikh."

He stood a couple of paces away, his bearing as proud as on the first occasion she had met him, his gaze as elusive, fixed on a spot beyond her shoulder. She put up the umbrella, feeling a sudden need for some form of shelter. Not from the sun but from the scorch of the sheikh's presence, his unwillingness to engage in social niceties.

She answered the question he had not asked.

"Yes, all is going well. You see that the women attend," she said. "They listen. They take the rations we've been able to find since the vicar's welcome change of heart. You were right, Sheikh, about the food. Some of the children are improving now, in their health. In everything. The next thing will be to get them to school."

He nodded. His silence was unnerving her.

"I am grateful to you," she said. "Without your encouragement, they might never have come."

"The time is finished for this work."

"What do you mean?"

"Your work here is over, Sitti."

Yael peered at him. She could understand the words he spoke but not what he meant by them. Half a dozen more little children played in the dust close to where they stood, the corners of their eyes studded with flies, their hands sticky with dirt. She felt a surge of indignation, like heat.

"Oh, no," she said, shaking her head. "The work is not over, Sheikh. Far from it. It has only just begun."

"You must close your clinic. It is time to go home."

Putting down the umbrella, she looked him straight in the face. "Don't you care for your people?"

"We care for them, and for those who would help them. I am trying to inform you of something."

"I do not care to hear it, Sheikh Hamada."

Yael went back inside, controlling her urge to slam the door, closing it quietly behind her. Shaking with anger, she tied her apron strings behind her back and resumed her seat, holding out her hands to receive a little boy. He seemed not to see Yael as he arrived on her lap. His swollen eyelids were stuck together with dried yellow secretions and his ribs, clearly visible, narrow as matchsticks, rose and fell with each breath. He sat still, not, Yael sensed, from an absence of fear but from a state of weakness too great to allow for bawling.

"Claptrap, sir," she called toward the door to the street, baptizing the fresh cloth in the clean water, squeezing it out. "Drivel, twaddle, and bunkum." She wiped her own eyes on her sleeve and, with the greatest gentleness, began to clean the little boy's eyes. "Jack fell down and broke his crown," she whispered. "And Jill came tumbling after."

FIFTY-FOUR

There was a tap on wood and Harriet jumped up. She put down her book, opened the door of her room, and looked into a pair of kind, soft-edged brown eyes. Disappointment spread through her like ink in water. She could barely get the words out.

"Monsieur Andreas. Good morning."

"Mademoiselle." He smiled at her over a wooden tray on which were a lace cloth, a sprig of bright flowers in a vase, and a battered teapot. "How are you this morning?"

"Quite recovered, thank you."

He nodded.

"The *Amon-Ra* has moored. There is a cabin available. They sail this evening, Miss Heron," he said. "I have informed Mama."

Harriet nodded, unable to speak as she took the tray. Closing the door, she put the tray on the table by the bed and sat down. She had believed Dr. Woolfe would come. She felt he had something to say to her, something urgent.

The next knock on the door was unmistakably Louisa's. She came in, her head wrapped in her green veil. Her body looked altered and it crossed Harriet's mind that Louisa didn't have on her stays, her bustle. She looked flatter and thinner. Harriet had been speechless when she first saw Louisa's cropped head. It seemed to make her a different person. Louisa could give no explanation for why she had done it. Only said she'd thought she had no need of hair, no need of anything. "And fortunately, I was right," she'd added.

"Good morning, Mother."

"We shall leave tonight, Harriet, on the *Amon-Ra*. I have spoken to the captain."

"I am not ready, Mother. I don't want to go."

"Harriet, I am your mother. I am taking you to your aunt. Pack your trunk and prepare to leave."

Louisa spoke in the stilted voice that Harriet recognized from when they were still in London, as if she needed careful handling, could not be trusted to bear the truth.

When Louisa had gone, Harriet leaned on the windowsill looking out over the river. In the urgency of his grip, the way he held her to him as if they were one flesh, she'd understood something she'd never understood from his conversation. She had seen Eberhardt Woolfe as a teacher, someone who could lead her into the world she had longed to enter. Until she stepped out of the darkness, blinking at the awful brilliance of the light, she had not seen him as a man.

The west bank had almost disappeared in a haze of heat. It looked colorless, the hills displaying none of their complexity. She turned away from the window and filled the ewer, splashing water over her face and rinsing her hands, examined the cuts and grazes that covered them. What had she imagined that he might have to say to her? He had told her, early in their acquaintance, that he was married. Have you left a wife behind in Germany, she heard herself asking. She groaned, remembering how little she had meant by the question, and the unexpectedness of the answer.

In the garden below, someone was beating rugs with great hollow thumps; farther away, the muezzin cleared his throat and commenced his singing summons to prayer. The heat was oppressive; it was 120 degrees Fahrenheit by the thermometer on the wall downstairs in the lobby.

Harriet had a familiar sense of what she longed for being out of her reach. The clarity she'd experienced in the darkness about what she would do if she lived was being eroded, supplanted by the feeling that she must look after Louisa. That it was her responsibility to keep her mother safe, get her home to London. Louisa wasn't herself. She'd had a reckless air about her since the shooting, compounded by her strange appearance now that she'd cut her hair. Harriet wondered again if her mother was losing her mind.

The trunks were stowed in the cabin; Harriet and Louisa stood side by side on the deck of the *Amon-Ra*, under the canvas awning, holding the railing. In front of them, on the bank, Monsieur Andreas waved a white silk handkerchief in the still air. Louisa held the posy of roses that he'd presented her with, lifting it in the air as Monsieur Andreas kissed his hand, hurried along the bank under the trees, calling *au revoir*. He had asked to be permitted to keep the painting of Harriet that Mr. Soane had abandoned in the gazebo. It would remind him, he said, of her mother. Harriet had agreed.

The last blue-robed sailor climbed up onto the stern of the boat, the sails filled, and the *Amon-Ra*, with its rowing boat being pulled along behind, forged its way toward the center of the river. The inundation grew greater every day; the Nile looked as wide as a sea. Harriet moved to the other side of the deck and looked out at the west bank, her eyes searching the shore for a tall figure, running, commanding the *rais* to bring them ashore again. The shore on the other side of the river remained empty but for a couple of donkey boys, a group of women bent over their washing, pounding it with stones. She gazed beyond them, at the splendor and stillness of the mountains, held on to them with her eyes until the familiar contours were lost to view. She felt as if she was being torn from Thebes like a tooth.

Louisa sat in a deck chair, leaning her head against the wooden frame. Fouad stood a little distance away, his polished shoes laced on his feet, facing north. He had recovered from his fright once he knew they were returning to Alexandria. Harriet threw herself down on the chair next to Louisa's, wrapped her scarf around her head.

"At last," Louisa said. "We are on our way home."

"Yes, Mother. It seems that we are."

Harriet felt empty. She was well, for the first time in her adult life. Her breath ran freely and silently into her body, it left without effort. She could breathe like anyone else. But good health was only part of being alive. Going back to London seemed to mean the end of her life, not its beginning. She had regained her health in Luxor but she had not succeeded in starting to live.

Her book rested on her lap in its pocket, one corner digging into her thigh. Harriet did not reach to touch it. It seemed disconnected from her, mocked her with its corners, its implacable, closed cover, its self-contained and secret existence. It was nothing more than a book, leather and paper stitched together, the words meaningless marks, not words of power at all.

Rising from the deck chair, she moved to the railings again and took the book out of her pocket. She held it out over the water. She was about to release it, drop it into the Nile, when some instinct prevented her from doing so. Gripping the cover between her fingers, she opened the book and looked at the title that she had written in red, months earlier, for the book of spells to help her not in death but in life. *Magic for the Living.*

There was no magic for the living, Harriet told herself, feeling something shrink and shrivel inside her, some vital part of herself slip into sleep or death. They were just words on paper. Doing up the ties, she replaced the journal in her pocket. Then she went to the cabin, knelt on the floor by her bunk, and wept.

FIFTY-FIVE

From his house on the hillside, Eberhardt Woolfe watched through his binoculars as the *Amon-Ra*, the vivid flash of orange on its deck, was lost to view. He threw down the binoculars and went inside, banging the screen door. Sitting down at the Bösendorfer, he adjusted his jacket so that it hung over the back of the stool, placed his foot on the pedal. He ran his fingers up and down the ivories and the notes rang out freely through the room, animating the air, conjuring Europe even in their disorder, their raw form.

Leaning over the keys, he embarked on the broken chords of the nocturne with his left hand, the songlike melody with the right. His fingers, as always at first, were stiff and reluctant, but as he played, he forgot his fingers and was aware only of Chopin's music, felt in his bones its subtle insistence on beauty, its call to the soul to rise, venerate the world.

Nocturne Opus 9, No. 2, had been his favorite from when he was a young man, from the time when he had no cause for melancholy but found it anyway. Eberhardt had a feeling of loss. Not the usual dull ache of Kati's absence, her interminable silence, but a new sense, strong and present as the smell of fresh paint, of something missing. An absence that put all things awry.

He shut the music book and moved to the desk.

"*Ach*, Kati," he said. "She is gone. And now I have lost her also."

Lighting the lamp, the tall one that he used for close work, he unwrapped the new piece he was working on, a shabti. Picking up the dry paintbrush, he began to work at it with the tip of sable, coaxing dust from the crevices. He occupied himself for some time at the work, then laid down the figure. He was nothing more than a shabti himself, a man of clay, serving corpses.

The goal he had been working toward was almost achieved. He would be able to enter the tomb himself the following day. The aperture was enlarged sufficiently, the structure safe. All was ready. And yet he didn't have the heart for it. He wanted to walk out of the house, despite the midnight hour, padlock the door behind him, instruct the guard to remain at his post at the tomb entrance until his return, and cross the river. Board the first craft that was leaving for Cairo. Chase after Harriet Heron. Find her and invite her—implore her, if necessary—to stay by his side.

Returning to the piano, Eberhardt Woolfe played until his fingers hurt, dispelling the silence that surrounded him, the endless darkness. Longing was as real as archaeology. Feelings as important to excavate as artifacts and more valuable. He had lost something precious. This time it was his own fault. He had let her go. He closed the lid, let it drop with a thud of spruce on spruce.

Moving onto the verandah, he looked out at the few remaining lights of the village on the opposite bank. A sickle moon, bright and heartless, floated on its back over the dimly outlined pillars of the Luxor temple, half submerged now by floodwaters.

Back inside, in the bedroom, he pulled down the small suitcase from the top of the wardrobe. He did not go to bed but sat in the leather chair in the large room with his eyes closed. As he waited for what was left of the night to pass, an image came to him of Harriet, walking out of the tomb, decked in yellow gold, holding a pomegranate in her hands. She walked purposefully. He was in the moving picture too, hurrying behind her as she walked on through a white Theban valley. He ran as fast as he could but was unable to lessen the distance between them.

The sun rose over a river that was high and swollen; the fast-flowing, mud-charged water appeared opaque, careless of the small sandal that skidded over its pulsing surface, its sails filled, carrying Eberhardt Woolfe sitting on a plank laid over the stern, his suitcase at his feet.

FIFTY-SIX

Harriet studied her hands, the scratches and scabs on her knuckles and fingers and palms. Lines of ingrained dust still lingered underneath her nails.

"Coffee, miss?"

"Thank you."

She pushed forward her cup. The waiter was the same one who had brought them their coffee when they last stayed in the hotel; the breakfast of cold beef was identical and she recognized most of the other guests by sight. She and Louisa faced each other across the breakfast table under the high molded ceiling of the Oasis Palace Hotel dining room.

They had arrived the evening before, after ten days on the *Amon-Ra*, the journey downriver more rapid than the one upstream. The world, which had grown so immense, was contracting again. All that remained was the reunion with Aunt Yael in Alexandria, the passage to England, followed by the train journey to London. The house in Canonbury. Lifting her cup to her lips, Harriet pictured the wall by her bed, its plaster that was the color of old snow. She saw in her mind's eye the raised pattern of the paper on the ceiling, inhaled the remembered smell of thorn apple and niter.

"Look who it is," murmured Louisa, her eyes fixed on the far side of the room.

Mrs. Cox was hastening toward them, edging around the hooded chairs and walking sticks, past hovering, aproned nurses.

Harriet jumped to her feet.

"Good morning, Mrs. Cox," Louisa said, dabbing her mouth on her napkin as the Coxes arrived at the table.

"Miss Heron, will you come for a stroll?" Sarah Cox said, after a brief exchange of pleasantries. "There is a bloom in the garden that I wish to show you."

"Do sit down, Mr. Cox," Louisa said. "And tell me all the news. It seems as if we have been away for such a long time."

Mr. Cox pulled out a chair.

"Nothing but bad news," he announced, "from the point of view of the man of business."

Harriet followed Sarah Cox's neat silk bustle through the dining room, through a pair of large open doors, and down the stone steps from the terrace. Mrs. Cox wore a hat trimmed with poppies and carried a red silk parasol looped over one arm. She looked what Rosina would call blooming. As they reached the grass, she turned to Harriet and took hold of both her hands.

"I want to hear absolutely everything," she said. "I know already that Mr. Soane pursued you to Luxor. Did he . . . ?"

"Did he what?"

"Propose, Harriet. Propose."

Harriet shook her head, unable to speak.

"He didn't ask you to marry him?" Sarah Cox sounded incredulous.

They walked under the shade of a line of sycamore figs, their trunks limed white. A tune played in Harriet's head—the steady tapping of a trowel, overlaid by the sound of the wind, fluttering leaves among the tombstones. She pictured the bleached valley, the stack of palm-leaf baskets inside the entrance to the tomb. Perhaps at this very moment, Eberhardt Woolfe was entering the chamber, lamp aloft, one of the Egyptian workers walking behind with a pan of magnesium, ready to ignite it and illuminate the painted walls in a brilliant, momentary flare of light. She imagined Dr. Woolfe's green eyes gazing in wonder at the sights she had seen and felt an ache in her chest, as if she had been thumped.

Mrs. Cox was speaking again. "I saw it so clearly in the cards. That you would join with a man you encountered on a nautical voyage. I would have staked my life on it. I'm sorry, Harriet."

"Perhaps the cards were mistaken, Mrs. Cox."

Harriet looked at the tough green grass under their feet. Mrs. Cox knew nothing about Dr. Woolfe. She'd been ill, confined to the surgeon's quarters, by the time he boarded the *Star of the East*. It was too late to confide in her now. There was nothing to say.

"Whatever happened to your hands?" Mrs. Cox said. "You look as if you've been building a pyramid."

They ascended the steps and entered the hushed comfort of the Oasis Palace. Seated next to Harriet in the dim lobby, around a round brass tray embossed with a complicated Arabic script that seemed to fly and dance its meaning into being, Mrs. Cox ordered two glasses of lemonade. She leaned back and linked her fingers over her stomach, the diamonds on her ring glinting.

"I have news, Harriet."

"Are you . . . ?"

Mrs. Cox nodded, and when she looked up, her eyes glittered like her ring. "The doctor confirmed it this morning. We're going home as soon as Zebedee has finished his business. The baby will be born in England."

"When will you leave?"

"As soon as possible. Zebedee says it's becoming unsafe."

"What does he mean?"

"Oh, you know. The natives are so angry with everyone. Zebedee says they've no one to blame but themselves if they can't pay their taxes." Sarah Cox gave a sad, silvery laugh. "I'd be angry too, if I were in their position. I would hate us more than they do."

"We're going home as well," Harriet said flatly. "We're taking the train to Alexandria this afternoon."

"Will you come and see me, Harriet? In London?"

A bent old woman slumped sideways in a wheelchair approached, the chair propelled through the lobby by an attendant, the iron wheels rolling silently over the smooth expanse of marble. Turning back to Mrs. Cox, Harriet forced herself to smile. She reached out for her hands and squeezed them.

"Of course I will visit you and the baby. I'm so glad for you, Sarah."

FIFTY-SEVEN

Yael had altered. The sleeves of her dress were loose on her arms and her waist had emerged from its long hiding. Her face, framed by the coils of silver hair, looked older and more serious. Arriving at the villa the previous day and finding her in the drawing room, writing letters, Louisa had wondered for an instant who this dignified-looking person was who rose from the table, pen in hand. From the look on her sister-in-law's face, Louisa had remembered that she too was not immediately recognizable. They had embraced, then stepped back to look at each other again. Louisa couldn't think of a time when she had been so glad to see Yael.

The air in the garden was still, heavy with the scent of the white mulberry blossom on the branches over their heads. Louisa unclenched her fingers from the arms of the wicker chair and patted the short ends of hair on the nape of her neck. She'd taken to going without the head covering while she was in the house and garden. Yael had appeared barely to notice that her hair was gone and Harriet insisted that it became her. Harriet was with Suraya in the hovel at the back of the kitchen yard, helping to prepare supper.

Louisa lowered her voice. "We're in June. It's been five months, Yael. If you're not prepared to go home now, when will you be?"

Yael's chair creaked. "I cannot say. The situation deteriorates by the day, Louisa. Most of the children are surviving on the ration of beans and rice we give out at the clinic. Nearly all our families are in the same situation. I cannot leave them at present."

Louisa straightened herself in the chair. She might embark on the steamer and then die on the journey home. She had to get Yael to return with Harriet, see her safely back to London.

"They are Egyptians, Yael. There are millions of them. You cannot save them all. You must come back with us."

Since Harriet had been found alive, Louisa's certainty that it was her own death that was near had been reconfirmed. For those hours when Harriet had been missing, she had believed—despite herself, unable to suppress the realization—that she'd had a reprieve; along with that came the terrible understanding of the price of her renaissance, that she would be condemned to live a blighted life, a life against nature, in which she outlived her own daughter. When Harriet had been found, brought back to Dr. Woolfe's strange house on the mountainside, Louisa had sent up weary prayers of thanks that it was indeed she whose days were numbered. She who would soon go to meet her maker and her mother.

The heavy scent of the blossom reached her again on a current of air and for a moment she had a vision of growing a mulberry tree herself, in the south-facing spot in the corner of the garden. Then she remembered that things of the future were in the past for her now. Only the present moment was available to her. She rose from the chair and snapped off a twig of white flowers, held them to her nose. The scent of flowers had always been one of life's sweetest pleasures.

"Miraculous," she said, holding the stem out to Yael. "But we must go home now."

Yael blinked at her. "Our work at the clinic is important, Louisa. It matters to me and to our families. This is their hour of need."

If Yael refused to come with them, it might be only Harriet who arrived back in England. Louisa pictured Blundell on the quay, meeting one woman in the place where he had dispatched three. It would break his good heart. She flopped down again into the chair, her legs weak.

"I cannot return without you, Yael. Blundell would never forgive me."

"It's not your decision, Louisa, dear. I have made that clear, in the letter I have already written to my brother. I sent it before you arrived."

259

Despite her smaller form, Louisa could not escape the sense that Yael had grown larger. Her sister-in-law had a presence and authority that were never apparent before. For some minutes, the women sat in silence. Yael's face in the moonlight appeared distracted when she spoke again.

"Our friend Mr. Soane is back in Alexandria."

Louisa laid the sprig of blossom on the table. "Oh?"

"He attended the service last Sunday, with a young lady. Reverend Griffinshawe informs me that she is his sister."

Louisa felt faint. She thought for a moment that she might be about to die now. Here. This moment.

"Did you . . . Did you have the opportunity to speak with them?"

Yael shook her head. "I didn't seek it, dear."

The lump in Louisa's throat threatened to close it. She swallowed.

"Did Mr. Soane's sister look well? Does she . . . resemble her brother?"

"Not altogether."

They sat in silence again, the wicker chairs creaking as they moved, until Yael began to speak.

"Once upon a time, Louisa, when I was still very young, another girl told me a story. She shouldn't have done so, because it was not her story to tell. But nonetheless, she did. She told me of a girl she knew who had fancied herself in love with a man. A powerful man used to having his way in all matters. The man did what many would. He seduced her and afterward he went away. He left her and her family to try to cover up what had happened, put things right."

"There are so many foolish girls." Louisa's voice was a squeak. She didn't recognize it. "Foolish and immoral."

"Do you believe so?" Yael rocked backward and forward, in a leisurely way, as if the question might occupy her thoughts for some time. She sighed. "I always felt pity for that girl. I had sympathy for what befell her when she was little more than a child herself."

Louisa's hands were clenching the arms of the chair so tightly that her fingers hurt. The scent of the mulberry flowers was overpowering, the sawing of the crickets louder than she had ever noticed before.

"Who told you the story?"

Yael hesitated. She held her chair at the farthest incline of its backward tilt, then allowed it to roll forward again, and came to rest.

"It was Lavinia."

"My own sister? I don't believe you."

"She meant no harm, Louisa. I was a child myself at the time, of twelve. She made me swear on the Bible never to repeat the secret to another living soul and I never have done. Except one."

Louisa rose from her chair in a single rapid movement, as if pulled up by a string. "You mean me? Now?"

Yael sighed. She rocked for some moments without speaking. "On the same day as I heard it, I told my older brother the whole story. I believed that before he married, he had a right to know."

Louisa cried out as if she had been struck. Then there was silence.

FIFTY-EIGHT

Harriet stood next to her aunt, in the front pew of St. Mark's. The church was pleasantly dim and cool, the air permeated by a faint, woody aroma, the walls lined with stone plaques to memorialize English people who had died in Alexandria. Some of the tablets were inscribed in both English and Arabic; the curling, fluid lines of the Arabic looked graceful, more fitting to eternal spirits, Harriet thought, than the straight lines of the Roman letters.

Yael's voice was off-key, sharp in Harriet's ear. The last strains of *England's green and pleasant land* died away and Yael put the hymnbook on the slanted wooden rest. As they sat down, side by side, Harriet glanced over her shoulder at the men of business and their wives, the bespectacled administrators and palm-helmeted hunters, the military families en route to India. Even here, she could not help searching for Eberhardt Woolfe, her eyes scanning the rounded, stooped, and stout figures for a tall angular one. She breathed in the smell of incense and closed her eyes, praying to God, briefly and urgently, to let her see Eberhardt Woolfe again.

She wanted to apologize to him for her stupidity in entering the tomb. Explain that she'd been intending to ask him a question. Let him know that she had wanted to stay.

The thought was too painful to pursue. She and Louisa were leaving that night, for London. Aunt Yael was remaining in Alexandria. Harriet opened her eyes and looked up. In front of them, set high in the wall, was a stained-glass window. Jesus was on the cross, his head hanging, his pale limbs drooping with a balletic grace, toes pointing down toward the brow of the hill of Calvary. Below, a blue-cloaked Mary kneeled on the ground, her face upturned. The light poured through the gold and red and blue glass, each splintered piece jewel-like and translucent.

At the lectern, the Reverend Griffinshawe raised his arms in the air. Harriet hadn't seen him since the day he called at the villa. The Reverend looked well, his face filled out and his surplice starched and spotless.

"As many present here today know," he said, "we have in recent weeks launched a collection for our less fortunate neighbors in Alexandria. People cannot apply themselves to the study of the Bible or the English language when their stomachs are empty. Our sister Miss Heron"—he gestured in the direction of Yael—"has taken it upon herself to distribute rations to the poor mothers and infants in her ophthalmia clinic. If you'd care to say a few words, Miss Heron, for the benefit of those who are new."

"Thank you, Reverend." Yael stood up, holding her prayer book in her hands, and turned to face the congregation. She peered at them through the thick spectacles and Harriet had a momentary vision of her aunt, depicted in stained glass, looking down at the congregation through a pair of horn-rimmed glasses, her feathers forever aloft over her head.

"As Christians, it befits us to love our neighbors as ourselves. It makes no difference if those neighbors are Mohammedans, who, after all, worship the same God as we. And before spiritual hunger can be met, bodily needs must be furnished. Through no fault of their own, the mothers I've been fortunate to become acquainted with are unable to feed their children at the present moment. They feel the same hunger that we feel. Suffer the same frailty of the flesh. If our Christianity is worthy of its name, I hope we will all do what we can to come to their aid. Thank you."

She sat down, unflustered, as the worn blue velvet pouch began to make its way along the pews, passed from hand to hand, the chink of coins audible as the Reverend began his last reading. Aunt Yael had been a figure of fun in London, in her comical bonnet, setting off for out-of-the-way church halls, volunteering at the home for fallen women. Harriet thought that her parents, not through words, had told her an untruth about her aunt and what she was made of. Until now, she hadn't had eyes to see the truth for herself.

It was past noon by the time they stepped out of the doors of the church. The sun was high, white in a white sky, the light blinding, the heat radiating up from the sandy ground. A line of carriages waited outside the church, their drivers stretched out on the seats, the horses' heads hanging, motionless apart from ears that twitched, tails that flicked over their haunches.

Two black-shrouded figures standing in a doorway called out greetings to Yael; she lifted her hand in a wave. She turned to her niece, took her hand, and drew her under the shade of a spreading tree.

"Harriet, dear," she said, looking at her through her thick lenses, raising her voice over the rattle of the wheels of a passing carriage. "Is it your wish to return to London with your mother?"

Harriet shook her head. "No, Aunt Yael, it isn't."

"You know that I shall be staying on in Alexandria for the foreseeable future. I shall be moving to the house where we hold the clinic. I could provide a home for you, a modest one, if you feel your health and spirits are better here."

"Could you, Aunt? Do you mean it?"

"Yes."

Harriet felt a great rush of hope spring in her chest. Almost as soon as it arrived, it began to subside. She pictured Louisa's sun-browned face, the shorn hair that had given her mother the air of a martyr, the alteration in her, so absolute since their departure from London. Louisa had cast off her stays and bustle, her high standards of housekeeping, her concern for Harriet's every breath. She wanted only to gaze at the flowers in the garden of the villa or watch Suraya's children playing. Sometimes she sang.

"Mother isn't herself, Aunt Yael. I have to look after her."

Yael did not disagree. She fingered the crucifix she wore around her neck, holding the two outstretched arms of the cross between her thumb and forefinger.

"Don't make the mistakes I made, Harriet. If you are not to marry, then don't spend your days doing what the world wishes you to do. Find out what the Lord wants for you, dear, now that you are well again. And *do it with thy might*. Did you care for Mr. Soane?"

Again, Harriet shook her head. "I thought I did. I care for someone else. Do you remember the man with his piano, Aunt?"

"Indeed. Did it arrive safely? Very difficult items to transport, pianos."

"I think of him day and night."

"Does he wish to marry you?"

Harriet averted her eyes.

"I believe he has a wife already."

"I see. Well then, you must put him out of your mind entirely, Harriet."

Harriet nodded, unable to meet the gray eyes that mirrored her own.

Yael patted her hand.

"Marriage is not the only way to a life. And you know that what I have will one day be yours."

"Thank you, Aunt. But that is a long way off."

"I daresay."

Yael raised her hand for a cab and a brougham drew up beside them. It was their final farewell. Yael was going to distribute rations at the clinic; she opened the place every day. She and Louisa had said their goodbyes after breakfast; Harriet had been surprised by the affection that seemed to have grown between them.

Yael spoke to the driver in Arabic and helped Harriet up onto the seat. As the driver cracked his whip on the ground, the horse raised its blinkered head and moved away from the church, under a thin avenue of trees, their leaves unmoving, drooping with thirst. Harriet turned and waved.

Sitting alone in the cab, passing on into the old part of the city, Harriet stared out. Merchants sat cross-legged in front of empty shops and children played marbles in the dust; veiled women stood in twos and threes in dark doorways; beggars slept on straw mats in the shadow of the mosque. The city looked strangely lifeless, as if in wait for something.

In the Cairo railway station, Eberhardt Woolfe stood in a place from which he could keep an eye on the great clock. He had a cup of Turkish coffee in his hand and his suitcase was on the ground at his feet. It was empty. He had not been able to think of anything that he required, other than to find Harriet. The train for Alexandria departed in fifteen minutes and his ticket was in his pocket. On arrival he intended to go directly to the office of the Anglo Ottoman Bank, find out the whereabouts of the villa, and go to her.

The clock struck the half hour and he finished the coffee and hurried toward the platform.

FIFTY-NINE

❧❦❧

Yael stood at a table, running the last of the round green lentils through her hands, feeling the seam at the bottom of the sack. It was mid-afternoon and the rations were almost finished. The women and children had come in a rush, departed without lingering for their usual chat with her and one another, the stories for the children. Only a few of them remained, including Um Fatima, helping out, as she sometimes did, in Suraya's place. Her husband had been released and was close to being able to walk again.

Yael felt subdued. Bidding farewell to Louisa at breakfast time, and then to Harriet after the service, she had put on a cheerful enough face. It was her choice, made of her own free will, she reminded herself, to stay on alone. But she felt daunted nonetheless.

"'Thy kingdom come,'" she said silently. "'Thy will be done, on earth as it is in heaven.'" She poured the last scoop of lentils into a cloth bag, added a dozen papery-skinned onions from the wooden crate at her feet. She heard a rumble from outside that sounded like thunder, and wondered if there was a summer storm brewing.

Spooning rough gray salt into a cone of newspaper, she twisted the top shut, then dropped the salt into the bag on top of the onions. Yael had torn pages from the Arabic version of the Bible and was using them to wrap the slivers of soap that she gave to the women with the food. Cleanliness was next to godliness.

She looked up at the last of the mothers waiting for rations. It was Nur, her child standing next to her, her feet bare on the floor. When Yael had begun the clinic, the women who walked through the doors had been indistinguishable to her. They had all looked the same, in their black veils held between blue-tattooed lips, black-and-blue-striped gowns, slippered feet. She knew each one of them now by name. Nur's name meant *light*, and when she smiled, she radiated light, a dignity in the face of adversity that Yael found Christlike.

The child's face was clean and so was her loose cotton garment. Her hair was combed and divided into two fine plaits, her face curious. Yael leaned forward over the table and touched the little girl's cheek.

"Sacrebleu. Abracadabra. Here, Sitti Nur."

She pushed the bag across the table and the woman dipped her knees in a kind of curtsy, reached for Yael's hand, and touched it to her forehead, saying something in Arabic. Yael did not recognize the words but she understood the sentiment behind them.

She nodded. "Greenwich Mean Time. Polly, put the kettle on. Forever and ever. Amen."

The distant rumblings outside the window intensified and the woman, instead of hurrying away with her provisions as the others had, spoke to her again, more urgently, in a stream of Arabic.

"*Je ne comprends pas*," Yael said, straightening up. "Ave Maria. Mazel tov. God bless you and God bless your daughter."

The woman took up the bag, balanced it on her head, the weight of the beans drooping down on each side of her face, and left. Um Fatima had gone already.

They had run out of oil, sugar, tea, onions, lentils. Soap. She would go to the market in the morning with Suraya. Alone in the room, Yael sat at the table and wrote a shopping list. Retrieving the donations from the congregation, from the back of the drawer, emptying the heavy mass of coins into her Gladstone bag, she raised her nose in the air and sniffed. Something was burning that was not meant for burning. Yael closed the drawer and let herself out. Locking the door behind her, she set off for home.

• • •

Louisa sat on one of the two striped couches in the drawing room of the villa, looking out of the open French doors at the garden beyond. The trunks were packed and locked, sitting by the front door. She and Harriet had eaten lunch together, after Harriet returned from church. Harriet had been subdued during the meal, as if preoccupied. She'd been to Yael's church with her and said goodbye to her aunt there. Louisa assumed she was sorry to leave her. She'd been sorry herself, felt a wrench at parting from her sister-in-law that she would have believed impossible. It felt wrong to be leaving without Yael, but she had been resolute. After their conversation in the garden, Louisa had not tried anymore to persuade her.

It was four in the afternoon. Mustapha had gone out to get a cab to take them to the harbor; the boat sailed first thing in the morning and the passengers had to embark before nightfall. Sitting on the couch, her handbag on her lap, Louisa felt at peace. There was nothing to do but wait for Mustapha's return, take the carriage to the harbor, then embark on one of the small boats that would carry them out to the steamer. Her death would come when it came. She prayed that she would be spared to see Blundell once more, to look on his face, feel his arms around her.

She sighed. Harriet was so quiet.

"Did you have enough lunch, Harriet?"

"Yes, Mother."

"Is everything packed?"

"Yes, Mother."

Harriet was wearing the peat-brown travel skirt that she had worn for the journey out. She had washed her hair and been sitting in the sun in the garden, allowing it to dry. For once, Harriet had requested Louisa to brush it for her, as she used to when she was a little girl. Louisa had been glad to oblige, had enjoyed standing behind Harriet, drawing the brush through her soft hair, arranging it in a plait that ran down her back and fell on her newly laundered white cotton shirt. Harriet wore the orange scarf over her shoulders and, at her neck, the brooch that Anna had sent from India, the garnet fruits hanging from the branches of the silver tree. Her pocket with her book in it was tied around her waist. Despite her eccentric costume, Harriet looked well, in better health than Louisa had seen her for many years. Louisa took comfort from that. It was what she had wanted. It was what they had come to Egypt for.

"I can smell burning," Harriet said.

Louisa sniffed the air. Laid over the lingering odor of the fried fish they'd eaten at lunchtime was the harsh smell of smoke. "Someone having a bonfire, I expect," she said.

Mustapha tapped on the door and entered the room.

"Is the cab out—"

Louisa stopped and stared at the housekeeper in astonishment. In the dim golden light that found its way through the curtains, he stood very straight before them. He was dressed in his customary long white robe, his feet were as usual bare, and at his waist was a long curved sword, sheathed in leather. She wondered for a moment if he intended to murder them.

"What is it, Mustapha? Is the cab outside?"

"Madame, there is trouble in the town. It is better to stay here."

"The steamer leaves tomorrow. I have the tickets." Louisa reached into her bag, produced an envelope, and held it in the air. "We must go now."

"No ships can leave tomorrow. You must hide."

Outside, the sound of gunfire ripped through the air, the shots crowding impatiently into the atmosphere, tripping over each other.

Louisa rose from the sofa. "Whatever can be happening?"

The air in the room thickened to a haze and Harriet took Louisa's arm.

"Don't be alarmed, Mother. What kind of trouble is it, Mustapha?" she said.

"Bad trouble." Mustapha held open the door, instructed them with a movement of his head to pass through it.

"Come, Mother."

Harriet pulled Louisa out of the room. They hurried behind Mustapha through the kitchen, out the back door, and through the mud yard where he and his family lived. Children's clothes hung from the branches of the tree in the middle and chickens scratched in the dust. Mustapha held open the curtain at the doorway to the apartment.

"No, Harriet," Louisa whispered. "I cannot go in there."

"Go on, Mother. Quickly."

Harriet gave her a push and Louisa stepped over the threshold. In the dimness, Suraya rose from a stool, laid down a new baby. She wiped her right hand on her robe and extended it to Louisa.

"*Ahlan wa sahlan,*" she said. "Welcome."

Straightening the cover on a low wood-framed bed, smoothing the pillows on it, she gestured for them to be seated. Louisa looked around her at smoke-blackened mud walls, a collection of earthenware jars on an open shelf, a copper kettle on a fire. She turned to Harriet as the commotion beyond the walls grew louder. Mustapha appeared again at the door and said something in Arabic to Suraya, his voice low and urgent. He let the curtain drop again. Underneath it, Louisa could see his feet walking across the yard among the fowls.

Gunfire sounded again, sharp, so close it might have come from the garden. Suraya gestured urgently and wordlessly that they should hide under the bed.

Harriet pushed Louisa under the bed, then crawled in behind her. They lay side by side underneath the sagging rope weave, the mud floor hard against Louisa's hips and shoulders. It was hot in the small room, and airless. Louisa's body was rigid. She had believed her life would simply expire, like a clock that ceased to tick. She had not imagined she would die like this. By violence. She felt a mortal fear that was new to her and whimpered.

Harriet took hold of Louisa's hand. "No one will look for us here," she whispered. "If they do, they won't find us. Don't be afraid, Mother."

"If only Yael were with us," Louisa whispered back.

"She will be all right, Mother. She will remain at the clinic until it passes."

"I should feel so much easier if she were with us."

SIXTY

The streets of the old city teemed with people. Not people, Yael corrected herself. Men. Men and boys. Women and small children were nowhere to be seen. The doors of the narrow houses were closed, the windows shuttered, and the latticed, overhanging galleries dark with watchers.

Despite the crowds, their insistent movement in one direction, like a river, there was a stillness and a sense of concentration, of purpose, that was alien here. No laughter. The silence, punctuated by shouts of *Allahu akbar*, *God is great*, didn't match the volume of people. It was eerie, despite the bright sunshine. God is great, Yael repeated to herself, trying to ignore the prickle of fear in her spine. She had the same disturbed feeling as when she had seen the brown cloud of the dust storm approaching, of something impending, a natural force.

The crowd was moving as one, a shoal of men and boys surging through the narrow alleys. Some had wooden staffs in their hands, or curved, sheathed knives at their waists. Boys stooped to wrench long-anchored stones from the dust; one child of six or seven ran past Yael with a stick in each hand. She recognized him from the clinic. He had come several times with his mother and a line of little sisters. Yael had washed his face herself.

She called to the boy. "Go home," she said, her voice soft. "You shouldn't be here."

The boy turned a pair of lustrous eyes on her. Stared for a moment, then darted off.

"It's not safe," she called after him.

Approaching the main path leading to Bab el Bahr, the Gate of the Sea, the mood altered. Shouts and cries rose, joined with more distant sounds of firecrackers and again the rumble that sounded like thunder. The crowd surged onward, moving rapidly through the dust and flattened stalks of straw, over cobbles blunted and polished by the tread of feet, toward the Frank quarter. Yael was forced almost to run to keep pace. Smoke was drifting overhead and the sun beat strongly. The air was still and stifling. Sweat poured down her forehead and made her eyes sting; the inside of her bodice clung damply to her skin.

As they converged on the gate, the tide slowed. Yael wiped her face with her handkerchief. She was almost home. There had been nothing to worry about. She took a deep breath as the people pushed and jostled from behind; the press of bodies grew tighter and then the pressure eased as the men in front of her streamed under the old stone archway; she followed them, past iron-studded doors, down the hill, into the broad streets and tall solidity of the Frank quarter.

Stumbling on, still trying to keep pace, afraid of falling and disappearing under a thousand feet, Yael gasped aloud. The windows of Otto Huber's apothecary had been smashed and men were crowding inside, grabbing at tins and packets, toppling the stoppered glass jars. She heard shouting, a frightened European voice, and sent up a prayer that the voice was not that of dear Mr. Huber, who had ceased to charge her for the zinc and alum powders, who had advised her so patiently on trachoma.

Many of the shopwindows were shattered. Poor-looking, barefooted men were clutching new leather shoes to their chests; teenage boys ran down the street with bottles of wine and whisky in their hands. The sound of the crowd had altered to something deeper and angrier, more discordant. Some were trying to prevent the looting, others intent on breaking into the shops of the Greek and Turkish merchants.

As the Place des Consuls came into view, Yael's heart missed a beat.

"Oh, Lord," she said. "Oh, dear Lord."

One of the elegant white buildings was ablaze. Dense black clouds billowed from between the charred roof beams; plumes of thinner smoke poured out of broken windows, their lace curtains aflame. The little wooden kiosk in the middle of the square, where the father and son sold coffee and hard biscuits, was reduced to a charred heap, with two smoke-blackened iron chairs still arranged around a wrought-iron table.

The square was empty of its usual inhabitants. No opulent closed carriages rattled through the square with liveried footmen running in front to clear the passage. No fashionable women strolled arm in arm under the jacaranda trees. The Arab quarter had come to the Frank quarter. The fellaheen, in their ragged navy robes, their turbaned heads, were massed in front of a wide building on the south side of the square, which was guarded by spiked iron railings, a pair of stone lions. A white hand waved a white flag from a first-floor window and disappeared.

Yael had felt as if she were experiencing the scene in perfect silence. She was wrong, she realized, coming back to her senses. The noise was increasing. Her ears were ringing, half deafened with chants, shouts, and a roaring whose source she still could not fathom, that sounded now like the sea but was not the sea. It was the sound of rage, she understood. Her legs felt weak. She would have fallen, if it were not for the crush.

"Think," she said under her breath. "Please, Lord, help me to think."

She wasn't far from the villa. She could reach it, if she could get through to the edge of the crowd. Muttering English apologies, praying that Harriet and Louisa were safely on board the ship, she began to inch her way among the people. Her face streamed as she pushed her way through, ignoring muttered words and hostile glances. An elbow in her ribs. A hand that grasped her flesh through her petticoats. As her eyes roved over the heads and faces, searching for the edge of the crowd, Yael tripped. Putting out her hands to save herself, she stumbled into a youth.

"Pardon me," she said. "I am so terribly sorry."

He wasn't more than fifteen. A boy, without a beard. His eyes were bloodshot and his face thin and starved. As he raised his arm in the air, a man stepped in front of her. Yael heard him invoking the Prophet by his title, *Rabir*. The youth looked past the man at Yael and spat on the ground.

Although the burning sun had not dimmed, Yael felt cold, the dampness of her dress chilly and clinging. She stood still, gripping her handbag to her chest. As she did so, another man, dressed in a long white robe that was starched and pressed, prodded her arm. His sharp fingers pierced her flesh painfully through her sleeve. He grabbed at the bag, pulled it open, and the collection coins rained to the ground.

"Thief," he shouted, opening the bag wide, shaking out the rest of the money.

"No, sir," she protested. "That is not right—"

The cry was taken up by others. They pressed around her, shouting into her face, their breath hot with fury. "Thief. Thief. Thief."

Yael turned in a circle, trying to speak, explain. Her mouth was open but no words came. Hands were claiming her, invading her. The bag fell to the ground. Her black umbrella was seized from her hand. As her shawl was dragged from her shoulders, she felt herself falling; she flailed with her hands for help that didn't come, and hit the ground painfully. Trying to right herself, get back to her feet, she felt a kick in her side and heard a tearing of cloth as a hand ripped open the bodice of her dress. One of her shoes was gone.

On her knees, her arms clutched over her breasts, she looked up and saw a familiar face. A beard stained orange; eyes darkened with kohl. Eyes that looked at her. Relief flooded through her. I am saved, she said to herself. The Lord has saved me.

"Sheikh," she called, her voice high and feeble. "Sheikh Hamada."

He waded through the press of bodies toward her, his stick lifted in the air. The youths shrank away, standing back in a circle as he arrived in front of her. The sheikh looked at Yael with an expression that was not what she had anticipated. That was not different from the expression of the men who did not know her.

"Help me, Sheikh," she whispered. "In the name of your God and mine."

He looked away, then spoke in Arabic, deliberate and brief, his voice harsh. The youths pressed forward and Sheikh Hamada turned his back as Yael lost her footing for the second time and fell into a sea of hands.

Yael found she was walking naked through the grounds of her childhood home. It was autumn and through the trees she caught a silver glimpse of water, moved toward it on bare feet over a soft, undone jigsaw puzzle of oak leaves. The ground under her feet made it possible to walk, she understood for the first time. It was not the movement of her legs that constituted walking, it was the stillness of the spinning earth rising to meet them.

Broken sunlight lay in shards over the surface of the lake, rising and glinting off the branches of the old trees that abided by the edges of the water, their roots mingled in it, their crowns inclined toward its opaque blackness.

Noise hit her, a tide of sound that she could not read, translate. The wind in the trees, she told herself. Thunder and the cracking of a mighty oak, its trunk rent by lightning end to end. Reaching the edge of the water, she continued, feeling the coldness introduce itself to her feet, her ankles, sensing it and not sensing it, detached, unsure if the water cooled her or if she warmed the water.

This was truth. This cold was truth. Truth was not found in language, in human voices, not in prayer or song. Truth was in the water, its cold embrace. She kept on, the mud soft between her toes, the ducks incurious around her. Oak leaves were here too, floating on their backs, lightly, strangers on the water, bobbing with the borrowed movement of the ripples. She was in deep now, the water beginning to lift and carry her, her feet rising from the mud, floating like the leaves of lilies. She could see her toes, white, above the surface. She rested her head back and a fleeting, partial apprehension of peace made itself known to her, like a promise, a whisper, a glimpse through a veil of fog or smoke.

Smoke. The vision was lost. Something hard and heavy struck her head. And another. The cool water turned to warmth, trickling thick and slow on her face; the roaring filled her ears. Rocks, the rocks. Hitting her skull, her curled back, her fingers. Something slicing, carving. Blood pooling and darkening in the dust where she lay. She cast about for help. Not with her hands, which were useless now, immobile. She cast about within and caught the silver glint again through the heavy-limbed trees.

Yael dipped her face forward into the cold blackness that rose to meet her as the birds, the whole chattering world, fell silent. There was stillness over the earth. It was not the lake of her childhood that was the dream, she understood with a sweet, sharp current of regret. It was the life that followed it, that had patiently and on a circuitous path led her back. The waters had been waiting for her. She was released from the dream. She had woken. Jesus was near, perched on a low, overhanging branch, his black wings spread out to dry, his hungry beak pointing the way to heaven. In the place where he had pierced it for the sake of his young, his feathered breast bled.

She opened her eyes to a mass of faces, the faces of the saints, a shard of brilliant blue sky, and closed them again.

"Hallelujah," she cried, throwing back her head, opening wide her own beak, flexing the muscles of her gray wings, and feeling herself lift, weightless, soaring toward the heavens. "*Agnus Dei. Resurgam.*"

SIXTY-ONE

Harriet peered through black gauze as the cart moved past the high padlocked gates of the houses and villas in the Frank quarter. The watchmen's huts were abandoned, the sleeping mats empty. The sun was still below the horizon, the sky streaked with crimson and purple. The voice of a muezzin cut into the air from somewhere close by. Pulling the black muslin folds of Suraya's veil more closely around her, Harriet looked straight ahead, as Mustapha had instructed.

Louisa sat beside her, her face covered, her white hands hidden from view. Suraya had borrowed a second veil for her. Only their feet, swinging over the ground from the back of the cart, were visible under the hems of the black robes. Fouad had dirtied Harriet's boots with earth from the garden. Louisa's light summer shoes, ruined already, needed no disguising.

Behind them, piled high on the cart, was a heap of green animal fodder. Harriet leaned her back against its damp bulk, breathed in the scent, sour and fresh against the lingering smell of ash in the air. Mustapha's curved sword was hidden underneath the clover and they were under strict orders to keep quiet if anybody at all stopped the cart, on any pretext whatever.

"You must be dumb," Mustapha had said before they left. "Deaf and dumb."

Mustapha urged on the ass with a stick, his voice tense; Fouad sat next to him, with Dash under his arm, the dog's collar removed. Harriet and Louisa had spent the night hiding in Mustapha's quarters;

Suraya had woken them before dawn with tea, wrapped them in the black veils.

They traveled on through the city to the sea, where the cart pulled up. After a few words with one of the fishermen on the shore, a chink of coins, Mustapha helped them into a boat. Fouad hoisted the sail, avoiding Harriet's eyes, moving it around until it caught the air. The boat was low in the water, sea slapping its sides. The gentle sounds contrasted strangely with the shouts and shots of the previous day and night. Yael had not returned but Mustapha had been informed by his cousin that a number of Europeans had taken shelter at the church and were waiting out the trouble there. God willing, he'd said, Sitti Yael was among them.

Harriet and Louisa sat close to each other on the plank seat laid across the rowing boat. Louisa had her handbag on her lap, containing the tickets for the journey. Harriet had her journal in her pocket and, at Louisa's insistence, held the medicine chest on her lap. They'd left the trunks behind for Yael to send on.

The steamer came into view. It was the SS *Tanjore*, Harriet saw, the ship whose china they had used on the way out. She felt a movement in her chest, at the strangeness of life, its large patterns.

She squeezed her mother's fingers and, for an instant, laid her shrouded head on Louisa's shoulder.

When they were within twenty yards of the ship, a man dressed in sailor's uniform leaned over the railings, a speaking trumpet held to his mouth.

"Declare yourselves."

Louisa threw back her veil. Her head was bare and her shorn hair in the morning light gave her face a naked, vulnerable look. The boat lurched as she stood up and waved her hand in the air.

"Please let us aboard," she shouted. "We are English people, going home to England. Myself and my daughter. We have tickets for the passage."

There was some commotion on deck; figures moving to and fro, shouts exchanged. A rope ladder was thrown over the side, hitting the water with a splash, the bottom rungs floating out toward them as the rowing boat bumped the iron hull of the SS *Tanjore*.

"Good morning, ma'am," came a voice with the accent of an officer. "The two ladies may come aboard. But not the Arabs."

"Thank the Lord," Louisa said, her voice flat. "Climb up, Harriet." Dash crouched in the bottom of the boat, whimpering, as Fouad slackened the sail, pulled on the oars to bring the boat to the end of the ladder. He leaned over and grabbed it, then looked at Harriet, his face impassive.

"*Kwayis*, Miss Harry?"

"*Kwayis*, Fouad."

Louisa gestured for Harriet to begin the ascent. Harriet pulled the veil from her own face.

"You first, Mother."

"Would you rather?" Louisa said.

Harriet could not speak. She stood to embrace Louisa, pressing her cheek against her mother's, feeling the softness of her cheek and inhaling her familiar scent, the scent that lay under her cologne, of her own skin and self. Taking hold of her hands, she squeezed them, kissed their backs.

"Go carefully."

"I shall." Louisa turned to Mustapha. "Thank you, Mustapha, for all you have done for us. Please take care of my sister-in-law when she returns."

"God bless you, madame," said Mustapha. "And thank you, Fouad, for accompanying us."

"Good, madame," Fouad said.

Louisa grasped the sides of the ladder, put one shoe on the bottom rung, and pulled herself upward. Her foot slid sideways on the wooden tread and Harriet grasped the end of the ladder, held it steady as Louisa got both her feet on the rungs. Clinging to the ropes, she began to ascend, her traveling coat billowing in the sea breeze, the veil streaming out from her shoulders.

"Up yer come, lady," shouted a sailor's voice over their heads. "Steady as she goes."

At the sound of the voice, Harriet's resolve weakened. It was London and every man in it. It carried her brothers and her father, the husband she might have had. The voice was home. Every instinct commanded her to follow her mother, to grasp the sides of the ladder and begin climbing.

"Easy does it," said the voice.

The man reached over and caught hold of Louisa's arms, pulled her safely onto the deck.

High up above, Louisa stood looking down over the railings, the black folds of the veil still lying on her shoulders.

"Your turn, Harriet. Don't be afraid. It's not as difficult as it may appear."

Harriet let go of the end of the ladder and sat down again on the plank seat. She opened her arms to Louisa in a gesture she didn't fully understand, as if to say that things were as they were and couldn't be helped, as if to embrace nothing and everything.

"I'm not coming with you, Mother."

Louisa's face changed. Harriet had the sense of it disintegrating. Her mother's voice floated down.

"Harriet, you must . . . You cannot . . . Please, hurry . . ."

"I'm staying here with Aunt Yael. Tell Father I'll write."

"I am ordering you, Harriet."

"Goodbye, Mother."

"Harriet, I am begging you."

Pulling the veil back over her head, Harriet gestured toward the shore.

"Tell him, Fouad," she said as Dash crouched at her feet.

Fouad spoke to Mustapha in Arabic and Mustapha looked at her. "Sure?"

"I shall remain with my aunt, Mustapha. The trouble is over now. You needn't worry."

Using the oar, Fouad pushed the boat away from the steamer. In minutes, they were back in open water, the sail taut. If Louisa cried out for her again, Harriet did not hear her. Facing the harbor, she pulled the dog onto her lap and hugged his warmth against her, feeling with her other hand for the pocket tied around her waist, the soft, solid promise of her journal. She would stay for a while with Yael and, when she could, as soon as the time was right, find a way to return to Thebes.

She did not look back and no sound reached the boat from either the ship behind or the land in front. There was only the sound of the wind in the patched sail, carrying them toward the shore, where the outlines of the city were becoming clearer with every minute that passed.

Harriet inhaled the warm, salty air, breathing it not just into her lungs but into her whole self, so deep she felt she might float up into the atmosphere, released to float on the currents of her own life and fate. "One, two, three," she counted aloud. "Four, five, six, seven, eight, nine . . ."

Her heart beat slow and strong in her chest, marching at its own curious pace into the years ahead.

Arriving back at the villa, she found not, as she had expected, one woman waiting for her but two men. Eberhardt Woolfe and the Reverend Griffinshawe had arrived at the gate of the villa at the same time and both stood in the drawing room, each with the air of having urgent news to impart. She looked from one to the other, joy and fear rising in her in equal measure.

Reverend Griffinshawe spoke first.

"Your aunt," he said. "I should say—do take a seat, Miss Heron— your late aunt." He drew a handkerchief out of his pocket, blew his nose. "Forgive me, I considered her a friend, you see."

Dr. Woolfe sat next to Harriet on the striped sofa.

"I am here, Harriet," he said. "I have come for you." He laid down his hat, took her hand in both of his. "Tell us, Reverend," he said. "Tell us what has happened."

SIXTY-TWO

Louisa allowed the sailor to lead her belowdecks; he showed her into a cabin with six bunks.

"The other ladies'll be 'ere soon enough," he said. "Make yerself comfortable."

Louisa sat down on the only bunk that had no personal items on it. She reached automatically to the back of her head, felt for the falling coils, and found, for the thousandth time, their absence. She had only her handbag and the old green dress she stood up in, the traveling coat that she had worn on departing England. Feeling in the pocket of her coat for a handkerchief, she discovered something hard and sharp and smooth. She drew it out. It was the carved green beetle that Dr. Woolfe had presented her with. The symbol of rebirth. She held it on the palm of her hand, looked at its humble, industrious form.

Louisa had a curious sense of lightness, as if a part of her had been amputated. She looked around the cabin, unable to believe that Harriet was not there. Was elsewhere. She hugged her arms over her chest, as if healing a wound. She barely knew how she felt. Alongside the shock, the pain, she had another feeling. It was relief. Harriet had moved into her own life.

The door of the cabin opened and a dark-haired woman stepped in. Louisa put the scarab back in her pocket. Glancing up at the woman, she felt even more odd, as if she had so deeply immersed herself in remembering, examining the past, herself as she had once been, that she was now conjuring her own ghost, in pale flesh and warm blood. She had the most curious feeling, as she stood up, held out her hand for shaking, of coming face-to-face with herself.

"I'm so sorry to disturb you," said the woman. "Did I startle you?"

"Not at all," said Louisa, as the woman moved to the basin and poured water into it from the ewer, began to splash her cheeks.

"It's rather cramped," said the woman, looking around, drying her face on a towel. "But we will manage, I'm sure. We are so fortunate to be going home, safely."

She removed her hat and began to adjust her hair, pulling the pins out of a chignon on the back of her head.

"Yes," said Louisa. "Yes, indeed."

Sitting on the edge of the bunk, watching as the woman brushed out her long hair, stroke after stroke, Louisa felt overcome with tiredness. The collapse she had felt coming for so long had arrived. Perhaps this was the moment of her death. She lay down, pulled the rough blanket over herself, and fell asleep.

By evening, the weather deck was shrouded in a sea mist, the temperature fresh. Louisa moved to the railing, gripped it with both hands, and looked in the direction of the sea, invisible in the vaporous atmosphere. She might have been at the very birth of the world.

Two figures were walking toward her out of the mist, close by each other, their heads bent. It took Louisa a minute to see that they were man and woman. Another to understand that one of them had an arm in a sling, inside a brown velvet jacket. Louisa moved toward them until she came within a yard of Eyre Soane. Like his father before him, he was a little man. Unremarkable. With no power over her.

"Good evening, Mr. Soane."

Louisa spoke without fear. She turned to the woman and saw the one who had entered the cabin earlier, who for most of the day had rested on a nearby bunk.

"Mrs. Heron," said Eyre Soane. "Allow me to introduce my sister. Mrs. Julia Summers."

Louisa reached out for her hand. "I believe we have met before."

"Probably." Mrs. Summers smiled, taking Louisa's hand, shaking it. "I've met so many people in the last twenty-four hours that my head is spinning."

She was the same height as Louisa. Dark-haired and red-lipped, slender as a reed, but with her father's broad, flat face. Her dark hair was parted to show an irregular peak on the right of her forehead. Louisa looked down at her own body, in the old green dress, under the traveling coat. She had the curious sensation that her breasts were leaking milk. That it ran wetly down over her belly, trickled past her legs, would at any moment begin to drip on the tops of her shoes, spill over the deck, flood the sea, and turn it white.

"Julia!" she said. "I have always been fond of that name."

"Are you feeling all right, Mrs. Heron?" Julia Summers said. "What an awful time we've all been through. But we must count ourselves fortunate to emerge alive."

"Indeed," said Louisa, making herself let go of the warm hand, raising her head. She looked at Eyre Soane. "You can have no idea how I've longed to meet your sister."

"Really?" he said.

Louisa stared at him, locking her eyes onto his.

"I have the strangest feeling," she said slowly, "as if I have always known her. Isn't that the most peculiar thing, Mr. Soane?"

Eyre Soane looked at her. His eyes turned back to Julia. Then again to Louisa.

His face blanched. His mouth opened.

Louisa continued to speak. "And do you know, Mrs. Summers, that I once met your mother. It was just around the time you were born. She showed me a kindness that day and I have never forgotten her grace."

"That sounds like Mother," said Julia Summers. "She has a sense of what's right."

"Will you take my arm, Mrs. Summers?" Louisa peered past her into the mist. "We can walk for a little way together."

ACKNOWLEDGMENTS

I'm deeply grateful to everyone who helped me with *The Sacred River*. Special thanks to my agent, Ivan Mulcahy; my editor, Jessica Leeke; and Egyptologist Olive Hogg.

ABOUT THE AUTHOR

Wendy Wallace is a writer and award-winning journalist. Her journalism has appeared in magazines and newspapers, including the *Times*, the *TES*, the *Guardian*, and the *Telegraph*. In 2001, she was Education Journalist of the Year. Her book on life in an inner-city school, *Oranges and Lemons*, was published by Routledge in 2005. *Daughter of Dust: Growing Up an Outcast in the Desert of Sudan* was published by Simon & Schuster in 2009. Her short stories have appeared in anthologies published by Methuen and Iron Press. She is also the author of *The Painted Bridge*, a novel set in Victorian London, published by Scribner in 2012 and longlisted for the 2013 Desmond Elliott prize. She lives in London and has two sons.